STAMPEDE

The Rocking R Ranch Westerns
by Tim Washburn

The Rocking R Ranch

The Devil's Rope

Stampede

STAMPEDE

TIM WASHBURN

PINNACLE BOOKS
Kensington Publishing Corp.
www.kensingtonbooks.com

PINNACLE BOOKS are published by

Kensington Publishing Corp.
119 West 40th Street
New York, NY 10018

All Kensington titles, imprints, and distributed lines are available at
special quantity discounts for bulk purchases for sales promotion,
premiums, fund-raising, educational, or institutional use.

Special book excerpts or customized printings can also be created
to fit specific needs. For details, write or phone the office of the
Kensington Sales Manager: Attn.: Sales Department. Kensington
Publishing Corp., 119 West 40th Street, New York, NY 10018.
Phone: 1-800-221-2647.

PINNACLE BOOKS and the Pinnacle logo are Reg. U.S. Pat. &
TM Off.

First Printing: December 2021
ISBN-13: 978-0-7860-4571-6
ISBN-13: 978-0-7860-4572-3 (eBook)

10 9 8 7 6 5 4 3 2 1

Printed in the United States of America

CHAPTER
1

After a recent rash of cattle rustling at the Rocking R Ranch, Percy Ridgeway was aiming to put an end to it and if that meant a necktie party for the rustlers then so be it. It certainly wouldn't be the first time he'd administered some frontier justice and, deep down, he knew it probably wouldn't be the last, either. Up before the roosters had even thought about crowing, he had rousted his son Chauncey and his brother-in-law Leander Hays out of their beds and after checking their weapons and saddling their horses they had departed shortly before daybreak. And it hadn't taken long for them to catch their first break when they had found a cut fence and the rustlers' trail.

Now midmorning, Percy was continuing to push the pace, having already covered nearly fifteen miles. Speed was essential if they were going to recover the six stolen steers before the rustlers could alter the brand or worse, slaughter them. Although the number of stolen cattle represented a tiny fraction of the Ridgeways' enormous herd, Percy was a stickler for details, and he knew if he let one group get away with stealing cattle then the floodgates would be opened.

Fending off rustlers wasn't a new problem for Percy and the rest of the crew on the Rocking R Ranch. The reasons were many, but the overriding problem was the ranch's location. Situated hard against the Red River in northwest Texas, most of the problems stemmed from what was on the other side of that muddy stretch of water—Indian Territory. Dubbed the most dangerous place in the country, the Territory offered refuge to some of the most wicked and vile people to ever walk the earth. It was infested with killers, robbers, rapists, and thieves, a majority of whom had no legal right to be there. Those lands were reserved for the indigenous people who had been rooted out of their ancestral homes, making Indian Territory the endpoint of all the many Trails of Tears. So, in addition to the other two-legged vermin inhabiting those lands, there were thousands of Indians from dozens of different tribes, many of whom were only a generation or two removed from raping and killing at will.

Hitting a patch of rocky ground, Percy slowed his horse to a walk and the other two matched him as they tried to parse out the trail. Although they had covered a lot of ground, they wouldn't officially leave ranch property until they crossed Holliday Creek, a little over a mile away. When you owned a ranch that sprawled across sixty-four thousand acres, long days in the saddle were the norm.

Leander Hays took off his Stetson, pulled a faded red paisley bandanna from his back pocket, and mopped his face. "If them rustlers had been smart, they'd have stitched the fence back together. We wouldn'ta been none the wiser till somebody made a count."

"How many smart rustlers you met?" Chauncey asked, pulling his tobacco and rolling papers from his shirt pocket.

"Good point," Leander said, stuffing the bandanna back into his pocket. A former Texas Ranger, he had hung or arrested more than a few cattle rustlers in his time. He scanned the ground as he rode, and they eventually picked up the trail again. "Where do you think they're headed, Percy?"

"No idea," Percy said. "I'm just glad they didn't head north for once." Having been on the trail for hours they now knew two things—they were after three men and they were headed east.

Once Chauncey had his cigarette rolled to his liking, he lit up and the three men rode in silence for a while. The trail eventually led them to a log house perched on a ridge overlooking the Little Wichita River, and Percy called a halt forty yards out. After nudging their horses into the trees, they climbed down to survey the scene.

"Don't see no steers," Leander said.

"Could be holed up in the timber somewhere," Chauncey said. "Same with their horses."

"Don't make no sense, though," Leander said.

"Why's that?" Percy asked.

Leander pointed at the log house and said, "I just don't see 'em hangin' around knowin' somebody was gonna come lookin' for them stolen steers."

Percy wrapped the mare's reins around the limb of a blackjack and said, "Guess we ain't gonna know until we go for a look-see."

Leander and Chauncey tied off their horses and the three men worked their way through the trees for a closer look. The timber petered out about twenty yards short of the house, so they squatted down behind the trunk of a large cottonwood and spent several minutes watching and listening. It was obvious the house hadn't been there long, the cut end of the logs still oozing sap. Although the house wasn't very big, it did have a nice view of the river.

Chauncey pulled out one of his two Colts and slipped a cartridge into the empty chamber. "How you wanna play it, Pa?"

"You two stay here," Percy said, "and I'll work my way around to the other side to make sure there ain't no surprises."

Chauncey reholstered that pistol, pulled out the second one, and repeated what he'd done with the first. He had worn a two-gun rig since the age of seventeen and Percy knew his son's revolvers had put more than one man in the ground.

"Place looks empty to me," Leander said.

Percy looked at Leander and said, "You got a better plan?"

"Save a lot of time if we was to go straight at it."

Percy thought about that a moment and said, "Well, I reckon we can sneak up to the window for a peek."

The three men stood and crept forward. When they reached the nearest corner, they snuggled up against the side of the house, waiting to see if they'd been spotted. After several moments with no response to their approach, Percy eased around the corner and snuck up to the first window, the other two following behind. Percy took off his hat and eased up for a quick look only to find a piece of furniture blocking his view. He ducked back down and looked at Chauncey and Leander and shook his head.

Leander tugged on his earlobe and Percy nodded. He could hear better out of his left ear, so he turned his head slightly and eased back up. After listening for a moment or two, he leaned forward and whispered, "Sounds like somebody's moanin'."

Leander must have heard it, too, because he pulled his pistol, stepped past Percy and Chauncey, and slowly pushed the door open before stepping inside. Percy and Chauncey followed him in, and once Percy's eyes adjusted, he saw a young woman lying on the bed, her dress torn and spotted with blood and her right eye nearly swollen shut. Percy quickly holstered his pistol and held up his hands. "We ain't gonna hurt you." He saw her one good eye focus on him, and the woman curled up in a ball and began frantically pushing against the headboard, trying to make herself as small as possible.

"Easy," Leander said. "You're safe now."

The three men held still, unsure how to proceed. The woman had obviously been traumatized and their first instinct was to comfort her, but they all knew that might be the one thing that might push her over the edge.

"It's over now," Percy said in a soft voice. He continued to talk to her, and the woman slowly relaxed enough to turn loose of the headboard. "Can you walk?" Percy asked.

The woman nodded and pushed herself up to a sitting position as fresh tears filled her eyes.

Percy offered her his hand and she took it and he pulled her up and helped her over to a chair. It took a long while to get her calmed enough to even find out her name which they learned was Molly Harris. She and her new husband of two weeks, Tommy, had moved into the cabin only a few days ago. Tommy had left before daybreak to pick up some supplies in town.

The other three men had arrived shortly after dawn.

Answering Percy's questions, Molly said yes, the men had some cattle with them and no, they hadn't been gone too long.

Glancing down, Percy saw a puddle of blood pooling around her feet. "We can take you to the doctor," Percy said softly.

Molly shook her head as fresh tears began coursing down her cheeks.

"No one would have to know what happened here," Percy said.

"No doctor," Molly said.

A few minutes later, Percy, Chauncey, and Leander exited the house, now armed with a description of the three rustlers. Percy pulled his leather gloves out of his back pocket and began pulling them on. "They got more than a hangin' comin'."

"Agreed," Leander said.

They stepped off the porch and went after their horses.

CHAPTER
2

Spring at the Rocking R Ranch was a busy time of the year for Emma Turner. Having taken on the job of improving the ranch's equine bloodlines several years ago, this spring she had thirty-one mares who were going to foal sometime in the next three months. Luckily, only a few of those mares would be foaling for the first time and those soon-to-be mommas would need to be watched closely. Now seated at her kitchen table and working on the endless paperwork the horse breeding business generated, Emma stood and walked over to the stove to warm up her coffee. She loved working with the horses but despised the administrative work even though she knew it was a necessity. Because of her detailed records of the sires and dams for every horse foaled on the ranch, she could trace a horse's ancestral bloodlines through multiple generations. She added a spoonful of sugar to her coffee and reluctantly returned to her chair.

Emma hadn't known the first thing about horse breeding when she had first started, but with the help of her uncle Eli and a few of his college buddies who were scattered across the country, she now had a library of horse-related material that was the envy of horse breeders all across the Southwest. But it wasn't just the library that others envied. Early in the process, Emma had purchased a Thoroughbred stud and two Thoroughbred mares from a well-respected Kentucky breeder and now her carefully bred horses were highly coveted and often sold for exorbitant sums. At a time when a good saddle horse might sell for a hundred dollars, Emma's horses often started at a thousand dollars and went up from there. Her highest sale to date was a three-year-old Thoroughbred stallion she'd sold last year for ten thousand dollars. And because the family allowed Emma to keep a generous portion of each sale, Emma, at the age of twenty-eight, had already banked thirty-six thousand dollars. Not bad for a single mother and a former Indian captive who had been kidnapped by the Comanches at the tender age of thirteen.

Not that she didn't still have nightmares about her year of captivity, but something good had come from that time, too—her son, Simon. Emma had been fourteen when she had given birth to her son inside an Indian teepee, deep in the bowels of the Palo Duro Canyon out in the Texas Panhandle.

Now fifteen, Simon was an extremely intelligent and curious young man and Emma was very proud of him, even if his curiosity sometimes caused her heartache. Lately, Simon had been pestering her for the name of his father, but it was a question Emma couldn't answer. It could have been any of a dozen Comanche men who had assaulted her and that wasn't something a mother could tell her child. So, round and round they went, and the only respite was when Simon was at school, as he was today. Finishing the last of the paperwork, Emma gathered up all the papers and pushed to her feet. After dumping her cup into the washtub, she stashed the papers in one of the bookshelves and headed for the front door. It was time for her to check on the mares.

After pausing by the front door long enough to strap on her gun belt, she slipped outside and headed for the barn. Being kidnapped by Indians changes a person and Emma never strayed far from home without being well armed. It didn't take her long to realize the north wind had a bite to it, and she returned to the house, grabbed a jacket, and slipped it on before exiting again. Predicting the weather in early April was always tricky. It could snow one day and be ninety degrees the next.

When Emma reached the barn, she slid the large door back and stepped inside. A large ranch required a large barn and the Rocking R's was enormous. Sixty feet wide and over a hundred feet long, the interior was sectioned off with the tack room on the right, just inside the door, and the wagons and buggies parked on the left. Beyond that was a large workshop and blacksmithing area followed by four rows of stalls, two in the center and one each along the exterior walls. Everything had a place and, with her uncle Percy in charge, it was kept tidy and neat at all times.

Emma headed toward the stalls at the back of the barn. All the mares that were expected to foal soon had been cut out of the herd and were now either inside or in the large corral attached to the barn. For safety, Emma thought it important for the mares to foal in a stall and with more horses than stalls, she would have to rotate the horses through based on where they were in the foaling process. It sounded much easier than it actually was. There were signs to look for, such as the hollowness around a mare's hips as her pelvic muscles relaxed, but each horse was different. After a careful look at the mares inside, Emma filled a couple of buckets with water and made sure she had a bar of soap handy. As ready as she could be, all she could do now was wait.

CHAPTER
3

Despite hemming and hawing about going to school, Simon Turner actually enjoyed his time in the classroom, especially on the days when Nellie Hawkins was in attendance. Fifteen and with long, dark, curly hair and big, beautiful blue eyes, Nellie had a smile that could light up the room. It was a bit awkward that she was a head taller than he was, but his mother kept telling him he hadn't hit his growth spurt yet, so he was hoping to catch up to her soon. As an added bonus Nellie happened to be best friends with Simon's closest confidante and cousin, Autumn Hays. Both fifteen, he and Autumn had been close since birth.

Simon wasn't sure how Nellie felt about him because he'd never asked her. Not that he exactly knew how he felt about her, either, although he could feel an undercurrent of something whenever he was around her. Occasionally, he would ask Autumn a question or two about Nellie, trying to gather some usable information, but it was like his cousin was wearing blinders and she could never seem to connect the dots that he might have an interest in Nellie. He didn't have the courage to come right out and ask Nellie if she liked him, mainly because he feared what her answer might be.

Slim and lanky with coal black hair and nut-brown skin, Simon brushed a strand of hair out of his eyes and looked up from his reading assignment, searching for Miss Abigail Thompson, their teacher. Deeply religious, Miss Thompson didn't tolerate any intermingling of the males and females, so when he saw her on the other side of the room helping another student, he turned in his chair to look at Nellie. She was in the next row over and three seats back, the mandatory dividing line between boys and girls running between them. Tossing a piece of chalk, it ricocheted off the top of her desk and Nellie looked up and scanned the classroom to find the culprit. When her eyes landed on Simon, she smiled, and his heartbeat accelerated ever so slightly. Using the first two fingers of his right hand, he mimicked a walking motion and pointed at his chest then at her. Nellie nodded then scolded him by placing her finger against her lips. Simon smiled and turned back around. Sometimes she would let him walk her home and other times she wouldn't. He didn't know what the deciding factor might be, but he was glad he got the go-ahead for today.

Simon, Autumn, and Nellie had blown through the eighth-grade curriculum long ago and were now working their way through the secondary-education material, what the folks in Wichita Falls called *high school*. It was a relatively new concept that was sweeping across the country and it was far different from the old standard when a student's education ended in the eighth grade. To install their new plan, the city fathers in Wichita Falls had moved the school to a larger building on the corner of Tenth and Scott streets and had separated the students, the younger ones in one room and the older ones in another. The new format meant the town had to hire two teachers and that was more than fine with Simon because he didn't much care for Mrs. Agatha Whitehurst, the dried-up old prude who had taught them through eighth grade.

A voracious reader, Simon loved the challenge school presented and he fully intended to continue his education by attending college, hopefully as soon as the fall. And that thought saddened him some. He doubted Nellie had the same ambitions or if she did, it was highly unlikely they'd end up at the same school since most wouldn't admit females. Still, that didn't dampen his desire to spend some time with her.

He was still daydreaming about Nellie when he heard the floor creak a moment before someone punched him hard in the back of the head. Momentarily stunned, he looked up to see Crazy Eddie Miller shuffling past, a big, stupid grin on his face. A recent arrival to town, Eddie had started school this spring, and he'd been a thorn in Simon's side since day one. Although he was only thirteen, Eddie was a head taller and probably forty pounds heavier than Simon and he was the typical bully, using his size to intimidate those around him.

Reading at maybe a fifth-grade level, Crazy Eddie was a dimwit who got a charge out of calling Simon names. Last week it had been Half Breed and this week he seemed to be stuck on Chief. It certainly wasn't anything Simon hadn't heard before and he mostly ignored it. But that punch to the back of the head escalated their feud to another level and it couldn't go unanswered.

Simon began plotting his revenge.

CHAPTER

4

Grace Ferguson looked up when the little bell above the front door dinged. A tall, thin man with muttonchop sideburns and a droopy mustache entered, took one look at her, and said, "Brandy?"

Grace froze at the name, but quickly recovered. "Excuse me?"

The man slowly approached her desk. "Is your name Brandy?"

"I'm sorry. I think you have me confused with someone else. Can I help you?"

The man gave her a long look and shook his head. "Just so you know, you've got a twin out there."

Grace smiled and said, "Good to know. Now, how can I help?"

"Is Mr. Ferguson in?"

"He's over at the courthouse but should be back after

lunch." Grace pulled a pencil from behind her ear. "Would you like to make an appointment?"

The man looked at the clock on the wall and thought about it a minute. "He handles divorces, don't he?"

"Yes, he does, among other things. Will one o'clock work for you?"

"Sure, I guess."

"Your name, sir?"

The man gave her another long look and said, "You sure we've never met?"

"I'm certain. Do you live around here?"

"No, I live over in Fort Worth. Don't trust any of them lawyers over there, though."

"Do you want me to pencil you in for one?"

"Sure. Name's Oliver Grigsby."

Grace wrote his name in the appointment book. "We'll see you at one, Mr. Grigsby."

Grigsby's eyes lingered on her for another moment before he turned and walked back to the door, the bell dinging again when he exited. Grace took a deep breath, held it a moment, and then let it out. Oliver Grigsby was a scoundrel who owned about half the buildings in Fort Worth's red-light district, Hell's Half Acre. It was an area Grace knew well because she'd once worked as a parlor house girl using the alias Brandy Bordeaux.

Grace's legs were trembling when she stood. She'd had a few awkward encounters over the last few years, but this had been the first one in a long time. Grigsby had been a regular patron of The Belmont, the name of the parlor house, and she wasn't at all surprised the old skinflint was getting divorced—again. But why here? she wondered.

She stepped over to the front window of their small office and watched as Grigsby disappeared down the boardwalk.

If Grace had to guess, it had something to do with money. She had learned working in her husband's law office that the root cause of most legal matters was money. She knew Grigsby had plenty of it, but she also knew he was so tightfisted he squeaked when he walked. She turned away from the window and walked back to her desk.

The office her husband, Seth, rented in Wichita Falls wasn't much, maybe ten feet wide and twenty feet deep with a small apartment upstairs where he could sleep over if he got tied up and couldn't make it home. Other than a couple of desks and a few chairs, the interior was sparse. But the best thing about the office was the cheap rent because the Ridgeway family, her in-laws, owned the entire block. Another plus for that particular office was the location, right across the street from the city marshal's office and the jail.

She looked down at Grigsby's name in the appointment book and thought about scratching it out. However, she resisted the urge, knowing Seth would be upset if he found out later, she'd turned away a client. Although Seth's law practice was doing okay, most of it was just paperwork and she knew he was itching for something with a little more meat on the bone. And what could be better than a nasty divorce with a substantial sum of money involved? If Seth played his cards right, Grace thought, maybe he could gig the old miser for a large retainer.

Grace looked at the ceiling, unconsciously rubbing her sore, swollen breasts as her mind turned from Grigsby to the baby girl asleep upstairs. After having three kids, Grace thought her breasts would have been better conditioned, but no, that same fullness and pressure was there and the only way to relieve it was to nurse her daughter. She stepped over to the front door and turned the lock before making her way up the stairs.

Tiptoeing across the hardwood floor, she looked down at their daughter, Lizzie, sleeping in her crib. Warmed by a muted slash of sunlight shooting through the window, Grace bent down and gently lifted the six-month-old out, snuggling the baby against her swollen bosom. Seth and Grace also had two boys, Andrew, four, and Edgar, three, but they were too rambunctious to bring to the office on the days Grace worked. Instead, they remained at home under the watchful gaze of their babysitter, Alejandra Garcia, the seventeen-year-old daughter of two longtime ranch employees. Grace walked over to the rocking chair and sat. In addition to the crib and the rocking chair, they had wedged an old sofa into the small room, a place where Seth could lie down if he was staying over.

Lizzie began wailing before Grace could get her dress undone. She smiled and said, "You're an impatient child, aren't you?" She finally freed her left breast and Lizzie latched on like she hadn't eaten in days.

Working two to three days a week, Grace spent most of her time keeping Seth organized. She loved her husband dearly and he was probably the smartest man she had ever met, but his desk often looked like a hurricane had passed through with papers and books frequently spilling onto the floor. But Grace didn't mind, and she actually enjoyed her time puttering around the office. It was a world removed from where she had once worked.

Grace was burping Lizzie when she heard the doorbell ding. She assumed it was Seth, after having locked it, and her assumption proved correct a moment later when he came bounding up the stairs.

"My two favorite girls in the world," he said. He leaned down and kissed Grace on the lips then gently picked up Lizzie and took over burping duties as they moved over to the sofa. "Did I miss anything?"

"You might have a new client. He's comin' back at one," Grace said as she licked her fingers and smoothed down Lizzie's hair.

"Who is it?"

"A man named Oliver Grigsby. He's from Fort Worth." Seth gave Grace a long look and said, "You know him?"

"Unfortunately, yes."

"Did he recognize you?"

"He thought he did, but I assured him we had never met. I'll be sure to make myself scarce when he comes back."

"It's been a long time, Grace. Does what you did in the past really matter anymore?"

"Probably not, but Grigsby probably owns half the buildings in the Acre. I don't want him spreading nasty rumors around."

"Well, I hope you're not doing it for my benefit," Seth said, "because I don't give a damn about what people think. You're a terrific wife and mother and that's all that matters."

Grace leaned in and kissed Seth on the cheek. "Thank you for that. If it was anybody else, I'd agree with you, but Grigsby's got a bad habit of runnin' his mouth."

Lizzie finally burped and a couple of seconds later both parents heard her fill her diaper. Seth tried to hand her back and Grace laughed and said, "The holder's the changer. There's clean diapers in the bag."

Seth scowled, but he stood and laid Lizzie in the crib while he wet a rag and grabbed a clean diaper. He removed the safety pins, cleaned up his daughter, and put on a clean diaper. As he worked, he looked back over his shoulder and said, "What does Grigsby want?"

"A divorce. And I don't think it's his first, either."

"Well, it sounds like he has some assets. Maybe we'll actually get paid."

"Better get it up front," Grace said. "He's a real skinflint."

"Duly noted." Seth picked up his daughter and handed her to Grace. "I'm not sure the old diaper is salvageable."

"Throw it out, then. I think your mother orders them by the gross."

Seth chuckled as he wadded up the dirty diaper and set it aside to take outside later. After washing his hands, he plopped back down next to his wife. "You find us a tent?"

"Had to order one through the hardware store. Should be here next week sometime. When are we heading up?"

"The Land Run is Monday, April twenty-second, so we probably ought to head up a couple of days before then. I need to familiarize myself with the land claim process and get all that ironed out."

"How many people you think will show up?"

Seth shrugged. "A bunch, that's for sure. News of the opening spread like wildfire. And people are crazy for land, especially *free* land. So, they'll be coming out of the woodwork and the way the rules are laid out, I'm predicting absolute chaos."

Little did Seth know how prophetic that statement would turn out to be.

CHAPTER
5

The rustlers' trail eventually disappeared into a dense stand of trees along the Little Wichita River, a couple of miles west of Henrietta, Texas. Percy called a halt and the three men nudged their horses close so they could talk without being overheard.

"I'm gonna cross here," Percy said in a quiet voice, "and ride a big circle to see if I can pick up their trail on the other side."

"What do you want us to do?" Chauncey asked.

"Might do a little snoopin' around to see if they're holed up in the trees," Percy replied.

"And if we find 'em?" Leander asked.

"You wait for me." Percy spurred his horse into motion, and he crossed a small creek then the larger river and, as he rode up the far bank, his nostrils picked up the first hint of smoke. With all the trees it was impossible to see where the smoke originated, so Percy kept on riding. The area was cut through with small creeks and dry washes and it took him a while to work his way through the mess.

He eventually broke into the clear and he scanned the ground as he rode, searching for any trace of the rustlers' trail. A half an hour later, after riding a large circle, he arrived back where he had started and found Leander and Chauncey sitting on a downed tree.

"Their trail dead-ends here, so they gotta be in there somewhere," Percy said as he climbed down from his horse. He wrapped the mare's reins around a low-hanging limb and turned around. "You two see any sign of them?"

Leander nodded and said, "I reckon that's the good news."

"What's the bad news?" Percy asked.

"Looks like they's joined up with some of their buddies," Chauncey said. "Not that it matters all that much to me."

"How many men we talkin' about?" Percy asked.

"Seven," Leander said. "And they done butchered one of the steers. They're all sittin' around the fire fillin' their gullets."

Percy pushed his Stetson back off his forehead. "Well, that complicates things, don't it?"

"Far as I'm concerned," Chauncey said, "if they's all eatin' it, they's all guilty."

"There's a difference," Percy said, "between a man ridin' onto our property and stealin' cattle and a man eatin' some meat if it's offered."

"Why?" Chauncey asked. "They all know them steers was stolen."

Percy gave Chauncey a hard look and said, "I got no trouble stringin' up a rustler but I ain't gonna hang a man 'cause he was eatin'."

"From the descriptions Molly gave us," Leander said,

"we can cut out them three rustlers and turn the rest loose."

"The other four men armed?" Percy asked.

"Yep, they's all wearin' side irons like they's a bunch of gunfighters," Chauncey said.

"I can't see them others sittin' by the wayside while we give their three buddies a necktie party or whatever we decide to do," Percy said. He looked at Leander and said, "How far you reckon to Henrietta?"

"Two, maybe three miles," Leander said. "Think they's gonna take the rest of the meat into town to try and sell it?"

"Makes sense, don't it?" Percy said.

Chauncey pulled out one of his pistols and slid a .45 cartridge into the empty chamber. No smart man rode around with the pistol's hammer sitting on a live round. He reholstered that pistol, pulled out the other one, and said, "I say we go in there and punch them rustlers' tickets and if the others wanna get involved then so be it."

"You make it sound so easy, Chauncey," Percy said.

"Well, it is, ain't it? You seen what they did to that woman. Don't that make your blood boil?" Chauncey asked.

"What about the other four that took no part in it?" Leander asked.

"We take their guns and cut 'em loose," Chauncey said. "It sure beats the hell out of tryin' to take 'em in town."

"You got a point there," Percy said. He walked around his horse, untied his rope, and slipped it over his shoulder then pulled his rifle from the scabbard. "You two grab your ropes and rifles and we'll go for a look-see."

After the other two had grabbed their gear, Leander

led them into the trees. Although most of Percy's focus was on the upcoming encounter, he also felt it was important to study the surrounding area to get a feel for the place. The area they were walking through was a mix of elms, oaks, a few walnuts, and several dense patches of cedar trees that were clumped along the riverbank, and Percy thought they'd make a good fallback position if they needed one.

After walking about two hundred yards, Percy saw a small clearing ahead and Leander held up his hand, bringing them to a stop. Percy could smell smoke again but hadn't yet seen the fire. Leander stepped up close to Percy and whispered, "They's camped along the river there to the right about thirty yards ahead."

Percy nodded.

Veering right, Leander led them closer to the clearing and when they were close enough to have a good view, the three squatted down behind the edge of a cedar to observe. Molly had given them good descriptions and it didn't take long for Percy to identify the three men who had assaulted her. They were older than he thought they'd be, and Percy guessed they were in their early forties, which was somewhat unusual. Most cattle rustlers got caught sooner rather than later, severely skewing that group's average life span to the younger side. Percy also noticed there were enough similarities between the three men—the same thinning hair, similar statures and movements—that they were probably related, maybe brothers or close cousins. As Percy widened his perspective to include the newcomers, he noticed that all seven of the men had several shared traits and that didn't really surprise him all that much. He had learned over the years that thieving was often a family business. Although not surprising, it did complicate matters. If they'd all been just friends it would have made separating them easier, but it was another matter entirely when it came to kinfolk.

One of the rustlers stood, walked over to his horse, and grabbed a running iron tied on behind his saddle. A heavy piece of metal about three feet long and formed into a J shape on one end, the running iron was used to alter the stolen cattle's existing brand. Percy had seen men hung for having one in their possession so some rustlers had started using cinch rings or a heavy piece of wire, both of which they could carry around in their pocket.

Percy tapped Leander and Chauncey on their shoulders and when they turned to look at him he pointed over his shoulder with his thumb. They eased back up and retraced their steps. When they had covered enough distance to avoid being overheard, Percy called a halt and said in a low voice, "Looks like we're dealin' with a bunch of kinfolk."

Chauncey shrugged. "So?"

"It complicates things," Percy said.

"You gettin' soft?" Leander asked.

Percy glared at Leander. "I ain't gettin' soft. But I am too damn old to be lookin' over my shoulder all the time. We string them three rustlers up, we could be startin' a feud that could run on for months." Percy paused and looked off into the distance for a moment before turning back. "We got 'em caught red-handed so maybe we ought to round 'em up and turn 'em over to the law."

"Why?" Chauncey asked. "So they can serve a few months in jail then get out and start thievin' again?"

Chauncey had already made his position clear, so

Percy ignored his comment and turned to Leander. "What do you think?"

"I reckon we'd burn a bunch of daylight lookin' for a marshal or a Ranger. Since them rustlers started at the ranch, we got us some jurisdictional issues. Might could toss 'em in the pokey in Henrietta and wire for a Ranger out of Fort Worth or Dallas. Or we could take care of it like we always done. Up to you."

Percy looked down at the ground for a few moments, thinking. He'd lost the taste for killing as he'd grown older. The world had become more civilized since the old days when rustlers and other outlaws were hung with little thought about legal issues. But all that was changing and there was now more scrutiny of those who doled out their own justice. The last thing Percy wanted was the headache of a trial or other lengthy legal proceeding. He looked up and said, "We're goin' to disarm 'em and turn them three rustlers over to the law in Henrietta."

Chauncey crossed his arms and gave his father a long look. "What about Molly? She goin' to get any justice?"

Percy sighed. "Well, I reckon the law can charge 'em with rape, too."

"And what if she ain't willin' to testify?" Chauncey asked.

"That's her choice," Percy said. "We can't cure all the world's ills, son."

"Maybe not," Chauncey said, "but we can make damn sure them three don't ever do anything like that again."

"I've made my decision," Percy said. "Let's get to it."

CHAPTER
6

Marcie Ridgeway dumped her breakfast plate into the washtub and paused at the front door long enough to slip on a jacket before exiting her house. She had promised to help Emma with the foaling and as she headed for the barn, she was still a bit peeved that Chauncey and the others had set out after the rustlers. The family had more cattle than a man could count in a month and five or six stolen steers weren't going to matter one whit. Not that she was worried about Chauncey's safety. He had proven over the years that he was more than capable, including against the three men he had dispatched in Fort Worth on the same day he'd proposed to her inside the parlor house where she had worked, The Belmont.

Like Grace, Marcie, too, had been forced to sell her body to make ends meet. Both women were well aware that having Chauncey and Seth propose to two women in the same parlor house in the span of a week was rarer than getting struck by lightning under a cloudless sky and both were, and continued to be, enormously grateful for their good fortune.

Now, five years later, both marriages were thriving. The only snag for Marcie and Chauncey had been the lack of offspring and it certainly wasn't for a lack of trying. It sometimes weighed heavy on Marcie's mind, wondering if her previous occupation had something to do with her inability to conceive. But in the end, there wasn't much she could do about it and she was just grateful that Chauncey wasn't pressuring her to get pregnant or get lost. As she neared the barn, which had been built on one of the few high spots on the property, she stopped and turned around.

Having grown up dirt poor on a tiny hardscrabble farm in Missouri, Marcie had never been exposed to a large ranching operation like the Rocking R Ranch. Although she had lived on the ranch for five years, she still found herself stopping at certain locations just to look, gazing in wonder at the vastness of it all. Cattle and horses in unimaginable numbers grazed along the gently rolling hills for as far as she could see, and it was almost impossible to believe it was all owned by one family. Knowing that more than a million people lived in Manhattan, she once looked up the island's size for comparison and discovered that the ranch was four times larger with a human population of less than fifty. It was mind-boggling to think about and Marcie couldn't imagine all those people crammed onto one small island.

Entering the barn, she walked through to the corral on the other side, hoping to find Emma. There was no sign of Emma, but she did see Eli Ridgeway and another man looking over a group of horses. She opened her mouth to ask Eli if he'd seen Emma and snapped it shut when the other man turned to look at her. Marcie's cheeks were flushing red as she turned quickly and hurried back inside. She was embarrassed, but she was angry, too. The man, Archer Keating, was a well-known cattleman from Fort Worth who had been a frequent visitor to The Belmont.

When Marcie had walked out of the parlor house for the last time years ago, she had known there would be awkward encounters ahead. But, damn it, was she going to have to hide her face for the rest of her life? Why didn't men like Keating face any consequences for their own behavior? Keating's frequent visits to the bordellos hadn't appeared to diminish his social status in any way. Why was it okay for him to pay for the use of a woman's body without any blame while the women he visited were branded with names like *soiled doves* or *fallen angels*, which were affixed to them like a permanent stain?

Keating, who now had to be in his late fifties, was a potbellied, bald man with a cruel streak. Stories had run rampant around The Belmont about Keating's hair-pulling, pinching, and biting. He was the type of man who thought paying for a woman's services included anything and everything. At that time, there had been little recourse for the women Keating had abused. But that was then, and the more Marcie thought about it, the angrier she got. She squared her shoulders and walked out of the barn and back into the corral.

"Eli," she said as she approached the two men, "have you seen Emma?"

Eli turned and smiled. "I believe she wandered off to her grandmother's." Eli gestured to the second man and said, "Marcie, meet Archer Keating."

Marcie looked at Keating and saw confusion in his eyes. She offered her hand and said, "Marcie Ridgeway. Nice to meet you, Mr. Keating."

Keating shook her hand, a small smirk forming on his face as his eyes widened with recognition. "Nice to meet you, Mrs. Ridgeway."

Marcie had to work hard to tamp down the urge to slap that smirk off Keating's face. "I'll let you gentlemen continue your conversation." Turning, she walked back into the barn, her shoulders square and her spine straight. She turned left and made her way to the back, where the stalls were. "That was stupid," she muttered to herself. However, she knew she couldn't unring the bell now. Walking from stall to stall and looking over the pregnant mares, she stopped when she discovered one of the horses in the process of giving birth. Leaning against the gate, she propped a foot on the bottom rail and settled in for the wait.

Emma was a firm believer human hands shouldn't be involved in nature's business, so Marcie would just watch for a few minutes to make sure things were progressing as nature intended. Having been involved in the foaling season since her arrival at the ranch, Marcie knew that once the foal's forelegs appeared the birthing process often proceeded rapidly, usually lasting no longer than twenty to thirty minutes. The chestnut-colored mare was lying on her side and didn't appear to be in any distress, but Marcie knew things could change quickly, and she was hoping Emma returned soon.

Hearing a loud splash from somewhere behind her, Marcie turned and hurried along the stalls to find a gray mare whose water had just broken. Things were about to get busy. Marcie was debating whether to go get Emma when she heard footsteps approaching. Thinking Emma had finally returned, Marcie hurried back to the chestnut's stall to check on her progress. Things were proceeding well, so she turned to check on the gray mare again and came face-to-face with Archer Keating.

The one habit Marcie hadn't been able to shake since her parlor house days was the need to have a weapon within reach, usually a knife. Now her hand drifted down to the right pocket of her skirt and she wrapped her fingers around the handle of the six-inch paring knife nesting there.

Keating, maybe two feet away, looked at her and sneered.

"What the hell do you want?" Marcie asked, her voice tight with a mixture of anger and fear.

"Well, being as I ain't been with a married woman other than my wife, how much for a poke?"

Marcie took a step forward, cocked back her right arm, and slapped him hard across the face, bloodying his mouth.

"Bitch," Keating said as he reached up and grabbed her by the throat. Blood was trickling out of the corner of his mouth when he smiled and said, "I guess you ain't forgot I like it a little rough, huh?"

Marcie yanked out the knife and jammed the razor-sharp edge against Keating's jugular. "Turn loose or I'll slit you—"

"Get your hands off of her," someone shouted.

With Keating's hand wrapped around her throat Marcie's head was immobilized, but out of the corner of her eye she could see Emma, who was standing ten feet away, her pistol up and ready to fire.

Keating's grip loosened and Marcie lowered the knife and stepped back.

"I don't know what's going on here," Emma said, "but, mister, I'll put you in the ground right damn now."

Keating turned to face Emma and said, "Ain't you a spunky one?"

"Emma," Marcie said, "he's got a pistol in a shoulder rig."

"I saw it," Emma said. "Not going to do him much good, though."

"You sound mighty confident," Keating said.

"Reach for that gun and you'll have maybe a half a second to understand why. Now, reach up with your thumb and finger and ease out your pistol and put it on the ground."

Keating glared at Emma for a moment, then did as instructed, tossing his revolver to the ground.

"I don't know who you are," Emma said, the gun never wavering, "but you're not welcome here."

Keating smiled. "You might want to talk to Eli about that seein' as I just made a deal for a half a dozen horses."

"Well, I just canceled that deal," Emma said. "Now clear out."

"You can't do that," Keating said.

"I can and I did. Start walking."

"What about my pistol?" Keating asked.

"Buy another one. Now move."

When Keating made no move to comply, Emma adjusted her aim and fired, the roar from her pistol loud in the cavernous barn. Marcie jumped at the sudden blast and saw blood sprout on Keating's neck. He slapped a hand over it, howling with pain.

Emma calmly recocked her pistol and readjusted her aim. "It's gonna sting for a while, but you'll live. That won't be the case if I pull this trigger again."

Keating glared at Emma a moment then began walking. "I'll remember you."

"I expect you will," Emma said, tracking Keating's progress with the barrel of her revolver as Eli came jogging down the center aisle.

He stopped and took in the scene, his face crinkling with confusion. "Has there been some type of misunderstanding?"

"No, his intentions were quite clear," Emma said. "And now he's leaving."

Eli, still confused, looked at Marcie then turned to look at Keating and a piece of the puzzle clicked into place. As one of the few who knew about Marcie's previous occupation, Eli also knew that Keating hailed from Fort Worth. Although this had been his first meeting with Keating, Eli could size a man up in moments and he had little doubt Keating might be a frequent visitor to the city's rowdy red-light district.

Keating stopped and scowled at Eli as blood leaked through his fingers and dribbled onto the collar of his shirt. "She runnin' this outfit or what?"

"Eli, I voided any deal he made," Emma said.

Eli nodded. "To answer your question, yes, Emma has equal input in all ranch-related matters."

Marcie was pleased to see that Keating's cheek was still red from her slap. "Get the hell out of here, Keating, and don't come back."

Keating curled his upper lip in disgust and looked at Eli. "You gonna let a whore tell you what to do?"

Eli, usually slow to anger, flared red-hot. Tall and broad-shouldered, Eli towered over the man as he took a step forward, invading Keating's personal space. His voice was low but urgent when he said, "What I'm not going to do is squander any more of my time talking to you. The sale of the horses is nullified, and our business is concluded. Leave now and if at any point you return you will be shot on sight for trespassing. Is that clear?"

"Big words from a man not packin' a gun," Keating said.

Eli took a step back, pulled out his pocket watch, and popped the lid. "You have exactly five minutes to exit the property."

Keating cocked his head to the side, a sneer on his face. "Or what?"

Eli looked up from his watch and locked eyes with Keating. "The manner in which you leave is of little concern to me. The way I see it, you have two choices: ride out on your horse or ride out in a wooden box. Either works for me. Four minutes, thirty-two seconds."

"I ain't gonna forget this," Keating said.

"I certainly hope you took what I said to heart," Eli said. "Four minutes, twenty-six seconds."

Keating spat on the ground, turned, and marched up the aisle and out of the barn. Eli, Emma, and Marcie followed. They stood near the barn door and watched as Keating untied his horse and mounted up. He turned his horse around and spurred it into motion.

"I'm going to make sure he heeds my directive," Eli

said. He grabbed a rifle from the small room they called the armory and exited the barn.

Emma stepped over close to Marcie and said, "What was that about? Did he just attack you out of the blue?"

"No, I have the misfortune of knowing him. He's a vile, cruel man and I would have danced on his grave if the path of your bullet had been a couple of inches to the left."

"If I had wanted him dead, he'd be dead. Am I going to regret not killin' him?"

"I don't see him comin' back here, but you'll need to keep an eye out when you're down around Fort Worth."

"I'll keep that in mind," Emma said. Although she wanted more information about what had happened, she quickly decided it wasn't any of her business. She'd heard rumors that Marcie might have had a difficult past and Emma was well versed on that subject. "You always carry a knife?"

"It's a habit I can't seem to break."

Emma lifted the hem of her skirt and stuck her left leg out to display the knife in her boot. "Me, neither."

CHAPTER
7

The seven men, including the three rustlers, were seated on the ground in a rough semicircle formation and still munching on the stolen steer meat when Leander, Chauncey, and Percy broke from cover, their weapons up and ready. Looking down the barrel of his rifle, Percy ordered the men to put their hands up and that's when one of the rustlers made the mistake of reaching for his pistol. Chauncey, who preferred his pistols for any close-in work, pulled one and spun, drilling the man in the heart. And the die was cast, as the other six men tossed whatever was in their hands and reached for their weapons.

Chauncey pulled his second pistol and his hands were a blur as he thumbed back the hammers and fired while Percy and Leander worked their rifles. All three men were excellent marksmen and it was all over in a matter of seconds, the seven men dead where they sat, having never fired a shot. The smell of spent gunpowder was heavy in the air when Percy lowered his rifle, his ears ringing from the roar of gunfire. All three men, seasoned warriors, immediately began reloading their weapons.

"Well, hell," Percy said as he fed fresh cartridges into his rifle's magazine, "that wasn't part of the plan."

"A bunch of dumb asses," Leander said. "What did they think was goin' to happen? We had the drop on 'em from the get-go."

"Don't make no difference now," Chauncey said, re-holstering one of his reloaded pistols.

Percy leaned his rifle against a tree trunk then pulled the makings from his shirt pocket and began rolling a cigarette. There was no need to check if the men were dead because all three men adhered to the old standard of shoot to kill. Percy flared a match with his thumbnail and lit up before walking a circle around the dead men, looking at the carnage. He was somewhat surprised to see that a few of the men had managed to get their pistols out and they lay where they had fallen. Having seen all he needed to see, Percy turned away from the gruesome scene and stared off into the distance for several moments as he finished his cigarette. Despite what some people might say, there was nothing easy about killing. Percy didn't mourn for the three rustlers because they got what they had coming for abusing Molly. But the other four men didn't need to die. However, Percy knew you could never predict what might happen when the lead started flying. After taking one final drag from his cigarette, he dropped it to the ground and snuffed it out with the toe of his boot. He turned to face Leander and Chauncey and said, "We got us a damn mess. We know where the other steers are?"

Leander pointed to his left and said, "They's in a makeshift corral back in the timber, there."

Percy nodded, still weighing their options, which were few. They could ride on and leave everything behind or one of them could ride into town and explain it to the marshal. Hoping to ward off any future potential problems he looked at both men and said, "I'm gonna ride into Henrietta to get the undertaker and to talk to the town marshal. You two stay here and don't touch a thing. I want 'em to stay just like they are." He started for his horse and then stopped and turned around. Something was bothering him, but he couldn't quite put his finger on what it was. Scanning the surrounding area, it finally hit him. He pointed at the bodies and said, "There's seven men there and I ain't seein' but three horses."

"Could be the others tied up their horses someplace else," Leander offered.

"Why would they do that," Percy asked, "when they can ride right up in here?"

"Why does it matter?" Chauncey asked.

"Think about it, Chauncey," Percy said. "Three horses and seven people? I rode a circle around this place and didn't see any wagons or any other horses so the only way those other four got here was afoot."

"Meaning they probably lived nearby," Chauncey said.

"Exactly," Percy said. "And with all that gunfire somebody's likely to come nosin' around. You two might ought to grab your horses and bring 'em up here."

Leander and Chauncey agreed, and the three men made their way back to their horses. Percy climbed aboard his and said, "You two keep your eyes open and I'll be back as soon as I can." He turned the mare and rode for town.

It wasn't long before Percy was steering the mare up Henrietta's main drag, looking for the undertaker's office. The small town encompassed only about six square blocks and it was anchored by the Clay County Courthouse, a three-story brick-and-stone structure that dwarfed everything in the vicinity. Percy studied the building from afar and had to admit it was a handsome building with ornately carved columns and a large, square clock tower on top as the crowning jewel. After a few moments of study, Percy turned his mind back to the reason for his visit.

He steered his horse down Gilbert Street and found the undertaker's office in the middle of the block between Main and Graham streets. Disguised as a carpenter's shop, Percy had to read the fine print at the bottom of the sign to confirm they also offered funeral services. As he climbed down from his horse he wondered what the undertaker's reaction would be when he found out he had seven graves to dig. Percy wrapped the reins around the hitching post and entered, a small bell above the door announcing his arrival.

There was no one manning the front counter and the scent of fresh-cut pine lingered in the air. The entry area was walled off from the rest of the shop and a moment later the door off to the right opened and out stepped a short, thin man wearing a stained shop apron and round, wire-rimmed glasses.

The man was wiping his hands on a rag as he stepped up to the counter. "Help you?"

"Busy?" Percy asked, trying to make conversation before dropping the bomb on him.

The man answered, but his German accent was so thick Percy had no idea what he'd said. *So much for an easy approach,* Percy thought.

"You have a wagon?"

"*Ja,*" the man said, nodding.

"Got some dead men I need you to pick up."

"*Ja, ja.*"

Percy sighed in frustration. "Anybody here speak English?"

The man tapped his chest and said, *"Ja, ja."*

Percy held up a finger and said, "I'll be back." He turned, pulled open the door, and exited, the bell dinging to announce his departure. He stood on the boardwalk and looked down the street. It looked as if the town petered out a block to the east, so he untied the mare's reins, walked her around the corner and up to the next block, then turned north on Ikard Street. He had a hunch the marshal's office would be near the courthouse and he found the building on the next corner, across the street from the enormous building.

After tying the reins around a different hitching post, Percy stepped up on the boardwalk and took a deep breath before pushing through the door. It was a small, cramped building with a single jail cell toward the back and the only furniture present was a large stove in the center and a small desk and a couple of chairs. The desk must have been sized for the man sitting behind it because he was a small man that couldn't have weighed more than 125 pounds. He stood as Percy pushed the door closed behind him.

"Can I help you?" the man asked.

"I sure hope so. You the town marshal?" Not only was the man light in the boots, he was short, too, the top of his head about even with the middle of Percy's chest.

"That's me." He stuck out his hand and said, "Cooper Wright."

Percy shook his hand. "Nice to meet you, Marshal. Name's Percy Ridgeway."

Wright waved to the chair next to his desk and said, "Please, have a seat."

Percy sat and Wright sank back into his chair and said, "How are things at the Rocking R Ranch, Mr. Ridgeway?"

"Percy'll do, Marshal. Well, I'll tell you, it had been pretty good until this morning."

"Uh-oh, what happened?"

"Had some steers stolen during the night and we tracked the rustlers to a spot on the Little Wichita about two miles west of here."

"How many rustlers we talkin' about?" Wright asked.

"Three men did the rustlin', but they met up with four other men fore we found 'em."

"Did you capture the three rustlers?"

"In a manner of speakin'," Percy said.

"How come you didn't go ahead and bring them in?"

"That's where things get kinda complicated, Marshal."

"How so?"

"Well, we went to apprehend the rustlers and a couple of them fools went for their guns."

"So, you're leavin' me with three dead bodies? Is that what you're tellin' me?"

"It's a might worse than that," Percy said. "When the shootin' was over, they was all dead."

"Jesus Christ," Wright muttered.

Percy went a little deeper into the details of what happened and when he finished, the marshal mulled it over for a few moments then stood, plucked his hat from the top of the desk, and put it on. "You better take me out there."

"Be glad to," Percy said as he pushed to his feet. "Tried to tell the undertaker to hitch up his wagon so he could fetch the bodies but, from what I can tell, he don't speak no English."

"That's Gustav Kirshbaum, one of the cabinetmakers who ain't been in the country for more than a month. Our regular undertaker took sick and is laid up in bed. Hadn't been a problem until now." The marshal gave Percy a hard look and said, "We get four, maybe five bodies a year in this town and most of them are old people who've hit the end of the line."

Percy shrugged. "Don't know what to tell you, Marshal. We had things planned out pretty good until it all went to hell."

The marshal was shaking his head as he stepped over to the door. He opened it, ushered Percy out, and then pulled the door closed behind them.

"Can you get through to the German that we need him and a wagon?" Percy asked.

"I can't, but there's a grocer on the corner that talks some German." The marshal paused while Percy gathered up his horse and they continued up the street, Percy leading the mare. "Any idea who the dead men are?" Wright asked.

"Not a clue, but they was pure evil. As we was trackin' them, the trail led us to a small cabin overlookin' the river about midmorning. It belonged to a young couple and the husband had started for town fore daybreak and the missus, a Molly Harris, stayed—"

Percy quit talking when the marshal stopped abruptly. He turned to look at Percy and said, "What did they do to her?"

"You know her?"

"'Course I know her. She's my niece."

"Well . . . uh . . . they roughed her up some, Marshal."

"What's roughed up?" Wright asked, his voice now tight with anger.

Percy swallowed and looked down at his boots, not wanting to tell Wright the grizzly details.

"I can see you don't want to say, but tell me this, then. Did they rape her?"

Percy nodded and looked up. "That and more."

Wright stared off into the distance for a moment, obviously trying to tamp down his anger. Percy let him stew for a moment then said, "They're dead now."

The marshal gave a slight nod and continued to stare down the street. Percy held his tongue and watched as the marshal inhaled a deep breath and slowly released it before saying, "She and her husband, Tommy, ain't been married but a week."

Percy, not knowing what to say, offered no response and eventually Wright turned to look at him as if seeing him for the first time. "I bet it was the Dillman brothers.

I should have killed them a long time ago. Them three rustlers all look alike?"

"Yes, sir." Having no idea how large the Dillman family might be, Percy was eager to get back out there. "Let's get the undertaker and ride out for a look-see."

The marshal nodded and they continued on their journey to the undertaker's.

CHAPTER
8

With their view obscured by the heavy timber along the river bottom, Leander and Chauncey had opted for a more suitable location to keep watch. They were now tucked back into the tree line near a bridge on the road connecting Henrietta and Wichita Falls, about a half a mile north of where the shooting had taken place. It was the ideal location because anyone approaching from town would have to cross the bridge if they wanted to stay dry.

Chauncey crossed his right leg over the saddle horn and pulled his rolling papers and tobacco from his shirt pocket and began rolling a cigarette. Once rolled to his satisfaction, he licked the edge of the paper to seal it and stuck it in his mouth. After striking a match on the bottom of his boot, he lit up and took a deep draw.

"We're assumin' them other four come from town," Chauncey said on the exhale.

"You think different?"

"Well, if them fellers was so busted they had to walk everywhere, how'd they afford to live in town?"

"Maybe they just like walkin'."

"Doubtful." Chauncey took another draw from his cigarette and said, "I'm bettin' they's camped somewhere along the river or they's nestin' in a couple of soddies somewhere."

Leander turned in his saddle for a look around before his eyes landed on Chauncey again. "You sayin' we ought to move to a different spot?"

Chauncey stubbed his cigarette out on the bottom of his boot and let it drop to the ground. "I am." He slid his right leg back where it belonged and picked up the reins. "Which way?"

"That's on you, after all that speculatin' you done."

Chauncey turned his horse and Leander followed as they rode back the way they had come. To make the riding easier, Chauncey steered away from the trees and they were about a quarter of a mile north of where the bodies were when a rifle shot shattered the stillness, the bullet plowing into the dirt a foot in front of Chauncey's horse. The two men immediately turned their horses and spurred them into the trees. Once they had some cover, they pulled their rifles and slid from the saddle.

"You see where it come from?" Leander asked as he dug extra ammo out of his saddlebag.

"Nope," Chauncey said as he stuffed extra ammunition into his pockets. "If they're shootin' at us, you gotta figure they found the bodies, so it has to be comin' from down that way."

The two men worked their way through the trees, angling toward the spot where the shooting had taken place. As they closed in on the river, Leander called a halt and they took cover behind the trunk of a large walnut and both men kneeled down on one knee while they studied their surroundings.

"We ain't got no idea what we're up against," Leander whispered.

"It don't matter, does it? Gotta play the hand we was dealt."

Looking ahead for any signs of movement, Chauncey said, "How do you want to—"

His words were drowned out by the roar of gunfire as a hail of bullets peppered the area all around them. Both men dropped to their bellies, waiting for the barrage to end. When the gunfire slacked off, Chauncey looked at Leander and said, "How many, you reckon?"

"Five, maybe six. Could be more, though." Leander pointed to a giant cottonwood to their left and said, "We need to move."

The two men belly-crawled twenty yards through the dead leaves and dirt before pushing up to their knees behind the cottonwood. Chauncey scanned the surrounding terrain and came up with an idea. "We get down into the river bottom we could work our way close to 'em without bein' seen."

Leander looked at the river, which was forty yards away, and said, "Means more crawlin' if we ain't gonna tip 'em to our plan."

"Gotta do what we gotta do."

Leander nodded and the two flattened out on the ground again and began crawling. Leander was looking in the direction of the shooters when he inadvertently brushed up against a patch of bull nettle. Immediately, it felt like the entire left side of his body had been lit on fire and he had to suck on his bottom lip to keep from cursing out loud. There was nothing he could do but keep crawling, the stinging hairs working deeper into his skin with each movement as bullets continued to pound the trees above them.

It felt like they'd been crawling forever before they finally slithered down the riverbank, which was about ten feet high. They paused to take stock of the situation. They had barely caught their breath when someone opened up from the other side of the river. Spotting a short sand dune off to their right that would offer some cover from that side, Leander said, "Follow me," and began crawling again.

They managed to arrive unharmed, but the situation was dire. It wouldn't be long before the shooters on their side of the river closed in. Trying to make himself as small as possible, Leander looked downriver and spied a large pile of driftwood that had accumulated at a short bend in the river. He looked at Chauncey and said, "They got us in a cross fire. We're going to have to wait it out and try to pick a few of them off. See that pile of driftwood yonder with the big sand dune next to it?"

Chauncey looked downriver and said, "I see it. I reckon this wasn't such a good idea after all."

"Ain't nothin' we can do about it now. Your pa'll be back soon, but we're gonna have to ride it out. We burrow down in there and we'll be okay." Leander, trying to ignore the pain, took a deep breath and said, "Cover me," before he lurched to his feet and took off running.

Chauncey pumped two rounds toward the shooter across the river then turned and began laying down heavy fire in the area where he thought the other shooters might be. He glanced to his left to track Leander's progress and saw that he was almost there. When his rifle clicked on an empty chamber, he dropped it and pulled his pistols, now pushing hot lead in both directions. When Leander dived behind the dune, Chauncey hunkered down and quickly reloaded his weapons.

With that task completed, he pulled his hat down tight and waited for Leander's signal. And he didn't have to wait long. As soon as Leander fired his first shot, Chauncey was up and running, an occasional bullet smacking the dirt around him as the man across the river tried and failed to keep up with a moving target. When Chauncey reached the sand dune, he dived to the ground and rolled over onto his back, gasping for air.

Leander looked down at him and said, "I'm twice as old as you and I ain't even breathin' hard."

"I'm a faster runner than you," Chauncey said, rolling over and pushing up to his knees. He took a moment to study the layout and liked what he saw. They would be vulnerable if anyone approached from the water, but Chauncey was betting if the shooters couldn't afford horses, they most likely wouldn't have a boat, either. "You get a feel where the shooters on this side of the river is?" He took off his Stetson and eased up to the top of the dune, next to Leander. The brush pile behind them would shield them from that direction, so Chauncey felt relatively safe focusing his attention on those closer at hand.

Leander pointed to the right. "There's one behind that deadfall there and," swinging his arm to the left, he said, "there's two or three in that stand of blackjacks."

Chauncey focused on the blackjacks, searching for

any hint of movement or anything that didn't belong. He didn't see anything at first, so he relaxed, letting his eyes wander from object to object, and still didn't see anything out of place.

"Them fellas probably been huntin' since they were old enough to carry a gun just to put food on the table," Leander said. "They're gonna be hard to root out of there."

"So we what?" Chauncey asked. "Sit here and wait for my pa to come?"

"That ain't what I said. They might be good hunters, but I reckon there ain't none of 'em never hunted anythin' that was shootin' back at 'em. We just need to be patient, is all I'm sayin'."

"I reckon we ain't got a choice, do we?"

"Nope. Keep lookin' and we'll thin 'em out a little fore Percy shows up."

CHAPTER
9

Although Indian Territory had been set aside for the Indians who had been forced from their native lands, there remained a section of fertile land in the heart of the Territory that had never been assigned to any tribes. Known as the Unassigned Lands, or Oklahoma to others, the area encompassed nearly two million acres of virgin ground that would-be settlers had been begging the federal government to open for years.

The land was cut through by as many as five rivers, which had deposited eons of sediment along their fertile banks. In addition, timber was plentiful along the watercourses, adding to the allure for those people lusting to own a piece of paradise. But not everyone was on board with opening the land to settlement and the most vocal critics were the Indians, who had been promised their lands for as long as the "grass grows and the water flows." The other group opposing the opening were the well-monied and well-connected cattle ranchers who had been grazing their cattle on the land for years, either for free or paying such paltry sums it was almost criminal. Their money had greased the skids in Washington, D.C., for decades, but even they and their paid-for politicians weren't immune to the public's insatiable hunger for land.

The groups pushing for the opening were many, but the loudest and most organized were known as the Boomers. Made up mostly of Kansans, the Boomers had lobbied the federal government for years to open portions of Indian Territory. To make their point, they frequently made incursions into the Unassigned Lands only to be expelled repeatedly by the U.S. Army. The driving force behind the Boomer movement had been a man named David Payne who had died of a heart attack before seeing his dreams come to fruition. Payne's death opened the door for another man, named William Couch, who took over the reins of the movement and ramped up the pressure.

It was unclear how effective Couch had been in his efforts, but his wish finally came true when President Grover Cleveland inked his name on a bill opening the Unassigned Lands to settlement. The when and how was left to President Benjamin Harrison, who assumed the office the very next day. Apparently with little thought to how the mechanics might work, Harrison announced on March 23, 1889, that the 1.9 million acres would be thrown open for settlement on a first come, first served basis at noon on April 22, less than a month away.

Before the ink on Harrison's signature was dry, word of the opening spread quickly, making front page headlines in newspapers across the globe. Settlement groups soon formed in most of the large cities and as far away as Sweden as surveyors went to work, mapping the free land into 160-acre tracts. The first to feel the effects were the Kansas border towns, which quadrupled in size seemingly overnight. One of those border towns, once a booming cattle town when cattle drives had been the order of the day, was Caldwell, Kansas, where William Couch and his Boomers chose to set up camp as the first few days of April peeled off the calendar.

Caldwell, slowly sinking into anonymity, was bustling again, at least temporarily. The area was quickly jammed with would-be settlers and to meet their needs, tent gambling halls, tent saloons, tent hotels, tent restaurants, tent churches, and, of course, tent whorehouses soon popped up. When added to the thousands of heavily armed men streaming into the city, it was a combustible mixture ripe for explosion. And with nothing much to do other than watching the clock tick down, violence soared, and a popular saying heard all along the border was "Give me my hundred and sixty acres or six feet, and I don't give a damn which." There was little doubt that blood was spilled, but how many people actually ended up six feet under was unknown.

And right smack in the middle of all that were William Couch and his Boomers. A short, thin man with dark hair and a handlebar mustache, Couch was a thirty-eight-year-old family man looking for a fresh start. Once prosperous with a bustling hardware store in Wichita, Couch was now busted. Camped along the Arkansas River that wound around the south side of town, he, his wife, Cynthia, and their five children were huddled in their tent, trying to ward off the chilly north wind.

There was also another Boomer leader in Caldwell that

day, and like everyone there he was also looking for a fresh start. When Gordon W. Lillie and his wife, May, had first arrived in Wichita a few months ago, they had been met by a brass band and a string of town dignitaries. It wasn't something the folks in Wichita did often, but with the famous Pawnee Bill and his wife rolling into town, city officials had thought the occasion merited a celebration. But that had been months ago, and much had changed since then.

Lillie, under the show name of Pawnee Bill, due to his years-long association with the Pawnee Indian tribe, had traveled the world as an interpreter and participant in Buffalo Bill's Wild West show until he had a falling-out with the show's founder, Bill Cody. Bill and May, who was dubbed the "Princess of the Prairie" for her shooting and riding skills, had tried starting their own Wild West show last year and it had been a financial disaster. With hopes of resurrecting their show in the future, Bill was now focused on staking a claim on a piece of free land to relieve some of their financial burdens. And he was bringing along a good number of people to do the same. Ever the showman, Bill had formed his own group of Boomers, which he had named the Pawnee Bill Oklahoma Colonization Company, and it was, by far, the largest organized group of would-be homesteaders in Caldwell.

Camped a few hundred yards upstream from the Couch family on Fall Creek, Bill and May were finishing up their noontime meal. Bill stood from his folding camp chair, carried his dinner plate over to the washtub, and dropped it in. He turned to May and said, "I'm gonna stretch my legs a bit."

May nodded and continued chewing the food in her mouth, never looking up from the newspaper she was reading.

She was in one of her "blue" moods again and he had long ago given up trying to placate her. He exited the tent and turned right for a walk along the creek. May's moods could change in an instant and he could never predict what might trigger the change. He suspected this one had something to do with all the children running around the camp, and that left him feeling helpless. On tour with Cody's show when May had given birth to their son, Bill soon returned home to find his son gravely ill and it had gone downhill from there. Six weeks later, they were burying their child and, because it had been a difficult birth, the doctor had been forced to operate on May afterward and the procedure had left her barren.

Pawnee Bill was jarred back to the present by a nearby gunshot. With nearly every man in the swelling city gunned up, it was a fairly common occurrence but that didn't make it any less startling. Bill stopped and looked around, trying to pinpoint the location of the shooter. It was an impossible task with hundreds of people milling about though he did notice that no one seemed overly concerned, so he continued on.

Having started with no real destination in mind, Bill changed course, deciding to pay a visit to the Couch family. It would have been much easier to have stayed home in Wichita until closer to the Run, but Bill had noticed a couple of the local bankers he owed were starting to give him the stink eye. The upcoming Land Run offered the perfect excuse to leave town for a while and Bill had jumped at the chance. With plans to pay every cent back, the angry glares only added to his stress and he looked forward to the day when he could walk into their banks, pay them off, and tell them to go to hell.

Someone shouted his name and Bill waved a hand and continued on. With his face plastered on show bills circulating around the globe, it was hard for him to go anywhere without being recognized. Although the attention was nice at times, there were other times when he craved anonymity. Having to always project a positive persona while in public was tiresome, but he knew it came with the job. There were no off days as a showman and he couldn't afford to alienate anyone, especially if they were going to resurrect the show at some point. He pulled his hat down a little lower as he worked his way around a maze of tents, and he waved to the Couch family when they came into view.

William stepped out to meet him.

"How are things down this way?" Bill asked, slowing to a stop.

"Crowded, noisy, and malodorous," Couch said.

"So not much different from where I am?" Bill said.

Couch chuckled and said, "I suppose not."

"Maybe we ought to pull out early," Bill said, "and camp elsewhere."

"Moving three thousand people is a pain in the ass."

"We're gonna have to do it at some point."

"I realize that, but I hate to do it more than once," Couch said. "Unless . . ."

"What?"

Couch waved a hand at the sea of tents and said, "Out

of all these people, I bet we're the only ones who have spent any time inside Indian Territory."

"You're probably right," Bill said, "but what difference does that make?"

"Well, with our knowledge of the area it would be fairly easy to slip past the army patrols."

"You talkin' about goin' in early?" Bill asked.

"Maybe. When it gets closer to the date, we could start staggering departures from here to keep it from being so obvious."

Bill mulled that over for a moment and said, "I don't know, William. We've worked awful hard to get the government to open the land up. It sure would be a shame to go in early and get caught and end up with nothin'."

"We don't need to decide today," Couch said. "Take some time to think about it."

CHAPTER
10

It seemed to take forever for the German cabinet-maker, Gustav Kirshbaum, to get his wagon hitched up. Percy didn't know if they did things different in Germany or what, but he was ready to strangle the man. And to make matters worse, he kept hearing distant gunshots and he hadn't been able to pinpoint where they were coming from. With the luck they'd had so far today, Percy had a bad feeling it was Chauncey and Leander. Not that he was worried, necessarily. Those two could take care of themselves. But he also knew there were times when being outnumbered had a direct impact on the outcome.

Percy, sitting atop his mare, fished out his watch and popped the lid. It was a little after noon and he looked at Marshal Cooper Wright and said, "Reckon we'll make it out there fore dark?"

Wright, sitting on his big gelding, frowned and shook his head. Percy knew he was frustrated, too. And not being able to converse with Gustav made it more maddening. The grocer had helped as much as he could before being called back to the store. Finally, Gustav looked up, smiled, and said, "*Ja.*"

Percy made a hurry-up motion with his hand, having given up on trying to talk to the German. Gustav scampered up to the seat, picked up the reins, and they were off. They passed a hardware store, a Chinese laundry, a saloon, and a hotel on the next corner and that was as far as they got when the marshal called a halt.

"What now?" Percy asked, exasperated.

Wright pointed at a young man who was standing in the doorway of a blacksmith shop down the street and said, "That's Molly's husband, Tommy Harris."

He was turned, looking at something inside, and hadn't see them yet. "Oh," Percy said. "How you gonna handle it?"

"You got any ideas?" Wright said.

Percy thought about it for a moment. It was a strange dynamic and he could see several sides of what looked to be a complex problem. If the men who had molested Molly had still been on the loose then the marshal would have had an obligation to begin an investigation and the details of what had happened to Molly would become public. But with the three rapists now dead, the only person who knew exactly what happened was Molly. Yes, she'd told Percy, Leander, and Chauncey some of what had happened to her, but they didn't have a stake in any of it. And now that she'd had some time to think about it, would she want people to know she'd been violently assaulted? Percy didn't feel comfortable telling her husband what had happened and since the marshal knew of the assault only because of what Percy had told him, he didn't think it was the marshal's place, either. The overriding question they couldn't answer was whether Molly would want her husband to know she'd been raped. She would have a black eye, but Percy thought that could be explained away with a few white lies.

The marshal cleared his throat and said, "Well, you come up with anythin'? He's gonna see us and I can't ride by without sayin' somethin'."

"There may be some things she might not want told. Might be best to tell her husband that . . . well . . . maybe that . . . she's hurt and needs tendin'."

"His next question is goin' to be how she got hurt."

Before he could respond, Percy heard gunfire again and there was no doubt where it was coming from this time. "I don't know what you ought to tell him, but I gotta ride. Cross the bridge and turn south and you'll find us." Without waiting for a response, he spurred the mare hard and she squatted for a millisecond before exploding forward. He loosened the reins and let her run.

As he drew closer, he began scanning ahead, searching for any signs of activity. Having no idea of where Chauncey and Leander might be, he was hoping to see a muzzle blast or a puff of smoke to pinpoint their location. But there was so much timber along the river, it was difficult to see much of anything. The horse flew across the bridge and Percy steered her off the road. As he drew closer to where he had last seen Leander and Chauncey, he slowed the mare to a walk, preferring not to ride into an ambush. Other than the wide strip of trees running parallel to the stream, this side of the river was wide-open country and he felt exposed knowing there were shooters in the area.

He hadn't heard any more gunshots and Percy didn't know if that was a good thing or a bad thing. That thought had barely registered when gunfire erupted again. Percy counted four shots, and, worse, none appeared to be from the same weapon, leaving him to wonder if the woods were infested with would-be killers. He zeroed in on where he thought the shooters might be and adjusted the mare's course before spurring her into another run. With about four hundred yards to the tree line, the horse gobbled up the distance quickly. Pulling her to a stop, he grabbed his rifle and slid from the saddle.

Although a voice in his head was urging him to hurry, Percy knew it was a good way to end up dead. Methodically, he worked his way through the trees, pausing every few steps to look and listen. He disliked going into battle when the number of opponents was unknown, especially in a dense forest that offered unlimited hiding places. His eyes constantly scanning, Percy worked his way closer to the river.

Twenty yards later, he spotted the first man. He was lying on his belly behind an oak tree about ten feet from the water's edge, his rifle snugged tight to his shoulder. A large cedar tree prevented Percy from seeing what the man was aiming at, so he slowly sidestepped to the right until he was directly behind the shooter. Following the barrel of the man's rifle, Percy saw a large sand dune fronting a larger stack of driftwood and assumed that was where Leander and Chauncey were pinned down. Shifting his rifle to his left hand, Percy pulled his pistol and eased up behind the man. When he was as close as he dared to go, he said in a low voice, "Hey, pardner."

The man turned as if stung by a bee and he was in the process of bringing his rifle around when the slug from Percy's pistol pierced the underside of his chin, launching a spray of blood, bone, and brains. Percy dropped to his belly before the echo had faded, as bullets ripped through the air above him. From the sound of it, he had a lot more work to do. He ejected the spent shell from his pistol and loaded a fresh cartridge then crawled over behind the cedar and pushed up to his knees as the firing tapered off.

Having no idea how many people he might be facing, he needed Leander and Chauncey out of their hidey-hole and back in the fight. Working his way from tree to tree and constantly scanning for threats, Percy slowly worked his way closer to their position. When he got as close as he could without exposing himself, he scanned the ground and picked up a good-sized rock. Not wanting to give away his position, he tossed the rock into the river and waited. A splash in the water could be explained away fairly easily.

After a few moments and nothing had happened, Percy searched for another rock and tossed it into the water. Waiting, he breathed a sigh of relief when Chauncey's face appeared around the side of the dune. It took a moment for him to find Percy and when he did, he smiled. Chauncey held up two fingers and pointed over his shoulder and then four fingers and pointed to their side of the river.

Well, hell, Percy thought. They were pinned down because they were caught in a cross fire. He hadn't counted on that. Percy held up four fingers and then dropped his index finger and Chauncey nodded. Percy pointed at his rifle then across the water and Chauncey nodded again. He gave his son a thumbs-up before melting back into the trees. He needed to take out the shooters across the river before he could free Chauncey and Leander.

The river was about 150 yards wide at that point, a long shot for sure, but Percy had made them before. First, he had to find out where the two men were hiding, and to do that he would need Chauncey and Leander's help. Working his way through the trees, Percy didn't want to get too far away from their hiding place, but he needed to find the right spot. He wasn't too worried about cover because if all went well, the men he would be aiming at wouldn't be returning fire. What he needed was some elevation that would allow him a better view of the other side. On the verge of giving up, he stumbled across an enormous oak tree, its long sturdy branches running almost all the way to the ground.

Although it had been a long time since Percy had thought about climbing a tree, he was out of time and out of options. He needed to get things settled before the marshal and the German rode into a firefight. Reaching up, he pulled himself up to the first branch and continued to climb. Finding a good spot where the tree forked, he wedged himself in and rested the front stock of his rifle in the notch of another branch, making it a perfect sniper's perch.

He assumed Chauncey and Leander would do something to draw fire from the other side of the river and that assumption proved correct a moment later when a rifle shot rang out from that direction. Percy marked the location of the muzzle blast and waited for the second man to fire before taking his shots. He didn't have to wait long and about ten seconds later the second man fired and Percy now had his targets. After quickly calculating the angles and allowing for bullet drop, he sighted in on the first man, took a deep breath, and fired. He quickly levered in a new shell and sighted in on the second man and pulled the trigger, the man's body jerking from the impact. Although he was fairly certain both were killing shots, at a minimum they were now out of action. Percy turned and began launching lead at the shooters on their side of the river as Chauncey and Leander broke from cover, their rifles up and firing as fast as they could cycle them. After reloading his rifle, Percy climbed down from the tree.

He joined up with Chauncey and Leander and they launched a withering fusillade as they slowly advanced. Looking through the trees, Percy saw two men on horses light out at a dead run and held up his fist, calling a cease-fire. Unsure if those two were the last of the shooters, Percy motioned for them to take cover behind a fallen tree and they sank down to their bellies, waiting for the smoke to clear.

"What took you so long?" Chauncey asked.

With his ears ringing from all the gunfire, it took a moment for Chauncey's words to register in Percy's brain. "A damn German, that's what. Him and the marshal ought to be along any minute now. Why'd you two let 'em pin you down?"

"A tactical error," Chauncey said, feeding more cartridges into his rifle. "We tried to shoot our way out but they was sneaky bastards and we couldn't get off many clean shots."

"Leander, you out of practice?" Percy asked.

"I might be a bit rusty," Leander said. "Gettin' too damn old for this stuff."

"We goin' after 'em?" Chauncey asked.

"Nah. I reckon they done had all the fight they wanted," Percy said.

"Means we're gonna be lookin' over our shoulders for a while," Chauncey said.

"Ain't the first time," Leander said. "They want more, we'll give it to 'em."

"Let's go see what kinda damage we did," Percy said, pushing up to his feet.

They picked their way carefully through the trees and found two more bodies. With the two across the river and the other one Percy had dispatched when he had first arrived, the morning's tally of the dead stood at twelve.

"Ain't gonna make the marshal none too happy," Percy said.

"Can't be helped," Leander said.

Percy reclaimed his horse and they moved out into the open to wait for the arrival of the marshal and the German. Just when Percy thought he was going to have to ride back to town, he spotted them, the German with that same silly grin on his face. Percy wondered if he'd still be smiling when they stacked the dead bodies like cordwood onto his wagon.

The marshal arrived a few moments later and climbed down from his horse. "What the hell happened? It sounded like the Battle of Bull Run out here."

"I guess some of the dead men's kinfolk wanted a little payback," Percy said.

"Jesus Christ," Marshal Wright said. He pushed his hat back on his head and said, "What's the damage now?"

"Twelve," Percy said.

Wright mumbled a few choice curse words then looked

at Percy and said, "You damn near wiped out half the county in a single mornin'."

Percy shrugged and said, "Don't know what to tell you. We didn't start none of it." Percy made the introductions and once that was complete, they spent several moments answering the marshal's questions.

Wright turned to check on the progress of the wagon and said, "Might as well wait on Gustav." He looked at Percy and said, "Can we get the wagon back in there where the first shootin' happened?"

"We can get close. If we'da known it was gonna turn out like it did, I reckon we'da planned it better."

The wagon arrived and Percy led the group through the trees, trying to pick a path that would accommodate the wagon's bulk. When they had gone as far as the wagon could go, the German set the brake and climbed down and they continued on. When they arrived at the first scene the marshal held up his hand, signaling everyone to stay where they were.

Percy saw that the flies had arrived en masse and they carpeted the corpses in a thick mat that almost made it look like the bodies themselves were moving. Several of the dead had begun to swell and the stench of death hung heavy in the air. Percy pointed out the three rustlers, and the marshal, holding his nose, moved forward for a closer look. After a quick look he stepped back and said, "Thems the Dillman brothers, all right. Furthest one on the right there, that's Michael Dillman, the oldest. Can't recall the other two's names but there ain't been a sorrier bunch of humans to ever walk the earth. The other four's nephews or cousins or half brothers or whatever. I ain't never figured out how that family tree limbed out. They got 'em three or four soddies over on Duck Creek and ain't none of 'em got two nickels to rub together."

"It look like it played out like I told you it did?" Percy asked.

"Yeah, it does. Saved me the trouble of huntin' those three bastards down. The rest of 'em probably got what was comin' to 'em in the end. No doubt they was guilty of somethin'." The marshal waved Gustav forward and the German began gathering up the guns and other personal effects, which he dropped into a gunnysack.

While they waited for the German to gather up the personal items, Percy stepped up close to Wright and said, "What'd you end up tellin' Molly's husband?"

The marshal gave Percy a sheepish look then looked down at his boots. "I didn't tell him nothin'. I *did* wave when we rode by." Wright looked up at Percy and said, "Think I'm a chickenshit?"

"Nah, it's a dicey subject and it's probably best to let your niece tell the story like she wants to. That said, I do think you ought to try to get her to go see a doctor."

Wright's brows arched with worry. "You think the Dillman brothers mighta give her the pox?"

"It's possible," Percy said. "You might ought to get that undertaker that's laid up or a doctor to take a look at the bodies."

Wright worked his fingers through his goatee, thinking. "Would you want to know you had the disease iffen it was you? I mean, there ain't no cure for it and all those so-called fixes ain't nothin' but snake oil."

It was actually a question Percy had thought about before. Over the last dozen years, Percy had made occasional trips to Fort Worth to spend some time with Josie

Belmont, madam and owner of a parlor house known as The Belmont. Although she had a very exclusive client list, Percy knew it would take only one bad apple to spoil the entire barrel. So yes, Percy had thought about it, but it wasn't a discussion he wanted to have with a man he'd just met. "That'll be up to her, I reckon. But if you find out they ain't got it, that might ease your niece's mind some."

"Good point. I'll get somebody to take a look," Wright said.

"We ready to load the bodies?"

"I suppose," Wright said. "I still need to identify the rest of 'em if I can. Want to show where the others are?"

"Two of 'em are on the other side of the river. Probably be best to finish up here before movin' on." Percy didn't know if the marshal was trying to avoid getting his hands dirty or what, but he wasn't going to leave Leander and Chauncey with the gruesome job of helping Gustav to load the bodies.

The marshal frowned but he joined in on the work and, with none of the dead being large men, it didn't take long to load them on. Percy thought Gustav might be a little soft in the head because the German smiled through it all, jabbering, "*Ja, ja*," repeatedly.

After stopping to retrieve the other three bodies, one of which the marshal identified as the Dillman brothers' father, they crossed the bridge and loaded up the other two before heading for town.

Townspeople, young and old, streamed out of their houses and a few of the businesses, swarming around the wagon, eager for a look at the gruesome scene. Blood and bodily fluids dripped through the wagon's floorboards and splattered in the dust. Why anyone would want to see such a thing was a mystery to Percy. He, for one, couldn't wait to get the hell out of there.

Gustav slowed in front of his shop, but the marshal waved him on, leading the procession out to the cemetery, and like thousands of other cemeteries the world over, it came complete with a white picket fence. Percy climbed down from his horse and wrapped the reins around a fence rail. The marshal moseyed up and said, "I couldn't see movin' 'em any more than we had to."

"Makes sense. If any of the people from town want to help dig the graves, I'll pay 'em."

"How much?" Wright asked.

"Whatever you think is best," Percy said. "How much am I gonna owe Gustav?"

The marshal mulled that over for a minute then said, "Forty dollars ought to cover Gustav. I figure a couple of dollars each ought to do for anybody wantin' to dig."

"Make it five dollars so we'll be sure to have some takers."

Wright made the announcement and he immediately had twenty men volunteer. Wright turned to Percy and said, "How many is too many?"

"Hire 'em all," Percy said.

"You sure?" Wright asked.

"I'm sure. Maybe it'll take their minds off of revenge if they're so inclined."

Wright made the announcement and several of the men shouted with joy before taking off to grab their shovels. Percy walked over to his horse, reached into his saddle-bag, and pulled out a drawstring bag. Untying it, he pulled out a handful of double eagles and walked over to Gustav and handed him three of them, more than the marshal had suggested but maybe, Percy thought, Gustav could use some of the extra money to pay someone to teach him some English. He counted out five more and handed them to Marshal Wright to dole out to the others. "Don't forget to have somebody look at the Dillman brothers."

"I won't forget," the marshal said.

Percy stuck out his hand and the two men shook. "Sorry about the trouble."

"Oh, hell," Wright said, "most of them killed had it comin' and the town folk can use the work. Looks like a winner all the way around to me."

"Well," Percy said, "if you ever need anything, look me up." He nodded at Leander and Chauncey and the three men mounted their horses and headed out of town.

As they were leaving, Percy pondered the morning's events. If anyone was sad about losing several members of the community, they didn't show it. And that made Percy a tad bit sad. That twelve men could have been so disliked that no one in town mourned their passing said something about human nature, and not in a good way.

CHAPTER
11

Although occupied with caring for the pregnant mares, Marcie was still reeling from her encounter with Archer Keating. As she watched a new mother bathe her foal, she contemplated the possible fallout from an altercation she had foolishly started. Eli had been crystal clear about what would happen if Keating returned to the ranch, but it was a vast space that stretched on for miles and there was no way a dozen ranch hands could patrol it all. And Marcie knew Keating's type. He'd want payback and it didn't matter if it came tomorrow, next week, or next year.

She was torn about mentioning it to Chauncey because she knew exactly what his response would be. He'd be on the first train to Fort Worth, his pistols loaded and ready for war. On the other hand, she didn't know how much Keating knew about the Ridgeway family. If he somehow learned she was married to Chauncey, then she was somewhat concerned Keating might go after him and she didn't want him blindsided. It was a quandary, but it wasn't so pressing she needed to make a decision today.

Besides, if worse came to worst, she'd put her money on Chauncey every time.

Her thoughts were interrupted when Emma shouted, "Marcie!"

Marcie hurried to the other side of the barn and found Emma in a stall with a mare who was lying on her side and in obvious distress. "What do you need?" Marcie asked.

Emma looked up and blew a strand of hair off her face. "I need a bucket of water and some soap and I need it now."

"On it," Marcie said. She raced past the stalls, grabbed a bucket and a bar of soap from where Emma had staged them, and hurried back, the water sloshing out and drenching her shoes. She lifted the heavy bucket over the gate and Emma took it.

"What's wrong?" Marcie asked, short of breath.

"Don't know yet." Emma quickly rolled up her shirtsleeve and began soaping up her arm. Foaling season demanded a change in attire and both Emma and Marcie were dressed in pants, boots, and long-sleeved shirts.

"Need me in there?" Marcie asked.

"Don't think so," Emma said. Once her arm was nice and slick from fingertip to shoulder, Emma kneeled behind the mare and slowly began pushing her hand inside the mare's uterus. After a few moments of grunting, cursing, and groaning, Emma, now drenched with sweat, slowly pulled her arm free and sat back on her heels. "Got it fixed, but I hope I didn't wait too long." She pushed warily to her feet, splashed some water on her arm, and dried it with a red neckerchief she pulled from her back pocket.

"I don't remember you having to do that before," Marcie said.

"It's rare. Usually Mother Nature does a good job takin' care of it."

"What was the problem?'

"One of the front legs had folded under. It's a tight squeeze through the birth canal even during a normal delivery."

"How do you know all of this?"

Emma shrugged as she opened the gate and stepped out. "Books, journals, whatever I can get my hands on. Let's give Momma here a little privacy while we check on the others."

They strolled passed the stalls, pausing at each one to check on the mares. All the horses appeared to be doing well so they stepped outside for a breath of fresh air. One of the buggies had been rolled out of the barn and they climbed up and sat down. It had been a busy day.

"Did you always want to work with horses?" Marcie asked.

"Not necessarily. I had the same dreams most young girls had—a husband, lots of children, and a house with a white picket fence." Emma stopped and turned to look off into the distance.

Marcie laid her hand on Emma's arm and said, "I didn't mean to pry."

Without turning, Emma said, "It's okay. Just give me a minute."

Marcie regretted bringing it up. Any conversations about Emma's past could circle around to her own.

After a few moments, Emma wiped her eyes and turned to look at Marcie. "I was damaged goods when I came home after being rescued. It didn't matter that I was taken against my will or that I fought like hell, it only mattered that I had been tainted by the savages, a permanent stain that I guess I'll take to my grave. The family tried to shield me from most of it, but even those people who spouted out about forgiveness and doing God's work, shunned me. So, I decided I'd devote my time to horses. They're affectionate, social animals who give a lot more than they receive and, more importantly, they accept me for who I am and don't give a damn what happened in the past. Does that make sense?"

"More than you know." What Emma had said touched something way down deep in Marcie's soul. She realized that everyone had some type of burden to bear, some much heavier than others. "We can't change our pasts no matter how much we may want to. I've done things I regret deeply, but all we can do is move forward. And for what it's worth, you're a remarkable woman who has done a terrific job raising your son."

"Thank you," Emma said.

The two women sat in silence for a few moments. The sun felt good on Marcie's face and it was a pleasant day with the barn blocking the chilly north wind. Ranch hands came and went, tipping their hats in greeting and that helped to lighten the mood.

Eventually, Emma slapped her thighs and stood. "We better check on the horses again."

"Before we go, I want your opinion on something."

Emma settled back on the buggy seat and said, "Shoot."

"I'm thinking about staking a claim during the Land Run."

Emma reared back in surprise. "We've got more land

than we know what to do with now. You and Chauncey ought to be able to carve out as much land as you want if you're looking to build a new house."

"It's not that," Marcie said.

"What, then?"

"Well, you were born into this family and I only married into it."

"That doesn't matter. You're family now."

"What happens if Chauncey gets tired of me? Or, God forbid, something happens to him? I have nothing, zero, zilch. But if I could stake a claim, I'd have something. Nothing compared to what we have here, but something tangible, something I could call mine."

Emma mulled that over for a few moments then said, "I can see wantin' to have something to call your own. When it comes right down to it, I don't have anything that I own outright, either, other than my house, I guess. But I'd lose that if somethin' happened to the ranch. What about the rules? Don't you have to live on it a certain length of time and do some other stuff?"

"If you build a dwelling, which could be almost anything, make a few improvements, and live on it for five years you get the land free and clear. But, and this is the important part, you can live on it for a year, build a flower bed or some other minor deal, pay a dollar and a quarter an acre, and it's yours."

"Would you actually have to live on it for a year?" Emma asked.

"How are they goin' to know? Pitch a tent and leave it up for a while and nobody would know any different. I think all the government cares about is the money."

"Huh," Emma said. She thought it over for a few moments and said, "When is this Land Run?"

"High noon on April twenty-second."

Emma thought about it some more and said, "If we can get all these mares foaled, I might just go with you. Think we can be neighbors?"

"I don't see why not."

Emma started to stand again, and Marcie grabbed her sleeve, pulling her back down. "I'd prefer you not tell anyone."

Emma looked at Marcie for a long moment and said, "Are you sure things are good between you and Chauncey?"

"They are, I promise. But . . . well . . . as you've no doubt noticed I haven't been able to get pregnant. I know Chauncey says it doesn't matter, but people change their minds all the time."

Emma settled back on the seat. "Have you been trying?"

"Oh yeah, plenty."

Emma's cheeks flushed with color and she tried to ignore it. "Have you been to the doctor?"

Marcie nodded and said, "They said they can't find anything wrong with me. But most of the doctors I've met don't know much about that stuff. A broken arm or a bad cut and you're in good hands. Not so much with everything else."

"Any reason you can think of as to why you can't get pregnant?"

And there it was—the question Marcie had asked herself ten thousand times. Now it was her turn to look off into the distance. She really didn't want to dive into the past and the only reason she was thinking about it now was the fact that Emma had spent years studying the horse breeding process. Although Marcie didn't even know if there were any similarities, there was always a chance that Emma had uncovered some nugget of information that could put her mind at ease. She turned to Emma and said, "I worked as a parlor house girl for almost two years."

When Emma didn't say anything right away, Marcie said, "You don't seem shocked."

"Word gets around, no matter how much we wish it didn't."

"Who else knows?" Marcie asked.

"I have no idea. I've never discussed it with anyone. Besides, I couldn't care less. You're like a sister to me and I'll love you until the day I pass from this world." Emma reached out, took Marcie's hand, and said, "Here's the thing, though. It takes a woman and a *man* to make a baby and Chauncey's role is just as important as yours, so it's not all your fault. Unfortunately, science hasn't advanced far enough to accurately diagnose where the problems might be and the only thing you can do is keep trying. I had a stallion I tried to breed for several years and he never could get the mare pregnant. So, stuff like that does happen and probably more often than we know."

Marcie gave Emma's hand a squeeze and said, "Thank you. I hadn't thought about it that way and I was thinking it was all my fault. You've eased my mind, and, by the way, I love you like a sister, too."

"Now can we go check on the mares?" Emma asked.

"Lead the way," Marcie said.

CHAPTER
12

Grace Ferguson was upstairs in the apartment when she heard the bell over the door ding and then Oliver Grigsby's voice. Despite the passage of time, a chill ran down her spine as she crept closer to the stairs. Lizzie was down for another nap and if she stuck to her schedule she wouldn't wake up for another couple of hours. Grace listened as the introductions were made then heard the squeak of Seth's chair as he settled into it.

"Where's the woman who was here earlier?" she heard Grigsby ask. He had a deep voice and it floated up the staircase and settled around Grace like a ghost from the past.

Seth's voice was softer, and she thought he said something about running errands.

"Her name's not Brandy, is it?" Grigsby asked.

Again, Grace couldn't hear Seth's reply, but she presumed he denied it.

She heard Grigsby chuckle and then she shivered when he said, "Too bad. I don't know where that girl got off to, but Lordy, could I tell some stories about her. There was this one time—"

"Get out!" Seth shouted. This time she had no trouble hearing her husband.

Grace heard the scrape of chairs being pushed back and Grigsby said, "What the hell's wrong with you?"

Seth sounded a little more composed when she heard him tell Grigsby that he wouldn't represent him.

"It's Brandy, ain't it?" Grigsby asked.

Seth was back to shouting when he reiterated his previous statement then tacked on, "And don't show your face here ever again."

Grigsby's voice was more subdued when he mumbled something about marrying a whore then the bell rang and the door slammed, and Grace sucked in a deep breath, held it for a moment, then blew it out. Would it ever end?

She pondered that question—again—as she descended the stairs. Seth's face was still red from the encounter as she walked over and wrapped her arms around his waist. "I'm sorry."

Seth gently cradled her face in his hands and tilted her head up to look her in the eyes. "You have nothing to be sorry about. That's the beauty of workin' for myself. I get to choose which clients I want to take on." He leaned in, kissed her softly on the lips, and whispered, "I'd marry you a thousand times over."

Grace broke the embrace and stepped back. "Me, too, but that isn't goin' to pay the bills. And because of me, a payin' client just walked out the door."

"Good riddance," Seth said. "I knew when I shook his hand, I wasn't going to represent him."

"Why?" Grace asked.

Seth shrugged. "He just rubbed me the wrong way, even before he opened that mouth of his." Seth settled back in his chair. "Besides, we're goin' to have more work than we'll be able to handle filing land claims after the Run."

Grace walked over to her desk, scooted behind it, and sat. She was hoping to move on quickly from what had just happened. She knew that Seth loved her, but she also knew, despite what he said, he was bothered that her past sometimes got thrown in his face. In the end, that wasn't who she was anymore, and she could no more change the past than anyone else could. "That's still a couple of weeks away."

"I've got a couple of wills to write and Uncle Percy has a couple of contracts he wants me to go over."

"I'm glad you mentioned that," Grace said, as the tension from Grigsby's reappearance slowly began to bleed away. "Why don't you approach the Waggoners and the Burnetts and take on some of their legal work? They're always doing land deals, and, like Percy, they contract their beef out to feedlots and meat-packers."

"I've thought about it," Seth said, "but they're our competitors, aren't they?"

"So what? Legal papers are legal papers, right? From what I've seen of the cattle business there aren't a lot of secrets about how they operate. In fact, since you grew up around it you'd have a better understanding of how it all works." Grace was a go-getter and she sometimes got frustrated with Seth's lack of drive.

"I suppose it wouldn't hurt to ask them. I'll run it by Percy to see what he thinks."

Grace almost rolled her eyes but caught herself in time. "What's Percy have to do with it?"

Seth sighed. This wasn't the first time they'd had this type of discussion. "He knows both Waggoner and Burnett really well. I'd like to have a little insight into how they operate before I ride out there like some greenhorn fresh off the train."

Grace thought about it for a moment then said, "I can see that, but don't wait too long, okay?"

"Yes, Mother." Seth leaned forward in his chair, moved a few papers around on his desk, and checked his calendar for upcoming appointments, then leaned back again, his heart not into lawyering at the moment. "I've been doing a little more research and I think we should head up for the Land Run a bit sooner than we had planned."

"How much sooner?"

"Three or four days, maybe. Leave here on Friday the nineteenth instead of Saturday."

"You know that Sunday is Easter."

"So what? It's not like we're a church-going family."

"I know, but it's always nice to spend time with the family, especially your grandmother. She's getting on in years and we ought to celebrate as many holidays with her as we can."

"It can't be helped. The Land Run is the next day and we need to be set up and ready to roll. From what I've read there are going to be two land offices where people can file their claims, one in Kingfisher and the other in Guthrie. We're going to Guthrie."

Grace stood and walked over to the window for a look outside. She spotted Mrs. Herbert Lawrence, the wife of a local banker, and watched as she crossed the street, her nose so high up in the air she could net gnats in her nostrils. Grace was almost disappointed when Mrs. Lawrence made it safely across without stepping in a pile of fresh horseshit. She smiled at the thought, turned from the window, and looked at Seth. "Let's take Grandma Frances with us."

Seth threw up his hands. "What? Three kids not going to be enough for you?"

Grace crossed the room and took a seat on the edge of Seth's desk. "Why not? She still gets around okay."

"Why would she want to go?"

"There's never been anything like this before. It was you who said the news had spread all across the world. Don't you think your grandmother would like to see it? We can take the train to Fort Worth and then north straight to Guthrie."

"Is she gonna want to sleep in a tent? You have to remember there are no hotels, restaurants, or any of the modern conveniences anywhere in the Unassigned Lands."

Grace slid off Seth's desk and onto his lap. She wrapped her arms around his neck and said, "I don't know, but you should ask her." She kissed Seth on the lips and looked deep into his eyes. "I love you." She tilted her head and was going in for a deeper kiss when they were interrupted by Lizzie's cries. Grace chuckled and stood. "Perfect timing, huh?"

CHAPTER
13

Simon Turner glanced up at the clock on the wall for probably the fiftieth time since the morning bell and was relieved to see that the school day would end soon. He usually wasn't so impatient, but he'd just found out that Autumn needed to head home as soon as school was over and that meant he'd be able to walk Nellie Hawkins home all by himself. That thought also terrified him a little, too. Without Autumn there to help steer the conversation, a heavy load would be placed on his shoulders. Normally that wasn't something that would concern him, being well read on any number of subjects, but even though he and Nellie had known each other for years, they hadn't had much alone time.

That lack of alone time could be attributed primarily to Miss Thompson, their teacher. Although he thought she was very knowledgeable and a good teacher, there was no doubt she ruled her small fiefdom with an iron fist. Simon had learned that the hard way a couple of years ago when Miss Thompson had dusted the seat of his pants with a willow switch for trying to talk to Nellie during recess. A stout, sturdy woman in her early forties, her gray hair was always wound into a tight bun and that fit with her personality. As far as Simon knew, Miss Thompson had never been married and he suspected the pool of potential courters had all but dried up. Although she was a good teacher, Simon didn't much care for all of her rules. How was he going to develop a relationship with Nellie if he couldn't even talk to her during the majority of their time together?

Simon turned to look at the clock again. Ten minutes until Miss Thompson would ring that silly handbell on her desk. And Simon knew they'd have to wait the full ten minutes because Miss Thompson didn't believe in turning anyone loose early. While he waited, he reached into his front pocket and felt around to make sure his silver dollar was still there and found that it was. Would Nellie want to stop by the general store to pick out a few pieces of candy or would she consider that childish? He didn't have a clue about Nellie's wants or needs, or those of any other girl, for that matter. He did know that Autumn still liked an occasional piece of candy, especially if she could get her hands on a small box of Whitman's chocolates. The only time they were readily available was during the winter, otherwise they were a melted mess by the time they arrived at the stores. It was now too late in the year, so chocolates were out. What else might pique Nellie's interest enough to delay, or at least slow, their journey to her house?

Before he could formulate an answer, Miss Thompson picked up the bell from her desk and gave it a shake. Simon reached under his chair to grab his Stetson then stood and turned to intercept Nellie as she made her way up the aisle.

When she was close, he whispered, "Let me grab my rifle and saddle my horse."

Nellie smiled and nodded. She brushed her fingers across the back of his hand as she passed and that caused a sudden bulge in his pants. He slid his hand over to cover it as he watched her walk through the door. *Damn, she's beautiful.* She was wearing a light blue calico dress that hit her midcalf and a pair of brown, lace-up boots that left just a hint of skin exposed. He realized he was staring and he looked around to see if anyone had noticed, but everyone was already outside. He turned and walked over to the closet where Miss Thompson made them stow their weapons.

Most of the kids enrolled lived in town and had no reason to bring a weapon to school. But for Simon and Autumn, eight miles was a lot of ground to cover, especially living next door to Indian Territory, the most dangerous place in the entire country. There was only one rifle left in the closet and it was his, so he grabbed it and exited the building. He paused to put on his hat and stepped off the stoop.

As he rounded the corner, Simon almost bumped into Crazy Eddie Miller. The nitwit loved trains and Simon thought he'd stand outside in the middle of a hailstorm to watch one pass by. Seeing that Crazy Eddie was distracted by the afternoon freighter that was pulling into the station, Simon took a quick look around and saw that they were alone. Gripping his rifle tightly, he stepped up beside Miller and, with all the force he could muster, he slammed the butt of the rifle into Miller's midsection.

Miller doubled over, suddenly gasping for breath. Simon leaned down close to Miller's ear and said, "Try anything like that again and I'll knock your damn teeth out next time. Got it?"

Still unable to catch his breath, the only thing Miller could do was nod.

Simon stood up straight and continued on. He had thought about smashing Miller's teeth in, but had changed his mind at the last second, opting for a more subtle approach. It would have been hard for Simon to plead his innocence if Crazy Eddie was walking around with a busted nose and a few missing teeth. Having gotten his revenge, he pushed thoughts of him from his mind.

The town's citizens had erected a small corral for student use and when Simon rounded the last corner of the building, he smiled when he saw Nellie sitting on the top rail, waiting for him.

"Did Autumn already leave?" Simon asked as he approached.

"She was riding out when I came around the building," Nellie said. "What did she have to do that was so important?"

"Something about a tailor comin' up from Fort Worth." Simon pulled his bridle off the fence and stepped through the gate to catch his horse while Nellie watched from her perch.

"Must be nice," Nellie said.

Looking over his shoulder, Simon said, "Rachel, her mother, is very particular about certain things." He turned back to the task at hand. Hiding the bridle behind his back, he approached the gray gelding with his left hand outstretched and talking in soft tones. A four-year-old quarter horse his mother had bred, he still had enough spit and vinegar that he required careful handling. When Simon got close enough, he rubbed the gelding's nose, slipped the bit into his mouth, and worked the straps over the horse's ears.

"What's it cost for a tailor-made dress?" Nellie asked.

"No idea," Simon said as he led the gelding over to the fence where his saddle was. "I can't imagine it's cheap."

Nellie climbed down and walked over, running a hand along the horse's neck. "And I bet she orders more than one, too."

Simon shrugged and said, "Probably so." He knew Nellie was jealous, so he said, "A dress is a dress as far as I'm concerned." He reached for the saddle blanket and placed it on the gelding's back before putting on the saddle.

"I suppose you're right," Nellie said. She rubbed the gelding's nose and said, "I love the name you gave him."

"Shadow?" Simon asked as he threaded the cinch strap through the cinch ring.

Nellie nodded. "It goes well with his gray color."

Simon looked up and smiled. "Thanks." He tugged the cinch strap tight, waited for the gelding to suck in a breath, and snugged it down tighter before tying it off. They exited the corral and Simon left the gate open so he and the other students could ride right in the next morning.

Leading Shadow, Simon and Nellie slow-walked their way through the town. It wasn't as awkward as Simon thought it might be and he was disappointed when they turned onto the road leading to Nellie's house. As they approached, Simon saw Nellie's body stiffen and she stopped, staring at her house as if she'd never seen it before.

Simon looked down the street and didn't see anything amiss. "What's wrong?"

Nellie turned to face him, her eyes wide with fear or surprise or something, and the smile on her face only a moment ago was gone. "I need to go. Thanks for walking me home." She glanced quickly over her shoulder then turned back. "See you tomorrow?"

Nellie was suddenly as nervous as a cat trapped in a doghouse and he couldn't figure out why. He nodded toward her house and said, "We still have a little farther to go." He started walking again and Nellie grabbed his arm, pulling him to a stop.

"You really must go, Simon."

Simon pulled his arm free and continued forward with Nellie reluctantly following along. Eyeing the bench swing hanging from the rafters of her front porch, he turned to her and said, "How about we sit on the porch swing and talk awhile longer?"

"I . . . uh . . . I have chores I need to do."

Now only a few yards from Nellie's house, Simon, his mind swirling with confusion, stopped and said, "Did I say something to make you angry?" He couldn't understand the sudden change in Nellie.

She reached for his hand and said, "No, not at all. But you need to trust me, okay? You need to—"

"Nellie!"

Both startled at the shout and Nellie immediately dropped his hand and turned to face the man who had stepped out onto the porch. He was dressed in a dark suit and Simon assumed it was her father and recalled that he did something with the railroads.

He strode across the wooden decking and stopped at the edge of the porch, his gaze remaining centered on Simon the entire time. "What's going on out here?"

There was a slight tremor in Nellie's voice when she said, "Pa, this is Simon. He . . . he walked me home from school."

"Nice to meet you, sir," Simon said, offering his best smile.

Instead of replying, he looked Simon up and down then turned to look at Simon's horse. There was a long, awkward pause then the man turned back to Simon and said, "Still got enough Injun in you that you can't go anywhere without a rifle?"

Stunned, Simon's cheeks flushed red with anger. Before he could form an answer, Nellie's father continued.

"I won't have my daughter hangin' around with some worthless half-breed. You get on that horse and get the hell out of here before I get my scattergun."

Confused, humiliated, and seething mad, Simon had to work hard to contain the rage surging through him. What he wanted desperately was to pull his rifle and send the man on his way to hell. Turning, he looked at Nellie and she refused to meet his gaze.

"Nellie, get in the house," her father said.

Still looking at the ground, Nellie hurried up the steps, brushed past her father, and disappeared inside.

"I ain't gonna tell you again, Half Breed," he said, crossing his arms. "Far as I'm concerned, the only good Indian is a dead Indian. And if I catch you hangin' around my daughter again, that's exactly what you'll be."

Simon, his body trembling with rage, turned until he faced the man head-on. He locked eyes with Nellie's father and said, in a low, menacing voice, "Not if I see you first." Simon touched the brim of his hat, turned, and mounted up.

Tears were streaming down his cheeks when he splashed across the Red River and entered Indian Territory. If he wasn't welcome in the white man's world, it was time to give the Indians a try.

CHAPTER
14

The Kansas border wasn't the only place where would-be settlers were gathering to claim their own pieces of paradise. People by the thousands were also camped along the Texas border, awaiting word from the army that they could proceed into Indian Territory. The rumor floating around the various camps was that the go day would be the Friday before and most were busy making preparations. Although separated by 250 miles from their fellow settlers in Kansas, the similarities between the two groups were readily apparent with about the same mix of people, horses, and wagons.

Among the thousands of people now camped along the southern border of Indian Territory was twenty-two-year-old Pearl O'Sullivan, a second-generation Irish American from Chicago. Unmarried and with suitable prospects limited in the hard-luck area of the city where she had grown up, Pearl had responded to a settlement group's newspaper ad and had joined up on the spot. In all there were about sixty people from Chicago, mostly families with a few individuals, like Pearl, thrown into the mix. Although they had varied backgrounds and various reasons for leaving, they all had one single thing in common—all were looking for a fresh start.

Now camped along the Red River a couple of miles north of Gainesville, Texas, Pearl was busy at the wash-tub, washing supper plates and wondering if she'd made a mistake in coming. It wasn't that she'd left anything behind in Chicago with both of her parents dead and her three siblings scattered across the Midwest, but what did she know about farming? Everything she owned was crammed into one small trunk. She didn't own a horse or a mule or anything that could pull a plow and she certainly didn't have the money to buy such, either. And that thought stoked a recurring worry that had nagged her from the beginning—how was she going to earn a living? During the trip, she had relied on the kindness of her traveling companions and she knew that was unsustainable. She could darn a pair of socks or sew on a button, but that was the extent of her sewing abilities. What else was there? Work as a laundress? A teacher? The latter would be unlikely with her limited education, but surely there was something she could do to earn some money. She had worked for a time in a shoe factory back in Chicago and that experience wouldn't do her any good here with the closest factory now hundreds of miles away. All of those things were weighing heavy on her mind as she absently ran a rag around a plate that was already dry. Then another thought wormed its way into her mind, and not for the first time. The easiest way out and the one thing that might solve all of her problems would be to find a husband.

Tall at five-eight and large framed, Pearl had long, curly, red hair, and gray-green eyes with a heavy dose of freckles splashed across her nose and cheeks. She knew she wasn't the prettiest woman around though she certainly wasn't the ugliest, either. At least she still had all of her teeth, which couldn't be said for some of the women she'd bumped into during her journey. She put the plate aside and dried her hands. With the upcoming Land Run, there were men aplenty and she decided to venture out for a closer look at a few of them.

Even if she failed to secure a man or stake a claim on her own 160 acres of paradise, she had decided there would be no going back to Chicago. And it wasn't just because she couldn't afford the train fare, either. Being out on the open plains had opened her eyes to a new way of living. The city was a filthy, smelly place full of meat-packing plants that required an enormous supply of ready animals, the hogs and cattle housed in large pens and adding another layer to the filth and foul odors that permeated the entire city. Add in the outhouses of a million people and the discarded remnants from the slaughterhouses that clogged the Chicago River and the entire city was one giant cesspool. She hadn't known any different, having grown up there, but now that she knew that people didn't have to live on top of one another, there was no going back.

With thoughts of possible suitors in mind, Pearl took off her apron and hung it up to dry. After smoothing down her dress and checking it for obvious stains, she decided it would do and exited the tent. The entire region was jammed with people and more were arriving every day.

Pearl had no trouble threading her way through the tents, wagons, animals, and people, well accustomed to crowded spaces.

Coming from Chicago, it would have made more sense for her settlement group to have begun their journey in Kansas. However, the leader of their outfit, a man named Henry McCoy, had meticulously studied maps of the land up for grabs and had determined the best available would be closer to the southern border of the Unassigned Lands. It meant a day or two of extra travel, but after a vote, it was decided the group would make the Run from Purcell, the southern entry point into the promised land. Pearl didn't know the difference between Purcell and Paris and all she wanted was a piece of land she could call her own.

A few moments later, as she was passing a tattered prairie schooner, she heard someone sobbing inside and paused. Usually not one to get involved, the anguish she heard registered somewhere deep inside of her. She turned and went back.

When she poked her head inside, she saw a jumble of mismatched furniture and, after her eyes adjusted, the faces of three young children, one boy and two girls, staring back at her. The young boy looked to be the oldest at five or six, and the oldest of the two girls was maybe four, and the youngest, and still sobbing, two or thereabouts.

Pearl reached in and took the young girl's hand. "What's your name?"

"Lill . . . Lilli . . . an," the girl stammered. She had dark, curly hair and the tears had cut trails through the dust on her cheeks.

"Are you hurt?" Pearl asked.

Lillian shook her head and wiped her nose. It appeared the crying was tapering off for now.

"I'm Pearl. How old are you, Lillian?"

Lillian held up her hand and it took her a moment to get the right number of fingers up. "Two," Pearl said. "Such a big girl." She turned to the other girl and said, "What's your name, sweetie?"

"Serena," the girl said. "I'm three."

Serena also had dark, curly hair and even though she was older than Lillian, she seemed frailer.

"Hi, Serena," Pearl said before moving on to the boy. "Hi, handsome. What's your name?"

"I'm Walter," the boy said. He had sandy blond hair, big brown eyes, and a firm handshake.

"How old are you, Walter?" Pearl asked.

"I'm five and a half," Walter said, puffing out his small chest.

"Mustn't forget those half years. Where are your parents, Walter?" Pearl asked.

"Ma's dead and Pa's gone off to find somethin' for us to eat."

"How long's he been gone?" Pearl asked.

"Seems like a long time and, well . . . it'll be . . . it'll be dark soon," Walter said.

Pearl could see tears shimmering in his eyes and it tugged at her heartstrings. "Want me to stay with y'all until he comes back?"

Walter nodded.

Pearl thought about it a moment, wondering if she really wanted to get involved. And what would the father say when he returned to find a strange woman tending to his kids? Although the unanswered questions remained, she couldn't just walk off and leave them. "Okay," Pearl said, "scoot over, I'm comin' in." She climbed inside and snuggled down next to the kids.

CHAPTER
15

After a long day spent dealing with the pregnant mares, Emma was exhausted when she finally exited the barn and turned for home. She glanced up at the sky and thought there was maybe twenty minutes of daylight left. But her work wouldn't end with the onset of darkness and she made a mental note to gather up a few extra lanterns after supper. Not having eaten since breakfast, she was starving, and she knew Simon would be hungry, too. Frazzled, she couldn't remember if she'd used the last of the bacon this morning, so she changed course and headed for the family smokehouse.

Stepping inside, she looked at the meat hanging from the ceiling, trying to decide what would be the easiest. There were a variety of items to choose from, including lamb, beef, and pork, with most of the space reserved for bacon and hams, the most popular cuts of meat. Emma reached up and pulled down a small ham and exited the building. Knowing she needed to get back to the mares soon, she hurried toward home.

She hadn't gone far before she got sidetracked when Percy, Leander, and Chauncey came riding into the yard, fresh off their pursuit of the rustlers. Percy, Emma thought, looked exhausted and for some reason that hit her especially hard. Percy was the rock they all depended on and she hadn't given much thought to him growing older. It was clear that aging and the stress of running a large ranch had taken a toll and she made a mental note to do more to relieve some of his burden. She hung around long enough to hear a few details about their trip before continuing on. Although shocked to learn of the shootout, she wasn't surprised by the high body count. All three men were crack shots and they were all seasoned warriors, and that included Chauncey, who was only a year younger than she was, at twenty-eight.

Entering the house, she was surprised to find it empty. Simon should have been home hours ago. She put the ham on the table and walked down the short hallway, hoping to find him in his room, but it, too, was empty. "Where are you?" Emma muttered as she turned and hurried back to the kitchen. She rested her hands on the back of a chair as her mind spun. She couldn't recall Simon saying anything about being late today and he was usually good about telling her his plans.

A tingle of fear started at the base of her neck and raced down her spine and all thoughts of food and pregnant mares faded from her mind.

Think, damn it! Where could he have gone? There were a couple of boys in town who had been out to the ranch a few times, but she knew most of the kids would be busy with chores after the school day was over. And living where they lived, next door to what the newspapers called the most dangerous place in the country, Emma had drilled into Simon the need to be home before dark. *So, where was he?* With her mind spinning through multiple scenarios—most of them bad—she hit upon another idea. She turned and hurried out the back door.

Crossing the yard, she climbed the steps up to Rachel and Leander's back porch, rapped on the door, and pushed on through. She crossed the kitchen in three strides and entered the parlor. Fabric samples were strewn all around the room and a short, bald man with a paper ruler draped around his neck was talking to Rachel, who was dressed only in a camisole and a pair of bloomers. The man's German accent was so thick that Emma couldn't understand what he was saying, not that she particularly cared at the moment.

Her aunt turned to look at her. "Hi, Emma. Want to have some dresses made?"

"Uh, no. Where's Autumn?"

"In her room. What's wrong?"

Emma ignored the question and hurried down the hall to Autumn's bedroom. She knocked on the door and pushed it open without waiting for a reply. Autumn was on her bed, reclined against the headboard, reading a book. She looked up and frowned at the intrusion.

Emma ignored that, too. "Have you seen Simon?"

"Not since school."

"Did he come home with you?"

"No. He wanted to walk Nellie Hawkins home and I had to come straight here to meet with the tailor." Autumn dog-eared a page in her book and closed it. "Is he not home yet?"

"No, and it's going to be dark soon." Emma had talked

to Nellie Hawkins at several school functions, but she knew little else about her. "Any chance he could have stayed for supper at Nellie's house?"

Autumn bit her bottom lip and shook her head. "I don't think so."

Emma sensed there was something off about Autumn's answer. "Why?"

"Well . . . uh . . . well—"

"I don't have time for a convoluted answer, so just tell me."

"Her father isn't a very nice man."

"Meaning he would be unlikely to invite someone like my son into his home?"

Autumn nodded and that tiny ember of anger in Emma's gut flared red-hot. "Did Simon know this?"

"I don't . . . don't think so. Her father's never around when we're there, but I've heard Nellie talk about him."

"If something did happen, any idea where Simon might have gone after that?"

"No, not really. Sometimes if we're killin' time we'll stop by Seth's office."

Emma hadn't considered that. But she also knew if Simon was upset about something, he wouldn't be hanging around Seth's office. "Where does Nellie live?"

Autumn explained where Nellie's house was, and Emma thanked her before exiting the house. On a normal day she might waste a few minutes wondering how much money her aunt spent on clothing, but that was insignificant when her son was missing. She stopped back by her house, strapped on her gun belt, took down her rifle, grabbed extra ammo for both, and headed for the barn. After quickly saddling a horse, a gray gelding she had bred that had the stamina of six horses, she led him over to Percy's house and found her uncle sitting on the back porch.

"Little late in the day to be headin' out," Percy said.

"No choice," Emma said. "Simon didn't come home from school."

"That ever happen before?"

"He's been late, but never this late."

"Any idea why?" Percy asked.

"Maybe. I know he's sweet on a girl named Nellie Hawkins and I just found out from Autumn that her father might have a mask, a funny-looking hat, and a long, white robe somewhere in his closet."

"He and Simon have words?"

"Don't know. That's what I aim to find out."

Percy pushed to his feet and said, "Let me get my gear."

"I'm not asking you to go," Emma said. "I just wanted to let you know what was going on."

"I know that. But I got a feeling things might get complicated."

"How so?"

"If Simon don't think he fits in here, he's liable to go lookin' elsewhere."

"Like where?" Emma asked.

Percy pointed beyond the river and said, "Where the Indians are."

CHAPTER
16

It took a while, but Pearl O'Sullivan finally coaxed the three children out of the wagon. She pulled some kindling out of the canvas sheet slung under the wagon bed and began making a fire. With the sun going down, there was a chill in the air. She was praying the children's father hadn't run off and abandoned them. She knew stranger things had happened. And she also knew desperate people did desperate things and it couldn't be an easy life for a widower with three young children.

Walter returned to camp dragging a piece of wood for the fire.

"Did your pa say where he was goin'?" Pearl asked.

Walter looked at Pearl and shook his head.

Pearl, thinking the family might be traveling with a group of like-minded people much like she was, scanned the surrounding wagons and tents, searching for clues that would suggest they were similarly equipped. Everyone in her traveling group had all bought the same brands of tents, cookware, and other items from the same vendor.

"Walter," Pearl asked, "did you come here with other kinfolk or maybe some friends?"

"Nope. Pa said he was done with all of it."

Pearl didn't know what *it* was and obviously Walter was too young to impart much information. "What's your last name, Walter?"

"Johnson," Walter said.

Well, that was no help, Pearl thought. The name Johnson was as common as ticks on a hound and she could immediately think of four people she knew with the same last name. Pearl stood. "You three sit tight and I'll be right back."

"You ain't leavin' us, is you?" Serena asked.

"I told you I'd stay until your pa comes back and that's what I'm gonna do," Pearl said. She pointed at the surrounding campers and said, "I just want to talk to a few of those other folks."

Serena stood and took Pearl's hand. "I wanna come."

Fearful people would be hesitant to talk truthfully with the girl in tow, Pearl squatted down to look Serena in the eyes and said, "I need you and Walter to tend the fire and keep an eye on your sister, okay? I promise I won't go far."

Serena gave a tiny nod, looked down at the ground, and pulled her hand back.

Pearl gave her shoulder a squeeze and stood. There were tents staked out and wagons lined up all along the riverbank and Pearl had to walk only about five feet and she was in someone else's camp. As she walked along the rear of the tent nearest them, she wondered why they had gone to the trouble of putting it up because it had more holes than a dead tree that had been swarmed by a flock of woodpeckers. She turned when she came to the end and saw that the sides had been rolled up. Sitting inside on kitchen chairs were two men and two women who didn't look to be much older than she was. Their clothing was as worn and tattered as their tent. Pearl waved and said, "Evenin'."

Pearl learned that the two men were brothers and the two women, their recently married wives. All four were hoping to stake a claim so the family could farm an entire section of land, something Pearl thought was rather greedy, but she kept that to herself. After chatting for a few moments, she moved on, visiting with a few more people who were camped nearby. In the end, they had all said basically the same thing—Levi Johnson was a good man in a hard spot.

Pearl circled back around to the kids as the last of the light in the western sky began to fade. She hadn't antici-pated staying out after dark and the thought left her some-what unsettled. Once darkness descended, she knew the liquor would begin to flow, and once the jugs were un-corked, trouble usually wasn't far behind. The fact that she hadn't yet met Levi Johnson did little to quell Pearl's growing anger. What type of man packed his three chil-dren off to parts unknown without stowing away the necessary provisions? Any fool could look at a calendar and count the days until the date of the Run and plan ac-cordingly. Not having done so, suggested Levi Johnson was either lazy or ignorant. And the more Pearl thought about it, the angrier she became. She stood and began to pace, her mind churning through all the things she was going to say to Mr. Levi Johnson when he returned.

Turning around, Pearl marched back toward the children and pulled up short when a man carrying a large crate of supplies came walking into camp. Her first impression in the fading light was that Levi Johnson was a bear of a man. The crate looked heavy, yet he carried it as if it were as light as a feather pillow. As the children swarmed around him, he put the crate on the ground and kneeled down, wrapping his long arms around his children.

"Sorry I was gone so long," he said, his deep voice echoing across the river bottom. He looked over at Pearl and said, "Evenin', ma'am."

Pearl was momentarily flummoxed because the real man was far different from the image of him she'd painted in her mind. She quickly regained her composure and said, "Evening."

He stood and stepped forward, sticking out his hand. "Levi Johnson."

He had to be at least six-four or taller and his hand dwarfed Pearl's when she shook it. "Pearl O'Sullivan, Mr. Johnson. Nice to meet you."

"Levi, please," Johnson said. "Thank you for lookin' after my kids, Mrs. O'Sullivan. I didn't intend to be gone that long."

"Call me Pearl, please. And you're welcome." He had a friendly face and light-colored eyes though she couldn't tell the exact shade in the growing darkness. She realized she was still holding his hand and she felt her cheeks flush as she pulled it free. "I don't usually stick my nose into other people's business, but I heard Lillian crying as I was walking by."

"Well, I'm glad you did. There was a line to get supplies and I couldn't come back empty-handed."

"I understand." Pearl wanted to ask why he hadn't stocked up before leaving wherever they had left from but didn't.

"You're stayin' for supper."

It was more an order than an offer and for some reason Pearl liked that. "Only if I can help."

"Deal."

Working together, they whipped up a quick meal and sat down to dinner with the children. There was a lot of the who, what, where, and when in their conversation with a good dose of laughter thrown in. Pearl discovered that Levi Johnson was a warm, friendly, entertaining man and she enjoyed being around him. Although she was curious to know the details of his wife's death, she knew that was a conversation best had in private.

After supper was finished and the dishes washed, the children stripped down to their skivvies and Levi gave Lilly a sponge bath while Walter and Serena washed themselves, using a bucket of water, a rag, and a bar of soap. Then it was into nightshirts and the three children climbed into the wagon. They begged Pearl to tell them a story, so she climbed in, nestled down beside them, and told them about Chicago and a lake that stretched farther than the eye could see.

It wasn't long before the children had drifted off to sleep and when Pearl exited the wagon, Levi was there to help her down. Levi held on to her hand and they stood and stared at each other for a moment, the firelight flickering across their faces. The spell was broken when one of the children moaned so they snuck away and took a seat by the fire.

Levi chuckled and said, "Now you got me wanting to visit that magical lake of yours."

"If it were only true," Pearl said. "But that's the fun part of telling stories, isn't it?"

"It is and it's nice to get their minds off the daily grind."

"You're a sage man, Levi Johnson." Pearl said. "Most people don't think about stuff like that."

Occasionally adding more wood to the fire, they sat and talked for a long time. Pearl felt like she could stay and talk all night, but she knew she needed to head back before the drunks began stumbling around. "I really should go," Pearl said.

"I know," Levi said, pushing to his feet. He reached for her hand and helped her up.

Pearl surprised herself when she stepped in for a hug and said, "Thanks for supper."

Levi wrapped his arms around her and said, "Thanks for lookin' after the kids."

They stood there hugging for a few moments and for the first time in her life, Pearl actually felt small in his arms. She finally broke the embrace and stepped back.

"Let me walk you back," Levi said.

"No," Pearl said. "You stay with the kids."

"Can I see you again?"

"I'd like that. Is tomorrow too soon?"

"Not for me," Levi said.

"Tomorrow it is, then." Pearl turned and headed back to her camp, her mind swirling with emotions.

CHAPTER
17

Although darkness had fallen, it was a clear night and the stars provided enough illumination for Percy and Emma to easily navigate their way to Wichita Falls. After steering their horses across a shallow section of the Wichita River, they rode into town.

"Once we get a handle on what happened with Simon," Percy said, "it might be best to wait till first light fore we set out lookin' for him."

"I'm not waiting," Emma said. She patted the unlit lantern looped around her saddle horn and said, "That's why I brought this."

"Speakin' from experience, that lantern ain't worth a damn when it comes to trackin' somebody. Light don't spread out far enough to see much of nothin'. All it'll do is tell everybody else where we're at and that ain't never a good thing if we have to cross over into Indian Territory."

"I'm not waiting, Percy. I'll go by myself if I have to."

Percy knew it wouldn't do any good to argue with her, so he let it go and they rode in silence for a while. There was no way he'd let her go alone and with so much on Emma's mind, he knew it was best to hold his tongue. It certainly wouldn't be the first night he'd spent in the saddle and his achy back hurt the same whether he was astride a horse or tossing and turning in his bed.

Percy's eyes drifted across the buildings lining the street as they rode. Lanterns were lit in most of the houses and the saloons they passed were doing a lively business. Emma, in the lead, turned right at the next intersection and Percy steered the mare around the corner. They made a left at the next road and Emma pulled her horse to a stop in front of a house in the middle of the block.

"This it?" Percy asked.

"It is if Autumn's directions were right."

"Well, I reckon she's been here a time or two," Percy said as he climbed down from his horse. He wrapped the mare's reins around the hitching post and waited for Emma to do the same before they both stepped up onto the front porch. Percy followed Emma to the front door, hanging back to see how things played out.

Emma gave the door a firm rap and a moment later a short, potbellied man swung the door open. He looked Emma up and down then turned his gaze on Percy and did the same, the corners of his mouth drooping to form a frown. "What?"

"That how you greet all your visitors?" Percy asked, taking an instant dislike to the man.

"You're interruptin' our supper." He was dressed in a pair of black suit pants and a white button-up shirt with black suspenders draped over his ponderous belly.

Percy peeked over the man's shoulder and saw a woman and three kids seated at the dinner table.

"I apologize," Emma said, "But we're here on an urgent matter."

"If you're sellin' somethin', we ain't buyin'," the man said.

"We're not selling any—"

Percy pressed in, cutting Emma off. "What's your name, pardner?"

The man glared at Percy. "You're the one that come to my house. Who the hell are you?"

"My name's Percy Ridgeway and this woman standing next to me and being too damn nice, is my niece Emma Turner." Percy saw the man's eyes widen in recognition at the mention of the Ridgeway name. He turned to face the man head-on, nudging Emma to the side. "Your name Hawkins?"

"That's right," the man said, "I'm George Hawkins and as far as I know I ain't got no business with neither of you."

Emma, angry about being pushed aside, bulled her way closer and said, "I'm Simon Turner's mother."

Hawkins smiled and said, "He went runnin' home to his mama, huh?"

Percy reached up and grabbed a suspender in each hand and yanked Hawkins out of the doorway. Transferring both straps to his left hand, Percy lifted until Hawkins was on his tiptoes then he reached out with his other hand and pulled the door shut. He turned and locked eyes with Hawkins and said, "I'd hate for your wife to see you gettin' your ass kicked. Now, you're gonna answer Emma's questions or I'm goin' to stomp a mudhole in your ass and walk it dry. Got that?"

Hawkins gave a quick nod and Percy turned loose and stepped back.

"What happened?" Emma asked.

"I caught your boy walkin' my daughter home and I told him he ain't welcome."

"Why?" Emma asked. "They go to school together and have for several years."

"Goin' to school's one thing. I ain't goin' to have no—"

"Careful, now," Percy said, cutting Hawkins off.

Hawkins looked at Percy then said, "As her pa, I decide who courts her and who don't."

"So, Nellie doesn't get a say in it?" Emma asked, her voice laced with anger.

"Not if she's gonna make foolish choices."

"And my son, only because he's half Indian, would be a foolish choice?"

Hawkins smirked again and said, "That's right."

Emma had to force down the urge to slap that smirk off his face. "What is it you don't like about the Indians exactly?" Emma moved in until she and Hawkins were nose to nose. When he didn't answer, she poked him hard in the chest and said, "Huh? What did the Indians do to you?"

"They're all lazy," Hawkins said, "and they're always beggin' for handouts. The army shoulda killed 'em all when they had the chance."

In an instant, Emma's pistol was in her hand and she jammed the barrel under Hawkins's chin hard enough to push his head back.

"Easy now, Emma," Percy said.

With her gaze still focused on Hawkins, Emma said, "I'm not gonna kill him today, but Hawkins, you talk to my son like that again and I'll splatter your brains all over this porch." Emma gave him one more hard jab with the barrel and then took a step back. After holstering her pistol, she turned, said, "Let's go, Percy," and walked off the porch.

Back on their horses, they rode in silence for a few moments before Emma said, "It's all my fault."

"How's that?" Percy asked. "It ain't your fault there's people in the world like Hawkins."

"It isn't just Hawkins. For his entire life, I've tried to shield Simon from anything Indian-related. At first, I was frightened the Comanches might try something if they ever found out about him. I lived with the Indians and I knew how much emphasis they put on family. As he got older those fears faded, but I still didn't want Simon mingling with the Indians, so I went out of my way to limit any possible interactions. And I see now that was a mistake."

"To be fair, you weren't . . . well . . . uh . . . not your normal self when we brought you and the baby home," Percy said. "No one could blame you for not wantin' to have anythin' to do with the Indians."

"It's not about me. Yes, I still have nightmares, but I should have expected that Simon would wonder why he looked different from everyone else in the family. Instead I ignored it. If I'd been open with him from the start, we wouldn't be where we are now. I should have introduced Simon to Quanah during one of his many visits to the ranch so that he could teach him some of the Comanche ways. But I didn't. I kept him locked away or busy doing other things whenever Quanah was around, silently praying the two would never meet. I was selfish and now

Simon's off searching for answers I should have provided to him long ago."

"You're bein' too hard on yourself. Hell, you was still just a girl when you come back. It takes a few years of livin' to get things figured out and, even then. you'll still get most things wrong. Just part of life. We'll find Simon and take him home. You can take 'im to meet Quanah and let him spend some time with him one of these weekends."

"Think Quanah would mind?"

"Oh, hell no. He's got kids runnin' all over the place up there. One more ain't gonna make a difference. And I know he's partial to you. I bet he'd get a kick out of it."

"That's all well and good, but first we have to find Simon."

They made a left, rode half a block, and stopped in front of Seth's office.

"Ain't no lanterns lit," Percy said.

"I really don't think he'd come here, but I'll go look through the window." Emma climbed down from her horse, stepped up on the boardwalk, and walked over to the large window that fronted the office. Cupping her hands around her face to block the light bleeding out of the saloon two doors down, she peered through the glass. It was so dark she couldn't see much of anything and she didn't think her son would be sitting in the dark. She stepped back, jiggled the door handle, and found it locked. She turned to look at Percy. "Think I should check the upstairs apartment?"

Percy tilted his head back to look at the second floor. "Naw, he ain't here. Should have asked that cocksucker,

Hawkins, what time Simon rode out. What time did school let out?"

"Two-thirty," Emma said as she walked back to her horse. She put her left foot in the stirrup and mounted up. "Why?"

Percy pulled out his pocket watch and popped the lid. There was just enough light to see the dial. "It's a little after seven now, meaning he's got a three-, maybe four-hour head start." He looked at Emma and said, "How long you reckon they farted around after school?"

"Not more than an hour, I bet."

"So, three and a half hours, then. A man could cover a lot of ground in that time." Percy stuffed the watch back into his pocket and said, "He carry any money around with 'im?"

"Usually, but not more than a dollar or two, if that."

"I reckon that nixes the train. Bad as I hate to say it, I guess we're headin' across the river." Percy looked up at the sky and said, "This time of the month, there ain't gonna be much of a moon, either."

"I'm goin'," Emma said.

"And I'm goin' with ya. All I'm sayin' is it's gonna be dicey as hell, especially if we have to light that lantern of yours."

"We don't have a choice, Percy. Get away from town and we'll be able to see enough to get by."

"Until one of the horses steps in a hole and breaks a leg," Percy said. "If we're lucky, Simon went to ground when it got dark."

"I think he would've come home if he was plannin' to quit when it got dark," Emma said. "He's stubborn when he sets his mind to something."

Percy looked at Emma and said, "Huh, I wonder where he got that from? Let's ride."

They turned their horses and rode out of town. A few minutes later, they crossed the Red River and entered Indian Territory.

CHAPTER
18

Although still deeply hurt and mad as a hornet, Simon began to regret his hasty decision to explore his Indian side as the night wore on. Riding through unfamiliar territory, he had no definite destination in mind and was unsure which direction he should even go. And really, what did he know about the Indians? He'd grown up around them and counted many of them as friends, but with all of that he still couldn't, at first or even third glance, tell the difference between a Comanche and a Cherokee. And he sure wouldn't be able to tell the difference in the dark and that thought led to a barrage of internal questions about his reason for being there. What exactly was he hoping to accomplish? From what little his mother had told him, he did know he had Comanche blood flowing through his veins and since he was now riding on that tribe's land, was he just hoping to stumble across a band of random Comanches?

"How stupid is that?" Simon muttered into the darkness. Although he hadn't been in the right frame of mind when he'd made his decision, he was too far into it to back out now, no matter how harebrained the idea had been. And he had to admit he was somewhat worried about the added humiliation he might face for returning home in the middle of the night.

Coming upon a small creek, Simon dismounted and led Shadow down the bank and let him drink. Although he had made his decision, it didn't alleviate the hunger pains and the chilly north wind cutting through the thin fabric of his shirt. He'd left his jacket at school again, and the temperature was dropping. But there was little he could do about it now and when Shadow finished drinking, he led him up the far bank and climbed back in the saddle.

He knew he was pushing his luck, riding around in the dark. He was a gopher hole away from being set afoot in a land well stocked with murderers and thieves. Although it didn't feel all that dangerous where he was currently, it did feel empty. There were large herds of cattle milling about, but there were no towns, no houses with the welcoming glow of a lit lantern, no sign of humanity at all.

With the sun long gone, he had lost his primary navigational tool and he wasn't exactly sure which direction he was traveling. He thought he was headed north, but as dark as it was, there were no certainties. As he rode, he looked up at the sky, trying to find the North Star. He knew it was there somewhere though he couldn't remember if it was the end of the handle for the Little Dipper or the Big Dipper. Things like that didn't merit much thought during the course of a normal day and he was now wishing he had paid more attention to some of that stuff.

With the temperatures continuing to plunge, it wasn't long before Simon was shivering. And, worse, he didn't know if he could find his way home now even if he wanted to. On the verge of panicking, he took a deep calming breath, held it for a moment, then slowly released it. It did help to settle his mind, but it didn't do much to improve his situation. Leaning forward, he wrapped his arms around the gelding's neck, trying to absorb some of the animal's heat. It helped enough to slow his shivering though it wasn't anywhere close to the heat a nice, warm fire would have provided back at home. He tried to push those thoughts from his mind as Shadow plodded onward.

A while later—he didn't know if it had been ten minutes or an hour—he caught a whiff of smoke. Sitting up, he looked around and didn't see anything obvious, but the scent grew stronger the farther he went. When Shadow rounded an outcropping of trees, Simon's hopes soared when he saw a grouping of teepees silhouetted against the night sky. There were the Indians he'd been searching for and his hopes suddenly dimmed when he was struck by another thought—Would they welcome him to their fire or slit his throat and take his scalp?

Before he could make a final decision, it was made for him when several dogs began barking. The dogs charged out of the camp and swarmed around his horse, barking, snarling, and nipping at one another. Simon pulled the horse to a stop twenty yards from the nearest teepee. As he waited for permission to enter, he reached down and rubbed the stock of his rifle. He'd leave it in the scabbard for now, but the reassurance it was still there offered a small measure of comfort.

It wasn't long before someone stepped around the side

of the teepee and approached. It was too dark to see much, but he didn't see any sign of a weapon and he took that as a good sign. Shadow, no fan of the dogs, was jerking his head up and down and stamping his hooves. As the person drew closer, Simon thought it might be a woman and that was confirmed a moment later when she shouted something at the dogs in her native tongue. The barking stopped immediately, and the dogs slunk back into the dark.

"Come, sit by the fire," the woman said.

"Thank you," Simon said as he climbed down from his horse. The gelding was well trained and didn't need to be tied up, so Simon slipped off the bridle and carried it with him as he followed the woman around the tent and into their camp. Simon counted nine teepees and they were spread out along what he thought was a small creek. There were a good number of people lounging around two large fires, but it was too dark for Simon to get a firm count. From what he could tell at first look, it appeared the men had a fire all to themselves and the other was reserved for the women and children. The woman led him over to where the men were seated and one of them rose to greet him.

The man tapped his chest and said, "Me, Quanah."

Simon was momentarily taken aback. Everyone in this part of the world had heard of Quanah Parker, the Comanche chief. He knew that Quanah had visited the ranch many times, but for some reason he couldn't recall ever meeting him. Simon stuck out his hand and said, "Simon Turner, sir."

Quanah laughed and shook Simon's hand. "No sirs here." Quanah studied Simon for a few long seconds, and he must have passed muster because the chief freed his hand and clapped Simon on the back. "Sit."

Before he could take the chief up on his offer, the woman who had led him into camp touched his arm. Simon turned and finally got a good look at her in the firelight. She was younger than he had thought, probably closer to his own age, and she was tall and thin. "What's your name?" Simon asked.

"Cynthia Ann Parker, but you can call me Ann. And your name is Simon Turner?"

"That's me. Quanah's your father?"

"He is," Ann said. "I'm named after his mother, but Cynthia sounds like the name of a seventy-year-old spinster, so I go by Ann. Are you hungry?"

"Only if you have something already made."

Ann smiled. "We're Indians. There's always somethin' cookin' in a pot, somewhere. Sit, and I'll bring you some stew."

"Thank you," Simon said.

Although he'd just met Ann Parker, Simon had already learned two things about her—one, she was well educated, and two, she'd give Nellie Hawkins a run for her money. Unsure if there was a seating hierarchy among the men, Simon chose a spot slightly behind and to the left of Quanah and as close to the fire as he could get without igniting and took a seat on the ground.

The men were conversing in Comanche, a language Simon couldn't begin to understand, so he sat and listened to the cadence of each speaker in a halfhearted attempt to decipher the subject matter of their discussion. Often one could pick out a word or two that sounded familiar when people were speaking a foreign language, but that wasn't possible with the Comanche language. It wasn't rooted in other languages such as English or Spanish and it almost sounded like a series of guttural grunts when the men talked.

It wasn't long before Ann returned. She sat down beside him and handed him a bowl of delicious-smelling stew along with a bone spoon to eat it with.

"They let you sit here among the men?" Simon asked.

Ann chuckled and said, "We can sit anywhere we would like. I think the women prefer the other campfire so they can gossip among themselves."

"You don't like to gossip?"

"New gossip, sure, but not the stuff I've heard a thousand times before."

Simon laughed and spooned some stew into his mouth. He chewed, swallowed, and said, "That's good. I'm almost afraid to ask what's in it."

Ann laughed again, her eyes sparkling in the firelight. "You've never had skunk stew before?"

Simon had to work hard to keep from gagging as he set the bowl aside.

Still laughing, Ann picked it up and handed it back to him. "It's beef, silly. A steer, to be exact."

With a sheepish grin, he took the bowl back and began eating again as he and Ann continued to talk.

They were briefly interrupted when Quanah turned to look at them and said, "Where Si-mon live?"

"My family has a ranch just south of the Red River."

Simon saw a look of confusion wash across the chief's face. "What ranch name?"

"I think you've been there before," Simon said. "It's the Rocking R."

Quanah pondered that a moment and it was obvious to Simon that he was troubled by something. He looked at Ann and said something in Comanche.

Ann listened then turned to Simon and said, "Roughly translated, he wants to know who your parents are?"

"It's just me and my mom, Emma Turner."

Ann translated that for her father and almost immediately, Quanah stood, turned, and walked away from camp.

"Is he angry?" Simon asked.

"I don't think so," Ann said. "I don't know what he'd be mad about."

Simon didn't, either, but something was up.

CHAPTER
19

Emma and Percy had no idea where they were going. They were just riding, hoping to stumble upon Simon somewhere along the way. It wasn't very efficient and it's not how Percy liked to run things, but this was Emma's show. She was hell-bent on finding Simon, so that's what they were going to do. They were operating on a hunch and Percy, now hours into the search, was questioning his assumptions. For all they knew Simon could be at home wondering where his mother was while they floundered around in the dark.

The inability to communicate with others was one of the most frustrating things Percy had to deal with. If he wanted to send a telegraph, he had to send someone into town to do it or go himself. He had given some thought to stringing a telegraph wire from Wichita Falls to ranch headquarters, but that presented a whole slew of head-aches, not to mention the enormous costs involved. Like most everything else, what sounded simple was anything but. As a result, Percy was hoping a new invention he'd read about in the newspapers would take root. Developed by a man named Bell, the telephone could change life as they knew it. He didn't know if it would reach north Texas during his lifetime, but just thinking about picking up something in his own home and talking to someone miles away was almost beyond comprehension. And it would've been damn handy now if they could have telephoned Simon to find out if he was home.

His reverie was interrupted when Emma said, "You're awful quiet. What are you thinkin' about?"

"Telephones," Percy said.

"Telewhat?"

"A telephone. Some fella named Bell come up with somethin' that lets you talk to somebody else even though they might be miles away."

"Like a telegraph?" Emma asked.

"Yeah, except you're talkin' to 'em in your own voice. Won't be no more tryin' to decipher a bunch of damn clicks and the average man'll be able to—" Percy stopped in midsentence then said, "Smell that?"

"Smoke," Emma said.

"That it is. You see anything?"

"No, but the wind's comin' out of the north. We keep ridin', we'll find it."

Dark shapes dotted the landscape in places, the cattle that roamed the area bedded down for the night. Percy and several other large cattle ranchers leased most of the land in this part of the country from the Indians and a good number of those sleeping cattle were wearing the Rocking R brand. Known as the Big Pasture, the area covered over 480,000 acres of prime grazing land, and it had taken Percy and the other cattlemen years to convince the Indians and the government to lease the land, despite offering substantial sums of money for the right to do so. After all that work and finally getting a deal done, the six-year lease would be expiring in a couple of months and there was some noise coming out of Washington that the government might not offer a renewal. If that turned out to be true, Percy and the others were going to be in a major bind with more cattle than land to feed them.

The smoke smell grew stronger the farther north they went, and Emma's statement proved true a few minutes later when they saw the silhouette of several teepees ahead.

"Think he'd ride up to an Indian camp?" Percy asked.

"You're the one that suggested Simon went looking for Indians."

"Yeah, I did, but the sun woulda been down by the time he made it this far, if my math's right. Reckon he'd have the moxie to do it in the dark?"

"I guess we're about to find out."

"I reckon we are."

When they were sixty yards from the nearest teepee, several dogs began barking and the noise increased in volume as they raced out of camp, swarming around the horses' legs. Someone finally shouted to call off the dogs and they scampered away, offering instant relief for Emma and Percy. Seeing no campfires, it took a moment for Percy to realize they were coming up on the rear of the Indian camp, validating his belief they were camped along the creek. He could see the shadow of someone walking around the edge of the nearest teepee, but that was all. Not quite sure what type of reception they would receive, Percy inched his hand a little closer to the butt of his pistol. It proved an unnecessary precaution because when they closed in on the person awaiting their arrival, a man said, "Per-cy?"

"It's me. Who am I talkin' to?"

"Quanah."

"What are you doin' this far south?" Percy asked.

"Huntin'. Quanah know you come. Who dat?" Quanah asked, squinting into the darkness.

"It's me, Quanah. Emma. Is Simon here?"

"He here. We talk, Taabe Piahp."

It was an order and not a request and Emma braced for whatever might come. Still, she smiled at the chief's use of the Comanche name he had given her during her year of captivity. It was one of the very few pleasant memories she had from that time. Comanche for "Sun Hair," it was more than appropriate for a redhead.

Returning to the reason for being there, Emma asked herself why, out of all the thousands of Indians, Simon had to end up in Quanah's camp. She was finally willing to lay out a few of the pieces in Simon's ancestral puzzle, but she certainly hadn't planned on doing it in the company of the one man who could contradict any white lies she might be forced to tell. She would have to be very, very careful going forward if she didn't want to lose Simon's trust.

She and Percy dismounted, and she stepped over and gave Quanah a hug and then he and Percy shook hands.

"Come," Quanah said. He turned and they followed him around the teepee to the campfire.

Simon stood to meet his mother and the two embraced

as Quanah added more wood to the fire so they could all see a little better.

"Are you okay?" Emma asked.

Simon nodded. "Sorry I caused you trouble. I got turned around and I was so cold when I smelled the smoke from Quanah's fires."

Emma wanted to scold him, to tell him how foolish he'd been for riding into Indian Territory, especially at night. Instead she said, "I'm just glad you're safe." She smoothed down his long, dark hair and kissed him on the cheek. "Your safety and well-being have always been my primary concerns."

"Is that why I've never met Quanah?"

"Let's move a little closer to the fire and sit down."

"Wait, I want you to meet someone." He turned to look at a young woman and she stood, wiping the dirt and leaves off her beaded buckskin dress. "Mom, this is Ann Parker."

Emma introduced herself and they shook hands. "Nice to meet you, Ann."

"Same here. How do you know my father?"

"That," Emma said, "is a long story and I'm chilled to the bone. Let's move closer to the fire and I'll tell you and Simon a little about how Quanah and I met. It's a story even Simon doesn't know." The short delay would also allow Emma some time to think on how she wanted to frame the story, even though she'd had almost sixteen years to do so. There was no easy way to tell her son the details of how he had been conceived without demeaning him or planting the seeds that he was unwanted. *Do I lie and tell him I had a loving relationship with a Comanche brave even though that was the furthest thing from the truth?*

I can't tell him I was used and abused by several different men for almost a year. It was a quandary she had pondered since she'd heard Simon's first cry as an infant back in that Indian teepee on the floor of the Palo Duro Canyon. Now here she was on the verge of telling some version of the story and she still hadn't figured it out.

What would Quanah say? She knew her perspective was far different from his. She had witnessed how the Comanches had treated their captives and, no matter how horrible it could be at times, the practice was embedded into their culture and beliefs. So, as far as Quanah and the rest of the Comanches were concerned, they hadn't done anything wrong.

In the end, Emma decided it would be best not to include Quanah in their conversation. Someone had dragged a dead tree trunk up close to the fire and they walked over to it and sat. Emma started off her story with the night she had been kidnapped by four Comanches while picking blackberries along the river. After talking about the first few days in captivity, she glossed over most of the details of her abuse, only hinting that she'd been mistreated. From there, she included a few items about the search to find her as told to her by Percy, then some finer details about the night Simon had been born before finishing with her return home, excluding any details about how difficult that transition had been.

Now she waited as Simon and Ann digested the information. She knew what was coming next and she had her response ready, one plucked out of thin air only moments ago.

"Who's my father?" Simon asked.

There it was—the question which had haunted Emma

throughout the years, and she was determined to put an end to it once and for all. "You have to understand that when I was being held captive, the army was on a constant hunt for the Indians and the group I was with was always on the run. Your father was one of the unfortunate ones who was killed in battle shortly after I learned I was pregnant." It took all of her willpower not to break eye contact with Simon and she prayed he'd accept the lie as truth.

"How was he killed?" Simon asked.

That wasn't a question Emma had anticipated so she had to wing it. "At that time, it was total chaos and details were scarce. I never heard how he was killed."

"But he's dead?" Simon asked.

"He is," Emma said.

"What was his name?" Simon asked.

This was actually a question she had anticipated, and she was ready with her answer. "His name was Pahiitu Huutsuu."

"Three Birds," Ann said.

"Correct," Emma said.

"Three Birds, huh?" Simon said. "I'll have to ask Quanah about him."

"Uh . . . well . . . uh," Emma stammered before pausing to gather her thoughts. She was kicking herself for even starting down this road with Quanah sitting only a few feet away. She took a deep breath and said, "I don't think . . . well . . . he was young and Quanah was on the move constantly and . . . well . . . he ran with a different group." Emma knew she needed to clean it up and fast. "All the different bands would get together on occasions, but that's a lot of people. I'm not sure Quanah even knew who he was."

"I can ask, can't I?" Simon asked.

"Sure," Emma said. "Just be forewarned that Quanah may not know him."

"Okay." Simon stood and walked over to where Quanah and Percy were sitting.

Once he was out of earshot, Ann looked at Emma and said, "You don't know who his father is, do you?"

Emma rolled that question around in her mind for a moment then said, "No, I don't."

Ann reached out and took Emma's hand. "I've heard a few horror stories about what my people did to their captives and I'm very, very sorry."

Emma worked to keep the tears at bay and said, "It's not your fault. It was a different time and place and I'm thankful that we, as a species, have moved on from that type of conduct. Bad people are still doing bad things, but overall, mankind has progressed."

Ann gave Emma's hand a squeeze and said, "It doesn't matter who Simon's father was, because you've raised a terrific young man."

"Thank you. Have you and Simon met before?"

"No, but I'm a quick study," Ann said.

Emma chuckled and said, "How old are you, Ann?"

"Fifteen."

"Same as Simon. You're both wise beyond your years."

Ann smiled. "Thank you. My father is a big believer in education."

"As he should be. It opens the door to an entirely new world."

"It does."

Ann withdrew her hand and they sat in silence for a few moments. Emma reflected on the reception Simon had received here and contrasted it to what had happened at the Hawkinses' home and her anger flared anew. Despite the circumstances of her pregnancy, Simon had been accepted into the family and was loved by everyone. Yes, there had been times when Simon had received hateful looks while they were out and about and, yes, he'd had a few scuffles at school after being teased about being different, but overall, it wasn't an issue and Emma hadn't wasted any time worrying about it. But what that asshole Hawkins had done was completely unacceptable and somewhere and somehow, she'd give the man a taste of his own medicine.

Emma was brought back to the present when Ann said, "Can I ask you one more thing about back then?"

Emma hesitated. Tonight's telling had brought it all to the forefront of her mind and she desperately wanted to lock it all away again and bury it deep. She sighed and said, "Okay."

"How old were you when you were taken?"

"Thirteen when I was kidnapped and fourteen when I had Simon."

"Again, I'm sorry," Ann said. "I hope having Simon has helped to dull some of those painful memories."

"It has. And it's not on you to apologize for someone else's behavior. At this point it's all water under the bridge for everyone involved."

Emma looked over at Simon and Quanah and saw that they were deep in conversation with another young Indian woman doing the translating. It made her wonder how many more lies she would have to tell before Simon was satisfied. It was a question she couldn't answer so she turned away and she and Ann talked for a while about life on the reservation and the house Ann's father wanted to build. Ann was in the process of describing the second floor when Simon returned, taking a seat between Emma and Ann.

Ann paused her story and looked at Simon. "What did my father say about Three Birds?"

"He said he might have met him a time or two," Simon said, "but he couldn't recall any details."

Ann and Emma shared a look, both wondering if that was the end of it.

Unfortunately, it wasn't. Simon looked at Ann and said, "Your father said he'd introduce me to some of the old-timers who might have known him."

"Well," Emma said, "all you can do is try."

Percy waited for Simon to leave before turning to business. "Have you started the house yet, Quanah?"

"No. Quanah start soon. Quanah build big house."

"I reckon you got the money to build whatever you want." Percy and three other cattlemen in the area had put up the money to build Quanah a house. The wily chief had been essential in negotiating the grass leases and if they hadn't had his backing it might not have happened. Percy knew some folks might call it a bribe or a kickback, but he and the others thought Quanah ought to be compensated for his efforts and considered the matter good business. In the end it was a win-win for both sides. The Indians made money and the cattlemen had grass to fatten their livestock.

"I hear grumblin' that the government's gettin' cold feet about renewin' the leases," Percy said. "What are you hearin'?"

"Quanah not hear about leases. Quanah's people heap mad with bill Great White Father sign."

"Which bill?"

Quanah made a chopping motion with his hand and said, "One that cut up land."

"The Dawes Act?" Passed by Congress and signed by the president in 1887, the Dawes General Allotment Act would parcel out reservation lands to individual Indians, usually in 160-acre tracts.

Quanah nodded. "They say not us other Indians. Quanah think white man lie again."

That immediately got Percy's attention. Although the Indians no longer had the numbers they once had, there were still enough of them to cause all kinds of hell. If they got all riled up there might not be a white person in three states with any hair left. "That what's goin' around the reservation?"

Quanah nodded. "Man with stars on shoulder say we live here long as water flow and grass grow. But Quanah not stupid. Land Run just start."

"The bill the president signed says it doesn't include most of the tribes in Indian Territory."

Quanah gave Percy a long, hard look and said, "President sign this, president sign that. Make no difference."

"So, what are you and the others gonna do about it?"

Quanah shrugged. "Quanah not know. Brothers no longer want fight. Great White Father only take. Quanah's people only give. Quanah not know end."

His statement that the Indians didn't want to fight eased Percy's mind some. And knowing that the government moved at turtle speed on most Indian matters, it made him think they were years away from having to worry about it. "If it ever comes to anything, I'll stand with you. The government has cheated you and your people seven ways from Sunday and that's gotta stop."

"Thank you, Per-cy. Quanah tired. Quanah want peace."

"Amen to that," Percy said. "You mind if we bunk with you and ride out in the mornin'?"

"You and family always welcome Quanah's camp."

"Thank you."

"Welcome." With catlike grace, Quanah went from sitting to standing in one movement. "Quanah now talk to Taabe Piahp."

"Take it easy on her. She was just doin' what she thought was best for her boy."

"Quanah know. But boy Comanche. He learn Comanche ways."

"I reckon that's up to him. He might not want nothin' to do with it. And if he does, I reckon you might get more than you bargained for." He nodded in Simon's direction and said, "Looks to me like he's took a fancy to your girl Ann."

Quanah turned to look then turned back and said, "Both young."

"But gettin' older every day," Percy said, taunting his old friend.

Quanah said something in his native tongue, smiled, and walked off. Percy didn't speak much Comanche, but he had a pretty good idea the chief wasn't telling him good-bye and that made him smile. He watched as the chief crossed over to where Emma was sitting. Quanah offered his hand, she took it, and he pulled her to her feet. As they strolled out of camp hand in hand, Percy was glad they were finally having a discussion they probably should have had long ago. After all, Simon deserved to know some of his Comanche heritage before it was lost to history.

CHAPTER
20

With only a week to go before the Land Run, Pearl O'Sullivan found herself spending more and more time in the Johnson camp. In fact, she did everything but sleep there and even that looked like it might change soon. Pearl couldn't deny there was a spark between her and Levi, and the only thing she could do was to see how it played out. Although she did have some reservations about stepping into a ready-made family, she knew deaths were common along the frontier and she certainly wouldn't be the only woman to hitch her wagon to a widower.

Pearl took the last plate out of the washtub, dunked it into the rinse bucket, and set it aside to dry. Having just finished dinner, it was now approaching Pearl's favorite time of the day. Lilly and Serena would soon be down for their afternoon naps and Walter would be off to play with his friends. It wasn't that Pearl didn't like spending time with the children, because she did. They often did or said things that kept Pearl laughing most of the time and they truly were a joy, but the afternoons were the only time she and Levi could talk without curious little ears listening in.

Pearl walked over to the campfire and added another log. A cold front had passed through during the night, bringing with it a blustery north wind. They were sheltered somewhat by surrounding campers, but they couldn't screen the cold completely. Pearl walked to the wagon and grabbed a blanket, draping it over her shoulders. Levi was inside, reading a story to the girls so she hovered near the rear, listening to his deep, baritone voice. If he was troubled about the idea of raising three children alone, Pearl had seen no evidence of it. In fact, he didn't seem to be troubled by anything at all. Nothing appeared to fluster him, and he was one of the most easygoing men she had ever met. She assumed he had a temper, but she hadn't seen any hints of one, yet.

After a few more moments, Levi stopped reading and the wagon rocked on its springs as he tried to climb out without waking the children. Although he was a large man, there was nothing clumsy about him. In fact, Pearl had noticed there was a certain grace to his movements. If she had to describe it, she'd say Levi was catlike—a very large cat, mind you, more along the lines of a mountain lion or a Bengal tiger, like the ones she'd once seen at a traveling circus.

Once he had extracted himself from the wagon, he took Pearl by the hand and led her over to the fire where they took a seat on the ground.

Levi looked around and said, "Where's Walter?"

"He's a couple of camps over, playing with his new buddies," Pearl said.

Levi nodded. "It's good he has someone to play with instead of always pestering his sisters."

"Agreed," Pearl said. "He definitely needs some time with boys his own age."

They sat and watched the fire for a few moments and Pearl was hoping he'd open up about the death of his wife and how he and the kids ended up here, waiting for the Land Run. However, she also didn't want to step on any toes since she'd known him for only a very short time. Hoping to start at the present and work backward, Pearl said, "What's your goal with the Land Run?"

Levi stroked his well-groomed beard for a few moments then said, "Well, I suppose it's the same as all the others. Stake out some land where we can put our roots down."

"Are you looking for a town lot or do you want the full hundred and sixty acres?"

"No town lots for me. I wouldn't mind living close to a town, though. I'm hoping to plant a few crops or maybe run some cattle."

"Have you farmed before?" Pearl asked.

"I have and I'll tell you, it's not for the faint of heart. There's a lot of things you just can't control. If the weather doesn't wipe you out, then it'll be the bugs, or the seed won't germinate, or a hundred other things. But if you can get a couple of good years strung together, a man can bank some money."

"How many good years have you had?" Pearl asked.

"Lately, I've had more bad years than good ones and that's why I'm lookin' for a fresh start. What about you? Town lot or a farm?"

Pearl shrugged. "I haven't decided. To tell you the

truth, I really just wanted out of Chicago. I don't know squat about farmin' or raisin' cattle, but I'm willin' to learn and I'm a hard worker. I think the idea of owning a piece of property is the most exciting thing because I've never had nothin' I could call my very own."

"I feel the same way. We mostly leased all of our farming land back in Missouri. Was Chicago that bad?" Levi asked.

"Worse. Even I didn't realize how bad it was until we got onto the train comin' down here. I'd never really been out of the city and the trip down here was a real eye-opener. I thought the sky was supposed to be gray, but out here on the prairie it's as blue as a sapphire and it looks like you can reach out and touch it. And don't get me started on the sunrises or the sunsets. Lordy, the colors are so bright and vivid, they're breathtakin'. You won't find anything like that in a city like Chicago."

"Biggest city I've been to is Kansas City," Levi said. "It's not anywhere near the size of Chicago, but I still didn't find much to like about it. I like havin' some space around me."

"I can see why," Pearl said. "You're as big as a bear."

Levi looked at Pearl and said, "Is that a bad thing?"

Pearl reached out and took his hand. "Not at all. If you haven't noticed I'm not exactly a delicate flower."

"You're what my pa called 'big-boned.' I like a woman who has some size to her. Makes her easier to get ahold of." Levi picked up a stick with his free hand and stirred the coals. "What are you gonna do if you don't stake a claim?"

"I don't know. Guess I don't want to think about that. What about you?"

"Oh, I'm gonna do all I can to stake a claim. Don't have any other options. But I'm workin' on an idea, in case it don't play out like we hope."

"What is it?"

"I'll let you know when I get it all worked out."

"Does it involve me?"

"It does." Levi tossed the stick on the fire and he pulled out his pocket watch to check the time. "Girls will probably sleep another hour. Want to go for a walk along the river?"

"I'd like that."

They stood and Levi reached for her hand as they headed toward the river, which was only about fifty yards away. When they reached it, they climbed down the bank, crossed at a shallow spot, and set out along one of the numerous sandbars that dotted the river bottom.

Levi pulled his hand free and wrapped his arm around her, pulling her close. For Pearl, it was nice to be held and she snuggled up close to him, wrapping her arm around his waist, no longer caring about appearances. Back East such things were frowned upon, but out here, Pearl had learned, nobody cared about such nonsense. And for the few who might make a stink, the entire area along the Texas border was jammed with strangers and no one knew who was married to whom and that anonymity created an air of freedom that circulated through the many camps.

Levi looked down, noticed her smile, and said, "This is nice, huh?"

"Very much so." Pearl tilted her head up and they kissed. Levi pulled her to a stop, and she turned to face him as he wrapped both arms around her. They kissed some more, and Pearl ran her hands up and down his broad back. Her blood ran hot and her heart was racing when she kissed him a final time and snuggled up against his chest. She had to stop or there was a chance she wouldn't. Every nerve was tingling, and she felt more alive than at any other point in her life as she took a step back and said, "Whew."

"That was nice, too, huh?" Levi said, his voice thick with desire.

"Oh yeah." She reached for his hand and interlaced her fingers with his as they continued down the sandbar. Pearl's emotions were all over the place. She had dated before, but she had never taken a lover and that inexperience was now causing her some confusion. With three children, Levi obviously had much more experience in that area and he probably had a good idea of the type of woman he was looking for. Was she that type or was Levi simply looking for someone to fill the vacant role of mother? It didn't feel that way to Pearl, but she knew she was a novice. She did have to admit it had been pretty convenient that she had shown up when she did and a small part of her wondered if Levi was exploiting her naïveté for nefarious purposes.

Again, it didn't feel that way to Pearl and those passionate kisses certainly felt like there was mutual desire. For Pearl, this was the part of dating she hated the most. The constant worry over whether that meant this, or this meant that, was exhausting, so she decided to confront it head-on. She turned to look at Levi and said, "I don't know what this thing is between us, but it feels different from anythin' else I've experienced. I know you've been married and you've obviously fathered children so I'm hoping you're not just trying to get into my knickers."

After pulling her to a stop, he turned to face her and said, "Of course not." He paused a moment as if gathering his thoughts then said, "I'm looking for something more. Me and Rose weren't a good fit from the get-go. Seems like I could never do anything right in her eyes and it was pretty damn miserable. Still, that didn' make her dyin' any easier, especially with three young'uns. But bein' married to her sure gave me a good idea about what I wanted in a woman if I was lucky enough to meet someone else."

"How did she die?"

"Don't know. About six months after Lilly was born, she went downhill fast. The doctor, if you could call him that, couldn't figure it out and she was dead within a week."

"I'm so sorry. That must have been terrible."

"It wasn't no picnic, I can tell you that. It really tore the kids up. But all of us know somebody that's lost a family member. Life's hard and there ain't nothing we can do but keep moving on." Levi freed his hand and fished his watch out of his pocket to check the time. "We should probably turn around and head back. The girls will be up soon."

"Okay," Pearl said, a thousand questions buzzing around in her head. She wanted to ask what those qualities were or how she might fit into those things he was looking for, but she didn't. Instead, she reached for his hand again and threaded her fingers through his as they walked back to camp. They crossed at the same shallow crossing and climbed the bank. They were reentering camp when he leaned in and whispered, "I would like to, eventually."

"What's that?"

"Get in your knickers."

Pearl could feel the heat rising in her cheeks. She smiled and said, "Well, that's good to know."

CHAPTER
21

Over the last week, there had been a steady stream of Boomers drifting out of Caldwell, Kansas, in preparation for the opening of the Land Run. As a group they numbered close to three thousand, a majority of them families though there were a good number of individuals, both men and women. Having begged, demanded, and agitated for the opening of the Unassigned Lands for years, their long-awaited reward was only days away.

Gordon Lillie, better known as Pawnee Bill, and his wife, May, were among those departing this morning. It was all part of a master plan hatched by William Couch to get most of the Boomers closer to the Oklahoma border without creating a big fuss. Bill knew Couch had every intention of entering the area a day or two early and there had been many heated arguments about that very issue, both for and against. If caught, any hopes of staking a claim would be gone and all their political wrangling would be for naught.

Driving a canvas-covered prairie schooner of questionable quality that he'd bought on the cheap, Pawnee Bill and May were hoping the shoddy wagon wouldn't fall to pieces the moment Bill cracked the whip come high noon on Monday.

For that reason alone, Pawnee Bill was contemplating an early entry into the Territory. The wagon might survive a slow, methodical trip, but there would be nothing slow or methodical about the upcoming Run. The first to arrive would win and with their perfect piece of ground already picked out, speed would be of the essence. Unlike most of the would-be settlers who had never laid eyes on the land they were clamoring for, the Lillies and their Boomer group had been evicted numerous times during previous forays into the Territory. Although they could never seem to stick, they did gain valuable information on the property that would be available on Monday.

Bill and May's favorite spot was located near a creek the Boomers had named Stillwater. In addition to sweeping views of the surrounding terrain, it had a water source and a ready supply of timber they could use to build their home. So cherished was that spot, they hadn't even told their closest friends where they were planning to stake their claim. Over the years the couple had developed many close relationships, but Bill knew that when it came time to stake out their futures it was going to be every man for himself.

Bill looked over at May, whose face was obscured by an overlarge sunbonnet, and said, "What do you think?"

Without turning May said, "About what?"

They hadn't been up long enough for Bill to know if

she was in one of her "moods" yet, but from her tone it wasn't looking promising. "About sneakin' in early."

"How many times do I have to tell you? You know what I think."

Yep, Bill thought, *she's definitely in one of her moods.* "I know you're against it, but I wish you'd think about it some more."

Still staring straight ahead May said, "If you wanna go in early, I'll take a train back to Wichita."

Bill sighed and decided to let it go for now. Maybe her mood would improve as the day went on.

But May had other ideas. She finally turned to look at her husband and said, "Why would you want to squander everything we've worked for? This is a chance to get some free land to make another start. And you want to screw that up by taking foolish chances?"

Bill kept his eyes on the trail and said, "Forget I asked."

"I just don't know why you'd want to take a chance. The army said they were gonna let everyone move up to the Oklahoma border a couple of days before the Run. I don't see that you'd gain much when compared to the risk."

"Well, you're the one's got a hankerin' for that one piece of property. What happens if we don't get it?"

"Don't tell me I got a hankering for it. You want that parcel just as badly as I do."

"You're right," Bill said, "I do want it. But I don't want you bitchin' and complainin' if we don't get it."

"It's my job as a woman to bitch and complain. If we have to, we'll stake out the hundred and sixty acres next to it. When we get the show problems ironed out, we'll be makin' some money and we'll buy out whoever it might be, if they claim it before we can."

Well, Bill thought, maybe things were lookin' up. At least she's being reasonable, but Bill also knew the day was young. "That's assumin' a lot. We lost our ass on the show this year."

"I'm well aware of that. I think we need to take the show to Europe. They can't get enough of the Wild West stuff."

"It's gonna take a passel of money to get everythin' over there."

"It takes money to make money. Bill Cody seems to be doin' just fine with his show."

"He's got the name, though. They been writin' dime novels about Buffalo Bill for years. Shoot, even I was readin' about him when I was a kid."

"Maybe we need to find someone to write a book about Pawnee Bill and his crack-shot wife."

"Not a bad idea. You know any writers?"

"No, but how hard could it be? We need to come up with some kind of hook that would draw the readers in." May paused for a moment and Bill could almost hear the gears grinding in her head. May looked at him and said, "Maybe we can use your connection to the Pawnees. Make the Indians the heroes for once."

"Would anybody want to read that?" Bill asked.

May shrugged. "I don't know. I'd read it. If not that then something else. It gives us another angle to think about."

They rode in silence for a long while and, looking ahead, Bill saw that they would eventually have to cross the Arkansas River to get to the new campsite. And he didn't much like river crossings. In fact, he hated river crossings especially in a wagon in less-than-stellar condition. Bill figured more people had been killed trying to cross a swiftly moving stream than all those killed in the Indian Wars. Although some people teased him about his aversion to river crossings, Bill would bet none of them had ever seen a couple of their buddies go under and never resurface. Those drownings had happened on the same day and in the same river—the Platte—during a cattle drive from Wichita, Kansas, to Valentine, Nebraska, back when he'd been seventeen or eighteen years old. He leaned out for a look ahead and saw that they were fifth in line and he was hoping the lead driver found a shallow place to cross.

After settling back on the seat, he glanced over his shoulder at all the holes in the wagon bed and mumbled a curse word or two. When he had bought the wagon, he had been thinking only of the small creeks they'd have to cross while in Indian Territory and hadn't paid much attention to the fact that they'd need to cross the Arkansas right out of the gate. He looked at May, nodded toward the back, and said, "Anything back there that can't get wet?"

"Oh, let's see, there's the flour, the sugar," May said, raising her fingers as she counted, "the tent, our clothes, the—"

"Okay, I got your point," Bill said, cutting her off. "Let's just hope the water's shallow."

"Did you even look at the wagon before you bought it?"

"Of course I did."

"Did you not see the holes in the bed and the rips in the canvas?"

And that's how quickly May's moods could change,

Bill thought. "I saw 'em," he replied, a tinge of heat in his voice. "You get what you pay for. Have you forgot we're flat-out busted?"

"How could I forget, riding around in this rattletrap? Couldn't you have shopped around some more?"

"I'll make a deal with you. You get to buy the next wagon." And that pretty much ended any conversation for the foreseeable future.

Fortunately, when they reached the river a while later, the water wasn't very deep, and the crossing was a breeze. However, that did little to lighten May's mood. As they approached the spot where they were going to camp, Bill said, "Where do you think I should park?"

"Wherever," May said.

He wanted to hand her the reins and tell her to park it, but he didn't. He steered to the left and chose a spot about ten feet from another wagon and set the brake. May climbed down and stalked off. Bill watched her for a moment then shook his head. He loved her, or thought he did, but sometimes he wondered why. He climbed down and set to work unhitching the two mules, wondering if he should cut May loose so she could find something that would make her happy. He had no idea what it might be, but maybe she did.

CHAPTER
22

Marcie, seated in their kitchen at the ranch, looked at Chauncey across the table, wondering if she should tell him of her plan. The Land Run was just a few days away and she was either going to have to find an excuse for being gone for a few days or tell him the truth. He was easygoing and she couldn't see him getting upset, but she didn't want to give him the wrong signal and have him think she was looking to move on when nothing could be further from the truth.

Having grown up on an enormous ranch and never wanting for anything, she didn't know if Chauncey would understand her desire to own something that would be all theirs. He, and by extension, she, did have their own livestock and their own brand as did a few of the others, but the cattle and horses all ran together, and the only time ownership mattered was when the livestock was sold.

Out of the corner of her eye, she watched as Chauncey wiped his plate clean with a piece of bread and popped it into his mouth. As he chewed, he leaned back in his chair and his gaze settled on her.

He swallowed and said, "You're awful quiet."

"I'm thinkin'."

Chauncey looked at the food still on her plate and said, "Can't think and eat at the same time?"

Marcie pushed her plate away and said, "Not real hungry."

"What's runnin' around in that noggin o' yours?"

"You're gonna think I'm crazy."

"Try me."

"You know about the Land Run next week, right?"

"Hard to miss. They's people by the thousands camped all along the border, all awaitin' their free piece of ground. Tell somebody you's givin' somethin' away and they'll flock to it like flies to a fresh pile of cow shit. Hell, I bet there's ten times more people than there is land."

"After sayin' that you're really gonna think I am kooky."

"Why's that?"

"I want to make the Run to stake a claim."

"What the hell for? We got over sixty thousand acres already. You can't do nothin' with them itty-bitty pieces of land they's givin' away."

"This ranch belongs to you and your family. If something happens to you or you someday decide to cut me loose I won't have nothin'."

"What are you talkin' about? I ain't cuttin' you loose, and I damn sure don't plan on dyin' anytime soon. Where's all that crazy talk comin' from?"

"None of us can see the future," Marcie said. She stood up, gathered up the plates, and scraped her leftovers into the slop bucket before dropping the plates into the washtub. She turned to look at Chauncey. "What if I don't ever get pregnant?"

Chauncey shrugged. He was lukewarm on the idea of having children and Marcie knew he thought she was making it a much bigger deal than it needed to be. "Then I guess we won't have no kids."

"You say that now," Marcie said as she walked back to the table. She pulled out a chair next to Chauncey and sat. "You gonna feel the same way five years down the road?"

"I reckon so. Ain't a damn thing we can do about it, is there?"

"*You* could always look for a new wife. Find you a woman who could have your children."

"How many times I gotta tell you it don't matter one way or the other? If we have kids, fine, and if we don't, fine. I ain't gonna lose any sleep over it, either way."

"I believe you," Marcie said, "but I still wanna stake a claim. We can do it together."

"What are we gonna do with it?"

"It'll be ours to have. Seth and Grace are going up so he can do his lawyer work. We should go along."

Chauncey pondered that for a few moments then said, "When they leavin'?"

"The Run is next Monday, and I think they're plannin' to go up Friday. That gives you a couple of days to think about it, but I really think you should go. It'll be fun."

"I don't know about fun." He mulled it over for a few more moments and Marcie knew not to overplay her hand, so she waited. If Chauncey thought someone was trying to steer him in a direction he didn't want to go, he'd dig in his heels. "Well," he finally said, "I suppose we could go up there with Seth and Grace. I don't know that I want to fool with stakin' a claim."

"You won't have to. I'll do it."

"Don't you gotta live on it and do some other stuff?"

"There's ways around it." Marcie didn't want to get into the specifics of it, knowing her husband didn't care about the land. Why would he? "I think Emma's goin', too."

"What she want with more land?" Chauncey asked. "Hell, we can't hardly manage what we got."

It wasn't Marcie's place to be telling anyone about Emma's business. "I think she just wants to watch what could be a grand spectacle."

"Oh, it'll be grand, I bet. Remind me to pack plenty of ammunition."

CHAPTER
23

Percy was out riding in one of the eastern pastures the next morning when he spotted a familiar rider approaching. He was too far away to confirm exactly who it was, but the big white horse was a tell. Percy clucked his tongue, put the mare into a trot, and rode out to meet him, crossing where the fence had been cut.

Over the last month, the pasture's fencing had been cut too many times to count, as land-hungry people surged toward Indian Territory. It had gotten so bad that Percy had ordered the livestock moved and the pasture abandoned until the Land Run hubbub died down.

As the two riders closed the distance, Percy smiled and waved at his old friend, Deputy U.S. Marshal Bass Reeves. The two men reined their horses to a stop when they were side by side and shook hands. "How ya doin', Bass?"

"I'm a-doin', Percy." He looked at the downed fences and the trampled grass and said, "If I didn't know most of the buffalo was gone, I'd think you been hit by a stampede."

"It was a stampede, all right, only it was caused by a bunch of two-legged animals."

"How far east you been?" Reeves asked.

"Far enough to know the army's gonna have their hands full come Monday. There's people piled up all along the border."

"Ain't just the army. Deputy marshals been ordered to help out."

"How many marshals and soldiers they sendin'?" Percy asked.

Reeves shrugged. "Don't matter. Whatever it is, it ain't gonna be enough. They's sayin' that when the bugle blows at high noon on Monday there could be sixty, seventy thousand people makin' the Run."

"Jesus," Percy said. "That's a passel of people."

"It is, and that's why I'm here."

Reeves smiled and Percy hated it when he did that before telling him all the particulars. If Reeves was working in the area, he'd occasionally ask Percy to go along with him to apprehend a criminal or whatever it was Reeves had been tasked to do.

"I'm gettin' too damn old to be chasin' around the country."

"Hell, Percy, you ain't that old. All we gotta do is keep the early birders out of the area they call Oklahoma till it's time. Plus, you'll be on hand to see somethin' ain't nobody's ever seen before."

Percy thought about it a moment and said, "When you goin' up?"

"Sooner the better. We's goin' to a place called Guthrie."

"You gonna be arrestin' these early birds?"

"Don't rightly know. The particulars on that's a bit sketchy."

"Great," Percy said. "It's soundin' better and better the more I hear."

Reeves laughed then said, "Hell, Percy, man's gotta live a little."

"All right if Leander comes along?"

"The more, the merrier. And Leander would be a good man to have around."

"You stay the night here and we go up in the mornin'?"

"Works for me," Reeves said, "But ain't you gotta ask Leander first?"

"He'll come. Rachel's about to drive him crazy."

Reeves chuckled. "That baby sister o' yours is a bit high-strung, for sure."

"That's an understatement," Percy said. He dug out his pocket watch and popped the lid. "It'll be about dinner-time when we make it back. You hungry?"

"I could eat," Reeves said.

"Let's ride." They turned their horses toward ranch headquarters and spurred them into a walk.

Born a slave, Bass had fled slavery during the war and had slipped into Indian Territory to escape. According to Bass, he had befriended the local Indians, chiefly Seminoles and Creeks, and had learned their languages and customs during the time he had spent with them. That had all changed when slavery was abolished by the Emancipation Proclamation and the later ratification of the Thirteenth Amendment. Once free, Bass had worked his way back home to Van Buren, Arkansas, where he had settled down and started a family.

His time in Indian Territory had proved invaluable when he later became a deputy marshal. Having established lifelong relationships with many of the Indians, Bass now had a vast network of contacts which he used to track criminals all across the Territory, making him one of the most successful deputies to ever wear the badge. If an outlaw had Bass Reeves on his trail, it was more likely than not that he or she would be captured—dead *or* alive.

Reeves looked at Percy and said, "You hear I had to sell the farm?"

"No, I didn't hear that. Hell, I'm sorry, Bass. Payin' that lawyer for your trial wipe you out?"

"That and the lost wages while I was sittin' in jail for six months."

"I'm still pissed you didn't wire me. I'd have bonded you out and paid your legal fees."

"I know that, Percy, but it wasn't your mess to clean up."

"It damn sure shouldn'ta been yours, neither. From what I read in the newspapers, that trial was a damn sham from the get-go. Filin' charges on you two years after accidentally shootin' your cook was downright dirty. It's that damn rebel fella that took over the U.S. attorney's office. They got beat fair and square in the war and now they can't stand a black man havin' a little success. It woulda never happened if you was white."

"Well, it's all done now and I'm clear of it."

"You're a bigger man than me. I'd be wantin' my pound of flesh from that asshole that filed the charges."

"I reckon they ain't none of us above the law. 'Sides, I ain't one to hold grudges."

"Well, maybe I'll punch that bastard in the nose if I ever run into him."

Reeves chuckled. "I reckon I'd pay to see that."

For the rest of the trip, the two men discussed old times, current events, and debated the plight of the Indians. Percy thought Quanah was right. Change was coming and both men thought the tribes would end up being screwed again. Although he and other members of the Ridgeway family had warred with Indians for most of their lives, the slow destruction of their way of life was a sad thing to watch.

After exiting through the last gate, Percy and Reeves walked their horses over to the barn, unsaddled them, and turned them out in the attached corral.

"Well," Percy said, "we've got chow in the bunkhouse or we could mosey over to my ma's house to see what she's cookin'."

"I ain't seen Miss Franny in a while. That gets my vote."

They crossed the large backyard the six homes shared and climbed up the back porch steps to find Frances Ridgeway asleep in one of the rockers. "Ma?" Percy said, hoping she really was asleep and not dead.

Frances opened her eyes and it took her a moment to focus. "Bass Reeves, you're a sight for sore eyes."

Percy saw her wince when she pushed out of her chair and that pained him. She was getting on in years and he couldn't hardly stand the thought of her being gone. She and Reeves hugged, and Frances sank back into her rocker and the two men took the chairs on opposite sides of her and sat.

"Just out here snoozin' away?" Percy asked.

"Must have drifted off." She looked at Reeves and said, "How's Jennie and the kids?"

"They's good, Miss Franny. Don't get to see much of 'em 'cause I'm on the road all the time."

"Ain't it about time you hung up your guns?" Frances asked. "I worry about you all the time."

"Gotta eat," Reeves said, "and I don't reckon the criminals is gonna put theyselves in jail. Ain't no reason for you to be worryin', Miss Franny. I reckon I can look after myself."

The three spent several minutes catching up and then Frances said, "How long you stayin', Bass?"

"Me, Percy, and hopefully Leander is headin' out in the mornin'," Reeves said.

Frances looked at Percy and said, "Where are y'all goin'?"

"Bass sweet-talked me into helpin' him with the Land Run," Percy said, still not completely sold on the idea.

"Is everybody on the ranch going?" Frances asked.

Percy was taken aback. "Who else is goin'?"

"Seth and Grace and the kids are leavin' on Friday and they're takin' along Chauncey and Marcie and Emma and Simon. They asked if I wanted to go, but I can't decide."

"How come I didn't know any of this?" Percy asked.

"'Cause you're always chasin' off after rustlers or whatnot." Frances turned to look at Reeves and said, "Bass, tell him it's time to pass the worry and work onto the kids."

"No offense, Miss Franny, but I reckon I'll stay out of that."

The three shared a laugh and when it faded, Percy said, "So you gonna go, Ma?"

"I'd like to see it, but it sounds like somebody needs to stay here and hold down the fort."

"Eli can do that," Percy said.

"No, he can't," Frances said. "He and Clara are leaving Saturday for Chicago."

"Damn, I forgot he was goin'. Not sure anything will come of it, but we'll see." Percy said, talking more to himself than to the others.

"What are you two cookin' up now?" Frances asked.

"Explorin' an idea to expand our operations. As it is now, we sell to cattle buyers then he takes a cut when he sells the cattle to the packin' houses then they take another cut when they sell the beef to grocers and local butchers. If we can get a piece of those other markets it'll cut some of our risk."

"This Eli's idea?" Frances asked.

"It is and it's a good one," Percy said. "But gettin' back to what I was sayin', if you want to go up for the Run, Jesse and the other hands can keep an eye on things."

Frances mulled that over for a moment then she looked at Bass and said, "Is there a hotel where you're goin'?"

"We's going to Guthrie and no, there ain't no hotels or nothin' else, neither. Ain't nothin' in Guthrie but a water tank for the railroad and a couple other run-down buildin's."

"Well, that settles it for me," Frances said. "I'm too dadgum old to be campin'. You all go and have fun."

"Probably ain't gonna be nothin' fun about it," Percy said.

"Miss Franny, is it just me," Bass said, "or does your eldest boy seem to get grumpier the older he gets?"

Frances chuckled. "No, it's not just you, Bass. I told him he needs to find a good woman to keep him company."

"Well," Bass said, "I don't reckon I'd go that far. Havin' a woman around might occasion a whole slew of new problems."

Bass and his mother had a big guffaw over that, so Percy waited until it tailed off before saying, "In case you two ain't noticed, I'm sittin' right here." Before either could respond, Percy decided it was time to change the subject. "Ma, did you cook anything for dinner?"

"Don't like havin' the reasons for your grumpiness debated?" Frances asked.

"No, not really," Percy said. "Food. Yes or no?"

"Oh, Percy, lighten up," Frances said. "There's ham, a pot of beans, and some corn bread on the stove."

Percy pushed out of the rocker and stood. He looked at his mother and said, "If you can stand one night in a tent, you could come up Sunday evenin' on the train, watch the Run Monday, then come back home." He looked at Reeves and said, "Think that's doable, Bass?"

"I don't rightly know. Probably be all right Sunday evenin', but I ain't got any idea what Monday's gonna look like. And, to tell the truth, I don't reckon anybody's got a handle on how things is gonna play out," Bass said, pushing to his feet. "But you can bet everybody's gonna hear about it. There's a whole passel of newspapermen comin' in from all over the country. The marshal's got a notion that we's supposed to keep 'em safe, too, and I don't rightly know how that's gonna work, neither." Reeves looked down at Frances and said, "If you want to come, Miss Franny, I reckon we'd figure a way to make it work. Up to you."

"Let me think about it," Frances said. "I'll let you know before you leave."

"Sounds like a plan," Reeves said.

Frances was struggling to get out of the rocker, so Percy offered her a hand and she slapped it away. "I don't need your help."

"Where you goin'?" Percy asked. "I reckon we can get our own grub."

"I expect you can." Frances finally made it out of the chair, and she held on to Bass's arm a moment to steady herself. "Seein' as Bass is here, I'm gonna make a pie for supper."

"Well, hell, I can't remember the last time you made *me* a pie," Percy said.

"Oh, hush. I made you a pie for your last birthday." She patted Reeves on the arm and said, "We don't get to see enough of Bass. Maybe if I bake him an apple pie, he'll come by more often."

"You don't need to go to the trouble, Miss Franny," Bass said.

"It's no trouble. And I do know, Bass, you stop by when you can." She gave his arm one last pat and stepped past the two men and they followed her into the house.

After filling their plates Reeves and Percy took a seat at the kitchen table. Percy fed a piece of ham into his mouth and chewed as he thought about the upcoming Land Run. He swallowed the ham, looked at Reeves, and said, "Who's in charge of this here Run?"

"Army, I reckon," Reeves said. He looked around to make sure Frances was out of earshot, then lowered his voice, and said, "All that talkin' got me to thinkin'. Pack your extra pistol and bring along that scattergun of yours, with plenty of ammo for both."

"You said we're goin' up for the Land Run, not to fight a war," Percy said.

"We are, but we might get a war whether we want it or not."

CHAPTER
24

The next morning, Percy, Bass, and Leander, who had been more than happy to go along, were in the barn saddling their horses when Eli came strolling in, a cup of coffee in his hand and his ever-present pipe clenched between his teeth. When he saw Reeves, he pulled the pipe out, and said, "How are you, Bass?"

The two men shook hands and Reeves said, "Still on the hunt, Eli. Miss Franny says you and Clara's headed to Chicago."

"Yes, we are. I'm not certain we'll accomplish anything, but it's worth a trip. I've read that Congress is considering the establishment of a U.S. district court in Indian Territory. Any truth to that?"

"I reckon it's close to happenin'. I think they's gonna put it in Muskogee up in the Creek Nation."

"Would you have the option of relocating there?" Eli asked.

"Don't reckon I've thought about it all that much,"

Reeves said. "But I'm kinda partial to Judge Parker so I reckon I'll stay there."

"Makes perfect sense." Eli took a sip from his cup and said, "Where are you three going?"

"Percy and Leander's gonna help me with the Land Run," Reeves said. "We're headin' up there this mornin'."

"Was this a voluntary assignment?" Eli asked Reeves.

"Not exactly," Reeves replied. "Most of us deputies got roped into doin' it."

Eli looked at Percy and Leander and said, "Are you two gluttons for punishment?"

Percy shrugged. "Bass asked us to go, so we're a-goin'."

"Do any of you have an idea what you are walking into?" Eli asked.

"Well, to tell the truth, no," Reeves said.

"Then allow me to explain," Eli said. "President Grover Cleveland signed the bill to open the Unassigned Lands in early March. Two days later he was out when Benjamin Harrison assumed the office. Now, keep in mind, this is a new administration and there are cabinet officials to appoint, judgeships to fill, and, not to mention, a country to run. So, during the middle of this hectic process, Harrison decides to proclaim, on the thirteenth of March, that those lands would be thrown open for settlement on the twenty-second of April, only five weeks after Harrison made the announcement. Are you three with me so far?" Eli asked, taking advantage of the brief pause to take a couple of hits from his pipe.

Reeves, Leander, and Percy nodded, some of the color draining from their faces.

"Good," Eli said, the smoke dancing around his

mouth as he continued. "Now, we all know that the federal government moves at a snail's pace, often taking years to accomplish even the smallest of things. Now, with all of that in mind, how much planning do you think the government has done for this opening of the Unassigned Lands?"

"Probably not much," Percy said, "when you put it that way."

"Correct," Eli said. "There simply hasn't been enough time for even minimal planning." Eli paused to take a draw from his pipe before continuing. "Take, for instance, the number of land offices they've designated for the event. Do any of you know how much land will be disbursed on Monday?"

Percy looked at Reeves and Leander and both men shrugged. Percy turned back to his brother and said, "How much?"

"Nearly two million acres," Eli said. "In other words, there will be thousands upon thousands of claims, and each one must be filed with one of the two land offices the government has provided."

"I already figured there was gonna be long lines," Percy said.

"But have you given any thought to the timing of how it will all work?" Eli asked.

"No, not really," Percy said.

"What is going to happen when they signal the start at high noon?" Eli asked.

"Everybody's gonna race out to stake a claim," Reeves said.

"Correct. And once they've staked their homestead or town lot, what's the very next thing they're going to do to ensure they are confirmed as the rightful owner of that particular piece of ground?"

"File it?" Leander said.

"Exactly," Eli said. "And if everyone has started at the exact time, they'll also finish around the same time, give or take a few hours, creating a nightmare scenario for those two land offices that could persist for days." Eli paused again for another sip of coffee then said, "If I were you, I'd do my utmost to avoid going to Guthrie or Kingfisher." Eli reached over and squeezed Reeves's shoulder. "A pleasure to see you again, Bass. Don't be a stranger."

"Good to see you, too, Eli," Reeves said. "You sure give us a lot to think about."

"Good luck. I have a feeling you're going to need it." Eli turned to Percy and said, "I'll send a wire if I have news."

Percy nodded.

Eli put the pipe back in his mouth, dumped the dregs from his cup, and exited the barn.

Percy looked at Reeves and said, "Where did you say we was goin'?"

Reeves, taking a sudden interest in his boots, said, "Guthrie."

Percy mumbled a string of curse words as the three men finished saddling their horses.

CHAPTER
25

By the time the calendar rolled around to the Friday before the Land Run, Emma Turner had watched thirty-one mares successfully give birth and she had only two more that hadn't foaled. The last two were older horses that had foaled multiple times and weren't expected to have any problems. Just in case, Jesse Simpson, the ranch foreman, had volunteered to keep an eye on those last two mares while she and Simon were away.

Now in her bedroom, she was trying to decide what to pack. They were going to be gone only three or four days, but the weather in April in these parts was as unpredictable as guessing when it might rain again. It could be seventy-two degrees one day and thirty-two and snowing the next. With that thought in mind and knowing how cold it could get at night, Emma pulled a pair of flannel long johns from her bureau and added it to her bag along with a couple of split skirts and three blouses and then she paused, wondering if she needed anything else. Deciding she didn't, she carried the bag into the living room and stopped at the sideboard by the front door. After loading in two boxes of ammunition for her pistol and two boxes for her rifle, she walked over to the mantel and grabbed her knife, which she slipped into a sheath sewn into her boot. Having been kidnapped by the Indians, Emma never ventured far from home without some type of weapon. And that knife wasn't just for show, either. It had spilled blood before, most notably when she had plunged it into the chest of the cruelest of her Indian kidnappers when he had attempted another attack a few years ago.

Trying to decide if she needed a heavy coat or not, she opted for a medium-weight jacket and took it down from a peg by the door and stuffed that into her bag. The last thing she needed was a hat and she had quite a collection. As a redhead, she was very conscious of the sun and had taken to wearing a broad-brimmed Stetson Silverbelly during the colder months, but she thought it might be too hot for this time of the year. Instead, she chose her flat-crowned, wide-brimmed sombrero and lifted it off the rack and set it on top of her bag. The last thing she donned was her gun belt, her .45 caliber Colt Single Action Army revolver already nestled in its holster. There was no need to check to see if it was loaded because it remained that way at all times.

"Why do you always have to strap on your gun?" Simon asked from the kitchen table, where he was finishing up breakfast.

"Just do," Emma answered. She adjusted the gun belt to her liking and opened another drawer—their shared junk drawer—looking for a compass she could use to navigate her search for a claim.

It had been a couple of weeks since she and Percy had traipsed across Indian Territory looking for Simon and things were finally returning to normal. She had noticed that some of the shine had apparently worn off Nellie Hawkins because Simon hadn't had much to say about her. Before, it had been "Nellie said this" or "Nellie did that," but Emma couldn't recall her name coming up at all the last few days. Although Nellie might have fallen out of favor, Ann Parker appeared to have taken center stage in Simon's mind and Emma didn't know how she felt about that. Not that Ann wasn't a lovely young woman, because she was, but she was also a full-blooded Comanche and if her son had thoughts about courting her, both would be forced to endure the scorn that seemed to permeate into all corners of white society. Emma finally found the compass and she tossed it into her bag before pushing the drawer closed.

"You takin' your rifle, too?" Simon asked.

"You bet," Emma said. And with that, she pulled the rifle down from where it hung and leaned it against the wall. She turned to face her son and said, "You have everything you're takin' packed?"

Simon nodded and said, "Don't need much."

"You pack a coat?"

"I did. Believe it or not, Ma, I'm old enough to pack for myself."

"I don't doubt that you are, but you need to remember there are no stores where we're going. If you forget something, you'll have to do without."

"Duly noted," Simon said, rolling his eyes. He stood, walked over to the washtub, and dumped his plate in. "We takin' horses along or are we all going to pile in the wagon for the trip to the train station?"

"The wagon will be too full, so make yourself useful and go saddle the horses."

"What time does the train leave?"

Emma glanced at the grandfather clock and saw that it was a little after eight. "Ten o'clock. We need to be on the road in the next few minutes."

"Won't take me long to get the horses ready," Simon said.

Emma glanced up to see his rifle still in the rack and she said, "You takin' your rifle?"

"Do I need it?" Simon asked.

"We don't really know how this thing is goin' to play out. I have a feeling it might get a little crazy. And with so much at stake, emotions will be running high and that's never a good mix. The whole thing could end up being a powder keg and I'd feel more comfortable knowing you had a way to defend yourself."

Simon reached up and took down his rifle then walked over to the sideboard to grab a box of ammo. "Now you have me worried," Simon said. "Are you sure we should be going?"

"Not a hundred percent sure, no. But you can't live your life bein' afraid of taking chances. Besides, Percy, Leander, and Bass Reeves will be up there, too, so we'll be just fine."

CHAPTER
26

Grace Ferguson scurried around the house, quickly collecting the last few items she needed for the trip. Traveling with three children was much more difficult than she had ever thought it would be. It didn't help that Guthrie had no stores or restaurants and they would need to take everything they thought they might need.

Seth stuck his head in the front door and said, "About ready?"

"Are the boys with you?" Grace asked as she hurried into the kitchen.

"Already in the wagon."

Grace scooped up a box of matches and grabbed two extra cups off the shelf above the stove and hurried into the parlor. "So, you're just waitin' on me?"

"Yep, everyone is ready to go." Seth stepped inside and said, "What can I help you with?"

Grace handed him the cups and the box of matches and leaned over to lift Lizzie out of her bassinet. As she snuggled the sleeping child to her bosom, she looked at her husband and said, "If you'll load the bassinet onto the wagon, I think we're ready to go."

Seth grabbed the bassinet with his free hand and the Fergusons exited the house, Grace closing the door behind them. Planning for a trip with very few known parameters had been difficult. They had no idea how long they might be there because it all depended on how much legal work Seth could drum up. Grace had a nagging suspicion they might be in for a long haul and she hoped she'd packed enough supplies to see them through.

Grace exchanged pleasantries with Chauncey, Marcie, Emma, and Simon, who were already mounted on their horses, and Seth helped her up to the wagon seat before going around to the other side. With a slap of the reins and a shout, they were off. The plan was to load the wagon and everything in it onto a railcar so they could roll it off in Guthrie and be ready to go.

Grace looked over her shoulder to make sure their sons, four-year-old Andrew and three-year-old Edgar, were comfortable and saw that they were snuggled down in a stack of blankets.

"Where we goin' again?" Andrew asked.

"A place called Guthrie, up in Indian Territory," Grace said.

"Is it far?" Edgar asked.

"Well, if we had to go by wagon like I used to have to do when I was little, it might take the better part of a week. But with the train, we'll be there before dark."

"Are there gonna be other kids there?" Andrew asked.

"I'm sure there will be, eventually. We're going up a bit early so your pa can get things set up. Think of it as an adventure." Grace turned back around before Andrew could ask another question. She loved him with all of her heart, but he could wear a person out with all of his questions. Of the three children, Andrew looked most like Seth, with the same eyes, and the same sandy blond hair. Edgar, on the other hand, had gotten Grace's curly, dark hair and her blue eyes. It was too early to determine who Lizzie was going to favor and there was still a chance her eyes could change from gray to the deep sapphire blue of her own eyes.

They made it to the train depot in Wichita Falls with plenty of time to spare. Railroad workers pointed out where they wanted Seth to put the wagon and he hauled on the right rein to steer the two-horse team where he wanted them to go. After pulling up beside a flatcar, he set the brake and climbed down. He quickly went to work unhitching the team so the railroad workers could hoist the wagon onto the flatcar with a block and tackle.

While Seth was doing that, Grace, still holding Lizzie, led Andrew and Edgar to one of the passenger cars and boarded. With it being Good Friday, the coaches were crowded with people going who knew where for the long Easter weekend. Thankfully, Chauncey, wearing his two guns and a scowl, had no trouble saving seats.

Andrew took a seat next to Simon and immediately began jabbering and Grace almost felt sorry for him, but he'd been like a big brother to the boys since they'd been born.

"Grace, do you want me to take Lizzie?" Emma asked.

"She needs to nurse first," Grace said, "but after that you can hold her till the cows come home."

Emma chuckled. "You forget how needy they are at that age."

"I know. It's not like you can just put her down and go on about your business," Grace said.

Lizzie must have known they were talking about her because she began squirming and stretching and Grace knew the crying would soon follow. She draped a small blanket over her shoulder, pulled her left breast free, and began nursing her daughter. Although Grace's breasts had been exposed to a good number of men during her time as a parlor house girl, now that she was married, it made her uncomfortable to nurse Lizzie in public. But hungry babies had to be fed and they didn't much care where it happened.

A few moments later, Grace jumped when the train whistle blew. Knowing that was the signal for departure, she turned, looking for Seth, and was relieved to see him climbing up the steps. He hurried down the aisle and she moved over so he could sit down. "Cut that kinda close, didn't you?" Grace asked.

"They had some trouble loading the wagon," Seth said. "I hope it's not a premonition of things to come."

"What happened?"

"One of the ropes broke and they almost lost it. Last thing we need is a broken axle before we even get started."

Seth was a worrier and she didn't want him gnawing on his bottom lip all the way to Guthrie, so she put a hand on his thigh and said, "Well, that didn't happen and everything's good now."

The coach jerked as the train began moving and it slowly picked up speed. For the residents of Wichita Falls and the surrounding area, train travel to anywhere other than the small towns along the route, required a trip to

Fort Worth no matter the final destination. The city was the hub and much like spokes on a wheel, trains entered and exited in a number of different directions. For most people, going to Fort Worth was not that big of a deal, but for Marcie and Grace, who had lived and worked there, it was fraught with danger.

Seth leaned in close and said, "You don't seem as nervous this time."

"Having that skinflint Grigsby show up at the office made me realize that I really don't give a damn what anyone thinks," Grace said, speaking more loudly than she would have liked to compensate for the roar of the train.

"I couldn't agree more." Seth glanced across the aisle to make sure Chauncey wasn't looking then leaned in closer, his lips almost touching Grace's ear. "But you know how Chauncey is about that stuff, so let me know if you see someone that looks familiar. I'd like to get in and out of Fort Worth without a killing."

Graced nodded and said, "How you goin' to stop him, though?"

"Distraction."

"Maybe we'll get lucky." As soon as she said that, Grace remembered Marcie telling her about the incident in the barn involving Archer Keating, a Fort Worth native. Although she hadn't shared that information with Seth and she highly doubted Marcie had told Chauncey, she knew secrets on the ranch were as rare as finding a diamond in a fresh cow patty. She wasn't all that worried because there was a good chance Chauncey didn't know what Keating looked like. Besides, Grace thought, what were the odds of running into Keating at the train station on any random day? A thousand to one? More than that? Although she wasn't a mathematician, she liked their odds.

However, the one thing Grace forgot to factor into her equation was the fact that it was a holiday weekend.

CHAPTER
27

As the other Ridgeway family members began their trek to Guthrie, Percy and Leander, already there, were regretting their decision to come. Working out of a satellite camp along the Cimarron River northeast of Guthrie, they were busy patrolling the eastern border of the area called Oklahoma and were having to change horses frequently just to keep a fresh mount under them. Working from daylight to dark, their days were spent chasing off the people who were trying to sneak in early. Known as Sooners—Percy preferred the term *cheaters*—they continually tested the limits and Percy was at the point now, he was ready to shoot a few just to make a point.

They had way too much ground to cover and it made for long days, especially knowing their task was as pointless as trying to carry water in a colander. Reeves, Percy, and Leander would escort the Sooners out of the restricted area only to have them sneak back in just as soon as their backs were turned. The army had sent out some soldiers to help, but the marshals were still woefully undermanned, and it hadn't taken them long to figure out they'd been tasked with a job that was impossible to fulfill.

To make matters worse, the area they were patrolling was lousy with small creeks, dry washes, and thick stands of timber, which made finding the cheaters extremely difficult. Almost like quail hunting, Percy, Leander, and Reeves had to comb through the gullies and brush hoping the Sooners would flush from cover. Not only was it laborious, it was also time-consuming and with a three-hundred-mile-long perimeter to guard, it would have been a challenge for ten thousand marshals, much less the seventy men currently out on patrol.

Although Percy, Leander, and Reeves thought the job pointless, they were making a good show of it as they worked their way south along Soldier Creek. Percy pulled the makings from his shirt pocket and began rolling a cigarette. "Eli pretty much nailed it, huh?"

"Yeah, and the shitshow ain't even started yet," Leander said.

"Speakin' of that," Percy said, looking at Reeves, "they gonna let all those people in Kansas and Texas move up to the startin' line fore Monday, Bass?"

Reeves nodded and said, "They was s'posed to get the go-ahead this mornin'."

"Terrific," Leander said.

Reeves chuckled and said, "We just gotta make it three more days, fellers."

When the cigarette was rolled to his satisfaction, Percy put it in his mouth and struck a match on his saddle horn to light it. He took a deep draw as he fanned the match out, and on the exhale said, "Why only three days? I reckon most of the action's gonna start after the Run. Them settlers will be all giddy till that bugle blows and then there's gonna be a bunch of jawin' and fighting about who claimed what."

"I didn' sign on for none of that," Reeves said. "Our job's to keep the cheaters out and I asked you two along mostly for the company. Y'all can cut loose anytime you want."

Percy looked at Leander and said, "You wantin' to cut out?"

"And miss all the fun?" Leander asked.

"We'll stick till the Run, like we said we would," Percy said, "but we ain't gonna leave you in a lurch, neither."

"I ain't aimin' to be in a lurch if I can help it."

Percy took one final draw from his cigarette, stubbed it out on his saddle horn, and slipped the remains into his shirt pocket. A fire this time of the year, before the grass really greened up, would burn for days. "What're your Indian friends sayin' about the Run, Bass?"

"They ain't happy, that's for damn sure. I'm just hopin' they don't take up arms."

"You hearin' rumblin's like that?" Leander asked.

"Some. But I don't really know what the Indians is gonna do. I don't reckon they got much fight left in 'em, but a man never knows for sure. Somebody gets to stokin' 'em up, ain't no tellin' what might crop up."

"Well, I hope like hell that don't happen," Percy said. "All this ground up this way's been watered in blood already. Last thing we need is the Indians goin' back on the warpath."

"Way I see it," Reeves said, "it'll be hard for the Indians

anyway. I reckon by the time Monday night rolls around they'll be outnumbered by all them folks comin' in."

"Ain't thought about that, but I expect you're right," Percy said.

The three men rode in silence for a while and as they veered a little farther west, the land opened up, the gently rolling terrain stretching farther than they could see.

"Hard to believe," Percy said, "that all this is gonna be crawlin' with people in a couple of days."

"I been ridin' this here land for a long, long time," Reeves said. "Can't rightly wrap my head around how it's gonna look. Reckon it's gonna take some gettin' used to."

In the distance Percy spotted two riders pushing a small herd of cattle their way and he said, "Riders comin'."

"I seen 'em," Reeves said. "Ranchers been tryin' to get all the cattle cleared fore they's all stampeded to hell and gone."

"They gotta be hurtin', losin' all this good grazin' land," Leander said.

"Can't be helped, I expect," Reeves said. "People's always wantin' more land. I reckon it ain't gonna end till it's all gone. Percy, you still got your grass lease with the Indians?"

"For now," Percy said. "Supposed to be renewed this year, but word is the government might be gettin' cold feet. I talked to Quanah a while back and he didn't have a feel for how it was gonna break."

"So, you're gonna need to sell some cattle?" Reeves asked.

"If we don't get somethin' worked out, yeah," Percy said.

"I'm bettin' the gove'ment ain't done cheatin' the

Indians out of more land, so you might ought to start sellin' a few cattle. How is ol' Quanah?"

"You're probably right," Percy said. "Quanah's the same, though he was mad at me when I last saw him."

"Why was he mad?"

"Well, it was more he was mad at Emma than me. You met her son, Simon?"

"I have."

"Well, Quanah hadn't until the boy wandered into his camp a while back."

"Boy's half Comanche, ain't he?" Reeves asked.

"He is. Emma ain't let him associate with the Indians none. Can't say as I blame her, though, after all she's been through."

The rest of their conversation ended when the two cowpunchers arrived. Reeves pushed his hat back on his head as he eyed the two men. He was the first to speak. "How ya doin', Bill?"

"I'll be doin' better, Marshal Reeves, when I get these here cattle back where they belong," the man said.

Reeves nodded and turned to the other man. "How's the world treatin' you, Charlie?"

"Fair to middlin', Marshal," Charlie said.

Percy had seen the tall, lanky man named Bill before, but couldn't put his finger on where. The other man, a head or two shorter and several pounds heavier, was a stranger. Percy looked over the cattle and saw they were all wearing the Bar-D brand.

Percy saw Reeves eyeing the cattle and then Reeves said, "You two ridin' for Mr. Drummond now?"

"We both hired on this spring."

"Did you now?" Reeves said. "Percy, Leander, this tall

fella here is Bill Doolin. The other one's Charlie Pierce. Fellas, meet my good friends Percy Ridgeway and Leander Hays."

"Me and Percy met once afore," Doolin said. "Nice to see ya again, Percy. Good to meet ya, Leander. You was a Texas Ranger, wadn' you?"

"I was," Leander said.

Percy nodded at the man named Charlie and said, "Nice to meet you, Charlie."

"You got a big spread south of the Red, ain't ya?" Charlie asked.

"We do," Percy said.

"Hear tell," Charlie said, "you 'n' Leander there shot up some rustlers a while back."

Percy and Leander shared a look, both knowing Charlie had most likely picked up that information from other rustlers. Percy turned back to Pierce and said, "I won't tolerate no thievin'. Man steals from me, he's gonna pay for it."

Charlie nodded and said, "Good to know."

"Well, I reckon we better get along," Doolin said. "Nice to see you again, Marshal." He touched his hat and said, "Same to you, Percy and Leander." Doolin and Pierce spurred their horses into motion. It took them a few moments to gather up the cattle again before they moved on.

Reeves watched them for a few more moments then turned to Percy and Leander. "I got a feelin' I'll be huntin' them two down one of these days."

"I was with you the last time I met that Doolin fella. You mentioned back then he might be doin' a little rustlin' on the side."

Reeves nodded. "Probably still is or worse. Both them fellas got a mean streak a mile wide. They's a whole passel of 'em that hangs around up at Ingalls about twenty miles northeast o' here."

"You got paper on any of 'em?" Leander asked.

"Not yet, but it's a-comin', I bet. Don't reckon either of 'em is gonna die from old age, if I had to guess."

"Their type never does," Leander said.

Reeves started his big white stallion off at a walk and the other two men matched him.

"What was Charlie talkin' about you killin' some rustlers?" Reeves asked.

"Ever come across the Dillman brothers?" Percy asked Reeves.

"I busted a couple of Dillmans for whiskey peddlin' a while back. If I recall, them two was brothers. There more?"

"Well, there was three of 'em, but there ain't none now. Marshal over in Henrietta said the oldest, Michael Dillman, was the ringleader."

"Sounds right. One of 'em I arrested was a Michael, if I recall. So, you killed all three of 'em?" Reeves turned to check their back trail, a habit that Percy knew was ingrained in his friend.

"Yeah," Percy said, "and a few more of their kinfolk."

Reeves's head snapped back to Percy and he said, "Do what?"

Percy and Leander told Reeves the details of the shootout and who was involved, and when they finished, Reeves stared at them for a long moment and said, "Maybe I ought to give you two my damn badge. Let y'all and

Chauncey clean out this here territory. I don't recall ever bein' in a fight that ended with twelve men dead."

Percy shrugged. "It happens in the blink of an eye. You know how it is. Me and you and Leander been in our fair share of scrapes."

"That we have," Reeves said.

When they arrived at a small creek a few minutes later, the three men split up, with Reeves and Leander riding one way and Percy the other.

Catching movement out of the corner of his eye a few minutes later, Percy turned the mare down into the creek and began searching. He glanced down to make sure his pistol was where he liked it and found it was. They hadn't had much trouble with the Sooners they'd run off so far, but up in these parts, Percy knew the cheaters were the least of their worries. Indian Territory was overrun with killers, robbers, and rapists, and a man never knew whom he was going to run into next. Although Percy hoped he was trailing a Sooner, there were no guarantees.

A little farther ahead, Percy spotted some tracks in the damp sand and followed them. They eventually dead-ended at a large cedar tree tucked into a side gulley. With his right hand drifting a little closer to his pistol, Percy said, "Come on out."

Limbs began moving and he heard a few grunts and mumbled curses before a woman emerged. Somewhat surprised, Percy looked her over for a moment before saying anything. It was difficult to judge her age with her face half shrouded by a floppy sunbonnet, but she looked pretty ragged with leaves and tufts of cedar clinging to the worn calico dress she was wearing.

"Are you armed?" Percy asked.

She put her hands on her hips and looked up at Percy, defiant. "No, sir, I am not. May I ask whom I'm addressing?"

"Name's Percy Ridgeway, ma'am."

"A pleasure, Mr. Ridgeway. I am Ruth Taylor."

Percy had to stifle a chuckle. If she was frightened it didn't show and for Percy it was a bit surreal, her acting as if they might be meeting for the first time in a bustling city rather than out here on a desolate prairie where she had been caught red-handed trying to cheat the system.

"Where are you from, Mrs. Taylor?"

"I lived most recently in Rolla, Missouri, Mr. Ridgeway. And you, sir?"

"Across the border in Texas. You got anybody with you who might still be hidin'?"

"I do not."

"You're here all by your lonesome?"

Taylor crossed her arms over her chest and straightened her spine. "I'm quite capable of caring for myself."

Percy saw her gaze drift up to the top of the creekbank and Percy turned to see Reeves and Leander pulling their horses to a stop, both grinning from ear to ear. Reeves pushed his hat back and said, "Caught you a Sooner, I see?"

Percy shot Reeves an angry glare and said, "Find any others?"

"No, sir," Reeves said. He nodded at the woman and said, "How'd you get the drop on her?"

Before Percy could offer a smart-ass reply, Taylor said, "Her has a name. I am Ruth Taylor. And you, sir?"

Reeves chuckled then said, "I'm Deputy Marshal Bass Reeves, ma'am."

"A pleasure, Marshal Reeves." Her gaze turned to Leander and she said, "Are you also a marshal?"

"Only part-time. My name's Leander Hays, ma'am."

"A pleasure, Mr. Hays. Does it always require three marshals to apprehend someone?"

Leander chuckled and said, "Not usually."

Ruth turned back to Percy and said, "Am I under arrest?"

"Undecided at the moment," Percy said. "You got a horse?"

"I do not," Taylor said.

"How'd you get here, then?"

"I relied on the oldest mode of transportation, Mr. Ridgeway, I walked."

Percy had to work not to smile. The woman had spunk, that was for sure. Although weary from travel, now that he could see more of her face, he thought she was very pretty with the bluest eyes he'd ever seen. "You got any belongings?"

"Indeed, I do."

"You leave it in that cedar behind ya?" Percy asked.

"I did not. I concealed them in some brush when I saw you approaching."

"Any weapons in what you stashed?"

Ruth paused a moment then nodded. "I have an old pistol that once belonged to my husband."

"You told me you was alone. Where's your husband?" Percy asked.

"Dead, Mr. Ridgeway."

She didn't offer any further details and Percy didn't

ask any more questions. "Grab your stuff and we'll meet you topside."

"So, you are placing me under arrest?"

"Still undecided," Percy said. "Just the same, we gotta escort you outa here."

"Very well. I will retrieve my things and join you in a moment."

"Leave that gun alone," Percy said for emphasis.

"I have no intention of doing anything with that gun, Mr. Ridgeway."

Percy turned his horse and rode along the bottom until he came to a game trail and he spurred the mare up the bank. He rode over to where Reeves and Leander were and pulled the horse to a stop. "Think we ought to let her go?" Percy asked.

"I reckon since she's your prisoner, that's up to you," Reeves said. He looked at Leander and they both started laughing.

"You gonna cuff her?" Leander asked.

That brought on more laughter and Percy let them have their fun.

Eventually, Reeves and Leander settled down and Percy asked his question again.

"Don't know. Damned if we do and damned if we don't," Reeves said. "Her bein' afoot's gonna eat into our time."

"She can double up with me."

"Might ought to check her for weapons, first," Leander said. That sparked more laughter, so Percy set to work rolling a cigarette.

When the laughter died down again, Reeves said, "You reckon she can cook?" The marshals had been taking turns cooking and they all were much better lawmen than they were cooks.

Percy stuck the cigarette in his mouth and lit up. After taking a draw, he said, "Now, there's an idea. And I reckon it'd be better'n her being out here by her lonesome, too."

"Hell, if she can cook at all, it'd be better than what we got," Leander said.

"I reckon we can ask her if she's got any interest in cookin'," Percy said. "Even if she don't, I'm thinkin' about askin' her to come with us."

"You've known her all of five minutes and you're already sweet on her?" Leander asked.

"Did I say anythin' about bein' sweet on her?" Percy asked.

"Don't have to," Leander said. "I can see it in your eyes."

"You two worry about your own business," Percy said.

They fell into silence as they waited for Ruth Taylor to return. Reeves, asking about the grass leases, got Percy thinking about them. As of now, they were running about eight thousand head on the leases and another eight to nine thousand head on the ranch. Cattle prices had spiked after the Big Die-Off during the winter of 1886 and '87 when cattle and other livestock had died by the hundreds of thousands during the most brutal winter anyone could recall. Since then, cattle prices had fallen back to their usual range of seven to eight dollars per hundredweight and Percy could still make a profit at those prices though the margins were slim.

However, that would all change if the government yanked the rug out from under him and the other ranchers. If the government ended the grass leases, he'd need to sell those eight thousand cattle quickly. And he wouldn't be the only one. All the big ranchers in northern Texas and southern Kansas were running stock on Indian lands and every one of them would be forced to sell, too, flooding the market and crushing prices.

Eli had been right when he had said the government operated at a snail's pace, but the exact opposite was true when they finally reached a decision and began issuing orders. The last time the Interior Department ordered all cattle out of Indian Territory they had given the ranchers only thirty days to do it. That sounded like a reasonable amount of time until one started the process of rounding up thousands of cattle that were mixed in with thousands of other cattle wearing a dozen different brands. For all those reasons, Percy needed a better handle on what the government was thinking and the best way to do that was to pay a visit to the Indian agent at the Kiowa and Comanche agency in Anadarko. But that would have to wait until after the Run.

Percy was brought back to the present when Reeves said, "Think she gave us the slip?"

"Been a while, ain't it?" Percy said.

Reeves clucked his tongue and put his big stallion into motion and Percy and Leander fell in beside him. Riding along the creek, they hadn't gone far when they spotted Ruth climbing up the near bank fifty yards ahead. She was carrying a medium-sized bag and Percy wondered how she was going to stake a claim and keep it without a tent or even a pot to cook her food in. She was either destitute, Percy thought, or extremely naive, which didn't jive with what Percy had seen of her so far. Usually not one to stick his nose into anybody else's business, there had to be more to her story, and he was intrigued to find out more.

When they caught up to her, Percy asked Ruth if she could cook and she replied she could. He offered her the job of camp cook and she accepted.

"Before we set out," Percy said, "I'd feel better if you'd give me the pistol."

"Certainly, Mr. Ridgeway," she said.

Reaching into her bag, she handed Percy an old, rusty, cap-and-ball revolver that wasn't even loaded. Percy looked at her and said, "Ever shoot this thing?"

"No, I have not."

"Good thing," Percy said, holding up the pistol for Reeves and Leander to see. "This here pistol is more likely to kill the shooter than the shootee." Percy slipped the worthless weapon into his saddlebag and lifted his left foot out of the stirrup. When he offered his hand, Ruth Taylor climbed up behind him without protest.

Percy looped the handle of her bag around the saddle horn, and they turned their horses and headed toward camp. With the dinner hour approaching, they'd find out real quick if Ruth could cook or not.

CHAPTER
28

The train carrying Seth, Grace, and the rest of the crew rolled into Fort Worth a little after noon. As they waited for the passengers in front of them to disembark, Grace focused her attention on the area around the depot, searching for any familiar faces from the past. It had now been five years since Grace and Marcie had walked out of the parlor house for the last time and the probabilities of running into a former client had diminished greatly. People moved on or they lost interest and no doubt some had died, but the possibilities still existed, and it required a heightened sense of awareness anytime they were in Fort Worth.

What Grace couldn't see was the inside of the building, and that was a problem. In order to board the next train to Guthrie, they would need to cross through the busy depot with no idea who might be lurking inside. With the path to the station clear, Grace and the rest of the group made their way to the exit and stepped down from the train.

Seth cut left to oversee the transfer of the wagon as the others made their way to the station. The rail yard was hopping, with people going every which way and trains coming in and others going out. With Seth gone, Grace asked Simon if he would help keep an eye on the boys and he agreed. Both boys were curious by nature and they'd been known to dart off for a closer look at whatever had caught their fancy. They made it to the building without issue and Grace took a deep breath and fell in behind Chauncey and Marcie as they entered.

The lobby floor was littered with bags and trunks of all sizes, but Marcie and Chauncey did a good job navigating through the mess. Keeping an eye on the boys and carrying Lizzie, Grace also tried to scan the crowd, searching for familiar faces. Thinking they were in the clear as they neared the exit on the other side, Grace was startled when someone in the crowd reached out and grabbed Marcie by the elbow.

Grace turned to see who it was, and her worst fears were realized when her gaze fell on Archer Keating, the man who had attacked Marcie in the barn.

Chauncey, unaware, had continued on, but Marcie shouted his name and he spun around. Grace could see the confusion on his face, but once he had a couple of seconds to assess the situation, she saw his eyes narrow and his face glazed over with an eerie calm.

"Turn her loose," Chauncey said, his voice calm and his hands resting comfortably on the buckle of his gun belt.

Sensing trouble, the crowd quickly melted away, leaving Chauncey, Keating, and Marcie alone, with about ten feet separating the two men.

Keating wrenched Marcie's arm harder and glared at Chauncey. "Who the hell are you?"

Frantic, Grace looked around for her sons and her shoulders sagged with relief when she saw Simon and Emma outside, her two boys in tow.

"I'm your worst nightmare," Chauncey said in that same even tone. "Turn her loose."

Marcie, taking advantage of the distraction, yanked her arm free and hurried outside.

Momentarily stunned by the situation, it suddenly dawned on Grace that she might be in danger, so she turned and hurried outside to join the others.

"Think you're a gunhand, do ya?" Keating said. "What's she to you?"

"My wife," Chauncey said.

Someone had propped the door open and they had a clear view of what was happening inside. Grace turned to Marcie and said, "Go stop them."

"No stopping Chauncey now," Marcie said.

"Try," Grace pleaded. "What happens if Keating kills him?"

Before Marcie could respond, they heard Keating say, "What kinda man marries a—" And that's when Keating reached for his gun.

Chauncey's hand was a blur when he pulled his pistol, cocked it on the way up, and fired.

Grace watched in horror as a hole appeared in the center of Keating's forehead a millisecond before the back of his head exploded in a spray of blood, bone, and brain matter.

The crowd inside recoiled in revulsion as the bloody

mist drifted down, coating them with a gruesome reminder of what they'd just witnessed. A woman screamed. Then another, sparking an explosion of activity as the crowd stampeded for the exits. Chauncey stood firm and like a boulder in the river, the frightened citizens cut a wide berth around him as they streamed outside.

The gunshot had awakened Lizzie and she began crying and squirming. Grace patted her on the back as she watched Chauncey calmly eject the spent shell before replacing it with a fresh cartridge. He seated his pistol, turned around, and calmly walked out the door, the expression on his face unchanged.

"Sorry you had to see that," Chauncey said. He reached out and took Marcie's hand and they continued on to the train as if nothing had happened.

Andrew, Grace's four-year-old, was looking at the dead man when he tugged on her skirt and said, "Mama, is that man dead?"

Grace, caught off guard by how quickly the encounter had spiraled into violence, was kicking herself for not shielding the boys from the shooting. She handed the baby to Emma and squatted down so she could look her boys in the eye. "Yes, that man is dead and I'm sorry you had to see it."

"It's okay, Mama," Andrew said, "I seen dead stuff before."

"I know you have," Grace said, "but it's a different thing to see it happen."

"Is Uncle Chauncey in trouble?" Andrew asked.

Chauncey was a second or third cousin to the children and technically not an uncle, but that's what they called him anyway. "I don't think so. It looked like a fair fight to me."

"But the other man never got his gun out."

"Well," Grace said, "sometimes it just happens that way."

Grace kissed each boy on the cheek and stood, wondering if what she had told her son was the truth. It sure looked like a fair fight, but the town marshal might think otherwise. Either way, she certainly wasn't going to stick around to find out. At her urging, the group proceeded on to the next train.

When they arrived, Emma, Grace, and the kids chose the row of seats across the aisle from where Marcie and Chauncey were sitting and once everyone was situated, Grace leaned in close to Emma, who was sitting next to her, and said, "Think Chauncey's in the clear?"

"I would hope so," Emma whispered, "but you never know for sure. The marshal might be havin' a bad day or maybe the mayor reamed him out this mornin' about rising crime rates and now he wants to set an example. Who knows what other factors they consider when making those decisions? But there were also plenty of witnesses, so I don't think he could make too big a deal of it. How big a rancher was that Keating fella?"

"Not nearly as big as the Ridgeways, but he used to hobnob with some of the city bigwigs. Don't know if he still did, but if anyone deserved a bullet in the head it was that man. I'm just sorry it took so long."

"How did you and Marcie come to know him so well?" Emma asked.

Grace had never discussed her previous life with any

member of the Ridgeway clan and she damn sure didn't want to talk about it now. Although she thought Emma was the one person in the family who might sympathize with the difficult choices she'd made, it wasn't the right time or place to have that discussion. She looked at Emma and said, "Fort Worth was a pretty small town when I lived there. It wasn't unusual to see the same people over and over again."

Hoping to avoid any more awkward questions, Grace steered the conversation back to the original topic. "So, you think Chauncey will be okay?"

"The best thing for Chauncey would be to get this train movin'," Emma whispered. "What time is it scheduled to leave?"

"One-thirty, I think."

Emma dug her watch out of the pocket of her skirt and popped the lid. "We've still got twenty minutes to go. Might be tight."

"All we can do is wait."

From what Grace could see of Chauncey, he didn't seem to be nervous about the possible arrival of the local lawmen. He sat easy in his seat, his left arm draped loosely over Marcie's shoulders. Grace thought if she had just killed someone, she would have been a nervous wreck, but not Chauncey. She'd heard stories about other shootouts he had been involved in and she wondered how many men he had killed. *Three? Six? Ten? Twenty?* The only way to know would be to ask him and Grace had no intention of doing that. Besides, it wasn't any of her business. Seth had told her a few stories about Chauncey and his pistols, but hearing stories was nothing compared to actually seeing it live.

She tried to push those thoughts out of her mind as she turned her focus to her sons. They were much more subdued than normal, and she wondered if they were suffering from shock. Grace made a mental note to keep a close eye on them over the next couple of days.

Hearing a familiar pattern of footsteps, Grace turned to see Seth coming up the aisle. She moved over to give him room and he sat down. He leaned in close and said, "Chauncey?"

Grace nodded.

"Who was he?"

Grace hadn't told Seth about the attack on Marcie in the barn, so she did so now. When she finished, she whispered, "Any lawmen outside?"

"Didn't see any, but they gotta be gettin' close if they're comin'. Tell me exactly how the shooting happened, in case I need to intercede as his lawyer," Seth whispered.

Grace told him every detail she could recall, including the fact that their two sons had witnessed the shooting.

"So," Seth said, "Keating went for his gun first?"

"He did, though he never had a prayer."

"Not many do against Chauncey. From what you told me, the local law might try to detain him while they conduct an inquest, but I don't see it going beyond that. Still, it might be dicey for Chauncey to be held here, in Keating's hometown. Was he well liked?"

"Most of the people I knew didn't like him and I'm bettin' not many are going to mourn his passing."

"How many men did he have workin' for him?" Seth asked.

"No idea."

Seth nodded and he and Grace settled in for the wait.

The next few minutes felt like an hour and finally, the engineer blew the whistle and the car jerked as the train lurched out of the station. Grace sighed with relief and settled in for the ride.

CHAPTER

29

After the army had given the would-be settlers in north Texas the okay to proceed to Purcell, Pearl O'Sullivan, Levi Johnson, and the three kids had finally crossed the Red River and were now officially riding through Indian Territory. It didn't look all that different to Pearl, but it did have a different feel, knowing the land belonged to the Indians. Everyone was on the move, the line wagons headed north stretching beyond the horizon and the white canvas covers looking like clouds floating along the ground. A sense of urgency rippled along the line, everyone knowing the importance of being near the starting point when high noon arrived on Monday.

Today was Friday and according to Levi, they had about ninety miles to cover before reaching their destination. If they had any hopes of making it before the start of the Land Run, they would have to push hard with very few stops. Everyone traveling north knew it was going to be a chore, but the mood among the homesteaders was giddy, each knowing there was a prize to be had at the end.

Although her future with Levi remained uncertain, Pearl had abandoned her fellow Chicagoans. Levi had made no promises, nor had she expected any after knowing each other for only a short time. But the few times they'd been able to sneak away for a few minutes of privacy, the kissing and cuddling had advanced to the point that it left them both hot and bothered. Was it love? That was a hard question for Pearl to answer, having never been in a serious relationship before. She did know she got butterflies in her stomach every time he touched her, so there was that. And Levi's earlier comment about wanting to get into her knickers always lingered somewhere in the back of her mind.

Having no real religious beliefs, Pearl had never given much thought to the "save yourself for marriage" idea. Obviously, Levi had already done the deed. Might he want to sample the goods before making any commitments? And that brought up the question of whether she wanted *him* to sample her goods. What if he didn't like the goods she had to offer? And that led to another question: Would it be better to delay the sampling until she had some firm answers about where the relationship was going?

The answers to any of those questions were problematic because she had no frame of reference on how an intimate relationship was supposed to work. But with no moral qualms about a roll in the hay and no worries about soiling a reputation that didn't exist, she was hard pressed to find a reason for not letting Levi sneak a cookie from the cookie jar. She had learned that people out here on the frontier didn't much care what you did or who you did it with, nor did they spend much time worrying about what you might have already done. Just eking out an existence required more energy than most people had and worrying about stuff like that never made it onto most people's lists of things that needed doing.

Pearl turned to look behind them. The wagons were spaced no more than ten feet apart and they were stacked up like a line of dominoes. She turned back around and spent a few moments watching Levi as he drove the wagon, the reins grasped firmly in his humongous hands. He was a bear of a man, yet he was as gentle as a kitten. It was a warm day and he had stripped down to his undershirt and she could see the muscles rippling in his broad shoulders as he steered the wagon around a mudhole. He turned to look at her and caught her staring.

"I have somethin' on my face?"

"No, I just like lookin' at you. I think you should shave your beard, though."

"We've known each other a couple of weeks and you're already givin' me groomin' tips?"

"Does that really matter?"

"What's that?"

"How long we've known each other?"

"I don't suppose it does. You got any bad habits I don't know about?"

"I don't think so. You?"

"Kids tell me I snore. I reckon that's about it, though I've been known to sip a little whiskey on occasion."

"Nothin' wrong with that."

Now comfortable enough with each other not to feel the need to fill any voids in their conversations, they rode in companionable silence for a while, the terrain relatively flat and easily traversed. They passed the small hamlet of Thackerville and were making good time. But that all changed a couple of hours later when the wagon train ground to a halt.

"What the hell?" Levi mumbled.

"I'll stay with the kids if you want to walk up there to see what the problem is," Pearl said.

"Good idea. We can't afford to be wastin' time." He set the brake, climbed down, and started walking, his long stride quickly eating up the distance.

Taking advantage of the break, Pearl coaxed the children out of the wagon so they could stretch their legs and go to the bathroom. Other families began spilling out of other wagons and it wasn't long before the once-desolate prairie was crawling with humans. Pearl saw a couple of people from Chicago and they waved, and she waved back. Although the wagon train had hit its first snag, the holdup had little effect on the mood of the people. Smiles were plentiful and the feeling they were on some grand adventure permeated the crowd.

Pearl spotted Levi coming back and she and the children met him back at the wagon. "What's the problem?" Pearl asked.

"There's some real rough ground up ahead," Levi said. "It's cut up with a bunch of creeks and dry washes and they're out now trying to find a better route."

"Want me to put on some coffee?" Pearl asked.

"No, I'm hoping we're not going to be here that long."

Despite what Levi had said, it took the better part of an hour to find a viable path forward and everyone loaded back into the wagons. The chosen route detoured a few miles to the west, but by the time they'd weaved their way through they'd had to cross only one small creek. After that it was smooth sailing for a while and then, a couple of hours later, they hit an even larger obstacle.

According to the old map Levi had, they were called the Arbuckle Mountains, but they were unlike any mountains Pearl had ever seen. She thought the name a misnomer because none appeared to be over eight or nine hundred feet tall. But whether they were nine hundred feet tall or nine thousand feet, they were impassible. So, again, the wagons were halted while a viable route was found. If this continued for the entire trip there was no way they were going to make it to Oklahoma before the Run.

"You think the wagons at the front of the pack have a newer map than this one?" Pearl asked, fluttering the paper in her hand.

"All we got to do is follow the railroad tracks."

Pearl pointed to the narrow opening cut into the rock and said, "We ain't gettin' the wagons through that lest we drive on the tracks. And that'd be a disaster waitin' to happen."

As if on cue, they heard the shrill notes of a train whistle in the distance.

"I reckon we're gonna hit some hiccups no matter what trail we follow," Levi said. "All part of it, I suppose. I do wish they woulda let us start a day or two earlier, but they didn't. We'll make it."

"You sound sure."

"I am. Even if we have to travel all night, we're gonna make it. Ain't got much choice. If I can't stake a claim, I'm gonna be in a hard spot."

Pearl worried about his use of *I* instead of *we* and she

wondered if she was going to need to stake a claim after all. With no form of transportation, she'd be forced to do it on foot, putting her at a significant disadvantage. However, she didn't have any other choice, either. Going back to Chicago was not an option.

Although she wanted desperately to know what Levi was planning, she also didn't want to put too much pressure on him, especially when he was already stressed about getting to Oklahoma in time. It was a delicate balance and she decided to bide her time for now. What she really needed to do was make herself indispensable and that was exactly what she'd do.

After a fairly short wait, someone came up with a new route, and the wagons were soon rolling again. They traveled west for a couple of hours and the mountains eventually petered out, which suggested they finally had someone at the helm who was familiar with the terrain. After making the swing back to the north, the traveling got much easier. A few moments later when they topped a small rise, Pearl looked into the distance and gasped. "Are they real?" she asked.

Spread out along a small creek ahead were fifty or sixty Indian teepees, the hides faded from years of use.

"They're real, all right," Levi said.

"They still live in teepees?"

"Some of 'em do, yeah. Most of the Indians in the eastern part of the Territory got houses and barns and such. These here," he said, nodding toward the sprawling camp, "don't got nothin'."

"How come?" Pearl asked.

Levi shrugged and said, "They spent their whole lives

wandering from place to place, so maybe they don't want nothin' that's gonna tie them down."

"Are they dangerous?"

Levi looked at Pearl and said, "They're okay most of the time as long as someone don't rile them up."

"And you don't think a long line of wagons with a bunch of white people in them isn't goin' to rile them up?" Pearl asked.

Levi thought about it for a moment then said, "Might be best if you was to pull out that shotgun from under the seat."

CHAPTER
30

   With the army giving the all clear to proceed to the Oklahoma boundary, the Boomers in Pawnee Bill's camp had been ready to roll out long before daybreak. Part of the group would be heading for Stillwater Creek when the gun fired at high noon on Monday, the rest, including Couch and his family, were planning to push farther south to Oklahoma Station, about thirty miles south of Guthrie. Couch, a born politician, had big plans to make that area the capital and he had already christened the area Oklahoma City. Bill didn't much care for the name, but he hadn't been consulted. Which was just fine. He had zero political ambition and all he wanted was a nice place where he could graze the stock for their traveling show.

   Now, midmorning, as they continued to roll across the prairie, Pawnee Bill was back to contemplating ways to make their Wild West show financially viable. If they launched another show, that is. Although he grew weary of May's many moods, she was a very intelligent woman and down deep he knew she would be the driving force if they were to succeed. He looked at May, who was sitting beside him, and said, "What changes should we make if we go back on tour?"

"We need to scale it down and change a few things, including the name."

"What's wrong with the name?"

"It needs more specificity. Right now, people see a playbill for Pawnee Bill's Historic Wild West show, and they associate it with Buffalo Bill's Wild West show."

"Well," Bill said, "they are similar. Does it really matter if they think they're goin' to Cody's show and end up at ours?"

"I don't think that happens as much as you think it does. If people are going to shell out money to go see a show, they're going to exert some effort to find out what they're paying for. No, what we need to do is provide the audience a unique experience, something they won't see at any other show. People love the Indian acts, but we need to restructure them and find a new approach. Perhaps we approach the Comanche chief, Quanah Parker, to gauge his interest in performing. His name alone would draw a large number of people and his story—born to a white woman the Indians had taken captive—is irresistible."

"Heck, Quanah wouldn't necessarily need to perform. Him sittin' his horse with a long eagle-feather headdress on would draw a huge crowd."

"He would need a larger role than that," May said. "You're thinking too small, as usual."

Pawnee Bill could sense her mood was beginning to turn so he steered clear of any further Quanah talk. "You want big ideas, here's one. What if we could lure Annie

Oakley away from Cody? She's a huge draw everywhere she goes."

"You'd risk starting a talent war, which would push everyone's expenses through the roof."

"Maybe she's lookin' for a change of scenery."

"I just said stealing each other's talent is unsustainable. Is there something about that you don't understand? All that time you spent with Cody has jaded your thinking. We need something different, something original that'll generate excitement, not the same old worn-out ideas that have been tried over and over again."

And with that, the conversation was over as far as Bill was concerned. Once she started sniping, he knew things would only go downhill. He shifted the reins to his left hand and reached under the seat to grab the canteen. He pulled out the cork and took a drink. He wasn't all that thirsty, but it kept his hands busy so he wouldn't be tempted to wrap them around his wife's neck. When some of his anger had bled away, he stoppered the canteen and put it back under the seat.

The northern border of Oklahoma was a little over eighty miles from Caldwell, and they had most of three days to get there, so the pace was brisk but not especially burdensome. Ideally, Bill preferred a Saturday-evening arrival to ensure they had a spot close to the front of what would no doubt be an enormous crowd. Although the Boomers numbered in the thousands, they represented only a tiny fraction of the people expected to arrive by noon, Monday. He had heard estimates that as many as a hundred thousand people would take part in the Run, but he couldn't fathom that many people showing up. Yes, two million acres of free land sounded like an exorbitant number, but once divided into parcels there would be far more people than land available—thus his desire to be near the front of the starting line.

He glanced over at May, who now had her nose buried in a book. She knew her sharp tongue cut like a knife and didn't seem to care. He had pleaded with her, to little effect, to soften her tone. If anything, it had gotten worse and any restraint she might have once had was now totally gone and she'd say whatever was on her mind no matter how hurtful it might be. It hadn't always been that way and he wondered if there was something medically wrong with her.

The wagon train veered west for several miles before turning back south. Having scouted Indian Territory for years, Bill knew the jog in their trail was to avoid a series of creeks that lay ahead. The Boomers had found and marked a trail that would allow them to bypass all the area's waterways until they arrived at the Salt Fork of the Arkansas River about twelve miles ahead.

The land they were now traversing was called the Cherokee Outlet, a huge swath of land ceded to the Cherokees when they had signed a treaty giving up all their lands east of the Mississippi River. The Outlet allowed the Cherokees to move unimpeded between their homes and the hunting grounds out west. But with the buffalo now gone, the Indians didn't have much use for the Outlet so instead they leased the land to several large cattle outfits. As a Boomer, Pawnee Bill had also lobbied for opening the Cherokee Outlet and he was fairly certain it would happen, and the only remaining question was when. And even though he and others had urged the federal government to open portions of Indian Territory, it saddened him some, too, when he thought about the impact on the Pawnees. Their way of life, which had so fascinated him as a boy, was disappearing and he knew the arrival of the white settlers would only accelerate the process.

It was midafternoon when they reached the river, one of the most treacherous obstacles they would face during their journey. Bill's stomach began to sour as he eased the wagon forward, waiting for their turn to cross. The river was up and the swirling, surging current was pushing the crossing wagons a hundred yards downstream before they could reach the other side.

"This old rattletrap gonna make it?" May asked, her first words in at least three hours.

"Guess we're gonna find out." When the team pulling the wagon in front of them regained their footing on the other side, Bill slapped the reins and shouted, to get his two mules moving. The river was about two hundred yards wide, and twenty yards in, the wagon began floating and the mules began swimming. The current was much swifter than it looked and by the time they hit the midway point they were well downstream. He glanced over his shoulder to see how much water was seeping into the bed and found it wasn't as bad as he had expected. Feeling confident they were in the clear, he loosened the reins to let the mules swim at their own pace.

However, Bill's confidence was shattered a moment later when he detected movement out of the corner of his eye. He turned to see a giant log barreling straight toward them. Had it been floating parallel with the water, they might have had a chance, but it wasn't, and it was going to hit them broadside like a fusillade of cannon fire during a naval battle. Bill looked at the log, nearly thirty feet long, then looked at the far bank and he knew the math didn't add up. "Hold on," he shouted at May.

With the mules swimming, they were still drifting downstream but not nearly as fast as the log. The mules were working on instinct and they would swim until they found firm footing and there was no way to soften the blow.

Wham! The log hit with a resounding thump, jarring Bill and May out of the seat. He grabbed the seat back to keep from falling off and he managed to grab May by the arm before she hit the water. Pulling with all of his might he finally got May back inside, but he was so focused on saving them that he didn't notice the mules were being dragged backward. The log was jammed against the side of the wagon, forcing them farther downstream. If he didn't do something right damn now the mules would drown.

People were running along the bank, trying to reach them, but they weren't gaining enough ground to make a difference. He stood in the footwell, his mind rapidly clicking through options. He had to separate the log from the wagon, or all was going to be lost. Holding on to the seat, he lifted his leg over the side and tried to push the log away with his foot and it wouldn't budge an inch. He peered over the side and his heart sank when he saw the log was jammed behind the wheels. The only way to get it out would be to pull it out, an impossible task in the current situation. The mules were thrashing and braying, and he watched in horror as one slipped beneath the surface. Thankfully, he popped up a moment later, but Bill knew it was only a matter of time.

Strangely, the wagon began to slow, and Bill couldn't figure out why. Then it hit him. The wheels on the other side must have hit a sandbar. With the force of the current and the added weight of the log, the wagon was seconds away from rolling over. He looked at May and shouted, "Get to the back of the wagon and jump off!"

"Why not here?" May shouted.

"Wagon's gonna roll."

May scampered over the seat and hurried to the back. Once she was safely out, Bill turned to jump and almost lost his grip on the seat when the wagon suddenly jerked to a stop. The right side was lifting out of the water when Bill took a deep breath and jumped.

CHAPTER
31

As the train approached Ardmore, a small town in the southern part of the Chickasaw Nation, Emma Turner was wondering if she was doing the right thing. Last Saturday, Quanah and his daughter Ann had arrived at the ranch for a daylong visit. The chief took to his role of teaching Simon some of the Comanche customs and had even given Simon a bow and a quiver full of arrows. Simon had a long way to go in his quest to become an archer, but it had been both heartwarming and confusing to see her son and Quanah together.

During the visit Emma had mentioned her plans to attend the Land Run and Ann had expressed an interest in also going. After some back-and-forth with Quanah, it was agreed that Emma and Simon would meet Ann at the train depot in Ardmore and she would accompany them to Guthrie. The only reason Emma was now second-guessing herself was the thousands of wagons they had passed on their trek north.

She knew the opportunity of free land would draw a

big crowd, but the number of people streaming toward Oklahoma was staggering. And Emma knew the same had to also be happening in other parts of the Territory and she was worried about her ability to keep Simon and Ann safe. There was no doubt the people now swarming toward the promised land would attract some unsavory characters whose only interest would be to fleece, con, or even steal everything they could from the homesteaders and she knew that might spark all types of violence and mayhem. Hell, Emma thought, there had already been one killing, and they were only a few hours into their journey. She decided to enlist some of the others to keep an eye on Simon and Ann, knowing she couldn't back out now.

The train eased into Ardmore station and jerked to a stop. Sure enough, Ann was on the platform, waiting. It took a moment for Emma to recognize her, not having seen her dressed in traditional white clothing. Ann was wearing a dark blue gingham split skirt and a light blue, pleated blouse and Emma thought she looked stunning. She and Simon exited the train to greet her. After hugs all around, Simon, ever the gentleman, took her bag and they reboarded the train. Simon introduced Ann to the family members she hadn't yet met then they chose a bench seat a few rows away and sat down. With restrictions on who could enter Oklahoma before the Run, the train was lightly populated and there was plenty of room to spread out.

Once Emma was resettled, she spent a few moments studying Ann and Simon together. There was no denying they made a handsome couple. Although she thought they were still too young to begin courting, Emma still had mixed feelings about them doing so if or when that time arrived. Emma had seen the nasty looks from some of the white passengers when they had reboarded with Ann in tow. It wasn't anything new, but it didn't make it any less hurtful. And if Simon was already being stigmatized for his mixed blood, Emma feared the two together would face a whole new level of hatred and hostility. However, Emma also knew she'd have little say in the matter and they both had their own lives to live.

It was late afternoon when the train rolled into Guthrie. Emma had been dozing on and off over the last hour, but she perked right up when she saw several men with badges pinned to their chests board the train. Her first thought was that they were there to arrest Chauncey and she began to panic. A gunfight in the close confines of the railroad car could get them all killed.

She looked over at Chauncey and saw him sitting easy, his legs splayed out and his hands resting comfortably in his lap. Okay, Emma thought, maybe he was going to give himself up. Whatever his plan, he gave nothing away. There were no tells and Emma had to zero in on his chest to see if he was still breathing. He was, but the tension in the coach was building. Even Emma was nervous, and she knew she hadn't done anything wrong.

One of the men stopped right in front of Chauncey and it took all of Emma's resolve not to push the children to the floor and dive on top of them. Studying the badge pinned to the man's chest, Emma saw that he was a deputy U.S. marshal and her eyes drifted down to the gun on his hip. She wondered if *he'd* be able to get it out before Chauncey killed him. The marshal looked at Chauncey then his gaze swept over the rest of the group. His clothing was grubby, and his mustache hadn't seen a pair of scissors since he'd started growing it. "All y'all travelin' together?" the marshal asked.

Seth stood and said, "We are."

"Ain't nobody allowed in here until high noon on Monday."

Seth dug around in his bag and came out with a piece of paper. He handed it to the marshal and said, "We have permission. I'm a lawyer."

The man didn't bother to look at the paper before handing it back. "All y'all lawyers?" the marshal asked.

Grace stood and said, "No, sir. We're here simply to assist."

The marshal gave Seth a long, hard look and said, "How many assistants you need?"

Seth shrugged. "It's going to be busy."

The deputy took one more look at the group then said, "Welcome to Guthrie." He turned, walked back down the aisle, and stepped off the train.

Emma sighed with relief. Chauncey stood and stretched as if he didn't have a care in the world.

Emma looked at him and said, "I thought they were comin' for you."

"I ain't broke no laws, leastwise not this month anyway," Chauncey said.

They gathered up their things and exited the train. As they filed off, each person paused to look around. They all knew there would be no stores or other modern conveniences in the area, but they had expected to see other signs of civilization, such as houses and such. Instead, the town of Guthrie was home to exactly four buildings and one of those was a railroad water tank. One of the other buildings was also railroad-related and that was the depot, which hadn't seen a paintbrush or nail and hammer since the day it had been put up. The third one looked newly built and Emma assumed it was the land office. The last building in the sprawling metropolis was a small run-down shack with a Western Union sign nailed over the door.

"Hell, it ain't nothin' but a wide spot in the road," Chauncey said. "Ain't even got a saloon."

"Alcohol is illegal in Indian Territory," Seth offered.

"Wonderful," Chauncey mumbled.

CHAPTER
32

The good news was that Pawnee Bill and May survived the disastrous river crossing. And there was one more bit of good news. When the wagon had rolled over, it broke into a dozen pieces and the mules were able to escape. But the rest of the news was all bad—the wagon and everything in it were a total loss. What didn't sink to the bottom was swept downstream and, after searching, Bill and May didn't even have a change of clothes. The tent, the cookware, the firearms, the stakes they were going to use to mark their claim, the hammer Bill was going to use to drive said stakes, and all of their provisions were gone.

Now riding in the wagon of another gracious Boomer with their mules tied at the back, Bill and May were trying to figure out what to do next. Well, at least Bill was. May hadn't spoken to him since he told her to jump. So, not only was it disorienting to be riding in the bowels of someone else's wagon, it was now as frosty as a Christmas morning inside.

"Nothing's really changed," Bill pleaded. "We can still claim the ground we wanted."

May's thoughts on the matter were revealed with a withering glare.

To say that things were tight inside the wagon would be an understatement. The people they'd hitched a ride with, the Padgett family, included three children who were also riding in the wagon along with, what looked like, everything the Padgetts owned. Bill stood and, using the wooden ribs that held the canvas aloft, delicately worked his way to the back of the wagon. He gave the mules the evil eye then slid over the back and started his legs moving before he touched down. He stumbled once, regained his balance, and continued on. It felt good to be out in the fresh air. The only complaint he had was that his clothes were still wet, and it wasn't long before he began chafing at all the pinch points. Still, it was nice to be out from under his wife's harsh glare for a few moments.

He angled away from the wagon to escape the dust. They would hit Red Rock Creek in a couple of hours, and he knew another water crossing would be a reminder of all they had lost, no doubt reigniting May's anger. With that in mind, Bill decided he'd better find someone else to hitch a ride with. He glanced over his shoulder to see who was in the wagon behind them and was surprised to see William Couch at the reins. He slowed his pace to match the wagon's and when Couch came alongside, he grabbed the side and climbed aboard.

"Sorry about your wagon," Couch said.

"Ain't a thing I coulda done different, except stay home. How many trips you reckon we made down this way?"

"A dozen, maybe more," Couch said, his voice muffled by the bandanna wrapped around his nose and mouth.

"You ever recall us losin' a wagon before?"

"Nope, but there's always a first time for everything."

Bill turned to say hello to Mrs. Couch and discovered the wagon was empty. "Where's your family?"

"They're scattered. Some are with my parents and the others are riding in my brother's wagon. I think they got tired of listening to all my plans."

"Mind if I ride along with you for a spell?"

"Fine with me," Couch said. "May still angry?"

"Oh yeah."

"I suppose that's what we get for hitching up with a couple of Quaker women."

"Ain't that the truth. Cindy have a temper?" Bill asked.

"Ever see a woman who didn't?"

"Good point." Bill pulled the bandanna wrapped around his neck up over his nose and mouth to block some of the dust as he settled in for the ride. He didn't want to burden Couch with his marital problems. He already knew there were no easy answers and no ready solutions short of a separation and that wasn't happening. May managed the finances and she would be crucial to relaunching their show. And that was part of the problem.

It might have been different if he and May hadn't spent every waking moment together over the last year. The logistics of moving the show from point A to point B was extremely stressful and when you factored in the financial difficulties they'd endured last year, it had been like living inside a violent storm, never knowing where the next twister might touch down. He suddenly realized he was tired of thinking about May and last year's failure, so he took a deep calming breath and tried to force it all from his mind.

"So," Bill said, "you're dead set on stakin' a claim somewhere around the Oklahoma Station?"

"I am," Couch replied. "Think of it, Gordon, being present for the birth of a city. Most cities and towns evolve over time, but Monday at noon, new cities all over Oklahoma will sprout from nothing. It's a chance to shape all the essential elements from design, to how it will be financed, and, more importantly, how it will be governed."

Couch was one of the very few who refused to call Bill by his stage name. "Sounds like a pain in the butt to me."

Couch laughed and said, "There will no doubt be some growing pains, but how many chances in life do we get to begin something that will continue to exist long after we're all gone? Oklahoma Station is the perfect spot for a city, and I could see it becoming the capital when the area we're calling Oklahoma and the rest of Indian Territory eventually becomes a state."

"You really think that's gonna happen?"

"It's inevitable, especially with the passage of the Dawes Allotment Act."

"But the language in the bill specifically excludes the Five Civilized Tribes."

"That's the only way they could get the bill passed at the time. It's easily amendable."

"Indians got a say in it?"

"Do they ever?" Couch asked. "I know you have many friends in the Pawnee Nation, but look around, Gordon,"

Couch said, making a sweeping gesture with his hand, "they're not using the land."

"Does that matter? They were promised their lands forever. I didn't have a problem campaignin' for the opening of the Unassigned Lands, but I'd hate to see the Indians lose what's theirs. Hellfire, the Cherokees have been here almost sixty years."

"I understand, but it's coming anyway, that I can tell you. I spent four years in Washington, D.C., and there are specific plans for dealing with the Indians. Why do you think the government forces the Indian children to attend boarding schools?"

"Haven't given it much thought."

"The feds have, that I can assure you. When an Indian child arrives at one of the boarding schools, their hair is cut, they're dressed in modern clothing, and they're assigned new American names. They're forbidden from speaking their native languages, and they're punished severely if they speak anything other than English. But the real key to the boarding schools is that they separate the children from all things Indian-related. The man, I believe his name's Pratt, who runs the Carlisle Indian School up in Pennsylvania coined the term 'Kill the Indian, save the man,' and that's a fairly accurate description of the government's attempts to assimilate the Indians."

"Sounds cold-blooded to me," Bill said.

"Oh, it is, especially for the younger children, but that's the plan that's been developed, and I don't see it changing anytime soon."

"Gives me a stomachache thinkin' about it," Bill said.

"The world's changing, Gordon. The buffalo are all gone and westward expansion is an unstoppable force.

The only way the Indians will survive is to follow our path."

What Couch had said had opened Bill's eyes to what was really going on and it made him angry. As a young man, he had lived among the Pawnees and they were kind, gentle people and many of the men had served their country with distinction acting as scouts for the army during the Indian Wars. As it was now, the Pawnees held their land in common and the thought of them being forced to accept a small allotment and have the rest of their lands sold to the government so it could be opened for settlement didn't sit well with him. It almost made him wish he'd never taken up the Boomer cause.

His thoughts were interrupted when Couch said, "I believe the federal officials have made some grievous errors in their planning for the Land Run."

"From what I can tell," Bill said, "they didn't do much plannin' at all."

"Agreed. But the biggest mistake was providing for only two land offices. As it is, I'll need to stake my claim and then travel to Guthrie or Kingfisher to file it along with thousands of others who will be trying to do the exact same thing. It would have made more sense to establish land offices at each likely town site."

"Most everything the government does don't make no sense. But with all those people trying to file their claims the tempers are gonna be running hot. You best keep that pistol of yours in easy reach."

CHAPTER
33

Ruth Taylor had passed the cooking test with flying colors. She had whipped up a tasty venison stew from a deer the marshals had killed, and all agreed it had been the best meal they'd had since arriving in Indian Territory. Their bellies now full, the group of marshals were lounging around the fire a few more minutes before returning to, what all agreed was, a futile task.

After the dishes had been cleaned, Percy and Ruth had drifted away from the rest of the group and were now seated on a small bluff overlooking the Cimarron. Now that the dust had been washed off her face and she'd had a chance to fix her hair and ditch the sunbonnet, Percy thought she was very attractive.

"How long you been a widow?" Percy asked.

"Two years, Mr. Ridgeway."

"It's Percy, please. What did you do back in Rolla?"

"I've taught school for many years, but recently lost the passion for it. I resigned at the end of the winter term. Have you always been a lawman?"

"No, I'm a cowpuncher. I just came up to help Bass out for a few days."

"You mentioned you had a place in Texas. Is that where you do your cowpunching?"

Percy smiled. "Yeah, our place runs along the Red River down around Wichita Falls."

"Is there a Mrs. Ridgeway back home?"

"Wife's been dead a long time."

"I'm sorry for your loss."

"Thank you. Same to you. Did you walk here all the way from Rolla?"

Ruth chuckled and said, "No, I took the train to Arkansas City and walked from there, catching an occasional ride if a wagon was passing by."

"Still a far piece."

"I had nothing but time, and one must make do with what one has."

"You hopin' to stake out a town lot or what?"

"I'd prefer the full parcel of one hundred and sixty acres."

"What are you gonna do with it?" Percy asked.

"Live on it, Mr. Ridgeway. I lost everything after the death of my husband. We had been renting a small house in town, but I couldn't afford to stay after leaving my teaching job."

"If you don't mind me askin', how'd your husband die?"

"He was shot."

Percy reared back in surprise. He was thinking maybe the man had died of a heart attack or maybe he had been thrown from a horse or he might have caught one of those infernal diseases always going around. He certainly wasn't expecting to hear her husband had been gunned down.

"Who shot him?"

"I did."

That was a double wallop. "Why'd you do that?"

"He laid his hands on me one too many times. In fact, he had his hands around my throat when I jammed the pistol into his gut and pulled the trigger."

"It wasn't the pistol you gave me," Percy said.

"It was not. I used another revolver."

"What'd the town marshal have to say about it?"

"He ruled it self-defense. It was no secret around town that my husband could be a volatile man, especially when he took to the bottle."

"Hell, I'm sorry you had to go through all that," Percy said.

"We all have some type of burden to bear."

"I reckon that's true, though some are a little heavier than others and I reckon yours was a heavy load. What happens if you don't stake a claim?"

Ruth shrugged. "I don't honestly know."

Percy watched the swiftly moving water for a few moments then looked at Ruth and said, "I'm gonna make sure you get your land."

"How are you going to do that?"

"Don't have it all figured yet, but this time Monday, you'll be sittin' on your own piece of property."

"Thank you, Mr. Ridgeway."

Percy pushed to his feet and extended his hand to help Ruth up. He was still holding her hand when he said, "One more thing. We're done with this Mr. Ridgeway business. It's Percy, okay?"

Ruth smiled and gave his hand a squeeze. "Percy it is."

"That's more like it." Percy released her hand and the two made their way back to camp. Although he traveled to Fort Worth on occasion to see Josie Belmont to satisfy his basic needs, it had been a long time since he'd just sat and talked to a woman who wasn't also a family member. He had walled off that side of his life after Mary's death, but he now realized that had been a mistake. Life was meant to be shared and Percy made a conscious decision to be more open-minded about letting a woman into his life. Whether that woman might be Ruth was undetermined, but he was willing to put in the effort to find out and that was a giant leap forward for him.

Percy had been so deep in thought he hadn't noticed that Leander and Reeves had walked up and were standing right next to him. "How long you two been standin' there?"

Reeves chuckled then said, "Not too long. You two have a nice chat?"

"We did, not that it's any of your business. We goin' back out?"

"Might as well. I reckon you can nab us another gal and then we'll have somebody to tend to our horses, too." Reeves laughed and, of course, Leander joined in. They were still laughing when Percy headed out to get his horse.

He found the mare grazing on a fresh patch of grass a hundred yards from camp and he retightened the cinch strap and climbed aboard. After walking his horse back, he waited for Reeves and Leander to mount up and they decided to head south.

"What'd you learn 'bout Ruth Taylor?" Reeves asked.

Percy decided to get the big news out of the way first. "Well," Percy said, "she shot her husband."

Reeves, who had been looking at something in the distance, slowly turned to look at Percy and said, "Dead?"

"As a doornail."

"What in tarnation?" Reeves looked at Leander to see if he was buying the story and he, too, had a skeptical look on his face. Reeves turned to Percy and said, "You're pullin' our leg."

"I'm not pullin' your leg. She killed her husband."

"Why'd she do that?" Leander asked.

"He had a bad habit of gettin' drunk and roughin' her up."

Reeves nodded and said, "I know the type. Town marshal clear her?"

"Accordin' to her, he did."

"You reckon you ought to check out her story fore you get in too deep?" Leander asked.

Percy scowled and looked at Leander. "For your information, I ain't *in* nothin'." He turned to Reeves and said, "What do you think, Bass? You think it's worth sendin' a wire up there to find out?"

"You trust her?" Reeves asked.

"Yeah, I do," Percy said. "I reckon she coulda lied and told me a different story, but she didn't."

"Then I reckon you got your answer," Reeves said. He looked at Leander and winked. "But you might ought to keep an eye on her in case she tries to draw down on you."

That set off another round of laughter and Percy spurred the mare into a trot. Both men were still chuckling when they caught up to him a few moments later.

"Ruth have any more surprises?" Leander asked.

Percy told them some of what Ruth had said before dropping back so they could ride single file down a creek bank. They crossed the small stream and steered their horses up another game trail on the other side. When they topped out, Percy spurred the mare forward and fell in beside Reeves and Leander again. "I don't reckon she's got two nickels to rub—"

Percy's last words were drowned out by a nearby gunshot. The bullet clipped a branch about four feet over their heads and, being seasoned warriors, they were off their horses in an instant.

"See where it come from?" Reeves asked as he reached up to pull his rifle out of the scabbard.

"Wasn't lookin'," Percy said.

"Leander, you see anything?" Reeves asked.

Leander, kneeling in the high grass with his rifle up and ready to fire, said, "Nope. I don't even know which direction it come from."

"Me, either," Reeves sad. "Keep your eyes peeled. I'm gonna lead the horses back down into the creek and tie 'em up."

"We'll cover you," Percy said.

Reeves duck-walked over to the horses and gathered up the reins and said, "I'm movin'."

Percy and Leander began levering off shots, fanning them in a 180-degree arc. Glancing over his shoulder, Percy saw Reeves and the horses disappear down into the creek and called a cease-fire. As they were reloading, another shot rang out and both men heard the bullet clipping the leaves overhead.

Reeves returned and dropped to a knee next to Percy and said, "See anythin'?"

"Gotta be shootin' from cover," Percy said. "Ain't seen no smoke or nothin'."

"Whoever it is," Leander said, "they can't shoot for shit. Had us dead to rights and missed."

"I don't think they're tryin' to kill us," Reeves said, his gaze steadily sweeping from left to right.

"So they're tryin' to scare us off?" Percy asked.

"Be my guess. I reckon they's at least fifty marshals within a half-hour ride of here. Ain't nobody stupid enough to shoot one of us, 'cause they know they'd be run to ground right quick."

"Well, I don't reckon the feller doin' the shootin' knows he's up against three old fellas that don't scare too easy," Leander said. "How you want to handle it, Bass?"

"Gotta find him first," Reeves said.

As if privy to their conversation, the shooter fired another round and they heard it thud into the tree above them. "Right there," Reeves said, pointing his rifle at a thick stand of timber about seventy yards away. "You see it?"

"I seen it," Percy said. "What do you reckon he's shootin' with?"

"Sounds like one of them ol' Springfields," Reeves said, "and I reckon that's why he ain't shootin' but one bullet at a time. What you two figure, two, maybe three seconds to reload?"

"Sounds about right, lest he's some kinda expert," Leander said.

Reeves looked at Leander and said, "What're the odds of that?"

"Slim," Leander said.

"Let's hope," Reeves said. "He shoots again, you two cover me. We gotta work our way closer."

Leander and Percy nodded, and they pushed up to their knees. A couple of seconds later, the shooter fired again. Percy and Leander began firing rounds into the timber around him as Reeves jumped to his feet and took off, using a line of trees for cover. Both men fired their rifles dry and immediately began reloading as they dropped back down to their bellies again.

Percy glanced up to see that Reeves had covered about forty yards, taking cover behind a large oak tree. Once Percy and Leander had filled the nine-round magazines of their 1886 Winchesters, both levered a shell into the chamber and fed in another cartridge as they waited for Reeves to give the signal. The gunman hadn't returned fire and Percy wondered if they'd gotten lucky. As soon as that thought entered his head, the shooter fired again, and this time the bullet plowed into the dirt two feet in front of them.

"That one was a little closer," Leander said. "Reckon he's done changed the rules of engagement?"

"Don't know," Percy said. "I reckon we're about to find out."

When Reeves waved them forward, Leander and Percy pushed to their feet and took off running as Reeves laid down cover fire.

By the time they reached Reeves, both men were gasping for air. "I'm too . . . damn old . . . for this . . . shit," Leander said.

Reeves smiled and said, "You two boys is gettin' soft. It does a man good to get his blood a-pumpin' every now and then."

"Yeah, until . . . it all starts . . . leakin' out . . . a hole in my . . . chest when . . . I get shot," Percy said.

Reeves and Leander chuckled as they searched for the precise location of the shooter.

Percy and Leander finally got their breathing under control and Percy said, "He ain't shootin' high no more."

"Seen that," Reeves said. "Think he's changed his mind?"

"Don't know, but that bullet hit plenty close," Percy said.

"You two ready?" Reeves asked.

"What's our aim here, Bass?" Leander asked. "We tryin' to catch him or kill him?"

"I'd like to get 'im to throw out his gun," Reeves said.

"And if that don't work?" Leander asked.

"Then I reckon we're gonna have to kill him," Reeves said. "Cover me."

As Reeves took off again, Leander and Percy began firing, and they used that same maneuver to hopscotch forward until they had the gunman's location in sight. The shooter was tucked down behind a fallen tree and the only thing they could see was an occasional glimpse of his rifle barrel.

"I'm a deputy marshal," Reeves shouted. "Throw your rifle out!"

"I ain't gonna," the man shouted back.

"Last chance," Reeves shouted.

"Or what?" the shooter shouted.

Although Reeves had no compunction about killing a man if it needed doing, he didn't think a few potshots merited a death sentence. But the shooter didn't necessarily need to know that. "You can leave here still breathin', or you can leave here slung over the saddle and your blood waterin' the ground. Makes no difference to me."

They had taken cover behind a couple of large elms and Reeves eased over to the right side, lifted his rifle to his shoulder, and braced the stock against the side of the tree.

"You gonna shoot him?" Percy whispered.

"Gonna try to take his rifle out of play," Reeves answered, his eyes still glued to the target.

"Can't see much of it," Percy said.

"So?" Reeves asked.

"I ain't sure Annie Oakley could make that shot," Percy said.

Reeves looked over his shoulder and said, "I was makin' shots like this here when Annie Oakley was still runnin' around in diapers."

Percy had seen Reeves shoot enough to know he was an excellent marksman but trying to place a bullet in a three-inch window that was constantly moving was almost impossible.

Reeves pulled the trigger and the man who had been shooting at them jumped up like his pants were on fire, screaming he'd been shot.

The three men fanned out and closed in on him.

"Hands up!" Reeves shouted.

"I'm shot, damn you," the man shouted.

"If I'da shot you, you'd be dead," Reeves said. "Hands up or I *will* put a bullet in you."

He was still hopping around when he reached for the sky. Percy could see a trickle of blood on the man's cheek and guessed he had caught some shrapnel. With Reeves and Leander covering him, Percy lowered his weapon and walked over to pick up the man's rifle. Reeves had been right—it was an 1873 Springfield and Reeves's bullet had shattered the front stock and collapsed part of the barrel. The old Springfield had fired its last round.

"Why'd you shoot me?" the man asked, having now calmed down a little.

Percy walked closer and showed the man his gun. "He didn't shoot you, he shot your rifle. You got hit by a piece of shrapnel."

Reeves lowered his rifle, preferring his two pistols if he had to do any close-in work. "You got any more weapons?" Reeves asked.

"Knife in my boot," the man said.

"Percy, pull it out," Reeves said.

"I'm on it," Percy said. He reached down, pulled out the man's knife, and tossed it into the brush.

"You can lower your hands," Reeves said, "but make any sudden moves, they'll be your last."

"I won't, Marshal. Ain't never seen nobody could shoot a gun with another'un." The man was almost as wide as he was tall, with muttonchop sideburns and a long scraggly beard.

"Name?" Leander asked.

"Danny Sparks," the man said. "Who are you?"

"I'm Leander Hays and that," he said, pointing at Reeves, "is Deputy U.S. Marshal Bass Reeves."

Sparks's eyes widened at the mention of Reeves's name. He looked at the marshal and said, "I reckon everybody in the Territory's heard of you. Just my damn luck it had to be you I was tryin' to scare off."

"That what you was tryin' to do?" Reeves asked. "The last shot come mighty close to hittin' my friends."

"I got scared when I seen you runnin' my way, Marshal." Sparks turned to looked at Percy and Leander and said, "I'm awful sorry 'bout that."

"You got two days till the Run. What exactly were you tryin' to do?" Percy asked.

"Don't rightly know," Sparks said, taking a sudden interest in his shoes. He thought about it a moment then looked up and said, "I reckon I was hopin' y'all wouldn't ride back this way iffen you was scared-a gettin' shot."

"How'd that work out for ya?" Reeves asked.

"Not too good. You arrestin' me?"

"Well, right now," Reeves said, "I could run you in for attempted murder."

Sparks's head dropped to his chest and his shoulders slumped. "How much time am I gonna do?"

Reeves looked at Percy and Leander and winked. "I reckon if convicted you'll get maybe fifteen years' hard labor. You like bustin' rocks, Danny?"

Sparks shook his head as tears spilled out of his eyes and wound down his cheeks.

"You got kids?" Reeves asked.

Sparks nodded and said, "Four."

"Look at me," Reeves said.

Sparks looked up and Reeves said, "I see you again, I'm a-shootin' first and there ain't gonna be no questions."

"You're turnin' me loose?"

"I am but remember what I said."

Sparks wiped his cheeks and said, "You ain't never gonna see me again, Marshal."

"Go on, then," Reeves said.

Sparks turned and hurried off. A few moments later they saw him break out of the timber, his horse running at full gallop.

Reeves turned to look at Percy and said, "What're you gonna do with that rifle?"

Percy smiled. "I reckon I'll keep it. Need to have somethin' to show my grandkids when I tell them the story of Bass Reeves."

"Ain't much of a story," Reeves said, "but I sure hope there's gonna be a happy endin' to it."

Percy and Leander chuckled and then Percy said, "I don't know about you two fellers, but I've had about all this fun I can stand for today. Let's ride over to Guthrie. Chauncey and Marcie and a few others is comin' in by train this afternoon."

"Works for me," Reeves said.

CHAPTER
34

As they approached another Indian camp, a tingle of fear started at the base of Pearl O'Sullivan's neck and raced down her spine when she saw a group of armed Indian men sitting on their horses, watching as the wagons rolled by. It was clear by the looks on their faces, they weren't there as a welcoming party, so Pearl leaned down and lifted Levi's shotgun from under the seat and settled it onto her lap.

"They won't attack," Levi said.

"How do you know?"

"They're outnumbered and they know it."

Pearl locked eyes with an older Indian man as they drove by and it chilled her to the bone. Although having grown up in Chicago she'd had zero interactions with the Indians, she could feel the man's visceral hatred and she had little doubt he'd kill her in a heartbeat if given the chance. Pearl looked away first when she turned to Levi. "They hate us, don't they?"

Levi nodded and said, "I reckon they do. Can't say I blame 'em, though."

"You got a soft spot for the Indians?"

"Maybe. If you traced how the Indians ended up here, you'd find nothin' but a trail of broken promises. And that's for both sides. I don't know all the details about who signed what, but the treaties they signed with the federal government were basically worthless before the ink was dry. And here we are, on our way to stake a claim on land that once belonged to them. They're not stupid. They know what's happenin' and there's not a damn thing they can do to stop it."

Pearl pointed to one of the teepees ahead and said, "But they can't live like that forever. The world's changing."

"They know that, too. I reckon it's hard to change when you've lived your entire life one way, and somebody comes along and says you can't do it that way no more."

"What other choice do they have?"

"None, I reckon, but I still don't like how they been treated," Levi said. "'Course, they ain't never killed any of my kinfolk and I ain't never had to go to war against them, so maybe I am being too soft on them."

"I'm tired of talkin' about the Indians," Pearl said. "Tell me what kind of land you're looking for."

"I'd like to have a nice creek bottom so I could put in some crops. Be nice to have a few shade trees, but there can't be too many. You?"

"I want a piece of land that has a view, a place where I could set on the back porch and watch the sunsets. My problem is, I can't quite envision how big a hundred and sixty acres is."

"There are four hundred-and-sixty-acre parcels in a square mile so a hundred and sixty acres would be a half a mile long and a half a mile wide."

"I get all that," Pearl said, "I guess I just can't wrap my head around it. I grew up counting city blocks and out here there ain't nothin' you can use for a reference. And it ain't like you got anything that says you've traveled such and such miles or whatever." Pearl decided to push a little to see if Levi would spill some of what he was thinking. "For instance, would it be possible to have a creek bottom and a place with a view close enough to be neighbors? Or am I gonna have to stake a claim a long way from you to get what I'm lookin' for?"

"I reckon it's possible to get both on the same claim. You'd just have to look at the lay of the land."

Pearl was frustrated he wouldn't come out and say what he was planning. He'd said he was working on something that would include her and she didn't know if that meant he was hoping to be neighbors or if there was something more. She hated playing these games, but she also didn't want to overplay her hand, either. It was enough to drive a person crazy. *Just ask him*. She opened her mouth to do just that and Walter climbed onto the seat between them.

"What you doin', little man?" Levi asked. He shifted the reins to his left hand and wrapped his arm around his son.

"Come up here to see what y'all are doin'."

"What're your sisters doin'?"

"We been lookin' for prairie dogs out the back."

"Prairie dogs, huh? Ground's too rocky around here."

"I reckon that's why we ain't seen any." Walter waited a beat then said, "Pa, is Miss Pearl comin' to our new place, too?"

Bless you, child, Pearl thought.

"We're talkin' about it," Levi said. "Do you want her to come with us?"

"Well," Walter said, drawing out the word, "I ain't seen you smile since Ma died. Leastwise not till Miss Pearl come along."

"I reckon that's true. We did hit some hard times there for a spell." Levi squeezed Walter's narrow shoulder and said, "We'll see what we can get worked out, okay?"

What does that mean? Work out what? Pearl's shoulders sagged, no closer to the answers she so desperately wanted.

"We'll probably hit softer ground in a little while," Levi told Walter, "and you'll probably see a whole bunch of prairie dogs."

Who cares about prairie dogs when my entire future is at stake? Pearl turned in her seat so that Levi wouldn't see the tears shimmering in her eyes. She wanted things to work out with Levi, but if that wasn't possible, the sooner she knew, the better. There was too much at stake and, even though she knew it was coldhearted, she would need to move on if things with him didn't work out. And that thought saddened her. She really did care deeply for Levi. He was such a gentle, kindhearted man and she knew he had feelings for her. The problem was, would it be enough? *What can I do different? Cook better meals? Take a more active role with the children to show that I'm indispensable?* Pearl wiped the tears from her cheeks as her brain churned through options.

As her mind began to slow, one idea stood out from the rest and it was one that was as old as time itself— maybe she should try seduction.

CHAPTER
35

Back in Guthrie, the wagon and the horses had been unloaded from the train, and the crew was busy trying to put up the large tent Seth and Grace had purchased. It was a job to sort out which pole went where or what needed to be staked down and what didn't. Seth, blessed with an overabundance of patience, was busy reading the directions while his cousin Chauncey paced like a caged lion.

The afternoon had gotten off to a fractious start when a couple of lawyers from Fort Worth, who had ties to The Belmont, had tried to set up shop right next door. Of course, most of the party didn't know that, other than Grace and Marcie, but Chauncey had a knack for knowing when something was off. He had noticed one of the men staring at Marcie and when he had confirmed who they were with his wife, he made it crystal clear to the two gents that they needed to set up somewhere else if they wanted to be alive for Monday's Run. They had taken his not-so-subtle advice and moved on.

"Chauncey, tighten the line that holds up the front-left-corner pole," Seth shouted from somewhere in the bowels of the tent.

"Your left or my left?" Chauncey asked.

"My left," Seth said.

Chauncey walked over and tightened the line. "Done."

"Okay, now the other one."

Chauncey complied and the tent began to take shape. He walked back and tightened the lines on the rear poles then the side poles and the large walled tent was up. He walked back around to the front and looked in on Seth and said, "Stiff wind's liable to blow it down."

"If we can find some men that might meet with your approval, they can set up next to us and that'll help."

Chauncey bristled at that. "I reckon you didn't want them two assholes next door any more'n I did."

"You're right, I didn't. Thank you. You're now in charge of security."

Chauncey smiled and said, "That come with a badge?"

"I'll get Andrew to draw one for you."

Chauncey chuckled. "I reckon I can do without."

"Speaking of Andrew," Seth said, "where did everyone go?"

"They went down to the creek to wash the soot off. You'd think the damn railroads would find a way to tamp some of that stuff down."

"They've built spark arrestors into the smokestacks, but I guess they can't catch them all. Let's grab some chairs."

Seth and Chauncey walked to the wagon and grabbed several of the folding wooden chairs and lugged them back to the tent. They did the same with the folding tables and then they carried in a half a dozen folding cots for the women and children and set them up near the back of the tent. Seth and Grace would work out of the front, so they strung a tarp across the inside to give those in the living quarters some privacy.

"I'm sure Marcie and Grace will want to rearrange things so let's call it good for now," Seth said.

Chauncey nodded. He stepped outside and scanned the tents that had been erected along the street and said, "Sure there ain't no saloon round here?"

"I told you it's illegal in the Territory," Seth said.

"Ain't illegal if you ain't caught. 'Sides, they's givin' this land away on Monday and that means it don't belong to the Indians no more."

"You have a point there, but this land is within the boundaries of Indian Territory and, therefore, the same rules apply. But if you want to go look for a saloon then have at it."

Chauncey rubbed the whiskers on his chin, thinking. After a few moments he looked at Seth and said, "Whatcha gonna do?"

"I'm going to try to build some kind of desk and then I'm going to have a chat with the land agent if I can find him."

"All righty," Chauncey said. "I'll be back in a bit." Chauncey turned and took a couple of steps before stopping and turning back. "You got a gun?"

"Think I'm going to need one?"

"Somebody from Fort Worth might come snoopin' around at some point. I'd hate for some of Keating's hands to show up and you not be armed."

Seth held up his hands and said, "Not my fight."

"They might try to make it yours whether you like it or not."

"Then I suggest you don't stay gone too long."

"Want my rifle? You know how I am 'bout my pistols."

Chauncey refused to let anyone touch the pair of matched Colts he carried and that even included his wife. "No, I don't want your rifle. I'm comfortable without a weapon."

"Suit yourself." Chauncey turned and headed up the street.

Seth, on a visit to see Chauncey when he had been hanging out around Fort Worth a few years ago, had watched his cousin gun down three men—all justified— in the span of a couple of hours and that had turned him off guns forever. Oh, he still had his shotgun and he carried a rifle on occasion when he was out riding, but he no longer walked around with a pistol in his pocket. It was much easier to talk his way out of a fight being unarmed, and he knew he wouldn't have a prayer against someone as lethal as Chauncey.

Percy, Leander, and Reeves rode into Guthrie late in the afternoon on Friday. Percy was surprised to see that a large number of tents had already been erected, especially with two full days to go before the Run. But Seth and the others were here somewhere, so he assumed the other tents belonged to lawyers, land agents, or others who were there in some official capacity. The army had set up camp north of the depot, the tents laid out in precise rows, each equidistant from the others. It had been a long time since

Percy had seen a military encampment and he marveled at the care the soldiers had taken in setting up their quarters. When he had ridden with the Texas Rangers all those years ago, they had slept wherever they fell with no regard for how the camp might have been laid out.

"Let's step inside the depot fore we go lookin' for your kinfolk," Reeves said.

"Works for—"

Percy's last words were drowned out when someone on a nearby locomotive blew the whistle. It was so loud that he could feel it vibrating through his body and the young mare he was riding didn't much like it, either. She tried to rear up, but Percy pulled her head around, killing her momentum as the steam and the smoke from the engine billowed higher into the sky. He rubbed her neck and talked softly to her for a moment before putting her in motion again.

"Them mares is gonna hurt you one of these days," Reeves said.

"Naw," Percy said. "Hell, *I* damn near jumped out of the saddle when that whistle went off. Ain't her fault."

Reeves chuckled and said, "Loud when you get right up on 'em, huh?"

"I'd say." The engineer blew the whistle again and a bell began dinging as the locomotive began moving forward. Percy nudged his mare a little closer to Reeves and still had to shout when he said, "Ever seen one of them engines after they blowed up?"

"Nope," Reeves said, "and damn sure don't want to hear about it now, with it bein' so close."

Percy laughed and said, "Superstitious, are ya?"

Reeves waited until the train was a little farther down

the tracks then said, "Ain't nothin' to be gained by tulip' fate."

The three men were still laughing as they climbed down from their horses and wrapped the reins around the hitching post. Percy took a moment to stretch his ailing back and then they stepped inside. Those who had just departed the incoming train were busy trying to retrieve their luggage and Reeves pointed to a couple of marshals seated at a table across the way and they walked over.

Percy recognized the two men instantly and they stood as the three approached. Reeves and Leander shook hands with the two men and then it was Percy's turn. "Heck, good to see you again," Percy said, pumping Heck Thomas's hand.

"You, too, Percy," Thomas said. "Still punching cows?"

"Always," Percy said. He turned to the other man. "Good to see you, too, Bill," he said, shaking hands with Bill Tilghman. Both marshals had dark droopy mustaches and the gun belts strapped around their waists were worn slick in areas from frequent use. Both had visited the ranch numerous times and Percy enjoyed their company.

"What'd Bass con you two into doin' this time, Percy?" Tilghman asked.

Percy looked at Reeves and said, "He told me it was gonna be a simple job. You'd think I'd know better by now, huh?"

Tilghman and Thomas laughed as they sat back down. Percy reached out and pulled over another chair and he, Reeves, and Leander joined them. They spent several minutes catching up and the depot echoed with their laughter. After a while the conversation turned to the upcoming Land Run and all the problems it presented. Marshal Heck

Thomas was in the middle of making a point when two men approached the table and stopped. Thomas stopped in midsentence, looked at the two men, and said, "Can I help you?"

Both were short, compact men, one with a mustache, the other with a mustache and goatee. Percy thought they shared enough similarities to be related and he pegged them as brothers.

"We're lookin' for a fella," the older of the two said, "that come in on an earlier train."

Thomas leaned back in his chair and said, "Bunch of folks been comin' in. What's this fella look like?"

"We heard he was tall and he was wearin' two guns like he's some kind of two-bit gunslinger," the same man said.

Percy, Reeves, and Leander shared a look, then Reeves leaned back in his chair and spread his suit coat open to display his two guns.

"We ain't lookin' for no nigger," the older man said.

Reeves let his suit coat fall closed, gave the two men a long look, and said, "Looks like you found one, anyway."

"Easy, now," Percy said in a low voice. The sudden tenseness in the air was tangible, and Percy knew all three marshals were as deadly as a den of rattlesnakes but, unlike a rattler, he knew there would be no forewarning.

"My brother didn't mean no disrespect," the younger man said.

"Yeah, he did," Tilghman said. He looked the older man in the eye and said, "You owe my friend here, Marshal Bass Reeves, an apology."

Percy could tell from their startled looks that they recognized Reeves's name and the older one was quick to remove his hat. He looked at Reeves and said, "I'm awful sorry, Marshal Reeves."

Some of the tension bled away, but not all of it.

"You two fellas have names?" Leander asked.

The older man said, "I'm Bud Keating; this here's my brother, Cole."

"Any kin to Archer Keating?" Percy asked.

"He was our brother," Cole Keating said,

"Was?" Percy asked. "Somethin' happen to him?"

"The fella we're lookin' for killed him," Cole Keating said. "We're aiming to make him pay for what he done."

"Any witnesses?" Thomas asked.

"A whole passel of 'em," Bud Keating said. "Our brother was gunned down in the Fort Worth train station."

"What'd the witnesses say?" Thomas asked.

"They said my brother never had a chance," Cole Keating said.

"Did they now?" Thomas said.

Cole Keating nodded and said, "They sure did."

"They say who went for their gun first?" Leander asked.

When neither Keating responded, Tilghman gave them a prod. "Well?"

Cole Keating shuffled his feet and the other brother took a sudden interest in the hat he was holding. "Well," Cole Keating finally said, "they say Archer mighta gone for his gun first, but he never cleared leather."

"Don't matter," Reeves said, getting back in the conversation. "You two best get on home."

"Don't think so," Bud Keating said. "Man's gotta pay for what he done."

Reeves leaned forward and propped his elbows on

the table. He looked at Bud Keating and said, "You got a wife, Bud?"

The older Keating nodded and said, "I do."

"Kids?" Reeves asked.

"Five," Bud Keating said.

"How are they gonna eat," Reeves asked, "when you're dead?"

Bud pointed at his brother and said, "They's two of us."

"Iffen there was a dozen of you," Reeves said, "I still wouldn't like your chances. Cole, your brother a gunhand?"

"He was pretty good," Cole Keating said.

"But not good enough, huh?" Percy said. "Bass is right, y'all ought to catch the next train out of town while you can. Otherwise, you two'll be goin' home in a couple of wooden boxes."

The Keating brothers looked at each other and then Bud said, "Talk all you want, but we ain't scared-a nobody."

"Well, I sure hope you two gave your families a kiss when you left," Percy said. "I reckon that'll give 'em somethin' to remember you by as they're shovelin' dirt onto your coffins."

"We ain't leavin'," Cole Keating said, puffing his chest out.

"Then don't say we didn't warn ya," Reeves said. "Now git."

The Keating brothers turned and headed for the exit.

"You three know the fella they're lookin' for?" Thomas asked.

"We know him," Reeves said.

"Well, who is it?" Tilghman asked.

"It's my son Chauncey," Percy said.

"Reckon he could take on two men by his lonesome?" Thomas asked.

"That boy can shoot like you ain't never seen," Reeves said.

"I seen my fair share of gunhands," Tilghman said, "and I ain't never seen no one faster'n you, Bass."

"Well," Reeves said, "I reckon you'll get a chance if them Keating boys hang around."

Percy pushed to his feet and said, "C'mon, you two. Let's see if we can keep them two knuckleheads from gettin' killed."

Percy ducked into the telegraph office and sent a message to Wichita Falls with instructions to forward it to the ranch before rejoining Leander and Reeves outside.

CHAPTER
36

Pawnee Bill felt bad he had to rely on someone else for his grub, but accidents happened, especially out on the unforgiving frontier. Bill understood that and he knew May did, too, but as he helped the Couch family set up camp for the night, May was nowhere in sight. If an afternoon away from him hadn't softened her up, then maybe, Bill thought, a couple of days would do the trick. Either way, he was tired of worrying about it. And he had decided he wasn't going to chase after her. If she came back, fine, and if not, so be it. He'd stake his own damn claim and she could do the same.

Bill returned to the wagon to grab some of the cooking utensils and carried them over to the fire. Couch's wife, Cindy, was dropping biscuits into a Dutch oven with a spoon and she looked up and said, "Where's May?"

"Don't rightly know," Bill said. "It's all my fault the wagon was busted to pieces."

Cindy put on the lid and used a horseshoe to grab the handle and moved the pan closer to the fire before standing. She smiled and said, "The men always get the blame, didn't you know that?"

"But it wasn't my fault," Bill said.

"Doesn't matter. Anything bad happens it's always the man's fault."

"So, if it started hailing right now, it'd be William's fault?"

"Sure, for not knowing it was coming."

"You womenfolk ever take the blame for anythin'?"

Cindy smiled again and said, "Not if we can help it." She laughed as she reached out and placed her hand on his arm. "May will snap out of it."

"You don't know her like I do," Bill said.

"No, I don't, but I do know she cares deeply for you."

"She's got a funny way of showin' it."

Cindy gave his arm a squeeze and said, "Just give her some time."

"Well, I reckon I got plenty of that now that I don't have a wagon to tend to."

"Oh, Bill, the wagon and everything in it is replaceable. You and May are not and that's the only thing that matters."

"Mind sharin' that with my wife?"

"Be happy to." Cindy gave his arm a final squeeze then turned and headed back to the wagon.

Not wanting to burden the Couch family any further, Bill took off after supper, searching for a couple of ropes he could borrow so he could stake out the mules to graze. It was embarrassing that out of all the wagons present, his was the only one lost and he was beginning to wonder if he'd been cursed. The death of their son, last year's financial disaster, and now the loss of the wagon with all their belongings had Bill questioning everything. Maybe, he thought, staking a claim would give them an opportunity to reset their lives and put all that bad stuff behind them.

Although May maintained a firm grasp on the family's purse strings, Bill had what he called a rainy-day fund stashed away in a mason jar that was buried in the backyard of their home in Wichita. To get it, he would need to hop a train as soon as he got his claim staked. He would prefer to file the claim with the land office before leaving, but he didn't have the money to pay the fourteen-dollar filing fee. The trip would require an overnight stay and he was struggling to find a way to do it without telling May. Not that he wouldn't share the money with her, but he didn't want her to know how much he had. The last time he'd dug it up to squirrel away some more money, he'd had a little over six hundred dollars. It wasn't a large sum, but it would tide them over for a while. And thinking of the money lifted his spirits. He stood up straight and squared his shoulders as he strolled through the camp.

Everyone there was looking for a fresh start and a low-level hum of excitement or hope or something pulsed through the camp, infecting everyone there. Even Bill had tapped into it and he was actually smiling when he spotted May sitting with the Jameson family, who were longtime friends. Although he told himself he was going to wait for her to make the next move, he was feeling conciliatory, so he walked over, offered his hand to May, and he was somewhat surprised when she took it. As he helped her to her feet, he said, "I'm sorry for everything."

"Me, too," May said as they walked around to the front

of the wagon for some privacy. Bill had no idea how long this version of May might last, but he'd enjoy it while he could. For once her eyes were bright and sparkly, replacing the dull glaze that often accompanied her mood swings. If he didn't know she was a teetotaler, he might have suspected she'd been sipping a little who-hit-John, so drastic was the change. After airing their regrets and their many mistakes they apologized to each other again and May leaned in and kissed him on the lips.

Bill savored that for a moment then said, "That mean we're a team again?"

"We are," May said. "Let me get my things and I'll come with you."

"Great, while you're doin' that, I'll talk to Bobby about borrowin' a couple of ropes."

"What do you need the ropes for?"

"To stake out the mules so they can graze a little."

May looked at Bill as if seeing him for the first time then said, "If you could have handled those mules better, we'd still have a wagon." And just like that, her eyes glazed over and the smile vanished from her face. "Are you going to buy another one?"

Bill threw his hands up and said, "We're out in the middle of nowhere. Where the hell am I gonna buy a wagon?"

"That's not my problem. Your carelessness got us into this mess and it's your responsibility to remedy it. Until then I'll be staying here."

May turned and took two steps before Bill grabbed her by the elbow and jerked her to a stop. "What the hell, May? Didn't we just talk about all this?"

May looked down at his hand and said, "Remove your hand."

Bill released her arm and shook his head. "I don't understand why you run so hot and cold. It beats all I ever seen." He stared off in the distance for a moment, still stunned by May's sudden change. Without turning to look at her, he said, "If you ain't forgotten, we're busted."

"You have two mules to bargain with. Figure it out."

May continued on and Bill stood and watched her, trying like hell to keep the lid on the cauldron of anger boiling in his gut. A public spectacle would only provide fodder for the rumor mill, so he held his tongue as he turned away in disgust. Deciding he'd find someone else to borrow the ropes from, he headed back to camp.

When Bill returned to the Couch camp alone, he could almost feel the eyes following him as he walked over to his mules. Using the two ropes he'd borrowed from another Boomer, he led the mules out to a fresh patch of grass and waited to see if they would graze. They'd been listless since the accident and Bill was concerned the mules had inhaled too much water. Not that he could do anything about it. The way his luck had been running, he wouldn't be surprised to wake up and find them belly-up.

Finally, one of the mules lowered his head and began grazing so Bill strung the ropes out, tied the ends to a wheel of a nearby wagon, and left the mules to fend for themselves.

The last rays of the sun were stretching across the heavens when Bill returned to camp. After filling a cup with coffee, he walked over to where William Couch was and sat down beside him.

Couch, smoking his pipe, took a draw and said, "No luck with May?"

"Nope," Bill said.

"She always been . . . so . . . huh . . . so . . . high-strung?"

Bill shrugged and said, "Seems to be gettin' worse."

"The way I see it," Couch said, "you've got two choices, Gordon. You can grin and bear it, or you can seek a more permanent solution."

"You talkin' about a divorce?" Bill asked.

"I am."

Bill thought about it for a few moments then said, "If we were a regular couple it might work, but we're kinda joined at the hip when it comes to our touring show. Although May can be moody as hell, she draws a big crowd everywhere we go."

"Then I guess you have your answer," Couch said. "You'll just have to make the best of it."

Bill sighed and said, "I was afraid you were gonna say that."

CHAPTER
37

As dusk descended on Guthrie, Percy was getting frustrated. He, Leander, and Reeves had been searching for Chauncey and the others and still hadn't found them. The area was jammed with people and it looked as if tents had doubled in number since their arrival only a couple of hours ago. And there wasn't much to differentiate one tent from another, so they had to slow their horses at each one for a peek inside. Time was slipping away, and they needed to find Chauncey before the Keating brothers did. Percy wasn't concerned about his son's safety because killing the two Keatings would be like shooting fish in a barrel for someone with Chauncey's skill set. But with army troopers in town and more marshals than ticks on a hound, Percy knew that any shooting would be thoroughly investigated.

Hearing some men shouting farther up the hill, the three men spurred their mounts into a trot and they finally found Chauncey and the rest of the crew. Unfortunately, so had the two Keatings and they were now squared off against Chauncey with only about ten feet of open space separating the would-be adversaries. It took only a second or two for Percy to get a read on what was happening, and he knew urgent action was required. The tent was full of Ridgeway family members who had been caught flat-footed and any gunplay would be disastrous. Percy spurred the mare forward, nudging her into that empty space between the two men and his son. Out of the corner of his eye, he saw Reeves and Leander dismount and pull out their pistols.

Percy looked down at the Keatings and said, "Someday you'll thank me for this. Now drop them gun belts and do it now."

Reeves and Leander had worked their way around to the other side, making sure those in the tent were out of the line of fire. Reeves lifted his pistol, cocked the hammer, and said, "You heard him. Unbuckle 'em and let 'em drop."

Percy looked down at his son and said, "You, too, Chauncey. Take 'em off."

Chauncey gave his father a long look but made no effort to disarm.

"I know what you're thinkin', son," Percy said, "but now's not the time or the place."

"I'd just as soon get it over with," Chauncey said, his hands resting comfortably on the buckle of his gun belt.

"If they're stupid enough to come at you again, then have at 'em. I don't doubt your abilities for a second, but neither one of us knows if them two can shoot worth a damn and there's too many innocent people standin' round here."

"They ain't gonna clear leather," Chauncey said.

"Just humor me," Percy said.

Chauncey thought about it another few seconds and nodded. He unstrapped his gun belt, rolled it up, and laid it on one of the tables they'd carried in earlier.

Reeves looked at the Keatings and said, "He's disarmed. Now it's your turn. You so much as look at them pistols, and I'll put a bullet right tween your eyes."

The Keatings kept their gazes locked on Reeves as they reached down and unbuckled their guns and let them fall to the ground.

Reeves, his pistol still up and ready, said, "Leander, you mind pickin' up the guns and checkin' for other weapons?"

"On it," Leander said.

Percy clucked his tongue and drew back on the reins, backing the mare up as Leander stepped forward.

After a quick pat-down, Leander felt around the tops of their boots and relieved them of their knives before scooping up the gun belts and stepping back. "That's it, Bass."

"What's you gonna do with our guns, Marshal?" Bud Keating asked.

Reeves holstered his pistol and said, "They'll be locked up in the train depot. You'll get 'em back when you two hightail it outa here."

Bud Keating nodded then turned to look at Chauncey and said, "You ain't seen the last of us."

Chauncey smiled and said, "Anytime, anywhere. And if you got any more brothers, bring 'em along, too."

"Cocky bastard, ain't ya?" Bud Keating said.

"Naw," Chauncey said. "Confident."

Reeves decided to put an end to the jawing. "You two fellas bring rifles with ya on the train?"

Cole Keating shook his head and said, "We just come with the pistols, Marshal."

"Good to hear. If we catch you two lurkin' round this here tent again," Reeves said, "there ain't gonna be no warnings. Got it?"

Both Keating brothers nodded.

"Go on, then," Reeves said.

The Keating brothers turned and walked down the hill as Percy climbed down from his horse. After tying the mare's reins to a tent pole, he walked over to Reeves and Leander and said, "You really think two men on a man-hunt ain't gonna bring no rifles along?" Percy asked.

"Not for a second," Reeves said. "We'll give 'em a little time to get their rifles then we're gonna take 'em away."

"You know where they're goin'?" Leander asked.

"Not exactly, but I'm bettin' they have a stash some-where round the depot."

"Makes sense," Percy said. "Holler when you two are ready."

Percy walked over to where Chauncey and Marcie were standing and said, "Keep an eye out."

"Shoulda let me end it here," Chauncey said.

"Poor timing," Percy said. "They get smart, they'll go on home. How'd this here feud start?"

Reeves and Leander stepped over to listen as Marcie and Chauncey explained what had happened, going all the way back to Marcie's altercation with Keating back in the barn.

When they finished, Reeves asked, "Why'd Keating come after you, Marcie?"

There was a long awkward pause. Of course, Percy and Chauncey knew of Marcie's prior occupation and Percy suspected Leander knew, too, but he'd never mentioned it to Reeves. There had never been a need and, frankly, it wasn't Percy's story to tell. Marcie was struggling to come up with an answer, so Percy decided to fill the void. "Marcie lived in Fort Worth for a spell, Bass."

"Oh, okay," Reeves said.

Percy looked at Chauncey and said, "Keep your eyes open. We'll be back in a bit."

"Want me to come?" Chauncey asked.

"No," Marcie said, beating Percy to the punch. "You're stayin' here."

"It ain't your mess," Chauncey said.

"Don't matter," Percy said. Before heading back out, Percy walked over to Emma and said, "Keep an eye out and make sure Simon and Ann stick around close."

Emma nodded and said, "Expecting more trouble?"

"Don't know, but it sure has a way of findin' us, don't it?"

CHAPTER
38

Pearl O'Sullivan rinsed the last of the supper dishes and set it aside to dry before taking a seat near the small fire Levi had built. The wagon train had gone into camp shortly before dark at a place called Davis, a wide spot on the trail situated next to the Washita River. There was a dry goods store nearby, but it might as well have been closed for all of the business it was doing. There was a reason all the would-be settlers were streaming toward Oklahoma for the *free* land—most were destitute. Everything they owned was traveling in the wagon with them or, in the case of those lucky enough to have an extra horse or a milk cow, tied on behind. And it was the same story for Levi and Pearl, too.

Levi didn't have the fancy folding camp chairs or a new tent with the canvas so bright it hurt your eyes if the sun hit it just right. In fact, Levi didn't have much of anything other than a few mismatched pieces of furniture and an old plow awaiting a fresh piece of ground to do its work. And Pearl had even less, with nothing in her bag but a change of clothes and a few other essentials. She did have a small money roll she carried on her person, but it didn't amount to much. There was little either could do to change the situation so they would get up in the morning, hitch up the horses, and continue onward.

She picked up a stick and stirred the coals, listening to Levi's deep voice as he told the children a bedtime story. Most nights it was a continuation of the story from the night before with the same cast of characters overcoming a new obstacle, but this one was different. This one was about the future and how different things would be this time around. Pearl didn't know how much of what he said he actually believed though he sure made it sound nice.

She listened closely to see if Levi would include her into the life he was describing to his children. He droned on about what types of crops they were going to raise and the type of house he wanted to build, but nothing about Pearl or what role she might play going forward. And that frustrated her to no end. She angrily tossed the stick into the fire and stood, all thoughts of seduction vanishing from her mind.

Pearl began pacing back and forth, her anger building with each step. She had been foolish to think a roll in the hay might make everything right. What she needed—no, what she must have—was an open and frank discussion with Levi about his intentions. And if those didn't include her, she would leave camp immediately.

The only problem was she had nowhere else to go. She had parted on good terms with her fellow Chicagoans, but there was nothing for her there. Although one of the families would surely offer to take her in temporarily, returning to them offered no long-term solutions. Yes, there had been a few single men in the group though none had taken a particular interest in her and she hadn't tried to cultivate any. The four single men she was thinking of had all seemed a little too eager to leave Chicago and Pearl suspected they were running from something, either the law or their own families and she wanted no part of that.

Her thoughts were interrupted when the wagon squeaked and began to shudder as Levi moved around inside. She stopped pacing and waited for him to exit the wagon, trying to tamp down the anger coursing through her body. An angry confrontation wouldn't do either of them any good. That said, she was tired of tiptoeing around the issue and she was determined to get some answers, even if they weren't the ones she wanted to hear.

Levi climbed down and turned around. "Finally," he whispered as he approached. He tried to take her hand and she pulled it away.

"Sounds like you got big plans," she hissed. "Unfortunately, they don't seem to include me."

She turned and walked away, and Levi followed. Stopping near the fire, Levi sidled up next to her and said, "Do you want to be in 'em?"

"In what?" Pearl snapped.

"My plans."

"Apparently it doesn't matter what I want."

"Of course it matters," he said, wrapping an arm around her and pulling her close.

She tried to pull free, but it was like wrestling with a bear. "It sure didn't sound like it to me."

"To tell the truth, I didn't want to paint a future with you in it and have the kids be crushed if you up and left."

Pearl stopped struggling and said, "Do you want me here?"

"I do. If we get us a claim, I want you to marry me."

"And if we don't get a claim? What then?"

Levi shrugged. He turned her loose and stepped back. "Without the land, I don't have nothin' to offer you. Why would you want to hitch your wagon to a man with three kids who's flat broke?"

Pearl stepped forward, wrapped her arms around his waist, and tilted her head back to look him in the eyes. "Was that a marriage proposal?"

"You'd marry me even if we don't get any land?"

"In a heartbeat."

"Well, I reckon it was, then." Levi leaned his head down and kissed her.

And that was the only spark they needed. It quickly progressed to a grabbed blanket, a quick walk into the trees, and a hasty removal of their clothing.

Their encounter was intense and raw, both with a hunger that desperately needed to be fed. Now, both spent, Pearl snuggled up against him and rested her head on his still-heaving chest.

Levi ran his fingers through her hair and said, "I didn't hurt you, did I?"

"It hurt a little bit there in the beginning, but no, you didn't hurt me."

"Good. I tried to be as gentle as I could."

"Thank you." Pearl ran her fingers through his damp chest hair. Having never been with a man before she didn't have a basis for comparison, but she did wonder how her performance compared to that of his late wife. For her, it had been awkward, especially in the beginning.

And it wasn't like there was a book that explained what to do and she assumed it would get better with time. If there was a next time, that is. Her privates were still pulsing with pain and if it was going to be like that every time, Pearl didn't know how much more of that she wanted. Yes, she had lied to him, but she knew he would be distraught if he knew he had hurt her. With so many unanswered questions and no ready answers, Pearl decided to see if Levi would fill in a few blanks.

"Was it okay for you?" Pearl asked.

He didn't appear flustered by her question and his response came quickly. "Yes, but it will get better for both of us over time. I reckon we was both nervous."

"You don't mind talkin' about it?" Pearl asked.

"No, I don't. It's important we be honest with each other."

"Okay, since we're bein' honest, I have another question for you. Is it always gonna hurt?"

Levi inhaled a deep breath and blew it out. "So, I did hurt you, huh?" He was quiet for a few moments then said, "I remember my wife sayin' it hurt the first couple of times, but I reckon it got better because . . . uh . . . we . . . uh . . . well, it wasn't long fore Walter come along. I'm really sorry I hurt you, Pearl."

Pearl kissed his chest and said, "I'll live. I reckon we'll have to give it another few tries to see if you're right."

"I sure do like the sound of that."

Pearl grasped one of his chest hairs between her fingers and yanked it out.

"Oww," he yelped. "What'd you do that for?"

"Don't want you gettin' too frisky before we hunt down a preacher."

Levi chuckled and said, "Reckon I'm stuck now, huh?"

She kissed the spot where she'd plucked the hair and said, "Yep, you're stuck and I ain't lettin' go."

Levi rolled over onto his side and brushed the hair out of her face. "Promise?"

She leaned in and kissed him on the lips and whispered, "I promise."

CHAPTER
39

Bass Reeves's hunch that the Keating brothers would return to the train depot proved correct. He, Percy, and Leander now had eyes on both of them and, as of yet, they had made no move yet to retrieve their gear—if they had any.

"They ain't experienced man hunters," Percy whispered. They were hidden around the side of the depot watching the Keatings, who were sitting on a flatcar that had been parked on the siding.

"There ain't a man alive dumb enough to bring only one gun along when they's lookin' to settle a score," Reeves said.

"We lost sight of 'em there for a bit," Leander said. "You reckon they done got their backup guns?"

"Don't know," Reeves said. "Hard to tell in the dark. But I reckon we ought to treat 'em as if they did."

Percy fished out his watch and popped the lid. He had to angle around toward the window and the lit lantern inside to see the dial and saw that it was a little after nine o'clock. Not terribly late, but most of the people in the tents had already settled in for the night. So, what was up with these yahoos sitting there as if waiting for a train that wouldn't arrive until midmorning tomorrow?

Percy looked at Reeves and Leander and said, "Somethin's afoot and I don't like it one bit. Looks like they're waitin' on somebody."

"Who? Ain't no more trains tonight," Reeves said.

"We know that, and they know that, but there they sit," Percy said. "Let's work our way round to the other side so we can see the main road."

"What're you thinkin'?" Leander asked.

"Nothin' good," Percy said. They worked their way around to the back of the building and took up a position on the opposite corner. It offered a good view of the Keating brothers and the main road, if it could be called a road. They hadn't been there long when they heard the rumble of hoofbeats in the distance.

"Company's comin'," Percy said.

"I hear 'em. Reckon they're comin' to see the Keatings?" Reeves asked.

The riders were close enough now they could feel the ground vibrating through the soles of their boots. "I do," Percy said. "Sounds like there's a passel of 'em, too. Be nice if Heck and Bill was to show up 'bout now."

Reeves kept his gaze centered on the road and said, "Hell, us three been around the block a time or two, ain't we?"

"That we have," Percy said. "How do you wanna play it?"

"Reckon it's better to stop them riders before they get all the way here?" Leander asked.

Reeves thought about it for a moment. He needed to

make a decision before one was made for him, the riders getting closer by the second. "We still don't know if the brothers rearmed," Reeve said. "I'd hate for them to get in behind us while we're tryin' to disarm the ones comin' in."

"Good point," Percy said. "We'll let 'em come and see what happens."

Fifteen seconds later, the silhouettes of several riders came into view. As they neared the depot, they slowed their horses to a walk, and, as they came around the corner, Percy counted twelve men, all well armed. They reined to a stop and the Keating brothers jumped down from the flatcar and walked over to greet them. Using the men's arrival as a distraction, Percy, Reeves, and Leander worked their way closer, ducking down behind a pile of trunks someone had left behind.

"Where the hell you been?" Bud Keating shouted at the riders.

"The law ordered us off the train in Purcell," one of the riders said. "Said we didn't have no permission to go no further. So, we off-loaded the gear, saddled up, and pushed the horses hard to get here as quick as we could."

It was too dark for Percy to see who was doing the talking.

The older Keating looked over the winded horses near him and shouted, "And likely killed some horses doin' it! Jesus Christ, what the hell were you thinkin'?"

"The telegram said come quick," the same man said.

"Did it say anythin' about runnin' the horses into the ground? Huh?"

When the man didn't immediately reply, Bud Keating said, "We need some damn light. Somebody get down and get a couple of lanterns goin' so we can see what the hell we're doing."

Two of the riders climbed down off their horses and set to work lighting the lanterns they'd brought along.

While they were doing that, Reeves, Percy, and Leander spent a moment strategizing.

"We need 'em to dismount fore we do anythin'," Reeves whispered. "Can't afford to let 'em scatter."

"I'm bettin'," Leander whispered, "them ranch hands are gonna be lookin' for an excuse to head back home soon as the ass chewin's over."

"I say we hit 'em now," Percy said.

"You think?" Reeves asked.

"I do," Percy whispered. "If we wait for them to dismount the horses are gonna be in the way."

As Bud Keating droned on in the background, Leander sealed the deal when he said, "While they're workin' to light the lanterns, I'm gonna work my way round to the other side. Percy, you cover the brothers, and me and Bass'll cover the riders. That work for everybody?"

"Yeah," Reeves said.

"Soon as they get them lanterns situated where they want 'em, we hit 'em," Leander said before slipping away into the darkness.

A couple of the riders closest to them got into an argument about something and Reeves took advantage of the outburst to lever a shell into his rifle's chamber and feed another round into the magazine.

When the two men got the lanterns going, they carried them forward and set them on the ground on either side of the spot where the brothers were standing.

Percy tucked the rifle tight to his shoulder and nudged

Reeves with his elbow. They stood and stepped out into the street.

"Hands up!" Reeves and Leander shouted as Percy zeroed in on the brothers, as he and Reeves advanced.

The Keatings now had jackets on, making it impossible to know whether they were armed. Out of the corner of his eye, Percy saw that the ranch hands all had their hands up and he breathed a little easier as he turned his focus back to the Keatings.

Percy saw Bud Keating slowly trying to lower his hands, so Percy centered the rifle on his chest and said, "Just give me a reason to shoot you."

His hands shot back up as Percy closed the distance.

"You done took our pistols," Bud Keating said.

"That don't mean you ain't got another one," Percy said as he came to a stop. "One at a time, I want you two to peel off them jackets real slow and easy, starting with old Bud there." Behind him, Percy could hear gun belts being unbuckled and thumping to the ground. Without turning, Percy said, "You got it under control, Bass?"

"Me and Leander's doin' just fine," Reeves said. "You?"

"Good so far," Percy said.

When the older Keating had his jacket off, he let it drop to the ground and Percy said, "That's good, now make a real slow turn to show me you ain't got any weapons."

Bud Keating was a quarter of the way into his turn when he yanked out a pistol from behind his back. Percy fired, levered another shell, and fired again. As the older Keating crumpled to the ground, he pivoted to the other brother who already had his revolver in his hand. He was already in the process of raising his arm when the rifle jammed as Percy tried to lever another round. Trying to tamp down the adrenaline now flooding his body, Percy dropped the rifle and, in one fluid motion, drew his pistol, cocked it on the way up, and fired just as the younger Keating pulled the trigger.

The two gunshots were no more than a half a second apart and Percy felt a stabbing pain in his left arm as the force of Keating's bullet pushed him back a step. Percy's first shot had hit Keating in the chest, and he was trying to lift his weapon again when Percy cocked his pistol and fired a second time. That bullet punched a hole in Keating's forehead, and he dropped like a bag of sand as Percy turned, looking for more threats.

The ranch hands who had already dropped their hands immediately reached for the sky again, so Percy holstered his pistol. For Percy, it felt like everything was moving in slow motion. He noticed that Reeves was looking at him and saying something, but Percy couldn't hear him, his ears still ringing from the gunfire. He looked down to see blood dripping from the fingers of his left hand and then he looked at Reeves again and said in a voice he couldn't hear, "I been shot."

Reeves, still busy disarming the ranch hands, looked at Percy and nodded.

Percy's hearing was gradually returning, and he finally heard Reeves when he said, "I reckon you're gonna live, but you probably ought to sit down while me and Leander finish up."

Percy nodded and made his way over to one of the benches at the rear of the depot and sat. It wasn't long before people began streaming into the area, eager to find out what had happened. Pain pulsed through his body with every beat of his heart and he was so hazy he didn't notice Heck Thomas was standing next to him until he spoke.

"Had yourself a little shootout, did you?" Thomas asked. "Sit still and I'll go grab one of them lanterns so we can get a look at your arm."

Percy nodded and Thomas walked over and picked up one of the lanterns. When he returned, he pulled out his knife and went to work on Percy's sleeve. Although Percy had been shot before, he couldn't remember it hurting as much as it hurt now. It felt like someone had run his arm through with a red-hot poker and he wondered if this injury was more severe than the others he'd had or if he'd just gotten too damn old to be gettin' shot. They'd know soon enough, Percy thought, as Thomas gently worked the severed sleeve down his arm and off. He bent over and looked at the wound and said, "Looks like it went clean through your muscle. Probably ought to get a doctor to clean it up for you."

"I will. Thanks, Heck."

Thomas stood, wrapped the sleeve from Percy's shirt around the wound, and tied it off. "Reckon that'll slow the blood some." Thomas walked over to the two dead men to take a look. After a few moments, he turned and looked at Percy and said, "Looks like they ignored your advice, huh?"

"That they did," Percy said. "Didn't plan on killin' 'em, but that's how it played out."

"Works that way sometimes," Thomas said. "Ain't nothin' a man can do but save his own hide."

Keating's men had all dismounted and Reeves and Leander had them lined up and sitting on the ground.

With Leander standing guard, Reeves stepped over to pick up Percy's rifle and carried it over.

He tried to hand it to Percy, but he shook his head and said, "Time for a new rifle."

Reeves leaned it against the bench and took a seat next to his old friend. "How bad is it?" Reeves asked.

"Bullet went through my bicep. Hurts like hell, but I'll live." Percy looked at the offending rifle and said, "Ain't never had it jam up before. It was poor timin' for damn sure."

"It happens," Reeves said. "I was tryin' to fix a jam on my old rifle and ended up killin' my cook."

"I remember. You get a new one?"

"Cook or a rifle?"

"Rifle," Percy said.

"The next day." Reeves pushed his hat up on his head and said, "Took a little longer on the cook. Don't know if there's any doctors round here, but we probably ought to look for one. Need to get that wound-a yours cleaned up."

"Be nice to have a shot of whiskey or two before we go lookin' for a doctor. Any of those whiskey peddlers you're always chasin' after live around here?"

Reeves chuckled and said, "Probably ain't any of 'em nowhere close with all the marshals around. But I reckon there's a few of them been known to tote a bottle round on occasion, though."

"That sounds promisin'." Percy nodded at Keating's men and said, "What are you gonna do with them?"

"Thinkin' about cuttin' 'em loose. What do you think?"

"Any of 'em look shook up 'bout the three Keating brothers bein' dead?" Percy asked.

"Nary a tear among the group. Still, it don't mean a few ain't mad 'bout what happened."

"I'm bettin' they're more worried about whether they're gonna have a job or not. But if any of 'em want to try their hand, let 'em. Cut 'em loose."

"You sure?"

"I'm sure," Percy said.

Reeves pushed to his feet. "Let me get 'em squared away then we'll go lookin' for a doctor."

"Can't wait," Percy said.

CHAPTER
40

It had been a long evening for the Ridgeway clan camped in Guthrie because of Percy's shootout and his subsequent injury. It was going to be an even longer night for Chauncey and Marcie, who were now on the road with Percy and Bass Reeves, hoping to make it to Fort Reno by daybreak. They all knew that the longer Percy's wound remained untreated, the higher the probabilities for problems. Reeves had doused the wound with whiskey before binding it up and, other than what ran down his arm, the rest of the whiskey was now slowly disappearing down Percy's throat. He wasn't drunk enough that Chauncey was afraid his father might break out in song, but they still had a long way to go.

Reeves had been chasing outlaws across Indian Territory for years and he knew every trail, every shortcut, and every nook and cranny within its borders. And according to Reeves, the distance between Guthrie and Fort Reno was almost forty miles, a significant distance on a good day and an even tougher one with Percy's injury, which required a slower pace. But to Percy's credit he was gutting it out and they were alternating between loping and walking their horses, trying to eat up as much ground as possible.

Chauncey hadn't heard all of the details of the shooting yet, so he nudged his horse forward and fell in beside Reeves. His father had drifted back some, but Chauncey still lowered his voice when he said, "Is the old man gettin' slow, Bass?"

Reeves looked around to see where Percy was before answering. "Hell, we're all gettin' slow, or slower, I reckon. But no, your pa's still one of the best I ever seen. If his rifle hadn't jammed, I reckon we'd all be rolled up in our blankets and sawin' wood 'bout now. That's the way it works sometimes. A man can't ever tell what's gonna happen in a gunfight."

"You shoulda let me in on the plan. It was my mess to clean up."

"Water under the bridge," Reeves said. "If you and Marcie get around to havin' kids you'll learn a thing or two. There ain't nothin' your pa wouldn't do to keep you from gettin' hurt. Same with my kids. And it don't matter if you're two years old or thirty-two, as long as your pa's alive he's gonna look out for you and your brother and sister."

"I can look after myself just fine," Chauncey said. "If Keating's bullet had hit six inches to the left, Pa woulda died and it wasn't even his fight. If I'd been there, them brothers would have never got off a shot."

"Maybe not," Reeves said, "and I reckon we'll never know for sure. But you coulda had a misfire, too."

"I would've still had eleven more rounds. That's why I wear a two-gun rig."

"My second pistol's saved my bacon a time or two for sure. Anyway, none of that other stuff matters. Your pa's gonna be fine."

"I know he will be. You think them Keating cowboys is gonna cause Leander any trouble?" Chauncey asked. Leander had volunteered to stay behind to guard the rest of the family.

"Doubt it," Reeves said. "If they do, he'll handle 'em. Leander ain't nobody to tangle with 'cause he'll put a man in the ground right quick."

"I've seen him in action," Chauncey said. "You know, for three old men, you, Leander, and my pa can still hold your own."

"Who you callin' old?" Reeves asked.

Chauncey laughed and dropped back next to Marcie. Deep into their ride, the eastern sky began to brighten with the coming dawn and the group crossed the North Fork of the Canadian River and entered Fort Reno. Constructed in 1874 to curtail an Indian uprising, the fort was situated near the Darlington Indian Agency, which provided oversight of the Southern Cheyenne and the Southern Arapaho tribes. Built with the usual military precision, the fort was laid out in a large square with a sizable parade ground at the center. And, if any of the four needed a reminder they were back in Indian country after leaving Oklahoma, in the distance was a large gathering of teepees, their conical forms silhouetted against the brightening sky.

Reeves pointed out a few of the various buildings as they rode, before they finally arrived at the post hospital, a large two-story structure with a wide front porch that was well stocked with rocking chairs. Wearily, they climbed down from their horses and wrapped the reins around the hitching post, the early-morning air filled with birdsong.

Somewhere along the way, Percy remembered stoppering the whiskey bottle and he was now, unfortunately, stone-cold sober. His arm throbbed in rhythm with his heartbeat and, to add to his misery, his back ached from the long ride.

Reeves opened the door and led them inside. They were greeted by a short, thin, young man wearing steel-rimmed glasses who took one look at Reeves and said, "Back so soon, Marshal?"

"Yeah, but this one ain't my doin'," Reeves said. He pointed at Percy with his thumb and said, "This here's my friend Percy Ridgeway and them other two is his son Chauncey and his wife, Marcie. Folks, this here's Riley Wheeler. He's a hospital steward studyin' to be a doctor."

After the introductions were over, Reeves said, "Percy's got a bullet wound we need the doc to take a look at."

Wheeler looked at Percy and said, "How did you end up with a bullet wound, Mr. Ridgeway?"

Percy wasn't in the mood for any small talk. "It's a long story. Is the doc around?"

"C'mon back," Wheeler said. He turned and led them down a long hallway and into a small examination room. It was a tight fit for all of them and Chauncey and Marcie lasted about fifteen seconds before they decided to go back outside. Wheeler exited the room and returned a few moments later with a short, portly man wearing a suit coat and a bow tie, whom he introduced as Dr. Stanley Beesley, the post surgeon.

The doctor looked at Reeves with a dour expression on his face and said, "You again, Marshal? Perhaps you should change your approach to apprehending criminals. Try more talking and less shooting."

Reeves took the rebuke in stride and said, "Ain't my doin', this time, Doc, but I'll remember your kindly advice."

"As you should." And with that, the post surgeon dismissed Reeves and turned to Percy. He eyed Percy's gun belt and said, "We're a civilized society and there's no need for men like you to continue carrying weapons. If you would have left your guns at home where they belong, I wouldn't have to spend my valuable time assessing your wound."

"See, you're wrong there, Doc," Percy said, locking eyes with Beesley. "If I hadn't had my gun, they'd be shoveling dirt on top of me about now. I appreciate you seein' me, but if it's all right with you, skip the lectures and get straight to the doctorin'."

Beesley puffed out his chest in anticipation of a reply, but he quickly deflated when he looked into Percy's eyes. "Very well, then."

"Good," Percy said. He walked over to a chair and sat down.

The doctor picked up a lit lantern from the desk, handed it to Reeves, and said, "Hold that."

Reeves took the lantern and walked over to where Percy was sitting, holding it up so the doctor could see what he was doing.

The doctor unwrapped the bandage Reeves had applied,

then reached over and picked up a pair of tweezers from a metal tray on a side table, and set to work without offering so much as a taste of laudanum or a shot of whiskey. If the doctor was hoping to use pain for a little payback, Percy was determined not to give him any satisfaction.

The doctor tweezed and picked, each touch sending a shock wave of pain arcing through Percy's body. It took all of Percy's willpower not to cry out and he briefly flashed on the idea of pulling out his pistol and shooting the doctor right between the eyes. But that quickly passed and after a few more moments the doctor finally leaned back and put his tweezers down.

"You done?" Percy asked.

Instead of answering, Beesley stood and walked over to a cabinet and returned with a clean dressing. The doctor began wrapping the wound and Percy looked at him and said, "You ain't gonna cauterize it?"

"Would you prefer to keep your arm?" the doctor asked.

"Well, yeah," Percy said.

"I'm a physician. Cauterizing wounds is for quacks."

The doctor tied off the bandage and stood. He looked down at Percy and said, "If you continue to carry a weapon in the future, I'll refuse to treat you." He turned and exited the room.

Percy stood, dug a twenty-dollar gold coin out of his pocket, and tossed it onto the desk. He looked at Reeves and said, "How did you run into this cocksucker?"

Reeves smiled. "If you ain't noticed, there ain't a whole bunch of doctors round these parts. Gotta take what you can get."

"He always act like that?" Percy asked.

"Mostly. He's a bit uppity, for sure."

"Somebody ought to knock him down a peg or two," Percy said. He didn't wait for a response because he wasn't expecting one. "Let's get outa here."

"You gonna leave him that double eagle?" Reeves asked.

"I am. Maybe he can buy a slice of humble pie with it."

CHAPTER
41

Grace, exhausted because the baby hadn't slept well last night, finally got Lizzie down for a morning nap. As she quietly slipped away from the crib, she was plotting how to get away for a couple of hours without making Seth suspicious. She still hadn't told him of her plans to stake a claim and she was running out of time to find a piece of ground. But hopefully that would change this morning if she could get away to join Emma for a quick ride around the area. After stopping by her cot to put on a blouse that didn't have baby throw-up on it, she parted the canvas sheet that separated the living quarters from the rest of the tent and stepped out.

"Lizzie still crabby?" Seth asked. He was seated on one of the folding camp chairs near the entrance, watching the boys romp around with some other children.

"Yeah, and I'm worried about her. She's never that cranky."

"Being away from home probably has something to do with it."

"Maybe. Will you keep an eye on her?"

"I will. Where are you going?" Seth asked.

"Me and Emma are going on a ride. She should sleep for a couple of hours, especially after being up half of the night."

"A ride, huh? Any particular destination in mind?" Seth asked.

"No, not really. We just want to get a feel for the place." She turned to look at her husband and said, "Is that okay?"

"Sure," Seth said. "Ride on."

"Thank you. We won't be gone long." Grace grabbed her wide-brimmed straw hat, leaned down and kissed Seth on the cheek, and exited the tent.

She paused long enough to pull the watch from her dress pocket to check the time. Although Lizzie often slept for a couple of hours during her morning nap, Grace didn't want to cut it that close. It was eight-thirty now, so Grace decided she needed to be back by nine forty-five. She dropped the watch back into her pocket and continued on.

Their horses had been staked out to graze down by the river, so she walked through the makeshift tent town and saw that it was growing by the minute. Several more people were busy putting up tents and she wondered what services they might be offering come Monday. So far, she'd seen mainly bankers, lawyers, and merchants selling a variety of things, with a few freight haulers and home builders thrown into the mix. She didn't know how much business any of them would do because most of the homesteaders she'd seen looked like they didn't have two nickels to rub together. Once clear of the tents, she veered left, heading for the Cimarron River that skirted the north side of Guthrie.

When she arrived, she was glad to see that Emma had already saddled a horse for her. "Sorry you had to wait," Grace said.

"No big deal," Emma said. "You're at the mercy of your kids. I remember those days." Emma was wearing a black split skirt and white pleated blouse with her ever-present pistol strapped around her waist.

The two women climbed aboard their horses and set off. Both women thought most of the land south of the river would end up being town lots, so they turned the horses west and crossed Cottonwood Creek.

"Have you told Seth you're stakin' a claim?" Emma asked.

Grace gave Emma a sheepish look and said, "No, because I know what he would say. He'd tell me it was against the law."

"But it's not," Emma said, "if we wait until Monday afternoon."

"Still, he'll say we had an unfair advantage, or he'll come up with somethin' else. I love my husband dearly, but he's as rigid as an iron bar when it comes to followin' the rules."

"So, you're gonna stake a claim without tellin' him?"

Grace thought about it a moment and said, "I guess I'm gonna play it by ear." After taking a long look at the terrain ahead, she turned to Emma and said, "Too many small creeks over this way. We might be better off headin' east."

"I'm game," Emma said.

They turned their horses around and put them into a

lope, slowing only to recross the creek. The two gray geldings they were riding were two of Emma's favorites. Not only were they fast, they had the stamina of a mule. They flew by the rapidly expanding row of tents and loosened the reins, letting the horses find their own rhythm. Grace was a capable rider, but she had a tendency to bounce around in the saddle a little too much. That wasn't the case for Emma, and it was almost like the horse and rider were one animal, fluid and graceful with no wasted movements. *Regal* was the term Grace came up with as she watched Emma ride. She had her chin strap on to keep her hat from flying off and her long red hair streamed out behind her, almost as if she had her own tail to match that of her horse.

It was almost impossible to carry on a conversation while mounted on a running horse, so Emma slowed hers to a walk and Grace matched her. "What are we looking for?" Emma asked.

"Well, we're gonna need water and I want a place with a view that's not goin' to be too far from town." Grace turned to look behind her and said, "How far east do you think the town will come?"

"Hard to say," Emma said as she turned her horse around and brought him to a stop. Grace did the same and they looked over the rolling grassland stretching out before them. There were a few areas dotted with heavy stands of timber, but it was mostly wide-open prairie, the unending blue sky vaulting high overhead. "I can't see the town comin' this far east," Emma said, "but I'm not seein' much of anythin' offerin' the view you're lookin' for."

Grace pointed to her left and said, "And it really flattens

out west of the railroad tracks, there." She pulled out her watch to check the time and said, "I've got about thirty minutes before I have to head back. Let's ride a bit further and see what we can find."

They turned their horses and spurred them into motion and a short while later they crossed a densely forested creek and they could feel the ground rising beneath them. When they broke into the clear on top of a large rise, Grace's jaw dropped open and she pulled her horse to a stop. She didn't know about Emma, but Grace had found her claim. With views that stretched on for miles in every direction, the terrain offered several large swaths of good grazing land with plenty of timber available for building. She turned to look at Emma and said, "Think it's big enough for all of us to stake a claim?"

"Sure looks that way," Emma said, trying to take it all in. It was a spectacular location and she could already envision the breathtaking sunrises yet to come.

"Is this it?" Grace asked.

Emma nodded and said, "If anybody else finds it, we're probably gonna have to fight like hell on Monday to get here first."

"We'll just have to figure it out," Grace said.

After picking out a few landmarks to help them remember the location, they turned their horses and headed back to camp. After recrossing the small creek, Emma stopped her horse and pulled a red bandanna from her saddlebag. She reached up and tied it to a tree limb so they would be able to spot it quickly during the Run. They loosened the reins and let the horses set their own pace.

"Simon seems to be smitten with Ann Parker," Grace said.

"I know," Emma said. "I've been tryin' to keep an eye on them without being obvious about it."

"Why? They're old enough to look after themselves, aren't they?"

"They are and that's the problem."

"How so?" Grace asked.

"It's complicated." Emma spent a few moments formulating her answer then looked at Grace and said, "Indians view life very differently than we do. What's acceptable in their culture might not be acceptable in ours. You've met Ann's father, Quanah, haven't you?"

"Of course," Grace said.

Emma turned in the saddle to make sure the bandanna was visible and saw that it was. She turned back and said, "Well, for Quanah and other Comanche men, it's perfectly acceptable to have multiple wives and not only that, they have no qualms about sharing their wives with their close relatives."

"What does that have to do with Simon and Ann?" Grace asked.

"That's just one example." Emma paused, trying to think of the best way to explain it. "The Comanches and many other Indian tribes allow—no, that's not the right word—let's say they encourage various forms of experimentation starting at a very young age. And it's not unusual for the Comanche girls, and later the women, to initiate the action."

Grace pondered that for a moment then said, "So

you're worried Ann's gonna entice Simon into having sex?"

Emma nodded and said, "Yes."

"Why?"

Emma was momentarily taken aback. "That's okay with you? What if she gets pregnant?"

"I don't think there's much you can do about it either way other than lock one of them up. And there are things they can do to reduce the chances of her gettin' pregnant. Have you talked to Simon about this stuff?"

Emma pulled her horse to a stop and said, "What do I know about it? I never had any say in any of it. They would come into the teepee, do their business, and then leave."

"You haven't been with a man other than the Indians who repeatedly raped you?"

Emma's eyes filled with tears, and all she could do was shake her head.

Grace nudged her horse closer and took Emma's hand. "I should have phrased that better and I'm sorry. But you've walled yourself off and you won't let anyone get too close and that has to change. You deserve to be happy."

Emma wiped her eyes with her free hand and said, "I know."

Grace squeezed Emma's hand and said, "You have to open your mind and your heart, and you have to be willing to take some chances. Will there be potholes ahead? Yes, there will be, but you've been traveling your own path through life and that's a lonesome journey."

"You're right," Emma said, pulling her hand free and drying the last of the tears. "I did take a chance on a man once, but he was killed right after we started courting. I think that pushed me over the edge." Emma clucked her tongue to put the gelding into a walk and Grace followed suit, falling in beside her.

Grace looked at Emma and said, "Do you want me to have a chat with Ann?"

Emma thought about it a moment then said, "No. If it's something she hasn't considered, I don't want you plantin' the idea in her head and have it take root."

CHAPTER
42

Having ridden all night, both the horses and the people riding them were exhausted as Chauncey, Marcie, Percy, and Bass Reeves rode toward the Oklahoma Station with plans to catch a train back to Guthrie. It would save them about thirty miles of hard riding and, more important, it would allow them a chance to get something to eat and maybe a catnap before the train arrived.

The group trudged up to the train depot and dismounted. Marcie had been napping when they had traveled through on the train, so she took a moment to look around. The town was larger than Guthrie, but not by much. Other than the tents that were going up, Marcie saw a few scruffy buildings, a cattle pen or two, and of course, the train depot. She walked over to where Chauncey was standing and said, "Ain't much of a town."

"I reckon it don't matter," Chauncey said, "if they got someplace where we can get some grub." He looked at Percy and said, "How's the arm, Pa?"

"I'll live," Percy said. He had fashioned a makeshift

sling for his left arm to keep it from moving around. Percy dug another double eagle from his front pocket and handed it to Marcie. "You mind buying us some train tickets?"

"Not at all," Marcie said, disappearing through the front door.

Percy looked at Reeves and said, "Bass, who's ram-roddin' down this way?"

"I think it's a fella named Needles, who's workin' out of the district court in Wichita. But I could be wrong. Him and Marshal Jones got into a pissin' match about who's in charge."

"Who won?" Chauncey asked.

"Don't rightly know," Reeves said. "They both appointed a bunch of extra deputy marshals that don't know one end of a gun from the other."

"People you ain't ever seen before?" Percy asked.

Reeves nodded and said, "Yep. Buncha dandies, if you ask me."

"Seems kinda strange, don't it? You reckon they're riggin' the Run?" Percy asked.

Reeves, dressed in his usual suit coat, vest, trousers, and white shirt, pulled a handkerchief from his back pocket and wiped the dust from his face. "Don't know, Percy, but there's a lotta things 'bout this that don't smell right. You got a gazillion railroad workers pourin' in, the new deputies I ain't never laid eyes on, and a bunch of folks millin' round that probably ought not be here, so, yeah, I reckon there's some shenanigans goin' on. Don't reckon there's much we can do about it, though. Supposed to be a bunch of bigwigs comin' down from Washington, so I reckon it'll be their problem."

Percy mumbled something about listening to Eli and let the rest of it go.

Marcie returned with the tickets and tried to hand the change back to Percy, but he waved her off.

"What time's the train?" Percy asked.

"Ten o'clock," Marcie said. "They got a nine o'clock freighter comin' through but there's no place to put the horses."

"Ten o'clock it is, then," Percy said. He looked at Reeves and said, "Where can we get some grub?"

"Ain't but one place and that's over at Gibson's," Reeves said. "They run the stage station. But I'm warnin' y'all, if his wife ain't doin' the cookin' then it ain't gonna be fit to eat."

"Any reason the wife wouldn't be doin' the cookin'?" Percy asked.

"Them two don't get along too well," Reeves said. "She'll get mad and light out for a day or two on occasion."

"Well, let's hope," Chauncey said, "they's gettin' along today 'cause I'm hungry enough to eat the ass end out of a skunk."

Reeves chuckled as he led them over to a slapped-together, single-story building that was surrounded by half a dozen cottonwoods, the only trees within a mile of the place. Reeves pulled the door open and held it, letting the rest of the crew file past. If it was possible, the building looked worse on the inside with daylight pouring through the cracks where the edges of the boards were supposed to meet. A dozen tables had been parked haphazardly around the room, all coated with a fine layer of dust.

"Hey, Marshal," a tall, rail-thin man said, stepping out from behind an old curtain that had been tacked over what looked to be the door to the kitchen.

"Mornin', George," Reeves said. "Fore we sit down, I gotta know who's doin' the cookin'."

"Janey's back there. Why?"

"Just wonderin'," Reeves said. He pulled out a chair and sat, the others joining him. "Let's start with coffee, George."

"Comin' right up," Gibson said before disappearing behind the curtain.

Marcie looked at the daylight pouring in then raked a finger through the dust on top of the table and said, "Is there a reason they didn't push the boards together before nailin' them?"

"Who knows," Reeves said.

Marcie's gaze drifted over to the two fly-specked windows overlooking the dirt yard and shuddered. The place looked like it hadn't had a good scrubbing since the day it opened.

She wondered sometimes about her obsession for cleanliness and she assumed it had something to do with working in a parlor house, where she'd had little control over anything, including her own body. As soon as that thought registered, she locked down the pump handle that was pulling those thoughts from the deep recesses of her mind, angry that after all this time, those things still flashed into her mind.

George Gibson returned with four coffee mugs and passed them around.

"Whatcha got to eat?" Chauncey asked, taking his cup from Gibson.

"We got flapjacks with bacon or ham with biscuits and gravy," Gibson said. "What'll you have?" Gibson asked.

"Both," Chauncey said.

"Both it is," Gibson said, as if it was a frequent request. He looked at Marcie and said, "Ma'am?"

Marcie had been battling recurring periods of nauseousness over the last couple of weeks and her stomach was a little unsettled this morning. "Do you have any toast?"

"I reckon we can scare some up." Gibson took the rest of the orders and returned to the kitchen.

"You sickly?" Chauncey asked Marcie.

"A little. It'll get better."

It wasn't long before the food arrived and those at the table fell silent, the only noise the scraping of the forks on the tin plates. Marcie, her stomach having advanced from unsettled to queasy, nibbled at the toast, knowing she would see anything she ate on the return journey. She pushed her coffee cup away and asked Gibson for a glass of water and he told her he'd be right out with it.

The front door opened, and Marcie turned to see two men enter. Backlit by the sun, she couldn't tell much about them, but she saw Reeves pull his hat down as they walked by on their way to a table in the opposite corner. Reeves looked at Marcie and whispered, "Go outside."

Marcie knew better than to ask any questions, so she nodded, stood, and made her way outside. She had no idea who the two men were, but the look on Reeves's face suggested they weren't a couple of traveling salesmen.

When she turned to look at the building, her mind clicked back to the memory of the sunlight streaming in and decided the paper-thin walls would be no match for a stray bullet. She turned, looking for something more substantial to hide behind, and hurried toward one of the large cottonwood trees. When she reached it, she squatted down behind the trunk and waited.

Back inside, Percy and Chauncey had been in enough battles to know when trouble was brewing. Neither knew exactly what that trouble might entail, but Reeves's body language indicated it was serious. He was in the middle of a story when the two men entered and other than pausing a couple of seconds to tell Marcie to go outside, he was still talking.

While Reeves droned on, Percy quickly calculated the angles. He was sitting closest to the aisle, sideways to the newcomers with Reeves to his left, his back to the corner. Chauncey was across the table, in between Reeves and the chair where Marcie had been sitting. Those two would be able to pull out their pistols unobserved, but Percy would have to pull his on the way up to his feet and then turn. Well rested and without a bullet hole in his arm, Percy figured maybe two seconds, tops. Now? Maybe three, four seconds? That was an eternity when the lead was flying.

Having seen Reeves and Chauncey in action many times, it was highly unlikely Percy's gun would even be needed. He looked down at the floor, wondering if he'd be better off just getting out of the way. To stay out of the line of fire, he'd need to dive to his left and just the thought of his arm smacking the hard floor sent a phantom pain shooting down his arm. Deciding that was the best option, he scooted his chair around, offering his back to the two men and screening Reeves enough to work out a plan.

Percy and Reeves had been friends for a long time, and they were well adapted to each other. Percy lifted his right hand and brought it close to his chest so the men behind him couldn't see it. Percy raised one finger then lowered it then raised two fingers. With his hand never leaving the table, Reeves raised two fingers, meaning he had warrants for both men. Percy looked at Chauncey and raised his eyebrows and his son nodded. He got it. Percy was trying to devise a way to find out what the warrants were for and decided it didn't matter. Reeves was known throughout the Territory as the one deputy marshal who always got his man and Percy knew today would be no different.

What was supposed to have been a few days of riding and visiting with his old friend had been anything but. The gun battle with the Keating brothers yesterday, the man taking potshots the day before, and now this, had Percy wondering if he was even going to be alive to watch the Run come Monday. Using a crude form of sign language, Percy, Reeves, and Chauncey worked through how the next few seconds would play out. Percy pointed a thumb at his chest then pointed to the floor to his left, telling them he was out of this fight. Both men nodded as they eased their pistols out.

Chauncey held up a hand and Percy heard Gibson talking to the two men behind him as he served them their meals. When he saw Gibson disappear back into the kitchen out of the corner of his eye, Percy held up three fingers and began counting down. When the last finger fell, Percy, trying to protect his left arm, twisted out of his chair and dived to the floor, landing on his right side as Reeves and Chauncey rose to their feet, their pistols out and ready for action.

"Hands up," Reeves shouted, aiming his pistol at the two men.

The two men shared a look and Percy thought they were going to give up, before the man on the right said, "Damn you, Reeves," and went for his gun.

Reeves and Chauncey fired almost simultaneously, the two shots loud inside the enclosed space. The man who went for his gun first had been leaning to his right and he toppled to the floor, a hole in his chest. The second man died with his hand on his pistol and he slumped in his chair, he, too, with a hole in his chest.

As Chauncey and Reeves ejected the spent shells and loaded in a fresh round, Percy scrambled to his feet.

Marcie, still hiding behind the cottonwood tree, flinched when the guns fired. She waited a few more moments to see if there would be any return fire and when there wasn't, she stood and hurried back to the restaurant. She had faith in Chauncey's abilities, but she also knew there were never any guarantees. She opened the door, stepped inside, and sighed with relief when she saw that her husband was still alive. He, Percy, and Reeves were sitting at the table finishing their breakfast as if nothing had happened. Crossing the floor, Marcie looked at the two men and said, "Who were they and what did they do?"

"They was wanted for train robbin'," Reeves said. "One on the left's a fella named Busey Jones and the other's Danny Ringo, a cousin of Johnny—"

Reeves was interrupted when Gibson poked his head out from behind the curtain and said, "Is the shootin' over?"

"It's done, George," Reeves said. "Come on out."

Marcie shied away from the bodies and went the long way around to get back to her chair as Gibson slipped past the curtain and walked over to look at the bodies. "I figured somebody was gonna kill them two sooner or later." He turned to look at Reeves and said, "But I sure as hell didn't think it was gonna happen in my restaurant."

"Sorry 'bout that," Reeves said. "We got the drop on 'em and still they went for their pistols."

"Them two been accused of a lot of things but I don't reckon anybody's accused 'em of bein' smart. What are you gonna do with 'em, Marshal? There ain't no undertakers within a hundred miles o' here."

"Want to earn a little extra money, George?" Percy asked.

Gibson thought about it for a minute then looked at Percy and said, "How much?"

"How much you want?" Percy asked.

"Twenty dollars a head?" Gibson asked.

"Done," Percy said.

"But y'all gotta help me get 'em into my wagon," Gibson said.

"We'll help you," Reeves said, "soon as we finish up breakfast. Your wagon hitched up?"

"No, I'm just gonna drag it over with a horse and hitch it up later," Gibson said.

"In that case," Reeves said, holding up his coffee cup, "reckon you could top me off fore you go?"

Gibson turned and walked back to the kitchen and returned with the coffeepot. He topped off the four cups, left the pot on the table, and went after his wagon.

"How can you three sit there and eat with two dead men in the room?" Marcie asked.

"They ain't goin' nowhere," Reeves said.

"Well, it's a little much for me," Marcie said. "Body count's pilin' up. You three keep it up and there won't be nobody left to make the Run." She stood, picked up her toast and coffee cup, and went back outside.

CHAPTER
43

While his mother fretted, Simon Turner was sitting with Ann Parker on a bluff overlooking the Cimarron River, feeling more confused than he'd ever been before. He was feeling things he had never felt before, and his mind was whirling with confusion. Since boarding the train in Davis, he and Ann Parker had spent almost every waking moment together, forming an inseparable bond that both thrilled and frightened him. There was no doubt Ann Parker was a beautiful young woman and the mutual attraction between them was undeniable, but it was clear they were from two different worlds. And Simon, being a very smart young man, knew there would be significant hurdles ahead if the relationship were to evolve into something more.

He could think of one hurdle right off the bat, and that was his desire to attend college back East. His original thought had been to follow in Seth's footsteps and study law, but more recently his thoughts had turned to medicine and that meant he had a long, hard road ahead of him. How would a relationship with Ann fit into those plans? Not easily, for sure. And with the altercation with Nellie's father still weighing heavy on his mind, Simon wondered if returning home would even be an option when it was all said and done. It might not have been an issue if they lived elsewhere, but living next door to Indian Territory, he knew he would face a lifetime of animosity simply because of the Indian blood running through his veins.

Another hurdle that would be difficult to overcome was the stark differences in their upbringing. From what Simon could gather, Ann had been raised without any of the inhibitions a white society imposed on its members and there had been very few restrictions, if any, on what she could or couldn't do. Her father did require her to attend school, but other than that it sounded like she was free to come and go as she pleased. It had been the exact opposite for Simon, whose childhood had been very structured, his mother always nearby and never shy about voicing her expectations. Looking back, Simon realized it hadn't been all bad and he credited that structure for his now-disciplined approach to not only school, but life in general.

He assumed that freewheeling attitude was common among Indian tribes, but he had silently cursed his mother a few times over the last few days for shielding him from his Indian heritage.

Ann slipped her hand inside his and said, "You're awful quiet. What are you thinkin' about?" Seated side by side, they were watching a small herd of cattle being driven north across the river.

Simon shrugged and said, "Pondering the future." He turned to Ann and said, "What do you want out of life?"

"Such a deep subject for this early in the day." Using her free hand, she tucked a strand of her long dark hair behind her ear as she contemplated her answer. "It's difficult to know. If someone had told my father twenty years ago that he and his people would now be living on a reservation, he would have called that person crazy before most likely killing him and taking his scalp. Those days are over, thankfully, but it's an example of how impossible it is to predict what might happen in the next five years, much less the next twenty and beyond."

"I'm not asking you to predict the future. I want to know what you dream about when you think about your future."

Ann picked up a rock and tossed it over the edge and waited to hear the *kerplunk* before continuing. "Are you suggesting I need some type of driving ambition for my life to have meaning? Why do I need to have some grand plan and not just take life as it comes?"

Simon thought that over for a few moments, suddenly aware of the sweat trickling down his back. It was unseasonably hot and what little breeze there was only stirred the heat around. Pushing thoughts of the weather from his mind, he focused on Ann's questions. Yes, he had grand plans, but maybe *he* was the outlier.

Before he could delve into that issue, Ann interrupted his thoughts when she said, "Look, going forward, you'll be afforded opportunities that, as a woman, aren't available to me. Tack on the fact that I'm a full-blooded Indian and my opportunities dwindle even more. I get it that you want to go to college and then study medicine, but the few colleges that admit women aren't looking for a Comanche woman from Indian Territory. Besides, the cost is more than my father could ever afford."

"I understand," Simon said. "Are you going to be happy being a wife and a mother?"

"Depends on who I marry." Ann gave his hand a squeeze then withdrew it before pushing to her feet. "It's too hot to be mapping out our futures. Let's go for a swim."

"I don't really want to get my clothes wet," Simon said.

"You won't," Ann said. "We'll do it the Indian way. Now, come on."

Ann grabbed his hand to help him up then they made their way down the bluff and chose a spot upstream from where the cattle had crossed. Ann, who was wearing a lightweight, blue gingham dress, slipped it over her head and let it fall to the ground.

Simon froze at the sight of her naked body and the only thing that moved were his eyes as they followed her as she entered the water. She walked out until the water was deep enough then sank down to her neck and turned around. "You coming?"

The question was enough to jar Simon into action. He turned around to hide his erection and quickly stripped off his clothes. Now the problem was getting into the water without her seeing his private parts. He looked over his shoulder and said, "Close your eyes."

Ann laughed and said, "Shy, huh? Don't worry, you don't have anything that I haven't seen before."

Simon could feel the heat creep into his cheeks. "Please?"

Ann laughed again and made a big show of covering

her eyes with her hands. Simon turned and hurried toward the river, using his hands to shield his privates. Running by the time he hit the water, he quickly worked his way out to deeper water and sank down.

"Can I open my eyes yet?" Ann asked.

"Yes," Simon said.

"Good," Ann said, dropping her hands. She swam over to Simon and locked her legs around his thighs and her arms around his neck and pressed her body against his as she began kissing him.

The shock of the cold water did have a shriveling effect, but that didn't last for long.

Emma and Grace returned to camp, still giddy about the perfect piece of land they had found. Grace still wasn't ready to tell Seth she was going to stake a claim so there would be no mention of their discovery around camp. Grace dismounted, gave Seth a kiss on the cheek, and disappeared into the tent to check on Lizzie.

Emma looked around and said, "Have you seen Simon or Ann?"

"Try the river," Seth said. "I heard them talking about it earlier."

"I'll check, thanks. I have another question for you."

"Shoot," Seth said.

"The railroads own their tracks and the rights-of-way, right?"

"A majority do, yes."

"So that would be considered private property?"

"Where you goin' with this, Emma?"

"Humor me."

"Yes, it would be considered private land, owned by the railroads."

"Meanin' it's not technically part of the Unassigned Lands?"

"Are you thinking about staking a claim?" Seth asked.

"Maybe," Emma said. "So, would it be legal or not?"

"The rules clearly stipulate that anyone caught trying to enter early forfeits any chance to stake a claim."

"The key word in what you just said is *caught*. How would anyone know?"

"It's all in the timing. If someone finds out you staked your claim at twelve-fifteen and you're twenty miles from the closest border, it's not real hard to prove you gamed the system. We're cousins, Emma, and I love you like a sister, but I won't be a party to your scheme. It would probably be best if you kept your plans to yourself."

"Duly noted," Emma said. The conversation had gone pretty much as she expected, and she couldn't be angry at Seth for not wanting to participate. "Need water, since I'm headed to the river?"

"We're good for now, but thanks. I'm glad you're not mad at me."

"Never," Emma said. She turned her horse around and set out for the river. She pondered what Seth had said about the legalities of it all. She knew Seth wouldn't want to be involved in anything if there was even a whiff of impropriety and she wondered how Grace was going to handle it. Maybe it would be best for Grace to lay it all out for Seth, but then she remembered the old adage that it was easier to ask for forgiveness than it was to ask for permission. Still, it was going to be next to impossible to keep Seth from finding out, especially if he was going to spend any time at the land office filing claims. It was something that would require further discussion because Seth's actions, if any, would have an effect on her and Marcie.

She steered the gelding up a bluff overlooking the river and pulled the horse to a stop. The stream was several hundred yards wide and was heavily timbered on both sides, making it difficult to see much of anything. Emma thought it unlikely they would cross to the far side, so she focused her search on the south shore. After searching and not seeing anything, she descended the bluff and picked up a game trail through the trees.

After navigating around a puddle of standing water, Emma heard someone laughing and she paused to pinpoint the location. It sounded like it was coming from the river, so she turned her horse to the right and picked her way through the trees. When she broke into the clear she saw Simon and Ann in the water about fifty yards away, so she eased her horse forward, taking cover behind a large cedar. Intertwined like mating snakes, it was readily apparent from their rhythmic movements that her hypothetical speculation was now reality. But what to do?

Emma pondered that for a few moments Her first instinct was to order them out of the water immediately and give them both a stern lecture on acceptable behavior. But she knew it would fall on deaf ears and she risked alienating both of them and for what? Was it fair to impose her moral code on a young woman who was raised without one? And, to tell the truth, could she *really* keep it from happening again? Emma felt like she was being ripped apart from the inside out, her mind a roiling pot of indecision. Both Simon and Ann would be sixteen in a few months, an age when it wasn't uncommon for young adults to leave the nest. And that thought triggered more, including the question of whether she had any legal rights to intercede.

The questions continued like a fusillade of bullets and there were no easy answers to any of them. Emma knew a rash decision now could have long-lasting impacts. Deciding there was nothing to be gained by confronting them now, she gently pulled on the reins to back the gelding deeper into the trees before turning the horse around. Still flabbergasted by her discovery, she couldn't formulate how the conversation with Simon might begin without him accusing her of spying. The excuse that she *just happened by* wouldn't hold water and she was a terrible liar anyway.

Another thought began to worm its way into her mind, and it persisted despite her attempts to quash it—What if she did nothing? Would she be shirking her parental duties by ignoring what she'd seen? Or would it be taking the easy way out? It's just sex, right? As she thought about that, she realized there was a teeny, tiny part of her that was envious of their relationship, and that angered her. She was supposed to be the adult, the one responsible for Simon's well-being. She inhaled a deep breath, held it a moment, then blew it out, trying to clear her mind. It had little effect and the questions were still buzzing around in her brain as she cleared the trees and rode for camp.

CHAPTER
44

With Grace back to look after the kids and having heard that the men who would be manning the land office had finally arrived, Seth set off in search of them. As he walked toward the newly built building, he wondered why land office workers were so late in arriving. With only two days until the Run, he would have thought the office would be buzzing, the workers going over surveys and making sure a plan was in place. But none of that was happening and Seth had a sinking feeling that Monday was going to be an unmitigated disaster.

It was going to be another sweltering day, and Seth's shirt was damp with sweat by the time he reached the land office. To his dismay, he found the door padlocked and there was no sign of the men he was searching for. He turned around and surveyed the area, wondering where they might be. Tents were continuing to go up and with no hotels in the area, he assumed they had established a camp somewhere, but where? Thinking they might have chosen a spot close to where they would be working, Seth chose the closest tent and walked over.

That tent was home to a stove salesman, his wares proudly displayed. The next tent he checked housed a man who claimed to be a dentist, the next a blacksmith, the next two barbers cutting hair. There was no method to the madness and the tents had been erected wherever the owners had found a patch of bare ground. Of the people he had talked to, none had seen the people who would be occupying the land office on Monday.

Frustrated, Seth continued his search and hit pay dirt half an hour later when he stumbled across two of the workers sipping coffee inside the train depot. After introducing himself, Seth shook hands with John Dille, a lawyer from Indiana who had been appointed as register of deeds and Cassius "Cash" Barnes, a former U.S. marshal from Fort Smith who had been appointed receiver of moneys. Dille pulled out a chair and Seth sat.

After a few pleasantries, Seth said, "I have to ask, how much planning was done for this event?"

The two men shared a look and Dille said, "To be honest, probably not enough. In fact, the office in Kingfisher isn't even finished yet."

"Is it going to be finished by Monday?" Seth asked.

"Supposed to be," Barnes said.

"But most likely not?" Seth asked.

Dille shrugged and thinking that would be the only answer he would get, Seth moved on. "How many people are you anticipating for Monday's Run?"

"Well," Dille said, "it's only been a month since the president announced the opening. I would think that would limit the number somewhat."

"I live just across the river in Texas, and I can tell you people were heading for the border of Indian Territory a day after the president's proclamation. When we came up on the train on Friday, we passed an unending line of wagons that was sixty, maybe seventy miles long. So, I'd guess there are twenty to thirty thousand people coming up from the south. Add that to the thousands of others pouring in from every direction and I wouldn't be surprised if there's sixty, maybe seventy thousand people now converging on this area."

"Surely that can't be right," Dille said, calmly taking a sip of coffee from his cup. "You said it was a guess. How much experience do you have estimating crowd sizes? I think you're vastly overstating the numbers."

Seth didn't care for Dille's pompous attitude. "Think what you want because it doesn't really matter to me. I was just trying to give you an idea of what might be comin' your way."

"And I appreciate it," Dille said. "Even if you're correct in your assessment, there's not a damn thing we can do about it, is there?"

"No, I guess not," Seth said. "Moving on, what's the plan if multiple people file a claim on the same parcel?"

Dille shrugged and said, "The claimant can file a contest with the land office."

"Then what happens?" Seth asked.

"Then we'll eventually conduct hearings and call on the witnesses to testify under oath," Dille said. "If a dispute still exists after that, the aggrieved party can appeal to the General Land Office in Washington, D.C., then to the secretary of the interior."

Seth's eyes widened in surprise. "So, you're telling me

there won't be anyone on-site to settle a claim dispute during the Run?"

"Correct. I certainly don't have the ability to know whose claim might be valid," Dille said.

Seth turned to look at Barnes and said, "Really?"

"Don't look at me," Barnes said, "I'm here to collect the filing fees."

Seth scowled and turned back to Dille. "If six people claim the same parcel, you what? Write the six names down and a few months later have a hearing?"

"Precisely," Dille said.

"That could take months or even years," Seth said.

"Not our problem," Barnes said.

Envisioning the coming nightmare, Seth said, "What about the army or the marshals? Couldn't they settle a claim?"

Dille shook his head and said, "They're not authorized."

Seth couldn't believe what he was hearing. He pointed to the vacant land out the window and said, "That ground might well become a killing field come Monday afternoon. Every homesteader I saw was armed to the teeth and with so much on the line, you can bet they'll fight like hell to hold on to their claims." Seth pushed to his feet, looked down at the two federal officials, and said, "If you didn't bring a gun, I'd suggest you find one." He turned and exited the building.

That city slicker from Indiana, Dille, had no idea how quickly things could turn violent out here in this country, Seth thought. He stalked back to camp, pulled Grace aside, and told her they were leaving in the morning.

"We can't," Grace said.

"We can and we are," Seth said. He told her what he had just learned then said, "The children aren't safe. As a matter of fact, none of us are safe."

"Chauncey and the others will be around to keep an eye on things."

"They aren't going to stop a stray bullet. Why are you so against leaving?"

That was the one question Grace had been trying to avoid. "Well, I want to be here to see it."

"And take a chance on our children being injured?"

"You're overreacting."

"No, I'm not," Seth said calmly. "Look, most of those people coming here are destitute and desperate. Everything they own is packed into those wagons, including their firearms. What happens if two people have a claim dispute and both literally have nowhere else to go? I'll tell you what they're going to do. They're going to fight like hell for what they think is theirs."

"Well," Grace said, "they had to come from somewhere, right?"

Seth took off his suit coat and hung it on a tent pole then rolled up the sleeves of his white shirt, all while studying his wife. "I don't remember the last time we had a disagreement about anything. Why are you fighting me on this?"

Grace sighed and stared off into the distance for a few moments before shifting her gaze back to her husband, knowing the game was up. "Me, Marcie, and Emma are goin' to stake a claim."

Seth cocked his head, looked at his wife, thinking he'd misheard her, and said, "Do what?"

"You heard me," Grace said, a tinge of heat in her

voice. After all, she was a grown woman capable of making her own decisions.

Seth crossed his arms, his brow wrinkling with confusion. "You plannin' on leaving me?"

"Oh, Seth," Grace said, stepping in to wrap her arms around him, her anger vanishing. "Not in a million years. You comin' along was the best thing that ever happened to me."

"So, what's the deal about wanting to file a claim?"

After one final squeeze, Grace broke the embrace and stepped back. "I want something we can leave for our children, Seth. Someplace where they can put down roots when they have their own families."

"And you weren't going to tell me?"

Grace's eyes drifted toward the ground, her cheeks flushing red. "I was gonna tell you afterward."

"Why not before?"

Grace looked up and said, "Because I know you're a stickler for details, especially when it comes to legal matters. Although I don't think we'd be doin' anything wrong by filing a claim, I'm fairly certain you'll think differently. Am I wrong?"

Seth nodded and said, "No, you're right. To file a legal claim, the claimant must be beyond the border of Oklahoma and can only enter at the appointed time."

"There's no wiggle room?" Grace asked, batting her eyelashes.

"Not that I'm aware of."

"How far away are we from the closest border?"

"We're about ten miles from the eastern boundary."

"How long would it take a man on a fast horse to cover that ten miles?" Grace asked.

"I know where you're goin' with this, but that still won't make it right."

"Humor me. How long?"

"Well, if the rider had no concerns about the well-being of his horse, maybe an hour or a little longer. But even if you waited an hour to stake the claim, you still have the issue of occupying the land for as long as five years and making improvements to it. How's that going to work?"

"After the first year you can buy the land for a dollar and a quarter an acre."

"Okay, but that still requires a year of occupancy."

"We've talked about that. We're planning to put up a tent on each claim until a man Emma knows can get around to building a more permanent structure. As for improvements to the land, the rules are vague, but if we have to hire someone to plow a field, we will."

"You three have it all planned out, huh?"

Grace nodded and said, "Are you mad at me?"

Seth thought about that question for a moment. He was more disappointed than mad that she hadn't shared her plans with him. But another part of him was proud she, Emma, and Marcie had taken the initiative. And he had to admit, it would be nice to have a piece of property all their own. Still, the legal hurdles remained. He looked at Grace and said, "I understand your reasons for not telling me, but I am sad you felt you couldn't confide in me because you feared what my response might be. We're in this thing together and, even if we disagree, you have as much say as I do. So, it's probably best if you don't share any more of your plans with me."

"So, we're stayin'?"

"We're staying. Trying to file claims will be a disaster, but maybe I can recoup some of our expenses by doing other legal work. But, you need to remember the kids come first."

"Of course. I'm very sorry for not telling you." Grace stepped in, kissed him on the lips, then whispered, "I don't know what I did to deserve you. I can't believe the thought that I might leave ever entered your mind because you're stuck with me until I breathe my last breath on this old earth."

CHAPTER
45

Pawnee Bill awoke in a state of confusion. Sometime during the night, May had climbed into his bedroll, both naked and eager. Although he hadn't known if she would be speaking to him come morning, he had obliged her, and it had been better than any encounter in recent memory. Before falling back asleep, he had spent some time thinking about it and he couldn't figure out if it was because he'd finally stood his ground or if it was just another of May's many moods.

Now both dressed and parked in the back of another Boomer's wagon as it rumbled onward, May was leaned against Bill, her head on his shoulder and a hand on his thigh. Talking was difficult with the bandannas wrapped around their faces to ward off the persistent dust and Bill thought that was probably a good thing. If he couldn't talk, there was a good chance of not making her mad again.

Bill turned his thoughts to what lay ahead. If all went as planned, they would go into camp on Big Turkey Creek sometime this afternoon. The campsite was only a half a mile from the northern border of Oklahoma, and they'd be able to rest up Sunday and make preparations for the Land Run on Monday. Despite what he'd told May, he knew he needed to buy another wagon and stock up on provisions, but Indian Territory wasn't exactly a shopper's paradise and, of course, there was the other issue of being flat broke.

Most of the Indian agencies had some type of trading post or mercantile store and he might get lucky and find a wagon, but he'd have to convince the owner to sell to him on credit until he could make it back to Wichita to dig up his stash. He and the Boomers had been in and out of the Territory many times over the years and he had a good handle on where most things were. Fort Reno and the Darlington Indian Agency was the closest place that might have a wagon, but Bill didn't know any of the merchants there and they would be less likely to extend him credit.

In the end, Bill decided the best course of action would be to stake their claim and then catch a train back to Wichita with the mules and try to buy a wagon and re-stock supplies there before returning.

His thoughts were interrupted when May pulled down the bandanna and said, "What are you thinkin' about?"

With May, that was always a loaded question. "Well, huh . . ." Bill stammered, searching for something that wouldn't set her off. He pulled his bandanna down and said in a low voice, "I reckon I was thinkin' 'bout last night."

May smiled and said, "It was nice, wasn't it?"

"That it was. Probably ought to do that more often."

"What are you sayin'?"

Uh-oh, Bill thought, recognizing the tone in her voice. "I was just sayin' how nice it was."

May sat up straight and said, "No, you're implying I've been neglectful of my wifely duties."

And that was Bill's clue to leave. "No, I'm not." He pulled the bandanna up, kicked his leg over the tailgate, and dropped to the ground. He immediately veered to the right, hoping to break free of the enormous dust cloud. The Great Plains was one of the windiest places on earth, but one wouldn't know that this morning. The dust particles hung suspended in the air and most eventually fell back to the ground a short distance from where they came, only to be kicked up again with the next hoof or the next wheel. His short legs churning, he finally gained some distance and slowed his pace. With his only goal to avoid May for a while, he didn't have a particular destination in mind, so he moseyed along as the wagons rolled on by.

As one of the Boomer leaders, it was difficult wrangling so many wagons and people and the constant strain on Bill and the other leaders was exhausting. They'd been at this for almost a month and now that they were nearing the end of the journey, he simply didn't have the mental energy to try and parse out what had just happened with May. Not that it would do any good anyway. The reasons for her sudden changes were often so obscure they were invisible to him and trying to figure it out was a waste of time. He tried his best to put May out of his mind as he veered back toward the wagons, deciding to catch up with William Couch.

With the wagons moving at a fairly slow pace, it didn't

take long to find him. Bill asked for permission to board and Couch waved him up.

After Bill had settled onto the seat, Couch looked at Bill and said, "Things between you and May any better?" His words were muffled by the bandanna covering his face.

"Well, they were until about twenty minutes ago and I'm done talkin' about it." He pulled his bandanna back up and leaned back, taking advantage of the shade provided by the canvas top. As usual, Couch was alone in the wagon and for the first time Bill wondered if he might be having his own family problems. They all seemed to get along, but who knew what went on behind the scenes? Bill didn't dwell on it for long because the state of Couch's family affairs had no bearing on his own marital problems.

The two men rode in silence for a while and as the morning progressed, the breeze freshened, driving some of the dust away. Although Bill and the Boomers had made several incursions into Indian Territory, this time it felt much different. This was the first trip where they weren't having to look over their shoulders all the time, and it felt weird. There would be no army escorts out this time, and they would be able to lay claim to a piece of property that would pass, for those who had children, from one generation to the next. Before, the best they could do was slap a few shanties together to ward off the weather and pray no one found them. But come Monday they would be able to build more permanent structures— at least for those with money—such as houses and barns and corrals and anything they wanted, knowing they couldn't be taken away.

Bill knew Couch and several other men had incorporated a company back in Topeka called the Seminole Town and Improvement Company to plat a town around the area where the Oklahoma Station was presently. Couch was hoping to name it Oklahoma City, which didn't sound very original to Bill, but thinking about it now, he lowered his bandanna and said, "Where's your surveyors?"

Couch looked around to make sure no one was in earshot and said, "They're already in Oklahoma City. Been there for the better part of a week."

"How'd they get in?"

"I can't tell you all my secrets. I will say it took some doing, though."

"Where are you makin' the Run from?"

Couch pulled down his bandanna and smiled. "Technically speaking, the railroad tracks are private property."

"So, you're bendin' the rules a little?"

"Maybe, but you know what, Gordon?"

"What?"

"The opening of the Unassigned Lands and the upcoming Land Run wouldn't have happened without our efforts. I walked the halls of Congress for years, pestering whoever would listen about opening the Indian lands to settlement. I realize that doesn't entitle me or you or anyone else to much, but I do believe our hard work earned us, at minimum, a head start."

"Others might not see it that way."

"Not my concern," Couch said. "Mark my words,

come noon Monday the woods all across Oklahoma will come alive with people who have snuck in early."

"Still don't make it right," Bill said. "How are you gonna get past the army?"

"No one knows this ground as well as we do, other than the Indians, maybe. There are a dozen different ways to get there, so I don't foresee any problems."

It sounded like Couch had it all planned out, but Bill knew plans seldom survived the harshness of reality. And Couch's cavalier attitude could come back to bite him in the butt. The two men fell silent again and Bill leaned back, studying a red-tailed hawk that was circling high overhead. It would be a feast day for him, Bill thought, the rumble from the long line of wagons scattering small game in all directions. As he watched the hawk floating along the currents, he reminisced about the ride he had taken in a gas balloon while traveling in Europe with Cody's show. It had been an eye-opening experience and he envied the hawk's abilities, soaring high above the primitive wagons and their earthbound occupants.

He was stirred from his reverie when Couch said, "You want me to hold a couple of town lots for you?"

"Hadn't thought about it," Bill said. He ruminated on that for a moment then said, "I aim to file on the hundred and sixty acres first. If I do that, aren't they gonna know if I try to claim something else?"

"Put May's name on one and your father's name on the other."

"My pa's dead," Bill said.

"So? They're not going to know that."

"I don't know, William. Kinda feel like I'd be pushin' my luck." Bill was seeing Couch in a whole new light and not in a good way. How many other shady things did he have up his sleeve? "I'll pass on the town lots, but thanks for askin'."

"Sure. Send me a telegram at Oklahoma City if you change your mind."

"Will do," Bill said, sensing trouble on the horizon for his friend. Hoarding a bunch of claims was a good way to get shot.

CHAPTER
46

When the train arrived in Guthrie, they unloaded the horses and Chauncey and Marcie went back to their camp as Percy and Reeves debated next steps. Additional army soldiers had arrived in their absence and they had set up camp on the hill north of the depot, making the marshals' pointless jobs even more pointless. Still, after all the gunplay the last couple of days, neither was eager to hang around now that their pistols had finally cooled off.

"I reckon," Reeves said, looking at the new army encampment, "we ought to ride over and see who's ramroddin' the show round here, then grab Leander and mosey on back to camp."

"I need to pick up something from the depot before we leave," Percy said.

"Want to do that first, since we's already here?"

Percy would have preferred to do it alone, but Leander and Reeves were going to find out anyway.

"Might as well," Percy said. "We need to walk around to the corral."

"You had a horse shipped up from the ranch?"

"I did."

"Who's it for?"

Percy ignored the question and turned right at the next corner, working his way around to the back of the building with Reeves following. There were only a couple of horses inside and only one of those was saddled.

Reeves took one look and started laughing. "A side-saddle?" Reeves asked. "You old softy. You're gonna give that horse to Ruth, ain't you?"

Percy bristled at the question and said, "I don't reckon it's any of your business what I'm gonna do with that horse." Percy opened the gate, stepped inside, untied the lead rope from the fence, and led the horse out, all while Reeves stood there, laughing.

"I need to circle a date on my calendar, too?" Reeves asked.

Percy brushed past Reeves like he wasn't there and led the gelding back around to the front. Reeves was still chuckling when he rounded the corner and Percy ignored him as he untied the mare's reins and climbed into the saddle. He finally looked at Reeves and said, "You comin'?"

"I'm comin'," Reeves said. He mounted up and they rode out to the army camp, Percy leading the new horse. After identifying themselves to the sentry and receiving directions to the commander's tent, they rode over and dismounted.

"I think it's nice," Reeves said, "you givin' Ruth that horse."

"I don't remember askin' what you was thinkin'," Percy said. His left arm pulsed with pain every time he moved and that made him a tad bit more irritable.

Reeves was still chuckling when they took off their hats and entered.

A thin, curly-haired man with a well-groomed mustache and captain's bars on his shoulders stood to meet them. "Captain Arthur MacArthur," he said, shaking hands with both of them. After the introductions were done, the captain waved toward the two chairs fronting his desk and said, "Please, have a seat," before working his way around to his own chair.

The captain looked at Reeves and said, "I've read several newspaper articles about some of your exploits, Marshal Reeves."

"Just doin' my job, Captain," Reeves said.

MacArthur turned to look at Percy and said, "What happened to your arm, Mr. Ridgeway?"

"It's a long story, but the short version is I got shot," Percy said.

MacArthur's eyebrows rose in surprise and he said, "Is that common in your line of work?"

Percy looked at Reeves and said, "Only recently."

Reeves smiled and Percy turned back to MacArthur and said, "I'm just a cowpuncher by trade."

Reeves chuckled and said, "Don't let him fool ya, Captain. I reckon he's got more cattle than the army's got soldiers."

They were interrupted when a young boy, probably nine or ten years old, entered the tent and approached, stopping next to the captain.

"There you are," MacArthur said, resting a hand on the boy's shoulder. "Men, this is my son, Douglas. He's going to follow in my footsteps and become an army officer one of these days, aren't you, Douglas?"

Douglas nodded and said, "I'm going to be a general."

"Yes, you are," MacArthur said. "Son, I want you to meet one of the finest deputy marshals working in Indian Territory, Bass Reeves and his friend Mr. Percy Ridgeway."

Douglas stepped around his father's desk and shook hands with Reeves then Percy. "A pleasure to meet you both," Douglas said. "Are you two excited for the upcoming Land Run?"

"Sure are," Reeves said, nodding his head. "You come along with your pa to watch it?"

"I did, sir. There's never been anything like it in the history of our country and I certainly didn't want to miss it."

"Did you need something, Douglas?" MacArthur asked.

The boy turned to look at his father and said, "No, Father. I saw the horses outside and wondered who you were talking to."

"Run along, then, and I'll be out shortly."

After telling Reeves and Percy it was nice to meet them, Douglas MacArthur turned and exited the tent.

"He's a fine young man," Percy said. He didn't know if the boy would ever make general, but he sure had some spunk.

MacArthur smiled and said, "Thank you. How are things out in the field?"

"A mess," Percy said. "We escort people out and they come right back in soon as we leave. How many soldiers are comin'?"

"Not near enough," MacArthur said. "By tomorrow we'll have fourteen companies of infantry and twenty troops of cavalry inside the border."

"How many men's that?" Reeves asked.

They waited as MacArthur did the math in his head. "Roughly, thirty-five hundred men," MacArthur said.

"They're gonna be spread thin," Reeves said, easing out of his chair, "with all the ground they got to cover."

"I agree," MacArthur said. "Let's hope it all goes smoothly."

Percy pushed to his feet and said, "I reckon it'll be considered a success if we all make it out alive."

They exited the tent and remounted their horses. They turned their mounts around and started the horses off at a walk and Percy said, "How many marshals you reckon are here?"

"Don't know the exact number, a hundred, maybe a hundred and fifty. Why?"

"The way I figure it, there's about three thousand square miles to cover. Sayin' we're spread thin don't quite do it justice."

"Ain't a whole hell of a lot we can do about it," Reeves said.

After swinging by to collect Leander, and after some more razzing for Percy, the three men made their way out to the camp. Ruth Taylor was the only one there and she was on Percy in an instant.

"What did you go and do?" Ruth asked.

Out of the corner of his eye Percy saw Reeves and Leander chuckling, so he tied up the mare and took Ruth by the elbow and steered her away from camp.

They stopped under the shade of a large cottonwood and Percy said, "Ain't so much what I did, it's what got done to me."

"Semantics," Ruth said. "Now, what happened?"

"Took a bullet through the arm."

"Let me see it."

"Done been to see a doctor."

"I didn't ask if you've been to the doctor. About ninety-five percent of them are quacks. Now, let me see it." Ruth began untying the sling and Percy stopped her by grabbing her hand.

"Been a long day. Mind if we sit down?"

"Of course." She led Percy into the shade of a large cottonwood and said, "Sit."

"Yes, ma'am." Percy took a seat on the ground and Ruth sat down beside him and finished untying the sling. "You some kind of wound expert or somethin'?"

Her touch was gentle as she unwound the bandage the doctor had put on. "You teach as long as I have, and you'll see a variety of injuries. Everything from cuts and scratches to broken bones to ruined joints."

"No bullet wounds?" Percy asked.

"You're my first. How's the pain?"

"Tolerable when I'm not moving around."

When she had the bandage unwound, she draped it around her neck to keep it from getting dirty and gently lifted Percy's arm for a closer look. "Well, wonder of wonders, you found a doctor who didn't try to cauterize the wound."

"He told me cauterizing was quackery."

"He's correct. Where did you find this wise man?"

"Fort Reno."

"So, he was an army surgeon?"

"Don't rightly know. He didn't have much to say, but I reckon he was if he was workin' there."

"Probably a safe assumption. He did a good job cleaning the wound, but I wish he'd stitched it closed."

"Why's that?" Percy asked.

"It's easier to keep clean." She rewrapped his arm with the bandage and said, "You mustn't submerge your arm in water until the wound's completely closed."

"What's water got to do with anything?" Percy asked, his brow arching with confusion.

"Are you familiar with germ theory?"

"What theory?"

"Germs."

Percy took off his Stetson and set it on the grass and said, "I got no idea what that is."

"Germs are microscopic particles that are thought to cause infections and some diseases by entering a person's body."

"You might just as well be talkin' in French. Where are these germs and how do you know about 'em?"

"The research is ongoing, and it will be years before they have all the answers. As to how I know this, well, I might be poor, but I do consider myself well read. Newspapers, textbooks, pamphlets—I'll read anything I can get my hands on. But returning to germ theory, I once read an article about a man named Snow who lived somewhere in London in the 1850s. His local community was having a terrible cholera outbreak and he was determined to find the cause." Ruth paused and said, "Am I being a boor?"

"Not at all. How did he find out what was causin' it?"

"Through hard work. He went around the neighborhood, plotting the location of each ill person on a map. After he had collected all of that information, he began looking for commonalities and eventually traced the illness to one of the public water wells in the neighborhood. To test his theory, he convinced the local authorities to remove the handle to prevent people from using it. And what do you think happened then?" Ruth asked.

"The cholera went away?"

"Yes, it did, eventually. Now, Snow had to find out what was different about that one well and why none of the others in the area were involved in the outbreak. He presented all of his research to the neighborhood officials and he convinced them to dig out the well to find the cause."

"He was a determined fella," Percy said.

"Yes, he was and that's what's required to make advances in our understanding of the world."

Percy leaned back on his right elbow, eager to hear the rest. "So, they dug out the well?"

"They did and found that the well had been dug next to an old, abandoned cesspit that was leaking raw sewage into the water."

"I'll be damned," Percy said. "So, you're sayin' the water in the creeks and rivers might have these germs just like that well?"

"Yes. Every time it rains, anything on the surface, such as animal or human waste, gets washed into the nearby streams. Although Indian Territory might be lightly populated, there are probably still some disease-causing germs in the water. By this time next week, with thousands of people coming in, I can assure you the waterways will be contaminated."

Percy looked at Ruth and was drawn in by her blue eyes. They were the same shade of blue as the sky after a cold front had scoured away the clouds. "You're one smart woman. Thanks for educatin' me."

"You're welcome."

Exhausted from being up all night, he eased back until he was flat on the ground, his mind swirling with a mixture of what Ruth had told him along with a heavy dose of Ruth herself. He watched her for a moment as she sat calmly, her hands in her lap and her eyes alight with merriment as she watched two squirrels spiraling around the cottonwood's trunk, their sharp claws scratching against the rough bark. "Would you be offended," Percy asked, "if I said you're not only smart, you're pretty easy on the eyes, too?"

Ruth stretched out beside him and they lay there, shoulder to shoulder, looking up at the rattling cottonwood leaves and the sky beyond. "Why, no, I wouldn't be offended at all."

"Good," Percy said.

They lay there in the silence for a few moments before Ruth said, "How come you never remarried?"

"Never found anybody I wanted to marry, I reckon." Percy thought about it some more and said, "Most was widows with kids to raise and my three was gettin' old enough to look after their own selves. What about you?"

"The most significant reason, I suppose, is fear. When you've lived with a monster, the last thing you want to do is to jump into a relationship with another."

"Was your husband always like that?"

"No, his transformation was more gradual. His desire for liquor eventually surpassed his desire for me. Do you drink, Percy?"

"On occasion. Never had a problem with it, though."

"That's good," Ruth said.

"Him being meaner than a feral hog the reason you didn't have kids?"

"It is. As I've said, I'm a voracious reader and I became an expert on birth control. I wasn't going to bring a child into that relationship."

"Why didn't you just leave?"

"I've asked myself that question a thousand times over the years, but the real answer, after final distillation, was money. He had some and I didn't. He eventually gambled it all away and that made him even more hostile." Ruth paused for a moment then said, "I'd prefer to talk about something else."

"How about we just lay here and not talk at all?"

"Works for me," Ruth said.

Percy reached out, blindly searching for her hand, and when he found it, he interlaced his fingers with hers. "That roan horse with the sidesaddle is yours."

"I don't take charity," Ruth said.

"Ain't charity. It's a gift from me to you."

"We'll discuss it later."

They fell into silence again and, after a few moments, Ruth heard him snoring softly and she gently removed her hand and sat up. After a few moments of studying Percy as he slept, she was hit with a sudden longing, something she hadn't felt in so long she couldn't remember. She leaned over and kissed him gently on the forehead and quietly rose to her feet. It was time to start supper.

CHAPTER
47

Emma was sitting in the shade created by the tent, an open book in her lap. She had thought reading would take her mind off Simon and Ann, but the words blurred on the page and she couldn't stop her brain from churning. Now she was second-guessing herself. Did she see what she thought she saw? Hugging and kissing while nude was bad, at least in her view, but did the way they were moving really mean they were doing the deed? The problem was that Emma had no frame of reference.

She dog-eared the page and closed the book. Melville was difficult to read even when she was focused, and she was anything but, at present. Maybe Grace had been right when she had said it wasn't that big of a deal. And, really, was it any of her business? Emma decided to see how it would play out when Simon and Ann returned from their outing. He had always been the type to share most things with her, no matter the topic. That thought had barely registered when she looked up to see the two almost on top of her.

"Hey, Mom," Simon said. "What are you doing?"

"Trying to read," Emma said as Simon and Ann sat down beside her.

Simon picked up her book, read the spine, and said, "Think you'll ever finish that book?"

"Doubtful. I really don't care for it, but I'll feel bad if I don't finish it."

"It's just a book and Melville will never know whether you finished it or not."

"I know." Emma looked at her son and said, "Your hair's wet."

Really, Emma? You want to start there?

"Ann and I were hot, so we went for a swim."

"Oh," Emma said. She could feel the anger welling up inside of her and she tried hard to tamp it down. Emma looked around and said, "Where's your wet long johns? You better hang 'em up to dry."

Color rose in Simon's cheeks. "Well . . . huh . . . I only brought the one pair and I didn't want to get them wet."

"Oh," Emma said. She turned to Ann and said, "Sweetie, do you have some wet things that need to be hung up?"

Without batting an eyelash, Ann said, "Why would I swim with anything on? That wouldn't make much sense."

Emma could tell from the way her son dropped his head that he knew she knew. But she didn't want to shame him any further, especially after the ordeal with Nellie Hawkins's father. If more needed to be said, she'd do it in private. "You two missed dinner. There's a pot of beans on the fire and some ham and biscuits in the Dutch oven."

Ann stood and said, "Thank you, I'm starving."

Simon pushed to his feet and hung back a minute as

Ann continued on. When she was out of earshot, he looked at his mother and said, "You saw us?"

"I did. I've been sitting here thinking about what I might say to you and I'm still drawing a blank. Was that the first time?"

Simon, looking down at his shoes, shook his head.

Emma blew out a long breath and said, "Do you think it will be the last?"

Simon shrugged. He finally looked up and said, "Are you angry because she's an Indian or because you think we've violated some type of moral code that doesn't even exist in her world?"

"That you would believe I harbored any animosity toward Ann because of her skin color cuts me to the bone. I raised you better than that."

"Yes, you did, and I apologize," Simon said. "I'm just trying to understand where your anger is coming from."

"Think about it, Simon. All of your dreams lie ahead of you—college next fall and then on to medical school. What happens to all of that if Ann turns up pregnant? I'll tell you." Emma brought her hands together and yanked them apart and said, "Poof, that's what. And what about all of her dreams, wants, and wishes?"

"She's not going to get pregnant."

"Famous last words uttered all around the world." Emma put a hand on her hip and said, "How, exactly, are you going to prevent it?"

"I don't know."

"Well, I don't, either, but you better figure it out."

As soon as Simon was gone, Emma rose to her feet and went searching for Grace. Although disappointed

Simon hadn't used better judgment, a very small part of her was curious to know what it had been like, there in the water and with both being willing participants. She knew what went where only because it had been forced on her, but she didn't know what it would feel like to actually want it to happen. Although she had some concept of desire and longing from some of the books she had read, they were still relatively foreign subjects to her. Did married people have sex because they wanted to or was it more of an obligation, a required element agreed to by both parties and enacted upon the completion of the vows? Or did they do the deed only in service of creating offspring and once they reached the agreed-upon number of children would it end? It was frustrating not knowing the answers, so Emma tried to silence her mind as she entered the tent and stepped through to the living quarters, where she found Grace nursing Lizzie.

Grace looked up and put a finger to her lips. Emma nodded and took a seat on the edge of a nearby cot. Even with the bottom of the tent rolled up, it was still hot. If there was no breeze, there was no breeze, and nothing could be done to change it. But she knew there was hope on the horizon. Electricity was slowly spreading its tentacles across the country and if it ever arrived at the ranch, the first thing she was going to do was buy an electric fan. She'd gotten a taste of it at a hotel in Dallas and she knew it would be life-changing, if it arrived during her lifetime.

After Lizzie finished nursing, Grace put her down for a nap and the two tiptoed out of the living area. Emma, eager for some privacy, suggested a walk and Grace agreed. After exiting the tent, they turned and headed toward Cottonwood Creek. As they walked, Emma told Grace the latest about Simon and Ann, including a detailed description of what she had seen down at the river.

"The river, huh?" Grace said. "That tells me it probably wasn't their first time."

"According to Simon, it wasn't. How did you know?"

"The first time is always awkward and it's usually over in about thirty seconds. What you described was something far different. You need to buy Simon some rubbers and do it quickly."

"What are rubbers and where do you get them?"

Grace stopped and stared at Emma. "Lordy, Emma, you really don't know what a rubber is?"

Emma looked around to see if anyone had heard, her cheeks flushing. No one seemed to be taking an interest in them, so she lowered her voice and said, "How would I know about them? The Indians who raped me didn't give a damn if I got pregnant or not."

"You're right and I'm sorry. Sometimes I forget what happened to you."

"I don't, not for a second." They continued on and Emma said, "Now, tell me about these rubbers and where I can get some."

"It's a rubber sheath the man puts over his pecker to keep the woman from gettin' pregnant. As for finding them, it's a lot harder now with that asshole Comstock spewin' his nonsense. I highly doubt you'll find any at the trading posts up this way, but I know where I can buy some in Fort Worth."

"How am I supposed to keep those two apart until then?"

"I don't know that you can."

Emma thought about it a moment and said, "It's only a couple more days. I guess I'll just have to keep an eye on them and hope some of the things I said to Simon sunk in."

"I'll help," Grace said. "Now, let's talk about you. This morning, I ran into one of Seth's lawyer friends from Dallas and I want you to meet him."

Emma groaned. "How old is he?"

"Late twenties, maybe."

"What's wrong with him?"

"What do you mean?"

"Late twenties and unmarried? Surely there's a reason."

"He was married but his wife died more than a year ago."

"Oh," Emma said. "Still, he probably has a passel of kids and he's probably only looking for a woman to ride herd on them."

"I don't think he has any kids," Grace said, "but you can't go lookin' for excuses before you've even met him. You need to open your mind and your heart." Grace stopped again and said, "In fact, let's go meet him right now."

"Now?" Emma asked.

"Yes, right now." Grace took Emma's hand and they reversed course.

"What makes you think he's gonna take an interest in me?" Emma asked, a slight whine in her voice.

"Why wouldn't he?" Grace said. "I'm done with you sellin' yourself short."

They hit the main road and made a right. Grace continued to babble about how much she liked the man and what a perfect pair they'd make, and Emma rolled her eyes. As they began to descend the hill, Grace said, "He's in the next tent."

At this point Emma just wanted to get it over with. As soon as the man found out that Emma had been an Indian captive, he'd bolt for sure. After passing the tent of a sign maker, they stopped in front of the next tent, which housed a single occupant. Grace said, "This is—"

"Hello, Reece," Emma said.

Reece Ford took off his Stetson, smiled, and said, "Hi, Emma. Didn't expect to see you up this way."

Grace looked at Reece then Emma and said, "You two know each other?"

"We do," Reece said. "Emma, there, breeds some of the finest horses in the country."

"How's that stallion workin' out for you?" Emma asked.

Reece waved toward a couple of vacant chairs and said, "Come on in and I'll tell you."

Grace gave Emma's hand a squeeze and said, "I'll leave you two alone."

She turned and headed back up the hill as Emma took off her straw hat and entered the tent, taking a seat on one of the offered camp chairs. Not having seen him in a couple of years, Emma took a moment to study Reece. He had kept himself in good shape, his wide shoulders tapering down to a narrow waist. His sandy brown hair and mustache were neatly trimmed, and Emma had forgotten how handsome he was.

"You know," Reece said, taking a seat on the other chair, "that stallion might have cost me an arm and a leg, but it's been a good investment."

"Are you being selective with the mares you're breedin'?"

"Thanks to you I am. You really opened my eyes to how important the breeding process was."

Reece had been to the ranch several times over the years to buy horses or to learn more about Emma's breeding habits and during those visits they had formed a close bond. She had even visited his place a couple of times, a five-hundred-acre spread just east of downtown Dallas. Remembering what Grace had said, Emma looked at Reece and said, "I'm sorry to hear about Laurie's passing."

"Thank you. I had a rough time with it."

"If you don't mind me asking, how did she die? I don't remember her being ill."

"She wasn't and I guess that's why it was such a shock. You know we were trying to start a family, right?"

Emma nodded and said, "You told me."

"Well, after years of trying, she finally got pregnant and it ended up killing her." Reece paused for a few moments, staring at something in the distance.

Emma had questions, but she waited. It was his story to tell and she'd let him tell it his way.

Finally, Reece wiped his eyes and said, "About five months in things started going sideways and there was nothing the doctors could do. After the burial a little over a year ago, I walked around in a daze for about six months and it still haunts me to this day."

The natural instinct is to offer comfort and Emma reached out and covered his hand with hers. "I know words aren't much of a consolation, but I *am* very sorry for your loss."

"Thank you." Reece looked down at her hand and Emma thought she'd overstepped, but he rolled his hand over and intertwined his fingers with hers.

To Emma it felt natural and they sat for a while, holding hands and watching the people come and go.

Eventually, Reece broke the silence when he looked at her and said, "Still packin' iron, huh?"

Emma smiled and it felt good not having to explain it for once. She'd already had that conversation with Reece on one of his visits to the ranch and he knew the entire story. "Always."

"Still carry the knife, too?"

Emma lifted her left leg and pulled up the hem of her dress with her free hand to show the knife strapped to her ankle.

Reece chuckled and said, "The Indians have been settled on their reservations for years."

Emma smiled and said, "Up in these parts, there's more than Indians to worry about."

They fell into an easy conversation about life in general and the prospects of things to come as they moved around Reece's camp, setting things up for the expected rush of legal work that would arrive on Monday afternoon. Reece had mentioned that two other lawyers had come along with him, but they were off somewhere, and Reece and Emma had the tent to themselves. When

Emma paused to check the time on her pocket watch, she was stunned to see that three hours had elapsed, and only then did she remember she had troubles back at her own camp.

"I should go," Emma said.

"Okay," Reece said. "Will you have Easter dinner with me tomorrow?"

"Can Simon and his friend come if they want to?"

"Absolutely."

"Then I'd love to. What time?"

"Come anytime you want, but we'll eat around, say, oneish?"

"Perfect. See you tomorrow, Reece."

"I'm looking forward to it," Reece said.

Emma turned to leave then turned back and said, "That was kind of awkward, wasn't it?"

"It felt that way to me, too."

Emma took a step forward and said, "I really enjoyed spending the afternoon with you."

"As did I." Reece also took a step forward and they were now only a couple of feet apart. "And it's not like we just met, either."

"That's certainly true," Emma said, her heart hammering in her chest. Although they had spent time together over the years haggling over horses or discussing breeding ideas, this time was much different because both were single after the tragic death of his wife.

"May I kiss you?" Reece asked.

"Please."

The distance between them evaporated when Reece leaned forward and kissed her on the lips.

"That was nice," Emma said, her voice husky with

desire. For the first time in her life she now understood what it felt like to want someone, to be able to actually envision the two of them, their limbs intertwined, his mouth on hers. Her entire body was thrumming, but she knew she needed to take it slow, thoughts of what the Indians had done to her always lurking somewhere deep in her mind. She took a step back and said, "Until tomorrow?"

Reece stood up straight, smiled, and said, "Come early if you want."

Emma was chuckling as she turned and exited the tent.

CHAPTER
48

As the sun rose on Easter morning, the long rays of light stretched across the landscape, slowly revealing the thousands of camps that had sprung up around the three-hundred-mile perimeter of Oklahoma. As people began to stir around, pastors called to their flocks for sunrise services while others filled coffeepots or started fires in preparation for a hearty breakfast. White, black, brown, there were people of all races and from all walks of life and despite their differing ideologies and perceptions, they were all there for the same reason—to stake a claim on their own small piece of paradise.

Some estimated the number of people at fifty thousand though the real number will never be known. But what was clear to everyone present was that there were far more people than available claims, putting the need to be first above all else. One of the very few not worried about such matters was Percy as he pulled his cup from his saddlebag and walked over to the fire.

"Did you sleep at all?" Ruth asked as she dropped biscuits into a Dutch oven at the back of the chuck wagon Reeves had borrowed from one of his rancher buddies.

"Not much, but I ain't never heard of nobody dyin' from a lack of sleep."

"Cranky, too, are we?"

"Maybe a little," Percy said. He poured a cup of coffee and walked over to the wagon.

"How's your arm?" Ruth asked.

"'Bout the same."

"I boiled some water and I'll clean the wound after breakfast."

"Okay. Put on some extra biscuits and a pot of beans for the marshals' dinner."

"Why?"

"'Cause I'm takin' you into Guthrie to have Easter dinner with some of my family."

"That an invitation or an order?"

Percy smiled and said, "Well, it was meant as an invitation. Leander and Bass'll be comin' along."

"I don't have a proper dress for meeting anyone, much less members of your family."

"Leander's family."

"That's different and you know it."

Percy took a sip of coffee and said, "It ain't gonna be nothin' fancy and we ain't fancy people."

"Forget fancy, I simply want to be presentable." She looked down at her dress and said, "This one has holes, rips, and tears not to mention the hem is permanently stained."

"Do you have another one? I'd buy you a new one if there was any stores around here."

"I do, though it's not much better. And you aren't to buy me things. I'm still angry about the horse." She put the lid on the pan and carried it over to the fire, nestling it in among the coals before shoveling a few on top.

When she returned, Percy said, "I'm gettin' the idea you don't wanna go."

"Nothing could be further from the truth." Ruth began slicing some bacon into a pan and said, "I simply don't want your family thinking you're consorting with a tramp." She spread the bacon around so it would cook evenly then looked at Percy and sighed. "Fine, I'll wear the other dress."

"Good." Percy picked up the pan and said, "I'll put the bacon on."

"There's some beans soaking in a pan under the seat. You mind putting those on, too, while I mix up another batch of biscuits?"

"Sure."

"Thank you."

He walked around to the front of the wagon, grabbed the bean pot, and carried it and the pan of bacon over to the fire. Carrying the pan with his wounded arm hurt, but he managed it. Other marshals were now up and milling around, most making a beeline for one of the four coffeepots Ruth had put on. All ten men working out of this camp were ready to call it quits and that included Percy, Leander, and Reeves. Woefully undermanned, their attempts to track down all the Sooners was like trying to carry water in a sieve.

Percy leaned over, stirred the bacon around with his knife, and stood back up. Reeves walked over and said, "She's got you doin' the cookin' now?"

"I offered, asshole," Percy said. "What time you think we ought to head to Guthrie?"

"After breakfast, I reckon."

Leander meandered over, an empty cup in his hand. He leaned over and filled it with coffee and stood back up. He took a sip and said, "You get a kiss for givin' her the horse?"

Percy looked at both men and frowned. "You two're so funny you ought to start a road show." He stirred the bacon around again and said, "Are we comin' back here?"

"We ain't doin' nothin' but chasin' our tails out here. Supposed to be some army troops comin' up this way in the mornin'," Reeves said.

"So that's a no? We ain't comin' back?" Leander asked. When Reeves didn't immediately answer, Leander said, "You worried the marshal overseein' this here hullabaloo is gonna take exception?"

"It ain't that," Reeves said. "If we're leavin', we all gotta leave and I'm not sure what the other fellers is thinkin'."

"Why's that?" Percy asked.

"Chuck wagon goes with me," Reeves said.

"Why, hell," Percy said, "they're all right around here, let's ask 'em." He turned and shouted, "Listen up!" and the other men turned to look at him. "If you're for quittin' this place, raise your hand."

Seven hands reached for the sky and Percy looked at Reeves and said, "There's your answer."

"If we're bustin' camp," Reeves said, "what're you gonna do with your woman?"

"First of all, she ain't my woman, but for your information, Mr. Nosy, she's goin' with us."

"You done asked her?" Reeves asked.

"That ain't none of your business."

Reeves and Leander shared a look and began laughing.

"Ha, ha, ha," Percy said.

"Hell, Percy," Leander said, "me and Bass is hopin' it works out tween you two. You ought to have a woman to boss you around some. It builds character, don't it, Bass?"

"It surely does," Reeves said, nodding his head. "What is it people say?" Reeves paused for dramatic effect then said, "I remember now—'It'll give your life some structure.'"

Leander and Reeves laughed again and Percy scowled and said, "Maybe you two could mix in a little marital advice when you hit the road with your comedy show. Watch the bacon." He turned around and walked back to the wagon.

"You hear all that?" he asked Ruth.

"I heard," Ruth said. "I guess that's the end of my cooking career."

"Gonna miss it?"

"Not for a second."

After breakfast, Ruth put the marshals to work washing the dishes and called Percy over to clean his wound.

"It's healing nicely," Ruth said after removing the bandage. She dipped a clean rag into the water she had boiled and gently cleaned the wound and the area around it. Using a clean strip of cotton fabric, she rewrapped the wound and tied off the ends. "Do we have an approximate departure time?"

Percy pulled out his pocket watch and popped the lid to check the time. "It's eight-thirty now and"—he paused to look around the camp to see how much stuff needed to be packed up before continuing—"I bet we're out of here by nine-thirty or ten. Why?"

She opened a drawer at the back of the chuck wagon and pulled out a bar of soap and said, "I'm going down to the river to freshen up."

"Want some company?" Percy asked.

Ruth thought about it a moment and said, "Uh . . . well . . . I was actually going to bathe."

"What if I promise to close my eyes when you get in and get out?"

"Can I trust you?"

"Sure, you can."

"No fooling around while we're there?"

Percy lifted his left arm and said, "You're the one that told me I couldn't get in the water."

Ruth walked around the wagon to grab a clean towel and said, "Come along, then."

Percy hurried over to where his things were, strapped on his gun belt, and caught up to Ruth.

Ruth looked down at his gun and said, "Are you expecting trouble?"

"I done been shot once since I been up here. I ain't takin' no chances."

"You any good with that thing?"

"Fair to middlin'," Percy said, downplaying the fact that he'd sent a good number of men to their graves.

When they reached the river, Percy found a spot in the shade overlooking the water and sat down. He hadn't been there very long when Ruth shouted, "Are your eyes closed?"

Percy angled his hat down to cover his eyes and shouted, "Yes."

He heard splashing and he was sorely tempted to take a look, but he kept his promise.

"You can open them," Ruth said.

He pushed his hat up and saw that she was submerged up to her neck about twenty yards away, close enough that they could talk without shouting. "How's the water?"

"A little chillier than I would like, but my body's adjusting to it."

"You figure out where you're gonna stake your claim?"

"Well, I would have if you hadn't caught me. I didn't have much time to look around before you came along."

"I think you'd want a place a little closer to where the town's gonna be. Make it easier to get on the train, too."

"I'm not worried about the train. Where am I going to go?" She lathered her hands up with the soap and scrubbed her hair.

Curious, Percy said, "Where are you puttin' the soap so it don't sink to the bottom?"

"Between my legs."

"Oh," Percy said.

They talked a bit about the type of land she was looking for and what she wanted to do with it. And the conversation branched off from there with no awkward pauses or dead spots. There were periods of quiet, but they felt natural and neither rushed to fill the silence. After a while, Percy said, "Are you gonna stay in there all—"

The words died in his throat when he whipped his pistol out, cocked it on the way up, and fired, the gunshot echoing across the river bottom.

Ruth looked down at the dead snake brushing against her leg and screamed. Her modesty instantly disappeared as she began swimming, her arms pinwheeling through the water.

Percy scrambled to his feet and hurried down to the shore, hoping the bullet hadn't nicked her. It had been close, that was for damn sure, but he was almost certain her reaction was out of fear and not due to injury. He slipped his wounded arm out of the sling and picked up the towel and unfurled it. When her feet touched the ground, Ruth came lunging out of the water straight into his arms.

He did his best to wrap the towel around her and then held her tight until the shivering subsided.

"Why . . . why didn't you tell me?" Ruth asked.

"Let's sit down for a minute."

She nodded and he guided her over to a large piece of driftwood and they both sat down.

"There wasn't time. He must have been sunnin' on a nearby log or somethin', 'cause I didn't see him until he was almost on you."

"Was it a cottonmouth?"

"Yep. Probably the biggest one I ever seen."

Ruth shuddered and said, "How could you tell?"

"You doubtin' my snake-identification abilities?"

"No, but it all happened very quickly."

"You can tell by the shape of their heads and cottonmouths are heavy-bodied snakes, much thicker through the middle than most water snakes." Percy chuckled and said, "I didn't know you could move that fast."

"People always say when you find one snake there'll be others nearby and that was all I could think about. I dropped the soap, too."

"I bet you did."

With her front half covered by the towel, her back half was exposed, and he couldn't refrain from stealing an occasional look.

"You lied to me," Ruth said.

"How so?"

"Only an expert shooter could make that shot, that quickly."

Percy shrugged. "I've fired a few rounds."

Ruth surprised him when she leaned forward and kissed him on the lips.

"Thank you," Ruth said. "Now close your eyes so I can put my dress back on."

"Sure you don't want to fool around a little?"

Ruth laughed and said, "I can't have you thinking I'm a pushover." Then she turned serious and said, "True intimacy requires trust and trust is earned through continuing interactions with one another over time. That's not to say we both don't have urges or needs or wants, but I want something more for us, if there is an us, than a simple roll in the hay. Does that make sense to you?"

This time it was Percy who leaned in for a kiss and, as he drew back slowly, he said, "It does."

"Good. Now close your eyes."

Percy pulled his hat down over his eyes, but this time he peeked, and he liked what he saw very much.

CHAPTER
49

Back in Guthrie, Emma was trying to decide what time to call on Reece Ford. Although she didn't want to appear too eager, she also didn't want to wait too long, possibly sending a message that she wasn't all that interested when that was the furthest thing from the truth. That single kiss had ignited something deep inside of her, sparking thoughts and feelings she'd thought were dead forever. Under the guise of wanting to help him prepare dinner, she decided she would depart at ten-thirty a.m. for the short walk to his tent.

Simon and Ann had declined the invitation to attend and were going to hang around camp, which she knew could mean anything. She had asked Grace to keep an eye on them, but in the end, there really wasn't much either of them could do to keep the couple from another romp in the river. Emma was just hoping Simon would show some restraint. Ann getting pregnant would not only have an effect on her and Simon, it would also have an impact on Emma's relationship with Quanah. How would he react to the news if it did happen? It was something she didn't want to find out.

What she needed to do was find Simon some rubbers. Grace had said they were hard to find and that got her to thinking. With hundreds of men in and around Guthrie and thousands more arriving tomorrow, might some of them have a rubber or two stashed in their saddlebags? *C'mon, Emma, are you going to walk around asking strangers if they have any rubbers you could buy?* Well, no, Emma thought. But what if the men who came up with Reece had a couple stashed somewhere? She hadn't met them yet and didn't know their marital status, but if they were single and thought they might be here awhile how strange would it be to pack some rubbers just in case? Or, Emma thought, Reece was single—might he have a couple hidden somewhere?

If she asked him and he admitted to having some what would that say about him? Ready to bed the next woman who looked his way? It didn't sound like the Reece she knew, but how well did she really know him? If a man was accustomed to having certain things, could he go for more than a year without a dip in the river, so to speak?

Stop it, Emma!

She took a deep breath. Those were waters she definitely didn't want to wade into. Asking a man on the first date if he had any rubbers would likely kill any hopes for a second one even if he believed she was asking for her son. She'd just have to hope Simon would be thinking with his big head and not the smaller one in his pants.

She pulled her watch from her skirt pocket and saw that it was time to go. After another debate if it was too early or not, she quickly decided it wasn't. She was tired of worrying about Simon and rubbers and what Quanah might think about something that hadn't even happened. She turned her focus to Reece as she pushed to her feet, smoothed down her skirt, and picked up the basket of fresh bread she had baked this morning. After telling Simon she'd be back later, she exited the tent and made her way downhill toward Reece's tent, hoping the two men who had come with him were elsewhere.

When she arrived at his tent, she saw that he was alone and that quickened her pulse a bit. Reece was reading a book and when her shadow fell across the page, he looked up and smiled. After dog-earing the page, he stood to greet her. It was another of those awkward moments with neither knowing whether to hug or shake hands, so Emma broke the impasse when she stepped in for a brief hug. She stepped back and said, "How long have we known each other?"

"Seven, maybe eight years."

"Long enough that we shouldn't be uncomfortable giving each other a hug?"

"I suppose," Reece said.

"Then why were we both stiff as a board just now?"

Reece shrugged and said, "Probably a mixture of embarrassment and uncertainty."

"I agree, so let's fix it."

"Get straight to it, huh?"

"Don't you think that's best?"

"May I take your basket first?" Reece asked, a sheepish grin on his face.

Emma had forgotten she was even holding it. She handed it to him and said, "Please." Reece was wearing another three-piece suit, this one a gray tweed, with a pleated white shirt and a royal blue paisley bow tie.

He took the basket and set it on the makeshift desk he had built. "Smells good. What is it?"

"Fresh sourdough bread."

"My favorite." When he turned around, he paused, looking Emma up and down. "No pistol?"

"Nope, and I feel naked without it."

"Well, I'm honored that you trusted me enough to leave your shooting iron back at camp."

"Don't worry," Emma said, lifting the hem of her skirt, "if you get too rowdy, I've still got my knife."

"Duly warned."

They both laughed and when the laughter died down, Reece said, "Would you like to sit before we begin dissecting the reasons for our awkwardness?"

Emma chuckled and said, "I would." She walked over to one of the folding camp chairs and sat.

Reece pulled his chair around, so they'd be facing each other, and sat. He studied her for a moment without saying anything and Emma began to prepare herself for bad news.

Uncomfortable with the scrutiny, she said, "Do I have something on my face?"

"No. I'm trying to recall if I've ever seen you with your hair down."

She slowly released the breath she had been holding and said, "Do you like it down?"

"Very much. It's a beautiful shade of red, reminiscent of a maple leaf at the peak of autumn."

"Thank you. It's not without costs, though. I'm sentenced to a lifetime of sunburns."

Reece laughed then said, "Do you have the fiery temper that allegedly comes along with it?"

"The only way you'll know that is to make me angry, something you should probably avoid, for now." Emma laughed, enjoying the back-and-forth.

"I'll file that away for future reference. Would you like a cup of coffee?"

"Please," Emma said.

Reece stood and said, "Sugar?"

"Yes, please. Would you like for me to get it?"

"Nope." He disappeared through the curtain that screened off the sleeping area and retuned a few moments later with two steaming cups of coffee. He handed one to Emma and returned to his seat.

Emma blew on her coffee and took a tiny sip and said, "Where are the men that came with you?"

"They're camped down on Cottonwood Creek with their families. Since it's just me, I offered to stay up here to keep an eye on things."

They sat in silence for a few moments, sipping their coffee before Emma said, "Okay, let's talk about embarrassment and uncertainty. Do you regret kissing me?"

"Not for a second," Reece said. "My only regret is that I didn't do it sooner."

"What do you mean by that?"

"You want to hear a secret?"

"I don't know, do I?"

"I hope so because I'm going to tell it anyway. I've been sweet on you since the first time I met you. When I got my mind clear after Laurie's death, the first thing I should have done was hop on a train and make a beeline to your place."

"Why didn't you?" Emma asked.

Reece looked off into the distance for a few moments, drinking his coffee and thinking. He eventually turned to look at Emma and said, "Fear of rejection, mainly. Another part of it was, knowing your history, I didn't want you to think I was pressuring you."

"So, you were waiting and hoping we'd bump into each other somewhere along the way?"

Reece set his coffee cup on the ground and leaned forward in his chair. "No, not exactly. At one point I had made up my mind I was going to pay you a visit, but then I took on a client who wanted to file for a divorce right around that same time. That case turned nasty, really nasty, to the point that the two litigants refused to be in the same room together and, worse, it dragged on for months. Being involved in all of that soured me on relationships for a spell. Does that make sense?"

"It does," Emma said. "And now?"

Reece leaned back in his chair and mulled the question over for a few moments. "To tell you the truth, I'm still a little gun-shy. I wouldn't want to try to start a relationship with someone I just met, but with you, it's different. We've always gotten along really well."

"That we have. You mentioned my history. That doesn't scare you off?"

"No, not at all." He leaned forward again, this time reaching out to take Emma's hand. "You were a victim, Emma. And it makes me angry when victims are stigmatized for the crimes of their perpetrators. You're a beautiful, caring, intelligent woman and if anyone deserves happiness, it's you."

"Thank you for that. So, what do we call this, courting?"

"If you want to," Reece said. "It's more than that for me. I know there are things that'll have to be worked out, but I'd stand beside you and say *I do* right here and right now." Reece smiled and squeezed her hand. "At least you know where I stand."

"Yes, you made that quite clear. So, how would it work with both of us living in separate places?"

"I'm willing to do whatever it takes to make it work. Either you move to Dallas or I sell the cattle and lease my place out and move in with you. I'd like to keep the horses if you'll let me turn them out on your land."

"Of course. What about your law practice?"

"I'll partner with Seth. We've talked about it before and with the train, I can travel to Dallas if I need to and still be back the same day."

Emma took a final sip of now-lukewarm coffee and poured out the dregs. "I do have to consider Simon's needs."

"Of course you do. He's a brilliant young man with a bright future and I'll support him any way I can."

"How long have you been thinkin' about all of this?"

"I've thought of nothing else since the moment I saw you yesterday."

Emma chuckled and said, "Did you sleep last night?"

"Not much. Seeing you, holding your hand, and even that single kiss made me feel alive for the first time in a long time. This is going to sound corny, but every time I'm around you, there's a current of something, I don't know exactly what, pulsing through my veins." He paused to take a breath then said, "Am I coming on too strong?"

"No, I felt it, too. For me it's like a low hum and I

didn't know what it was at first because I'd never felt it before. Whatever it is, my heart was racing like a Thoroughbred yesterday when you leaned in to kiss me."

Reece nodded and smiled. "Mine, too." He picked up his cup and took a sip then said, "Have you ever considered moving away from the ranch?"

"Having second thoughts?"

"No, not at all, but I have to admit that cutting the electrical umbilical cord will be somewhat difficult. Any talk around Wichita Falls about putting in a power plant?"

"I've heard some rumblings," Emma said, "but I don't see it happening anytime soon. Too expensive. I've used electric lights in some of the hotels I've stayed in and it's convenient, but does it really make that much of a difference?"

"Oh, it's life-changing, Emma, and we're still in the early stages of development. You flip a switch and the light comes on and you don't have to deal with the smoke and soot from a gas lantern. I even have an electric fan I can turn on at night to cool the bedroom down. It cost me a small fortune, but like the stallion you sold me, it was well worth the money. And they're inventing new devices seemingly every day, so who knows what's on the horizon?"

"Sounds like you're on the verge of talking yourself out of moving to the ranch, if we get that far."

"No, I said I'd do whatever it takes and as for getting that far, I'm already there, Emma."

"How can you be so certain?"

"Because I know the type of person you are."

It was all moving a little too fast for Emma. She pulled

her hand free and leaned back in her chair. Her last and only brief relationship had been years ago and though she had butterflies in her stomach every time she looked at Reece, she knew a twining of their lives would be much more complicated than he was suggesting. She had worked hard to establish herself as a respected horse breeder and if he balked at moving to the ranch, she'd be forced to downsize significantly if she chose to move to his place. Although five hundred acres sounded like a good amount of land, it was minuscule when compared to the sixty-four thousand acres under fence at the Rocking R Ranch. And, of course, there was Simon. Although he would be headed east to college in the fall, Emma wanted him to be able to come home to the only house he'd ever known.

"You're awfully quiet," Reece said.

She looked at Reece and smiled. "There's a lot to think about."

"Are you feeling stressed?"

"Maybe," Emma said.

He held up his hands and said, "No pressure. Let's just see how this thing plays out. Deal?"

"Deal," Emma said.

"You hungry?"

"Starving."

"Let's eat."

While they dined on ham, scalloped potatoes, baked beans, and Emma's fresh bread, they discussed the next day's Land Run and how that might play out, steering clear of any more talk about their budding relationship. And much like yesterday afternoon, the conversation was easy with much laughter involved, Reece describing some of the unusual cases he had handled and Emma telling him some of the fiascos she'd encountered on her search for suitable horses.

After eating, Emma insisted on doing the dishes and when she finished, they decided to take a walk down to Cottonwood Creek. The tent city was alive with activity, the afternoon weather perfect with a slight southerly breeze. Out on the flats near the railroad tracks, a horse race was under way and closer in, several people were tossing baseballs about, the smack of leather loud in the clear air. Everyone was whiling away the afternoon, waiting for the clock to strike high noon tomorrow.

When they arrived at the creek, they saw that several people were swimming, so they turned south and walked through the trees, looking for some privacy. They found a small rise overlooking a bend in the creek and decided that was the spot. Emma tucked her skirt down and lowered herself to the ground, using the trunk of a giant cottonwood for a backrest. Reece took off his suit coat, gently folded it in half, and laid it on the grass then topped it off with his Stetson, before sitting down next to Emma. He reached out and took Emma's hand and they sat and watched the current for a few minutes in silence.

Overcome by a sudden wave of emotions, Emma's eyes watered up and tears began spilling down her cheeks. It took Reece a few moments to notice and when he did, he wrapped his arm around her and pulled her onto his lap and held her while she wept.

When the tears began to taper off, Reece thumbed the moisture from her cheeks and said in a soft voice, "Want to talk about it?"

"I . . . I didn't . . . think this would . . . be possible . . . for . . . for someone like me."

Reece tilted his head down and looked into her eyes. "You mean the fact that you're beautiful, intelligent, caring, considerate, generous, kind, and did I mention beautiful?" he said, emphasizing each word with a soft kiss on her lips.

"You know . . . what I mean," Emma said, wiping her eyes. "I'm damaged . . . goods."

"Nonsense," Reece said. "You're a survivor who has built walls around herself, terrified to let anyone inside. But I'm right here, Emma, and I'm not going anywhere. I'll dismantle your walls brick by brick if I have to because that's how much I care for you."

For Emma, it was like a dam broke. To be in the arms of a loving man, someone who wouldn't hurt her and someone who chose to be there even knowing she'd been mistreated by the Indians ignited something deep inside of her. The years of hurt and despair melted away and she was left staring at the face of the man she wanted to spend the rest of her life with. She turned, straddled him, and wrapped her arms around his neck, pulling his lips to hers. Now, consumed by a hunger she'd never experienced before, she wanted all of him.

From there things progressed rapidly, and when it was over, they lay side by side, each staring into the other's eyes. "That was nice," Reece said, his voice still thick with emotion.

"It was better than that," Emma said, her mind a tumbling mass of emotions. She didn't feel dirty like she had all the times before and for the first time she had given herself willingly and with her eyes wide open, far different from every other time when she'd closed her eyes and prayed for the Indians to finish. She rolled onto her back, a smile on her face.

Reece scooted closer, snuggling up against her and draping an arm across her midsection. "Are you okay?" Reece asked softly.

There was a lot packed into that simple question and both knew it. Emma turned her head to look at him and said, "What you said earlier about saying *I do*, was that an actual proposal?"

Reece chuckled and said, "To clear up any confusion, Emma Turner, will you marry me?"

Emma rolled back onto her side and kissed him gently on the lips. She pulled back, locked eyes with Reece, and said, "I will."

CHAPTER
50

Although Sunday was a holiday, there were no cele-brations planned for Pearl O'Sullivan or Levi Johnson or for the thousands of others making the northward trek to the promised land. As they trudged onward, there were some real concerns they wouldn't arrive in time for the high noon start on Monday. For those who had the means, catching a train from Wynnewood to Purcell, the final destination, was an option and there were a fair number of wagons waiting to be loaded onto the next train. It was not, however, an option for Levi and Pearl. They might have been able to scrounge up the money for passenger fares for the five of them, but there was no way they could do that and pay the freight fees for the wagon and horses. So, they continued on, trying to set a pace that would get them there without killing the horses.

According to the map they had they had a little over twenty-five miles to go. On an average day, a wagon and a team of two horses could easily cover eighteen to twenty miles, but they'd done thirty-plus miles the last two days and both man and beast were tired. The one good thing was that the Arbuckle Mountains were behind them and the traveling was now much easier.

However, that wasn't necessarily true for Pearl's backside. Having never ridden more than a few blocks in a wagon back in Chicago, the day-after-day travel in Levi's unforgiving schooner had rubbed a blister on her left butt cheek. When combined with the continuing soreness of her private parts from their lovemaking two days ago, Pearl could not get comfortable. Even the saddle blanket she was sitting on offered little relief from the potholes or the other obstacles Levi seemed to hit with growing frequency. What she really wanted was a long soak in a hot bath, but she had neither a tub nor the time, so she'd have to grin and bear it.

Looking ahead through the dust, Pearl saw another river ahead and the sudden infusion of fear pushed the pain from her mind. She absolutely hated river crossings. Not only were they treacherous, but by the time it came their turn to cross, the trail would be so deeply rutted it was almost impassable. She looked at Levi and said, "Another river comin' up."

"I seen it," Levi said. He shifted the reins to his left hand and pulled out the map he was sitting on. After studying it a moment, he said, "It's the Washita."

"Knowing the name ain't gonna make it any easier to cross."

Still studying the map, Levi said, "I expect not, but the good news is this'll be the last big river before we make camp."

Pearl leaned over to look at the map and pointed to

another river north of the Washita and said, "What about that one?"

Levi looked up and smiled. "That's the Canadian, the southern boundary of Oklahoma. We'll have to take the wagon across eventually, but hopefully we'll be doin' it as new claim holders."

"I like the sound of that," Pearl said. "Do you know where you're gonna stake a claim?"

Using his finger, Levi traced the railroad tracks that were displayed on the map. "I'm thinking somewhere around here," he said, stopping his finger on a train stop called Norman. "Neither of the horses is real fast so I'll just have to see how it goes. We'll set up camp somewhere around here," he said, pointing to a spot on the river north of Purcell that was only about five miles from Norman. "I'm thinkin' somewhere near the Canadian, but far enough away that we won't have to worry about floods. What do you think?"

"I'd like it if you could find a high spot, so we'd have a view of the river."

Levi tucked the map under his leg to keep it from blowing away and said, "Don't know if there's any high ground around, but I'll look."

As they drew closer to the Washita, the wagons at the front began to fan out, searching for the best places to cross. Levi knew the wait would eat into their schedule, but river fording was risky business on the best of days. As the wagon driver, he had to worry about the current, the possibilities of hitting a sinkhole, and the dreaded quicksand that seemed to be as common as flies in this part of the country.

Normally all the wagons crossed at one spot, but time

was of the essence and that meant multiple fording spots were needed. And it wasn't long before several gunshots rang out, signaling those spots had been found. Usually it was a thoughtful and determined process, but today's rapidity added to Pearl's fear, knowing that one man's opinion of what was suitable usually didn't match up with hers. Despite what Pearl thought, the wagons began to roll out and lines began to form, and Levi put the team in motion, falling in behind the wagon in front of them.

As they waited, Levi began getting antsy, grumbling about maybe finding his own spot to cross. But Pearl nipped that in the bud right quick.

"We'll travel all night if we have to," Pearl said. "You try to go out on your own and get the wagon stuck we're done for."

"I know that," Levi said, "but I was hopin' we'd get there early enough to do some scoutin' around. I'd like to get a feel for the lay of the land, so I don't go chargin' off without a clue where I'm goin'."

"Like I said, we can travel all night. I'll drive the wagon and you can sleep."

Levi looked at Pearl and said, "Ever drive a wagon?"

"No, but I'm a quick learner. And it sure beats drownin' in some godforsaken river."

Levi looked at Pearl and said, "You can't swim, can you?"

"I grew up in Chicago. Where was I gonna learn to swim?"

"If I remember my geography, ain't Chicago right there on one of them big lakes?"

"It is, but you'd be a fool to swim in it. What's the first thing that pops into your mind when you hear Chicago?"

Levi shrugged. "I ain't never been there but I heard somewhere it was the meat-packin' capital of the world."

"That's what they say," Pearl said, "though I don't know why anybody would be proud of that. Now, just imagine them slaughtering thousands of animals every day. Where do you think all the blood and the guts and all the other stuff they didn't use ended up?"

"In the lake?"

"Exactly. Now imagine how that smelled."

"Awful, huh?" Levi said.

"Beyond awful. So, that's why I never learned to swim."

"I ain't gonna let you drown."

"The kids come first and I ain't gonna be able to help you." Pearl paused then said, "I don't even like talking about this stuff." She turned to look in the back and said, "The kids are awful quiet."

"They been dozin' on and off all mornin'," Levi said. "I don't think any of us slept too good last night." Levi looked at Pearl and said, "You tossed and turned all night. Havin' second thoughts?"

"No, just couldn't get comfortable." Pearl hadn't told him about the big blister on her butt because she didn't want him thinking she was a greenhorn, though that's exactly what she was. "Are you havin' second thoughts?"

"No, ma'am. Soon as we get a claim staked, we'll find us a preacher and get married. That work for you?"

Although it wouldn't be the wedding she'd dreamed of as a girl, if she had to say *I do* then turn around and cook supper, so be it. "Sounds perfect."

When they finally reached the river crossing, Pearl discovered all of her worry was for naught. The water wasn't more than two feet deep and they crossed easily.

After working their way around a stand of timber, they broke into the clear again.

The terrain was relatively flat, and they made good time, arriving at Purcell a little before five o'clock in the afternoon. After stopping at a local merchant's to pick up a plat map of the land to be given away, Levi and Pearl pushed on, both breathing a little easier knowing they were within striking distance of Oklahoma.

CHAPTER
51

Percy, Ruth, and the rest of the crew rolled into Guthrie a little before noon, all hungry for Easter dinner. As the other marshals peeled off to go their own way, Reeves steered the borrowed chuck wagon down the main road, cursing as he worked the reins, trying to avoid the haphazardly arranged tents and the throngs of people. If it was this crowded now, Percy thought, what was it going to look like tomorrow afternoon?

Those who had erected the tents hadn't given much thought to local traffic and Percy could tell Reeves was getting madder by the second, so he pointed to a patch of open ground and said, "Park it there."

"They'll steal the supplies," Reeves said.

"Then I'll pay to restock it," Percy said. "You ain't gettin' no closer in that thing."

Reeves nodded and turned the wagon. After setting the brake, he grabbed his rifle from under the seat and climbed down. Reeves looked at Percy and said, "What happens if they steal the whole damn thing?"

Percy mulled that over for a moment then said, "Maybe we ought to unhitch the team. We can turn 'em out with our horses down by the creek."

Leander and Percy climbed down to help and once they had the horses unhitched, Reeves untied his stallion from the back and mounted up. They found a nice shady spot down by the creek and they pulled their rifles and loosened the saddles before turning the horses out. They walked back up the hill and finally found Seth's tent again.

When they entered, Percy stopped short when he saw his mother sitting inside. "What are you doin' up here, Ma?" Percy asked.

"I was bored at home. Took the train up this morning."

"They give you any trouble about gettin' off here?" Percy asked.

"Tried to until I set 'em straight."

Percy chuckled and said, "They were probably glad to see you go."

"I expect they were," Frances said. "What happened to your arm?"

"Long story, Ma, but the short version is I got shot," Percy said.

"I swear, Percy. Aren't you gettin' a little long in the tooth to be goin' around lookin' for trouble?"

"I wasn't lookin' for nothin', but trouble has a way of findin' me, I reckon."

Percy would have preferred to wait and see how things played out with Ruth before introducing her to his mother, but that was out the window now. "Ma," he said, putting a hand on Ruth's shoulder, "this is Ruth Taylor. Ruth, this here's my mother, Frances Ridgeway."

Percy saw his mother give Ruth a quick once-over before she smiled and stuck out her hand. "Nice to meet you, Ruth."

Percy was old enough not to care what anyone thought, but he did breathe a sigh of relief when the two women shook hands and chatted for a few moments. From there it was on to Chauncey and Marcie and then the rest of the group.

Percy looked around and said, "Where's Emma?" Since finding Emma in an abandoned Indian camp where she had been held captive for over a year, he and his niece had formed a close relationship.

Grace smiled and said, "She's on a date."

Percy reared back in surprise. "Do what?"

Grace chuckled and said, "I know it's a shock, but it's true."

Percy looked at Simon and said, "You know about this?"

Simon smiled and said, "I did and I'm happy for her."

"Me, too," Percy said. "They broke the mold after they made your ma and I'm tickled pink to hear she's finally opened up a little." Percy looked at Grace and said, "Who's the lucky fella?"

"Reece Ford. He's been to the—"

"I remember him," Percy said, interrupting. "I thought he was married."

"His wife died over a year ago," Grace said.

"I'll be damned," Percy said. He looked at Leander and said, "You remember Reece?"

"I do," Leander said. "He's a good man and he'll do right by Emma."

"I expect he will," Percy said, "and if he don't, I'll have a chat with him."

"You hush, now," Frances said, waving a finger at him. "That girl can take care of herself. She doesn't need her uncle gettin' involved, period."

Percy smiled and said, "And the same goes for you, Ma."

"I have no intention of gettin' involved," Frances said.

"That's what you always say," Percy said, "but most of the time you wind up right smack in the middle of it."

"You just mind your own business and let me worry about mine," Frances said.

Percy chuckled and said, "Deal." He had been so focused on Emma that he almost forgot about Ruth. He stepped over close to her and said, "Ruth, here, is stakin' a claim tomorrow."

Expecting a few questions for Ruth, Percy was bowled over when Marcie said, "So are we."

"Who's 'we'?" Percy asked.

"Me, Grace, and Emma."

Percy studied his daughter-in-law for a long moment and said, "You got somethin' you need to tell me?"

"It ain't like that," Marcie said. "Me and Chauncey are just fine."

"What, then?" Percy said, a tinge of heat in his voice. "You done got sixty-four thousand acres. What are you gonna do with them piddlin' parcels they's givin' away?"

When she heard the number, Ruth's knees almost buckled. She stepped over close to Reeves and said, "He told me he was a cowpuncher."

Reeves chuckled and said, "I reckon he is. Only thing

different is he's got a lot more cows to punch than most people."

"Lordy," Ruth said. "He didn't say a word about it."

"I don't expect he would. Percy ain't like that." Reeves paused for a moment and then said, "I don't know what's goin' on tween you two, but you ain't gonna find a better man than Percy, there."

"That much, I already knew," Ruth said. She and Reeves turned back to the ongoing argument between Percy and Marcie.

"I don't expect you to understand, Percy," Marcie said. "You grew up knowin' that everything for as far as you could see belonged to you and your family."

"It's yours now, too," Percy said.

"And we'll live there until they bury me and Chauncey in the family cemetery," Marcie said. "Think of it another way. Let's call it an investment."

"Why does it matter?" Frances asked. "Let 'em stake a claim."

Ignoring his mother, Percy thought about what Marcie had said. "I reckon the investment idea makes some sense."

Eager to move on now that she'd won a concession, Marcie looked at Ruth and said, "Why don't you stake a claim next to us?"

"Do you have a location picked out?" Ruth asked.

"We do," Marcie said. "After dinner we'll ride out for a look."

"Sounds good," Ruth said.

Percy had a few reservations about that, having known Ruth for only a few days. If they all staked their claims in the same area, they would forever be intertwined. However, he also realized he didn't lack for resources and if things got squirrely between him and Ruth, he could always buy her out.

Percy turned to look at Chauncey. There was something different about him, and Percy couldn't quite figure out what it was. Then he did. He walked over and said, "You ain't wearin' your guns?" Percy couldn't remember the last time he'd seen his son out and about without his two-gun rig wrapped around his waist.

"They're handy like always, but it looks like we're gonna be sittin' around for most of the day. It's a little more comfortable without 'em."

"Seen any of the Keating men around?"

"Ain't looked. 'Sides, I don't know what any of 'em look like, but I reckon they can find me if they're of a mind to."

Percy looked around to make sure Marcie was out of earshot then turned back to Chauncey and said, "You on board with the claim stakin'?"

Chauncey shrugged. "Ain't that big a deal to me. Like you said, can't do much with it."

"So, everything's good tween you two?"

"Far as I know."

"Good to hear," Percy said.

It wasn't long before the women brought out the food. Percy looked over the offerings, his empty plate in his hand. There was ham, fried chicken, fried potatoes, mashed potatoes, fresh bread, and, of course, the requisite pot of pinto beans. But what caught Percy's eye were the four pies that were set off to the side. Two were cherry, the other two apple and Percy thought that was going to be a hard decision to make. He filled his plate and, as with most gatherings, the men congregated in one area, the women and children in another.

Only later would they realize how lucky they'd been it had worked out that way.

Moseying over to where the men were, Percy took a seat next to Reeves.

Reeves looked at Percy's plate and said, "Put some sideboards on that thing and you might could load on some more food."

"Funny," Percy said. "You might not pile up your plate, but I've noticed you go back two or three times. This saves me the trouble."

Reeves chuckled and said, "I reckon the secret's out." He forked a piece of ham into his mouth and chewed.

Percy, chewing on a piece of ham, looked at Seth and said, "You got a handle on how it's all gonna work tomorrow?"

Seth swallowed the food in his mouth and said, "I don't think anyone has a handle on it and that includes the government officials that're in charge of it."

"That bad, huh?" Percy asked.

"My only advice is to make sure your guns are well oiled," Seth said.

"Why do you say that?" Leander asked.

"The probabilities of multiple people claiming the same parcel are high," Seth said, "and there's no system in place to quickly validate who the legal owner might be."

"Oh boy," Percy said, giving Reeves the stink eye. "How are they goin' to decide, then?"

"The land office will eventually hold hearings with

sworn testimony to determine the legal owner, but that's probably months down the road. And when you factor in the lengthy appellate process, some of the disputed claims will take years to settle."

"Can't the army do somethin'?" Reeves asked.

"I asked the same question," Seth said, "and was told they weren't authorized. You three best be on your toes tomorrow."

"Can't wait," Percy mumbled. Looking across the tent, he saw his mother and Ruth sitting together, both chatting away. He could already hear the questions his mother would be asking him as soon as she got him alone and he made a mental note to make himself scarce as soon as the shindig was over.

After everyone had finished eating their dinners, the pies were cut up and the pieces passed out. Percy had requested a little bit of both, and he was trying to decide which to eat first when a rifle shot rang out and the left front leg of Reeves's stool shattered. Percy dumped his plate, pulled his gun, and shouted, "Everybody down," before diving to the ground. It had all happened so fast that he ended up landing on his bad arm. The jolt of pain that shot through his body was so intense he broke out in a cold sweat. After taking a couple of deep breaths, he refocused his mind on the situation at hand. He looked at Reeves and said, "See where it come from?"

"Hell, no," Reeves said, "I was tryin' to eat my damn pie."

"Ma," Percy shouted, "gather everyone up and y'all crawl out the back."

"We're movin'," Frances said.

"Leander, you and Chauncey see anything?" Percy asked.

"Nothin'," Leander said.

Percy turned to look at his son and wasn't at all surprised to see his pistol in his hand. "Chauncey?"

"Nope," Chauncey said, "but there ain't many places they could be shootin' from."

"Bass," Percy said, "take a look at the chair and see if you can calculate the angle of the bullet."

Before Reeves could move, someone shouted, "Reeves, come on out. We ain't got no interest in the others."

Reeves looked at Percy and said, "Any idea where that come from?"

Percy shook his head and said, "Hard to say."

Ignoring their demands, Reeves reached out and grabbed the chair and pulled it close. The leg was busted to pieces and there was no way to find the bullet's initial entry point.

Percy looked at Leander and said, "He said 'we.' How many you reckon?"

"Don't matter, does it?" Leander asked.

"I expect it don't," Percy said.

A few moments later, Reeves said, "They gotta be shootin' from up high somewhere."

"We're sittin' on the highest piece of ground in three counties," Percy said.

"I reckon the only place they could be is on top of the land office."

"You can't even see it from here," Percy said.

"You can if you get closer to the front of the tent where I was sittin'," Reeves said. To prove his point, he crawled forward about six feet and a bullet plowed up the dirt a foot in front of him. He scooted back and said, "They gotta be on the roof."

"Reckon they'll shoot now if they can't see us?" Leander asked.

"Don't know," Reeves said, "but I wouldn't get up and go to cuttin' a rug iffen I was you."

"How do you wanna play it?" Percy asked.

"We gotta get closer," Reeves said.

"How?" Percy asked. "They for sure know what you look like."

"They think they do," Reeves said. "Let's crawl to the back so we can move around a little."

When they reached the back wall of the tent, all four men scrambled to their feet.

"Why don't you let us handle it?" Percy asked.

"Me, you, and Leander," Reeves said, "been ridin' together for days. Good chance they know what you look like, too."

Reeves, a master of disguise, set to work transforming himself. After shucking off his suit coat and vest, he unstrapped his gun belt and pulled out his shirttail before tucking one of his trouser legs into his boot. The transformation continued when he unbuttoned his shirt and rebuttoned it, intentionally missing a few holes so that it hung crookedly. He rolled up one of his sleeves and, to finish everything off, he tucked his gun into the waistband at his back and walked over and picked up Emma's straw sombrero. He placed it on his head at a cockeyed angle, held out his arms, turned a circle, and said, "What do you think?"

"You look like a drunk," Chauncey said.

"Thank you," Reeves said. "After y'all grab your rifles

we'll go out the back and I'll cut left and you three cut right and come around on the other side."

"You want 'em alive?" Leander asked.

Reeves looked at Leander and said, "You say somethin'?"

"Nope, not a word."

After Percy, Leander, and Chauncey retrieved their rifles, they crawled under the back wall that had been partially rolled up and pushed to their feet. Reeves went left and the other three turned right.

Percy and the other two had more ground to cover and when they got as close to the land office as they could without exposing themselves, they saw that Reeves had already started his approach. There were two men on the roof, and they were ducked down behind the false front of the newly built building. Percy, Leander, and Chauncey didn't have a good enough angle to attempt a shot and they were out of real estate. If they tried to change positions it would put other people in harm's way.

Reeves's approach was slow, his body swaying from side to side as he shuffled forward. At one point he stumbled and almost fell down and then he began laughing and tossing his head about.

"Damn, he's good," Chauncey said. "I wouldn't even recognize him if I walked by him."

"He's the best I ever seen," Percy said, watching his old friend's progress. Seeing that Reeves would need to cross in front of the building and then turn around, Percy stepped out where Reeves could see him and waited. When he was sure Reeves was looking in his direction, Percy held up two fingers and pointed at the roof.

The only acknowledgment Reeves gave was a tiny nod

of his head before he began laughing again. Most people wouldn't have noticed it, but this wasn't the first go-around for Percy and Reeves.

Reeves finally cleared the front of the building and his demeanor changed in an instant. He spun around and had his gun out and cocked before the two men could react. "Drop 'em," Reeves shouted.

Foolishly, the men tried to raise their rifles and Reeves fired, drilling the first man in the chest. Half a second later, Reeves's pistol roared again, and a fountain of blood erupted from the second man's chest as he fell backward, his body tumbling down the other side of the roof.

When Percy, Leander, and Chauncey arrived, Reeves was calmly reloading his Colt.

"Recognize them?" Percy asked.

"Yeah, they was runnin' buddies with Danny Ringo."

"What do you want to do with the bodies?" Percy asked.

"Leave 'em for the undertaker," Reeves said.

Percy pushed his hat back on his head and said, "There ain't one."

"There ain't now, but I reckon by this time tomorrow they'll be a half a dozen of 'em round here just lookin' for somethin' to do."

CHAPTER
52

Monday, April 22, 1889, dawned to reveal a cloudless sky so blue it appeared endless. Today was the day thousands of people had been waiting for. And as the homesteaders began stirring around, preparations were being made—the harnesses were double- or triple-checked, the hooves of the horses were closely examined, and even a few bicycle tires were tested for sturdiness. If it walked or rolled there was a version of it somewhere along the three-hundred-mile perimeter of Oklahoma. These included everything from the handsomely built buggies and fringe-topped surreys, to the broken-down buckboards and the shoddy prairie schooners with their moth-eaten canvas covers. And for those less fortunate who owned neither wagon nor horse, they would be forced to rely on the oldest form of transportation to make their dash to a new destiny—their own two feet.

It was impossible to know exactly how many people were gathered there on Monday morning, but as varied as the modes of transportation were, so, too, were the people. From old war veterans to recently born babies, those waiting for the clock to strike noon were a cross section of American society. Rich, poor, young, or old, there was a rainbow of skin colors represented and they came in all shapes and sizes, from big and brawny to the slight and small. Whether male or female was of little concern, as were the reasons for being there, but for those traveling with family members or those who would be making the Run alone, they all had one common goal and that was to make a fresh start.

Pearl O'Sullivan, her hands coated with biscuit dough, had to laugh when she looked up to see Levi Johnson riding back in from his scouting trip. He was almost as large as the horse he was riding, the soles of his boots only about a foot above the ground. Pearl was hoping he had found some land fairly close to the river because he'd most likely come in dead last if it came down to a race. Dropping the last of the biscuits into the pan, she rinsed her hands in a bucket of water and dried them on her apron before carrying the pan over to the fire.

"Did you find us a place?" Pearl asked as Levi climbed off his horse. He had crossed over into Oklahoma before daybreak to avoid getting caught.

He wrapped the reins around a wagon wheel and said, "To tell the truth, it was pretty depressin'. Ain't no high ground around and there ain't many trees. It looks like a giant hay field and it's been grazed hard by the local ranchers."

Pearl's heart plummeted. "So, you didn't find any-thing? Do we need to go somewhere else?"

"Ain't time. I did find one place I liked that had a small

creek that feeds into a pond with a few trees where we could build us a place. The ground looks good and ought to work well for plantin', but there ain't nothin' with a view of the river that wouldn't flood if it come a hard rain."

"Not having a view of the river ain't a deal breaker."

"But it's what you wanted," Levi said.

"I want a million dollars, too, but I ain't gonna get it." She slipped her hand in his and said, "Is it a place we can make our own?"

"I reckon it is. There's a little rise overlookin' the creek that'd be a good spot to build on."

"Sounds perfect to me."

While they were talking, five more wagons had arrived, and it was obvious Levi would be in for a dogfight. People were stacked up all along the south bank of the Canadian River for as far as Pearl could see and more were arriving by the minute. "Do you think you can get there first?"

"I'm damn sure gonna try. I wrote down the township and range from the corner marker and I need you to help me figure out the legal description for the land office."

"Where's the plot map we picked up in Purcell?"

Levi reached into his back pocket and pulled out the map. "Right here, but I don't rightly know how it's supposed to work."

"I don't, either, but we ought to be able to figure it out. Get yourself a cup of coffee and we'll work on it while we wait for the biscuits to cook."

Levi walked over to the wagon to grab a cup and returned. After filling it he took a sip and said, "Kids still asleep?"

"Walter was stirrin' around, but the girls were still asleep the last time I looked."

Levi nodded and sat down on the ground. Pearl, mindful of her blistered butt, sat down beside him. They spent several minutes trying to figure out the map. There was a short primer printed at the bottom that tried to explain how to write a legal description for claimed property, but it might as well have been written in Chinese as far as Pearl was concerned. She looked at Levi and said, "You make any sense of it?"

"No, not really." He flipped the map over and studied the information he'd written down from the corner marker and shook his head. "I'm not gettin' it."

"Maybe you ought to ask some of the other people around here."

"Good idea."

Pearl pushed to her feet and walked over to check on the biscuits and decided they were done. Using an old horseshoe, she lifted the pot out of the coals and carried it to the wagon, where she set it on the tailgate. Levi refolded the map and stuck it back in his pocket and stood. He walked over to the wagon, looked at the single pan of biscuits, and said, "No bacon?"

"Ran out yesterday and we're about out of flour, too."

"Okay," Levi said, the dejection evident on his face. "Maybe I can do some huntin' this evenin'."

He forked a biscuit onto his plate, added a spoonful of jelly, and moved over to a shady spot and sat down. It was time to do some hard thinking. Money was tight and he still had to pay the fourteen-dollar filing fee when he registered his claim at the land office. He had that covered, but just barely, and the excuse there was nowhere to buy supplies would last only so long. He thought about asking Pearl if she had any money then decided against it. What type of provider would she think he was if he couldn't feed his own family?

It was a question he didn't want answered, at least not yet. He had done some blacksmithing so maybe he could catch on with one and work for wages for a while to put a little money in his pocket. He didn't have anything left to sell other than the wagon and the horses, but without those they'd be sleeping out in the open and he wouldn't be able to plant any crops. So that was a no-go, leaving him with very few options. His thinking was momentarily interrupted when Pearl walked over and sat down beside him.

"Kids are all up," Pearl said.

Levi nodded and stuffed the last of the biscuit into his mouth as his mind continued to churn. What if he sold one of the horses? A single horse might be able to pull the wagon if he took everything out of it and he didn't try to go too far. But how realistic was that? Especially when he didn't have any idea where the towns might spring up? Not very, he decided. And riding around in an empty wagon was as useless as not having one at all. But it wasn't just the wagon, either. Plowing with a two-horse team was much easier and faster and he was going to need both horses if he was going to haul some logs to build them a place to live. Having been inside a sod house or two over the years, he'd just as soon sleep outside if that's all they could manage. The constant dirt, the bugs, the roofs that dripped water every time it rained, they weren't fit for a dog to live in, much less a human. That being said, a soddy would shelter them from the weather, and they were extremely cheap to build, something that aligned well with his empty pocketbook.

As if reading his mind, Pearl slipped her hand inside his and said, "I've got some money."

"I ain't takin' your money. I'll get me a job somewhere."

"It's *our* money, now. Besides, where are you goin' to find a job around here?"

"There'll be some businesses comin' in once a town is staked out. If not that there's bound to be some people lookin' for help puttin' up their houses and whatnot."

"That won't buy us any grub right now, Levi."

Levi watched the kids chasing after a jackrabbit then said, "How much money you got?"

"Forty-three dollars," Pearl said. "That'll keep us in groceries for a while."

"I expect it would. It'd at least tide us over until I can get some money comin' in."

"That it would," Pearl said, "and it'll take some pressure off of you. Today is the day we've been waiting for and you've been moping around, worried about money. This is our chance to build a real life together."

Levi set the plate aside and said, "You tellin' me we was out of bacon and almost out of flour hit me like a board between the eyes. Been sittin' here thinkin' about what we could sell to get some more grub, but your offer of the money feels like a giant boulder's been lifted off my shoulders." He interlaced his fingers with hers and turned to look her in the eye. "I don't know what I did to deserve you, but I feel like the luckiest man in the world that you agreed to share this life with me."

"Same here," Pearl said, leaning forward to kiss him on the lips. "Now, mister, we're burning daylight. Pull out that plot map and see if you can find someone to help you with it."

After pushing to his feet, Levi offered her a mock salute and said, "Yes, ma'am."

CHAPTER
53

As Levi and Pearl made final preparations, others were doing the same all along the border of Oklahoma. Most of the activity was busywork, burning off nervous energy as people continually glanced at their wrists or fished into their pockets to check the time. It was as if time itself had collapsed as everyone waited for that one, single moment—noon.

A giddy expectation hummed through the crowds like an electrical current, everyone aware of the historical significance of this thing that had never been done before. No doubt it would go down in history as the most unusual land disbursement since the dawn of civilization. Plans were scrapped and new ones made, no one quite sure what to expect when the clock struck noon. Some of the would-be settlers argued over best practices, with some suggesting a claim be staked at the first available plot while others insisted the runners should go as far and as fast as humanly possible with an eye for only the best parcels. With this Run being the first, there was no previous knowledge to build upon and the various hypotheses about how it might play out were merely guesses, at best.

That buzz of excitement had even energized May Lillie, who was actually humming as she moved around camp, helping to pack away the breakfast pans. After camping elsewhere for the last couple of days, she had shown up early this morning, acting as if all was well with the world. Pawnee Bill, seated on a nearby camp chair, watched her out of the corner of his eye, wondering how long it would last. His strategy this time was to talk to her as little as possible. As long as his mouth was closed, there was little chance of setting her off again.

Now camped twenty-five miles due east of Buffalo Springs with other Boomers, Bill fished his watch out of his pocket to check the time—again. He had an hour until the designated time, so he pushed to his feet and began gathering his things. With most of their stuff lost to the river, it didn't take him long. He strapped on his gun belt and felt naked without his trusty Winchester rifle—it, too, lost in the melee. However, he didn't have a scabbard to put it in even if he did have it, his hand-tooled fancy saddle also gone. Instead of lamenting the things lost, he decided to turn his focus to securing the parcel of land he and May wanted. In that effort, he walked over to the wagon he'd been riding in to retrieve the four new stakes he had made. As he looked at his name and address that he'd written on them, he was trying to decide if that was the best course of action.

Already knowing the claim's quadrant, section number, township, and range, he had toyed with the idea of hopping on the train at Alfred and going straight to the land office in Guthrie to file it. Was driving in a stake with his name on it really all that important? Stakes could be easily removed, and it would be much more difficult for someone to remove his name from the official record book. The only downside he could see was getting the timing right. If he was later accused of being a Sooner, there would be a good chance they'd lose the claim. Did he really want to risk that, knowing he would face May's wrath for the rest of his life? That question was easy to answer, and it was a big, fat no.

He turned and walked over to the mule he had chosen to ride and tied the stakes to the back of the saddle he had borrowed. Seeing people already lining up at the rope the army had deployed about a quarter of a mile away, he decided it was time to mount up. The mule, unaccustomed to a saddle, balked when Bill spurred him, but a second spurring put the mule into motion. Before heading to the starting line, he steered the mule over to where May was and told her he'd meet her at the claim.

May looked up and said, "A kiss for luck?"

"Sure," Bill said. He leaned down for a quick kiss, hoping this version of May would stick around for a while. It sure made things a lot easier. He turned the mule and headed toward the starting line. Other Boomers were moving that way and Bill saw Avery Pittman astride the racehorse he had purchased a week ago for five hundred dollars. A short, pompous man, Pittman was a wealthy Kansas City businessman who needed free land about as much as he needed a hole in his head. Pittman liked to boast about how much he'd paid for the horse and it irked Bill to no end that he was even making the Run.

Pittman rode up beside Pawnee Bill, looked at the mule he was riding, and said, "Think you'll make it there by dark?" He burst into laughter and Bill had to work hard to tamp down the urge to punch him in the mouth.

"Laugh all you want," Bill said, "but I'd take this mule over that thin-legged horse of yours any day. You'll be lucky if he don't break a leg."

"You wish," Pittman said.

Bill showed him his middle finger and Pittman rode on, laughing.

CHAPTER
54

In Guthrie, most people were making final preparations to receive the expected onslaught of thousands of people. Others, Percy saw, were busy staking claims while another group of men was busy laying out the town and claiming lots along the way. Most of those jumping the gun were the deputy marshals who had been sent there expressly to stop such activity and that angered Percy, who was out for a stroll with Ruth.

"What are those men doing?" Ruth asked as they crested the only hill around.

"Breaking the law," Percy said, pausing to watch.

Ruth stopped beside him and said, "Where did they all come from?"

"They've been here all along. Most of 'em are marshals, but there's some others mixed in, too."

Ruth looked at Percy and said, "What time is it?"

Percy dug out his pocket watch and popped the lid. "Ten-thirty."

After watching the men for a few more moments, Ruth said, "They aren't even making an effort to conceal their activities."

Percy closed the lid and dropped the watch back into his pocket. "Why would they try to hide? They're the law around here."

"Will their claims be valid?"

"I don't have any idea about that." Percy reached out to take Ruth's hand and they continued their walk. "What did you work out with Emma and the others?"

"After looking at the map, we decided it would take someone about forty-five minutes to arrive here from the closest entry point. To be fair, we're going to make the Run from the train depot at one o'clock."

"Sounds good," Percy said. "You like the spot they picked out after seein' it?"

"I do, very much. Do you like it?"

"It don't really matter what I think, does it?"

Ruth pulled him to a stop and turned to look at him. "Yes, it matters unless I'm misreading things. Correct me if I'm wrong, but we did kiss yesterday, didn't we?"

Percy smiled and said, "We did, and it was nice, too. But both of us are used to makin' our own decisions and you ought to be able to make this one without worryin' about what I think."

"I'm not worrying about anything. I value your opinion."

"Okay, I think it'll make a mighty fine place."

"Thank you. I agree."

She turned and they began walking again. As they neared the depot, Percy was glad to see that someone had pulled the body off the roof. He still didn't know the names of the two men Reeves had killed, but it didn't much matter now.

"You know there is one thing that concerns me," Ruth said.

"What's that?"

"Trouble seems to follow you, especially when you're in the company of Marshal Reeves. I've only known you a few days and during that time span you've killed two men, been shot in the arm, and helped the marshal kill another two men only yesterday."

"Been a rough stretch, for sure. I can't recall the last time I even had to pull out my pistol fore this. But you have to remember where we are. Indian Territory's chock-full of wicked and vile people. Many of 'em would just as soon shoot you as look at you and when you add in the fact that Bass has put a bunch of them in the pokey, it makes for dangerous work." He was glad she didn't know about the two men killed in Oklahoma City or the rustlers they'd killed only a few weeks ago.

"Why do all the outlaws flock here?" Ruth asked.

"Because of a bunch of screwy laws. The Indians got their own lawmen, but they can't arrest a white man. And there ain't no local marshals or anything like that 'cause it's all considered government property. So, Bass and the other deputies are left to weed out all the criminals in an area that covers almost seventy-five thousand square miles. In other words, there's a lot of hidin' places up in these parts. It's like lookin' for one particular needle in a barn full of 'em."

"How many marshals are there?" Ruth asked.

"Not enough. There's probably only forty or fifty of 'em workin' in the Territory at any one time."

"I had no idea. Maybe the settlers coming in will drive some of the criminals out."

"Maybe," Percy said, "but I sure don't like the idea of you bein' up here by yourself."

"I'm quite capable of caring for myself."

"I reckon you are and it does help to know Emma and the others are goin' to be in and out."

"Speaking of Emma, why does she always wear a gun?"

Percy spent a few minutes telling Ruth about Emma's kidnapping, the subsequent search that ended before finding her, and how she was eventually found already in labor with Simon.

"My goodness," Ruth said. "Now I understand why she has the gun. And she knows how to use it?"

"You bet. That woman could shoot the wings off a fly."

"That's good to know."

They fell into an easy silence and it wasn't long before they were back at camp. When they arrived, Seth was in the middle of a story and Percy was glad to see his mother laughing. He knew she had aches and pains and they prevented her from getting out as much as she used to. He said good-bye to Ruth and left to saddle his horse. He hadn't taken more than three or four steps when he heard his mother calling his name. He turned around and walked back, taking off his Stetson. "How are you feelin' this mornin'?" Percy asked.

"Old," Frances said. "But I didn't come out here to talk about me."

"Okay, I'm listenin'."

"Ruth's a keeper, Percy. Don't screw it up."

Percy chuckled and said, "I'll try not to."

Frances stepped forward and wrapped her arms around her oldest son. "I haven't seen that sparkle in your eye since Mary died and that was a long time ago. You deserve to be happy, Percy." She kissed him on the cheek before breaking the embrace and stepping back. "Now, you listen to your mother and you do right by that woman."

Percy smiled and said, "Yes, ma'am. I'm glad you approve, but we'll have to wait and see how things play out."

"I didn't say you should get married tomorrow," Frances said. "I'm just suggesting you give it some effort."

"Duly noted." Percy put his hat back on and said, "Hear anything from Eli?"

"Got a telegram from him Friday. He and Clara are still in Chicago. He said talks were ongoing, but the prognosis is poor, whatever that means. Tell me again about the scheme you two have cooked up."

"I ain't got time to go into it too much, but the way it works now is the cattle brokers are the ones who buy up the cattle and then cut a deal with the meat packers. Eli's plan is to bypass the brokers and have the ranchers sell directly to the slaughterhouses."

"That's not going to make the brokers very happy," Frances said.

"Exactly. It'd put 'em out of business so they're raisin' all kind of hell. Listen, Ma, I need to saddle my horse so I can catch up to Bass and Leander. You got a safe place to watch all the people that's comin' in?"

"I'm not so far gone I can't look after myself. Don't you worry about me."

Percy chuckled and said, "No wonder you and Ruth get along so well, you're two peas in a pod."

"You hush, now," Frances said. "Be safe out there, son."

"I reckon if I've lived this long, I'll make it a little longer." Percy reached into his pocket and pulled out his watch to check the time again. "It's eleven now but I reckon it'll be closer to one fore there's much action here." He closed the lid and dropped the watch back into his pocket and said, "See you later, Ma." Percy turned and hustled down to the creek where they had been keeping the horses and quickly saddled his mare.

He found Leander and Reeves a short time later at the train depot. They'd found a spot of shade and they were sitting on their horses, watching the deputy marshals as they continued to stake illegal claims. Percy rode up beside them and pulled the mare to a stop. "Reckon anybody's gonna stop 'em?" Percy asked.

"Don't know who it'd be," Reeves said. He nodded toward a group of cavalry soldiers on the other side of the railroad tracks and said, "The army ain't too interested and it's making me sick to my stomach seeing it. Let's ride out to watch the start."

"Works for me," Leander said.

The three men turned their horses and rode due east toward the border. The area they were riding through was cut up with a multitude of dry washes and small creeks, and Percy knew the wagons were going to have a rough go of it. By the time they made it to the border, it was nearly noon. The once-vacant prairie was now inundated with humans, the horses and wagons and people lined up twenty-deep for as far as the eye could see. A cavalry officer was riding up and down the line, his pocket watch in his hand while his bugler sat nearby, awaiting his signal. Reeves led Percy and Leander over to a small grouping of trees and they pulled their horses to a stop.

"You reckon we won't get run over, here?" Leander asked.

"I reckon we're safe," Reeves said. "They'd have to plow down the trees to get to us."

Although Percy didn't have a stake in the outcome, he was still nervous and tense.

A short time later, the bugler lifted his instrument and the moment the mouthpiece touched his lips, all hell broke loose as the dense cluster of humanity exploded outward. Those riding horses whipped their mounts into a gallop, launching an enormous dust cloud. In the commotion, a few of the horses began bucking and one tossed his rider and took off at a dead run. Then the wagons began rolling out, the drivers whipping and shouting at their teams, the dust so thick it momentarily obscured the wagons themselves.

"The damnedest thing I ever seen," Reeves said.

It wasn't long before they witnessed the first wagon wreck, then another, and another and within fifteen minutes the prairie was littered with busted wagons. Thankfully, most of the drivers escaped without major injury and they limped on, most chasing after their teams.

Those on foot advanced next and they fanned out across the rolling terrain, firing their pistols in celebration after driving in their stakes.

Percy looked at Reeves and said, "How many, you reckon?"

"Lordy," Reeves said. "They's a bunch of 'em. I reckon eight, maybe nine thousand, but that's just a guess."

"And that's only what we could see. Think of how many are pourin' in all the way around this place."

"Gonna be a long day," Leander said as they turned their horses back toward Guthrie.

CHAPTER
55

Down south, Levi Johnson's boots were getting wet as he waited for the go signal from the middle of the Canadian River. And he wasn't alone. There were hundreds of others doing the same, mounted on their swiftest horses or driving their best buggies. Because of the quicksand, crossing in a wagon was treacherous at best and could be accomplished at only three or four places along that section of the river and the line of wagons waiting to cross stretched beyond the horizon.

Levi didn't have a watch and he startled when a rifle shot rang out. Unsure if that was the signal, there was a momentary lull of maybe a second before the line of would-be settlers charged forward. One man on a sleek black stallion was up the far bank and gone before Levi could even reach dry land. There was a cacophony of sound with the onlookers cheering, the wagon drivers cursing, and the sharp cracks of a thousand whips all echoing across the river. The man next to Levi was launched forward into the water when his horse stepped in a hole and Levi felt guilty for not stopping to help. But the race rewarded only those who arrived first and there wasn't a moment to lose.

When Levi crested the far bank, he spurred the horse into a gallop and loosened the reins. He had about three miles to cover, but he couldn't afford to run the horse the entire way. After a few minutes he slowed the horse to walk, satisfied he had caught up with a few of the other land runners.

Celebratory gunshots rang out every few minutes and he had to work hard to resist the urge to spur his horse back into a run again. He'd need both horses to get the wagon across the river and without it, they'd have no place to sleep.

When he finally arrived at the parcel he had chosen, he was relieved and thrilled to see it hadn't been claimed. He rode over to the cornerstone the surveyors had laid out and dropped the old bag he had been carrying. He knew leaving the claim after he staked it would be dicey, so he'd come prepared. He climbed down from the horse and set to work.

Inside the bag he had several stakes with his name on them and he used them to stake all four corners of the property. To make improvements to the land as the rules stated, he'd brought along a small shovel and used that to begin digging a well, though he had no idea if he was even digging in the right place. It looked like a toy in his massive hands as he plowed through the ground, digging a hole about three feet in circumference. It wasn't long before he had a mound of dirt that would be easily visible to any would-be claim jumper and he called it quits.

Wiping the sweat from his face with his sleeve, Levi went searching for sticks. When he thought he had gathered enough, he returned to the spot where he'd dug the hole and began poking the sticks into the ground, trying to create something that might look like a tent. When he finished, he draped a blanket over it and stepped back to take a look. It was without doubt the sorriest tent he'd ever seen, but it would have to do. He returned to his horse and mounted up. After one long, last look at his claim, he turned the horse and headed back.

At Oklahoma Station, which would be renamed Oklahoma City in a few hours, Captain Arthur MacArthur and his fellow officers settled in for a long wait. The closest border was miles away and they weren't expecting any arrivals for an hour or maybe an hour and a half. That assumption was based on calculations of time and distance, but the one thing they hadn't factored into the equation were the people already there. Shortly after the cannon fired, it was like the ground came alive as people began emerging out of the tall grass and the nearby creeks and gullies. MacArthur looked up in time to see a half a dozen men dropping out of a single tree and within fifteen minutes there were hundreds of people milling about.

Chase Russell, a lieutenant, looked at MacArthur and said, "What should we do, Captain?"

"Personally, I'd like to run them all out of here, but technically the Land Run has begun and it will be up to the land office to sort it all out."

"So, we're going to stand here and watch, sir?" Russell asked.

"I don't believe there's anything else we can do. As you can obviously see, there are a good number of deputy marshals and other federal workers involved. What I will do is send a message to the two land offices to suggest they record the precise time when a claim is filed. Our only focus from this point forward is to quell any violence that might arise."

As if to emphasize his point, a fight broke out between four men a short distance away and MacArthur ordered his troops to break it up.

"Going to be a long day, sir," Russell said.

"I expect so. Just keep them from killing each other, Lieutenant."

Russell snapped off a salute and said, "Yes, sir," before turning his horse and riding off.

Captain MacArthur had thought he'd seen it all until a full survey crew stepped out of the trees, complete with all the gear they would need to do their job. Curious, the captain spurred his horse forward just as a tall, skinny man with a bushy mustache and goatee began barking orders at the surveyors. He rode up close and pulled his horse to a stop, "You, sir," MacArthur shouted, "who are you?"

The man turned and approached. "I am Captain William Couch of the Seminole Town and Improvement Company."

"You served in the military, Captain?" MacArthur asked.

"No, I did not. It's more of an honorific title, sir."

MacArthur smiled. "Are you here legally, Mr. Couch?"

"I most certainly am," Couch said.

"Continue on, then." MacArthur touched the brim of his hat and turned his horse, knowing Couch was lying.

* * *

W. L. Couch, the leader of the Boomers, had made the Run from the railroad tracks, some one hundred yards distant. He had staked a claim on 160 acres of prime property just south of the train depot. It was there, he hoped, Oklahoma City would be born.

However, some people had other ideas, and it wasn't long before two other townsite companies arrived on the scene. Tempers flared, guns were drawn, and it wasn't until cooler heads intervened that things began to calm down.

A meeting was called to coordinate matters and it, too, ended in a shouting match. The men were separated, and the meeting was canceled only to be reconvened an hour later. The hour break had the desired effect and they did make some progress trying to combine the three opposing plans. Motions were made and seconded, then the votes were tallied, and they made more progress until they hammered out a plan that everyone could live with.

Now that they had a plan, they needed a few duly elected town officials to implement it. Men were nominated and others rejected and during it all, William Couch, who had spent four years roaming the halls of Congress lobbying for the opening of the Unassigned Lands, wielded all of that political knowledge to bend the crowd to his will.

After a final vote, William L. Couch was elected the first mayor of Oklahoma City.

CHAPTER
56

Emma, Grace, Marcie, and Ruth had gathered at the train depot and all were raring to go. With all the people that were already staking claims, they decided to shave fifteen minutes off their start time and they would depart at twelve forty-five p.m. Emma was in charge of the watch and that was something she regretted almost immediately when the others continually asked what time it was.

Chauncey, unwilling to let four women go off alone, was gunned up and mounted up, awaiting the signal. He still didn't think much of the idea, but sometimes a man had to go along to get along and it was a hell of a lot easier than arguing with Marcie. Although he didn't know how it was all going to work out with all the requirements, if Marcie was happy, he was happy.

Simon and Ann had climbed on top of a railcar parked on the siding and were ready to cheer the group on.

"Ten seconds," Emma said. She was mounted on one

of her favorite four-year-old geldings and when the second had struck twelve, she shouted, "Yeehaw!" and spurred her horse. The gelding squatted for half a second then leapt forward like he'd been shot out of a cannon. Emma heard Simon and Ann whooping and hollering behind her as the horse hit his stride. She looked back at the others and laughed, giddy with excitement.

The race to the land they hoped to claim wasn't even close, Emma smoking them all by a good quarter of a mile. They were in the process of staking their claims when the wave of would-be settlers arrived from the east. Chauncey, watching it all from aboard his horse, had to draw his pistol more than once to persuade potential claim jumpers that they'd live a lot longer if they moved on elsewhere. Fortunately, he hadn't yet fired his weapon, but he knew there was still a lot of daylight left. He steered his horse into the shade of a large cottonwood and rolled a cigarette as he waited for the next claim jumper to come along.

After pounding in her stakes, Ruth spent a few moments in the shade of a large oak tree, looking out over her property. She'd come a long way after surviving years of abuse and as she thought about that, her eyes watered up and tears began to spill down her cheeks. Although she didn't know how things might go with Percy, for the first time in a long time she was optimistic about her future.

Back in Guthrie, Simon and Ann were now sitting on top of the freight car, watching as the hordes of people came racing in. The burgeoning town was already jammed with people and more were arriving every second. Although it was exciting to watch, a small part of Simon regretted that the land had even been opened for settlement. He knew the pristine prairies where the wildlife had roamed unfettered for thousands of years would be forever changed in the span of a few hours, but he also knew the opening of the Unassigned Lands had been inevitable, whether it happened today or at some point in the future. The constant clamoring for land wouldn't end until it was all gone. Ann turned and smiled at him and he reached for her hand.

Simon had given the things his mother had said considerable thought and, once he had stripped away his emotions, he could see that she was right. They both had bright futures and being saddled with a child at such a young age would be devastating. But knowing what was right and trying to stick to it were two different things when the beautiful young woman in question was sitting right beside him. Although they hadn't known each other long, it was impossible to deny the deep emotional connection that had formed between them. He thought it probably had something to do with the Indian blood flowing through his veins, a type of deep ancestral pull that had drawn them into each other's orbit. That bond had allowed them to have an honest and frank discussion and both had agreed they would halt the sexual liaisons until they could acquire some type of protection that would greatly reduce the chances of an unwanted pregnancy.

Simon pushed those thoughts from his mind and returned to the chaos of the present. He had noticed the line in front of the land office had begun forming well before the clock struck noon, a strong indicator of the nefarious activity that was afoot. A prideful young man, he disliked the idea that someone would use their authority to game the system and he hoped those in line and others like them, the cheaters, would someday be stripped of their claims.

Their bird's-eye view allowed them to see a wide area and Ann turned and said, "Can you make any sense of the town they're trying to lay out?"

"From what I can tell, there are three or four competing groups that are trying to create a town using their own designs. According to what I read from the rules, a town can be no larger than three hundred and twenty acres. They're well past that already and they're only an hour into it." Simon looked at Ann and said, "How does it make you feel, seeing all of this?"

Ann thought about that for a long few minutes then said, "I hate it for my father and those of his generation who were promised so much and then had so much taken away. My father doesn't know his birth date or even how old he is because the Indians had no concept of time. They went where they wanted when they wanted and that was their entire existence, until the army decided otherwise. He and his peers were forced to assimilate into a culture that was as foreign to them as it would be for you, if you were to go to Africa. But they did that because they were tired of being hunted like a pack of wild dogs and because the government gave them a large swath of land that was to be theirs for as long as the, and I quote, 'grass grows and the waters run.'"

Ann paused to take a breath before continuing. "Then several years later, Congress passes the Dawes Act, which will grant each Indian their own small piece of land, called an allotment. Once that process is completed and with the government holding those allotted lands in a trust for twenty-five years because all Indians are deemed 'incompetent,' those same officials then turn around and say, in all their generosity, they'll buy all that extra land so the Indians won't have to worry about it.

"The Dawes Act was signed into law in 1887. When my father and many others raised a stink about it, the government told them, *Oh, don't worry. We're not talking about the tribes that relocated to Indian Territory. This is for the other Indians.* Ann made a sweeping gesture with her hand and said, "And this is just the beginning."

"Do you really believe they're going to force every tribe into accepting allotments?" Simon asked.

"Don't you, given their history?"

Simon pondered that for a moment and said, "You're probably right. You've obviously given all of this considerable thought. Why don't you try to do something about it?"

"Like what?" Ann asked.

"Become a lawyer."

"Can a woman do that? Become a lawyer?"

"I don't see why you couldn't. Surely there have been other women who have become lawyers and if not, someone needs to be the first."

"A full-blood Comanche woman as a lawyer?"

"Sure. Why not? Isn't that what this country is supposed to be about?"

"I wouldn't know where to even begin."

"You might not, but Seth will."

"Good point. He might even know some women who have done it."

"So, you'll consider it?" Simon asked.

"I absolutely will. Now, I'm hot. Let's go swimming."

Seth held up his pinky and said, "Pinky swear it'll be just swimming?"

Ann laughed, linked her pinky with his, and said, "I promise."

CHAPTER
57

On the northern border of Oklahoma, Pawnee Bill was jockeying for position along the starting line. When dawn had broken this morning, it had looked like they'd have an easy go of it. But as the hours passed as they counted down toward noon, the crowd of people all along the line had ballooned to unimaginable proportions. Normally, Bill wouldn't have been worried if he'd been riding his highly trained, fleet-footed, gray quarter horse, Silver, but that horse was back in the barn in Wichita and Bill was now mounted on a red mule of undeterminable age. The mule was what he had, and he was determined to make the best of it. To ease his mind some, he kept repeating two words from the story "The Tortoise and the Hare." "Tortoise, hare. Tortoise, hare," he mumbled under his breath. "Remember, fastest is not always—"

He was jarred from his thoughts by the explosion from one of the army's howitzers and the race was on. He spurred the mule and he took two steps forward and stopped, the land runners streaming past him in droves.

He knew flogging the mule wouldn't do any good, so he squeezed his thighs and gently tapped him with his spurs again. The mule began walking and another tap of the spurs put him into a trot and Bill was off. Thinking that was probably the best he was going to get, Bill settled back onto the borrowed saddle and let the mule set the pace.

People were surging past him, but the busted wagons now dotting the prairie in front of him were a reminder that slow and steady was better than fast and dumb. Looking ahead, he saw Avery Pittman on his high-dollar racehorse a moment before he disappeared down into a gulley. When he didn't reappear after a few moments, Bill steered the mule that way for a quick peek. As the mule trotted past the mouth of the gully, he saw that Pittman's horse was down, its front leg obviously broken. He felt terrible for the horse because it wasn't the horse's fault he had been purchased by an idiot. Pittman looked up and Bill showed him his middle finger again before passing on by.

As he closed in on the parcel of land he and May had dreamed of owning for years, anger flared in his gut when he saw that someone else had already staked it. Muttering a string of curses, he scanned the property looking for the trespasser. He didn't see anyone, but there was a thick band of timber that ran alongside Stillwater Creek, blocking his view of the back third of the property. He rode over to the corner marker and climbed down from the mule.

He yanked the stake out of the ground and read the name. "Well," Bill muttered, "John Wisdom, you asshole, you done staked the wrong claim." He picked up one of the nearby rocks and drove Wisdom's stake into the ground on the other side of the cornerstone and muttered, "But I reckon we can be neighbors."

Bill untied his stakes and drove one in where Wisdom's had been and then remounted the mule and hit the other three corners, moving Wisdom's stakes and replacing them with his own. With the tent and all of their supplies lost, he rode over to the nearest tree and tied a stained, white pillowcase he had found to one of the limbs and slid down from the mule.

As he worked to take off the saddle, he wondered what May was going to say. She and several of the other women had been studying the map for days, trying to decide who would claim what. According to their plan, the ground now under Wisdom's stake was supposed to have gone to Esther Robinson and her family. Bill thought she was a dried-up old prune who had a nasty habit of prying into other people's business and it certainly wouldn't break his heart if she had to find another claim. Although he didn't know who John Wisdom was, Bill thought he damn sure couldn't be any worse than Esther Robinson. He moved into the dappled shade of an oak tree and stretched out on the ground, deciding he didn't really care what May thought.

Pulling his hat down over his eyes, Pawnee Bill was on the verge of drifting off to sleep when he heard a twig snap. His Colt was in his hand in an instant and a woman shouted, "Don't shoot."

He pushed his hat back to see a pretty, dark-haired woman who looked to be in her late thirties. Bill sat up and said, "Can I help you?"

"I think you're on my claim?"

"Now, that can't be right," Bill said as he holstered his

pistol and pushed to his feet. He stuck out his hand and said, "I'm Gordon Lillie, but you can call me Pawnee Bill."

She shook his hand and cocked her head to the side. "Pawnee Bill?"

"Long story," Bill said. "Anyway, I didn't see no stakes."

"Well, they were here, and they had my name on it, too."

"What's your name?"

"Joan Wisdom."

"Huh," Bill said. "I reckon we ought to walk out for a look. You put it next to the northeast corner marker?"

"I staked all the corners."

"Huh," Bill said again. It was a short walk and when they arrived, Bill pointed at the stake he had moved and said, "That one yours?"

Wisdom leaned down to read the name and stood back up. "Yeah, it's mine, but I coulda sworn I put it where yours is now."

"Reckon you coulda gotten turned around?"

She didn't say anything for the longest time, and Bill could almost hear the gears grinding in her head. Glancing to his left, he saw the Robinsons' wagon in the distance, and he knew he needed to close the deal fast. Trying to nudge her along, he said, "I can't see that there's much difference between the two."

"The one you staked has a pretty waterfall on it."

"What if me and your husband was to build you a waterfall, too?"

"I'm a widow."

"Oh," Bill said, "Sorry for your loss."

"Thank you."

"Any kids?"

Wisdom nodded. "Three. My oldest boy ought to be along with the wagon in a bit."

Jeez, could the news could get any better? A pretty widow for a neighbor and a young man I could hire to help out if needed?

He decided to give her another nudge. "I bet me and your son could build you a waterfall."

She stared down at her stake for another long moment and then turned to Bill and said, "You know what, it doesn't really make much of a difference, does it?"

For an answer, Bill stuck out his hand and said, "Howdy, neighbor."

Wisdom chuckled and shook his hand again. "I will take you up on your offer."

"I look forward to it. Let me know if you need anything."

"Thank you. Are you married, Pawnee Bill?"

What he wanted to say was *Not for long*, but he didn't. "I am. My wife should be along shortly."

"I look forward to meeting her."

Bill turned and headed back to his spot in the shade. If he'd been alone, he would have stopped to dance a jig. "Esther who?" he mumbled before breaking into a smile.

CHAPTER
58

Percy, Reeves, and Leander made it back to Guthrie in time to see the first double-engine train from Arkansas City approaching. It was packed to the gills with people inside and there were others riding on top, on the platforms between cars, or anywhere a person could find a flat spot to stand, sit, or lie down. Percy counted twenty-three passenger cars and it looked like a giant centipede with all the people waving and shouting as the train slithered into the station.

Before the train came to a stop, luggage was being thrown out of the windows and that was followed quickly by the people who had done the throwing. People on top were jumping off and many of them crashed hard before getting back up and hurrying on. Like ants, people were scurrying every which way, many with no clue where they were going. It was absolute mayhem and the three men looked on in wonder.

Seeing how crowded that train was, Percy assumed the wave of land seekers would slowly taper off, but his assumption proved wrong when another train, just as packed, arrived a few minutes later. Then another train arrived shortly after that one and over the next couple of hours, six more trains chugged into the station from the north and Percy was beginning to wonder if there was anybody left in Kansas.

As he mulled that over, the trains from the south began arriving and when combined with the continuing on-slaught of arrivals via traditional means, the people in Guthrie were packed ass to elbow and people were still coming. The line at the land office stretched around the building and all the way down to the railroad tracks and tents were going up wherever people could find a patch of bare ground. Gazing out over the prairie, Percy thought it looked like a flock of giant geese had bedded down for the afternoon.

According to the rules, the towns were to be limited to 320 acres, but two hours after the start, the town-lot claimers in Guthrie had expanded the city boundaries by two miles with as many as a dozen claims on a single lot. There was no plan and the lot seekers had no idea if their lots would even exist when a plan was finally put in place. As the half a dozen townsite companies in Guthrie argued how the town should be laid out, another enterprising man chained two long logs together and hitched it to a team of mules and began laying out the streets, wiping out any-thing in his path as people scrambled to get out of his way. It was absolute chaos and would-be settlers continued to pour in.

It was a hell of a sight to see for sure, but Percy was quickly growing weary of the crowds. He could work around a large herd of cattle all day long and not bat an eye but being around a herd of people set him on edge right quick, so he said good-bye to Leander and Reeves and headed out to check on Ruth.

On his way out of town, he came across a merchant selling tents and he stopped and bought one. His left arm still in a sling, Percy tipped the merchant a dollar to lash the tent to his saddle before moving on. A little farther down the road, he passed two men who were having a heated argument and that got him to thinking. He and the rest of the deputy marshals had oiled up their guns in anticipation of having to use them, but there had been very little violence, so far. Yes, there had been arguments and yes, gunshots aplenty though none had been fired in anger that he could recall. He thought most of that was attributable to the fact there was no liquid courage to be had. The sale of alcohol in Indian Territory was strictly forbidden and even though the area was lousy with whiskey peddlers, most of them operated in the shadows and weren't readily accessible.

When Percy arrived at the place the women were hoping to claim, he was pleased to see they'd been successful, at least for now. He waved at Emma as he passed her claim and a little farther on, he spotted Chauncey and steered the mare that way. "Any trouble?" Percy asked, pulling his horse to a stop.

Chauncey pushed his hat back on his head and began rolling a cigarette. "There's been a few knotheads that needed some proddin' to move on, but it ain't nothin' I can't handle."

"Probably ought to camp out here for the night."

"Done planned on it," Chauncey said. He licked the edge of the paper and put the cigarette in his mouth. After pulling a match from his shirt pocket, he struck it on the saddle horn and lit up, the smoke curling around his lips when he said, "Still don't know what the hell we're gonna do with the claim, though. Waste-a time if you ask me."

"Ain't you learned nothin' durin' the years you been married?" Percy asked. "The woman almost always gets what she wants and sometimes you've just gotta bite your tongue."

"My damn tongue's chewed raw already."

Percy chuckled and said, "I expect it is."

Chauncey took another draw from his cigarette and said, "Speakin' of women, what's the story on you and Ruth?"

"It ain't fully written. Why? You mad?"

"Why the hell would I be mad? Ask me, it's 'bout time you had someone to boss you around like the rest of us. 'Sides, you could do with some company."

"Think so?"

Chauncey nodded and said, "I do. She looks to be a keeper to me."

"We'll see how it plays out. See ya later." Percy clucked his tongue to put the mare into motion. When he arrived at Ruth's claim, he found her sitting in the shade, a book in her hands. He climbed down from his horse and said, "Now that you're a landowner you just lazin' the day away?"

"It's not mine yet. I still need to file the claim and fulfill all the obligations."

Percy untied the tent, pulled it down, and said, "Got you a tent."

Ruth closed the book and rose to her feet. "What did I say about buying me things?"

"Well, I got to admit, it was partly selfish."

"How so?" Ruth asked.

Percy smiled and said, "Well, dependin' how things go, we might be needin' some privacy."

Ruth put her hands on her hips and said, "Is that so?"

Percy nodded.

"And I suppose, because of your injured arm, you'll be requiring my help?"

"I'd be obliged."

She left him hanging for a few seconds and Percy was wondering if he'd overplayed his hand.

Finally, Ruth smiled and said, "Let's get to it, then."

CHAPTER
59

Pearl, anxious to get there, looked at Levi and said, "How much further?"

Levi pointed at a clump of trees ahead and said, "Soon as we get past them trees yonder, you'll be able to see it."

Pearl wasn't the only one who was excited. All three kids were leaning over the wagon seat, their small heads turning every which way, eager for a glimpse of the place they would call home.

"You gonna build us a house, Pa?" Walter asked.

Pearl noticed that Levi winced at the question and she felt bad. What child wouldn't want to live in their very own home?

"Eventually," Levi said. He shifted the reins to his left hand and ruffled his son's hair. "Don't know what it's gonna look like yet, but I'm gonna build something to keep us out of the weather."

The area they were traveling through was buzzing with activity, some people busy erecting tents and others already busy plowing up the sod. When he made the turn around the trees, Levi tensed up and muttered, "Son of a bitch."

"I didn't know you had a tent," Pearl said.

"I don't," Levi said.

"Whose is it, then?" Pearl asked.

"We're about to find out." Levi set the brake, reached under the seat to grab the double-barreled shotgun, and climbed down from the wagon.

Seeing the shotgun and the determined look on Levi's face, Pearl panicked. Having known him for only a couple of weeks, she had no idea if he was going to start blasting or what. She hadn't yet seen that side of him, and she knew the stakes were high. Without the land, their future was dismal. When she saw Levi lifting the shotgun to his shoulder as he advanced on the tent, she knew she had to do something and went with the first thing that popped into her mind. There was no time for anything else.

After telling the kids to stay where they were, she stood and clambered down the side of the wagon. Lifting her skirt with her left hand, she took off at a dead run just as two men emerged from inside the tent. Willing her feet to move faster, she shouted, "No!" to draw their attention and to buy some time. She ran right up to Levi, threw her arms around him, and shouted, "Please don't kill anybody else. We've had enough trouble."

Pearl turned her head slightly so she could see how the two men had reacted and was pleased with the results. Both men had raised their hands and the larger of the two said, "Mister, we don't want no trouble."

Still looking down the barrel of the shotgun, Levi said, "From this distance, this ol' shotgun of mine'll punch a hole in you big enough to ride a horse through. Now, get gone."

"What about our tent?" the larger man asked.

"The cost of being claim jumpers," Levi said. "One."

"We're goin'," the same man said.

"Two."

The two men spun and raced for their horses, Levi tracking their progress with the shotgun barrel. They jumped on their horses and lit out at a dead run as Levi slowly dropped the hammers. He lowered his weapon and began chuckling. "Where did you come up with that?"

Pearl released her hold on Levi and stepped back. "It's the first thing that I thought of."

"Well, it worked, I reckon."

"You feel bad about takin' their tent?"

"Nope. Maybe they'll think twice about stealin' another man's claim." Levi looked around, nodded toward an approaching rider, and said, "Yonder comes the preacher."

"A preacher?" Pearl asked.

Levi smiled. "I told you we was gettin' married."

"Today?"

Levi looked Pearl in the eye and said, "Now that I found you, I ain't lettin' you go. You gettin' cold feet?"

Pearl reached for his hand and said, "No, not at all. You couldn't run me off even if you tried. Do I have time to take a bath?"

Levi winked at her and said, "I thought we'd slip off to the creek after we got the kids bedded down this evenin'."

Pearl smiled and said, "I like that idea better. Where did you find this preacher?"

"Met him this morning when I was out scouting. He staked a nearby claim, so I reckon we're neighbors."

When the preacher arrived, Levi made the introductions before he and Pearl gathered up the kids. There was a short discussion on where to have the ceremony and Levi suggested a spot down by the creek that cut through the property. Pearl agreed and after walking down there, they chose a spot in the dappled shade of a giant oak tree and the preacher opened his Bible.

Standing together with the three children in front of them, the preacher took them through their vows and pronounced them man and wife. Levi kissed Pearl then paid the preacher a dollar and sent him on his way.

Walter looked up at Pearl and said, "Does that mean I get to call you Ma now?"

Pearl squatted down so she could look him in the eye and said, "That's exactly what it means." She opened her arms and the children shuffled in for a group hug. She kissed each one on the cheek and said, "Thank you for lettin' me be a part of your family. I'm the luckiest woman in the world." She stood and reached for the children's hands and they all took a stroll around the property, their futures now inextricably linked forever.

CHAPTER
60

After returning to town to retrieve the wagon containing their supplies, Emma and Grace were busy assembling their tents as the sun began its steady downward march toward the horizon. Marcie and Chauncey had agreed to keep an eye on things so Grace and Emma would be returning to Guthrie shortly, Grace to care for her children and Emma to have a late supper with Reece Ford. She pounded in the last stake, grabbed the rope for the last corner post, and pulled it taut, looping the rope around the stake and tying it off.

She stood and studied her handiwork for a moment. The canvas was saggy in spots, but it would do for now. She tossed the hammer inside, tied the entry flap closed, and walked over to help Grace finish up. In an effort to make Chauncey's job easier, they had placed their tents close to the corner markers with only a few feet between them.

"What can I do to help?" Emma asked.

Grace held up a rope and said, "If you'll tie this off, I'll nurse Lizzie before we head back to town."

"You got it," Emma said. "She's been so quiet I almost forgot she was here."

"She's been the best baby," Grace said. She walked over to where Lizzie had been napping in the shade and scooped her up.

"Good enough that you're ready for another one?" Emma asked as she leaned down and tied off the last rope.

"Maybe, but I'd sure like to have Lizzie up and walking before the next one comes along." Grace sat down and pulled her right breast free. After Lizzie latched on, she looked up at Emma and said, "How are things with Simon and Ann?"

Emma shrugged and said, "I talked to him, but I'm not sure how much of it sunk in."

"He's an extremely bright young man so maybe he'll heed your advice. How are things with you and Reece?"

Emma sat down beside her and said, "Really good."

"Oh," Grace said. "Not just good, but really good, huh?"

Emma could feel the heat creeping into her cheeks. "We've known each other for years."

"It's nice that you have that connection. Are you warming up to the idea that it's okay to let a man into your life?"

"I am and it's much easier than I thought it was going to be. Of course, it might have something to do with who that man is. Reece is easy to get along with and he's pretty easy on the eyes, too."

"Yes, he's very handsome. Can you see yourself havin' a future with him?"

"There are some issues that need to be worked out, but

yes, I can." Emma looked at Grace and said, "Thanks for making it happen."

"You're welcome. I'm very happy for you, Emma."

Emma smiled and said, "Thanks. I know it's only been a couple of days, but I can hardly wait to see him again. Is that normal?"

Grace laughed and said, "Only for the lucky ones. I'm that way with Seth, too, and we've been married for years." Grace handed Lizzie to Emma and said, "If you'll burp her, I'll gather up my things and we'll go see them."

When they arrived back in Guthrie, they found Seth swamped in paperwork. Grace climbed down from her horse and said, "Seth, I thought you weren't going to do any land claims."

Seth finished what he was doing and looked up. "I wasn't until I saw that the town lots were being bought and sold. Each transaction requires some legal work so it's easy money. I'd be a fool not to do it."

While Seth and Grace talked, Emma slipped past and entered the living area at the back of the tent. After stripping off her clothes, she gave herself a sponge bath, brushed her hair, and pulled on one of her better dresses. As she was leaving, she suggested Seth put Simon and Ann to work and he readily agreed. *Maybe that'll keep them busy,* Emma thought as she exited the tent.

When she arrived at Reece's tent, she was disappointed to see the other two lawyers there and they, too, were up to their necks in paperwork.

"Are you too busy?" Emma asked.

"Not for you," Reece said as he pushed to his feet. "There's nothing that can't wait." He walked over and gave Emma a quick peck on the lips. "Would you like to go on a walk before it gets dark?"

"Are you sure you have time? I don't want to be a burden."

Reece took her by the elbow and eased her outside. "Think I'm goin' to miss a chance to spend some time with you? No way. Did you get the claim you wanted?"

"I did, but I still have to file it with the land office."

Reece turned loose of her elbow and reached for her hand, intertwining his fingers with hers. "Probably best if you wait a few days. The line to file a claim has swelled all afternoon and it takes hours to even get to the door."

"I'll take your advice, then. Lordy, I can't believe how many people are here."

"And they're still coming. Word is someone has already established a bank and someone else is working to put out the first newspaper. It's incredible, really, when you think about it. You know they say that Rome wasn't built in a day, but for Guthrie and the other towns that have sprung up, they were all created not in a day but in a single afternoon. Not only will the citizens of this town be able to pinpoint the exact day their city was born, they can narrow it further to the exact time, at least within a few minutes, of this city's founding."

"It is incredible and to think we were here when it all happened is crazy. We'll be telling our grandchildren about this one day."

Reece gave her hand a squeeze and said, "I like the sound of that."

They walked in companionable silence for a few minutes and when they topped a small rise with a view of the surrounding prairie they stopped and stared in awe. With the last of the sun's rays painting the landscape a purplish hue, what had been virgin prairie only yesterday was now lit with the light of ten thousand campfires.

"Strangers this morning," Reece said softly, "all of those people are now coexisting on land they could have only dreamed of owning yesterday."

"Imagine, the course of your entire life changing in only a few hours."

"You mean like mine did," Reece asked, "when Grace dragged you down to my tent?"

Emma turned to look at Reece and said, "She didn't exactly drag me."

"Oh, so you were a willing participant?"

"I was when I saw it was you," Emma said. She leaned forward and kissed him on the lips. "Reece Ford, you're about the best thing that ever happened to me."

"I feel the same, Emma Turner."

Emma chuckled and said, "It's a shame your tent is occupied."

"There's always tomorrow."

"What time?" Emma asked.

"The other two go eat with their families around noon."

"Noon it is. Now take me back before it gets too dark."

CHAPTER
61

As the days rolled on, it became clear the Land Run had been a very bad idea that had been executed very badly. Almost immediately land disputes arose and who claimed what was just a guess. The legal system was flooded with lawsuits and people who were once friends were now bitter enemies. Even the U.S. government had admitted its failures and vowed that any future land runs would be structured much differently. The idea of "the first one wins" was flawed from the outset and ripe for corruption as evidenced by the land grab made by the deputy U.S. marshals who had been there to manage the chaos, not create it.

Although born out of anarchy, Guthrie and Oklahoma City were thriving. By the end of June, Guthrie boasted it had six banks, seven hardware stores, forty restaurants, fifteen hotels, and more than fifty saloons. Farther south, in Oklahoma City, there were thirty-four grocery stores, eleven feed stores, five newspapers, and two men hawking lightning rods. Even with all those businesses thriving, there remained an undercurrent of anger over the disputed claims that might linger for years.

For Percy and the others who had ventured north for the Land Run, they were happy to be out of the turmoil and back in the routine at the Rocking R Ranch. But it hadn't been all wine and roses for Percy after the federal government pulled the rug out from under him and all the other big cattle ranchers when they ripped up their lease agreements with the Indians. That had left Percy with eight thousand head of cattle and no place to put them. After weeks of scrambling, he had finally shipped the last of the cattle off to an outfit in Wyoming only last week.

However, Percy wasn't thinking about cattle today. Now sitting in a buggy parked outside the Wichita Falls train depot, he fished out his watch and popped the lid to check the time. The train was late, a fairly common occurrence. On any other day it wouldn't have mattered, but today he was running on a pretty tight schedule.

Back at the ranch, Emma Turner was standing in front of the full-length mirror in her bedroom making final adjustments to her dress. Today was a big day for her, one she'd never expected to experience. When she had her dress the way she liked it, she tucked a flyaway strand of hair into the bun at the back of her head and spent a moment examining the freckles splashed across her nose and cheeks. They had multiplied and darkened since she'd been spending more time outdoors and she debated whether to rub some powder on them to dull their appearance then decided against it and exited the room. Reece claimed to love her red hair and freckles and he had kissed her cheeks and nose enough that she believed him.

Now that horse breeding season was over, she had more free time. She had spent most of last week in Guthrie overseeing the building of their getaway cabin, as she liked to call it. Although she loved her family dearly, she sometimes felt smothered and there were times when she craved privacy and the cabin would be an ideal place for her and Reece to find it. And with Simon off to college in the fall, they would be free to come and go as they pleased.

She did have some concerns about Simon's upcoming departure. He and Ann were constant companions and she had little doubt there would be heartbreak ahead, but that was for another day. Today was her day.

Opening the front door, she stepped out on the front porch and scanned the road that ran between the ranch and town, looking for Percy. He was due home any minute now, but she didn't see any sign of him, not even a dust cloud. Impatient and maybe a little nervous, she paced back and forth on the porch, knowing they were at the mercy of the railroads. It helped to know that her grandmother was entertaining the guests over at the main house and there was little doubt the liquor was already flowing.

Finally, the train from Fort Worth chugged into the station, fifteen minutes late. Percy climbed down from the buggy and hustled inside. It wasn't long before a porter wheeled in a load of luggage and, spotting Ruth's bag, Percy grabbed it so they could make a quick getaway. Scanning the windows of the passenger coaches, he saw

Ruth waiting to disembark from the third car back and scooted that way. He was waiting at the bottom of the step and when she climbed down, he gave her a quick kiss on the lips then grabbed her hand and hurried toward the buggy.

"Are we going to be late?" Ruth asked.

"Not if I can help it," Percy said.

When they reached the buggy, Percy helped Ruth up and hurried around to the other side. He handed her a folded blanket from under the seat and said, "Wrap that around your dress to keep some of the dust off."

Ruth did as he instructed and he popped the reins, putting the horse in motion. A chestnut Narragansett Pacer, the horse really hit its stride when they turned onto the road to the ranch. He loosened the reins, leaned back, and said, "Nervous?"

"No. I'm old enough to know what I want." She reached out and took his free hand and drew it onto her lap. "I feel like the luckiest woman in the world."

"I reckon we both got lucky. They get the water well finished?"

"Yes, they finished late yesterday afternoon and they were moving over to Grace and Seth's place this morning when I left."

"The man's makin' a killin' with all those homesteaders now lookin' for water. Maybe I ought to start me a drillin' company."

"You have more than enough on your plate. Speaking of money, I have those papers you asked me to sign."

"Thank you," Percy said. The papers were a legal document that Seth had created. With the entire family intertwined with the ranch, Percy thought it important to detail the specifics of what Ruth would be entitled to if he died. "Are you mad I asked you to sign 'em?"

"Of course not. You were more than generous and it's your family's ranch. In fact, I couldn't spend the sum you granted me if I lived to be three hundred years old."

Percy smiled and said, "You could always move to Paris and live like a queen."

She scooted over close and wrapped her arms around him. "Then I'd have to learn French."

The dust was thick and neither wanted to arrive with a mouthful of dirt, so the remainder of the ride passed in silence. A short time later, Percy steered the buggy onto the road that led to the ranch's residential area and brought the buggy to a stop in front of his mother's house. After helping Ruth down, he looked up to see Emma coming their way, so they waited and all three entered the house together.

The first person Emma bumped into upon entering her grandmother's house was Quanah Parker, who greeted her with a hug and a kiss on the cheek. It wasn't unusual for the Comanche chief to be there as he was often invited to many of the events hosted at the ranch. Still, it was a tad bit disconcerting for Emma, especially today. She and Quanah spoke for a few moments and Emma gave Ann a hug before wading into the crowd, searching for Reece. The house was jammed with family and friends and, of course, they all wanted to offer their sentiments, so Emma smiled and nodded, the sweat already trickling down her back.

She spotted Marcie across the room and she threaded her way through the crowd and grabbed Marcie's hand when she was close. "Congratulations," Emma said.

"Thank you and the same to you," Marcie said, leaning in to kiss Emma on the cheek. Marcie had announced earlier in the day that she and Chauncey would be having a child.

"Talk later?" Emma said.

"Absolutely."

Emma turned and pushed through the dining room then through the kitchen and finally escaped out the back door, where she found Reece.

"How long have you been out here?" Emma asked, walking over and slipping an arm around his waist.

"Not long. Needed some air," Reece replied. He looked Emma up and down and said, "You look beautiful." He leaned down and gave her a quick kiss on the lips. "You know it's a special occasion when you leave your gun belt at home. How about the knife?"

"Don't trust me?" Emma asked. She lifted the hem of her dress to show Reece she was knifeless.

"I feel honored," Reece said.

Emma chuckled and said, "I might have a hairpin or two," before leaning in for another kiss. They still had some issues to work through, but over the last month they'd been spending most weekdays at the ranch and most weekends in Dallas with an occasional trip to Guthrie thrown into the mix.

"I saw you talking to Quanah before I slipped out here," Reece said. "Is that awkward for you?"

"Today was the first time I'd felt that way in a long time. I don't know how to explain it exactly, but when I first saw him here it immediately rubbed me the wrong way. I thought how dare him for showing up on this day of all days after I'd nearly given up on having a normal

life because of the hell his people had inflicted upon me."
Emma paused to take a deep breath before continuing.
"But really it was just a flash in my mind and nothing
more. No matter how much we'd like to, there's no changing the past."

"Agreed," Reece said. "You're the strongest woman
I've—"

He was interrupted when someone began tinkling a
glass, indicating the ceremony was about to begin.

"I guess that's our cue," Reece said. He took Emma by
the hand and led her back inside.

This wasn't the first double wedding the Rocking R
Ranch had hosted. As Percy and Ruth made their way to
the front of the parlor, he recalled the day both Chauncey
and Marcie and Seth and Grace had exchanged vows. At
the time, Percy had been against the marriages because
of Grace's and Marcie's histories, but they'd been nothing
but model citizens since the day they had walked out of
that Fort Worth parlor house. In fact, he thought Marcie's
arrival was the best thing that had ever happened to his
son, and he'd say the same for Seth, too. Kind, caring,
warm, and often funny, both women now held a special
place in Percy's heart.

He was brought back to the present when Ruth gave
his hand a squeeze. He looked at her and said, "You still
have time to run away."

"You're not going to get rid of me that easily."

Pastor Steve Hickerson, a Methodist preacher from
Wichita Falls, called the room to order. He offered a few
words to those assembled then called for a prayer. It ran
on a little too long for Percy's taste, but after a round of
amens when he finally finished, Hickerson opened his

Bible and went to work. He married Emma and Reece first and as they were kissing, he turned to Ruth and Percy, waiting for the whooping and hollering to die down.

When the room finally settled again, Hickerson led them through their vows and pronounced them man and wife. Percy gave Ruth a quick peck on the lips and was booed for it. Laughing, he gave her a longer kiss and that was greeted with cheers.

Champagne was passed around and Frances Ridgeway was the first to offer a toast and Percy could see the tears shimmering in her eyes. He stepped down from the make-shift stage that had been built and made his way over to his mother. He waited for her to finish the toast and then he took a quick sip from his glass before wrapping an arm around her. "Why the tears, Ma?"

Frances wiped her cheeks and said, "Some are for Emma because I'm so very happy for her and the rest are for you. I can finally rest easy knowing you won't be alone when I'm gone."

"You ain't dyin' today, are you?" Percy asked.

Frances playfully elbowed her son in the ribs and said, "I wasn't planning on it."

"Good. Save me a dance, later." An early supper would be under way soon and later the two couples would be hosting a barn dance.

"I think my dancin' days are done," Frances said. "Now go find your bride and introduce her around."

"I think she's had about all the glad-handin' she can tolerate."

"Can't say as I blame her. You two going on a honey-moon?"

Percy nodded and said, "But she don't know it yet."

"Where are you taking her?"

"San Francisco."

Frances jerked back as if she'd been scalded. After a long look at her son, she said, "Lordy, Percy. Have you forgotten what happened when me and the girls tried to go out there? Worst mess I ever seen after them damn robbers derailed the train. For goodness' sakes, why don't you go back East?"

"Been back East too many times. I'll buy you a train ticket if you want to come along."

"No thank you. You couldn't mint enough money to get me back on that damn train."

Percy chuckled, kissed his mother on the forehead, and turned, looking for his bride. He spotted her in the dining room and threaded his way through the crowd. When he got close enough to snag her hand, he did and led her outside.

When they were clear of everyone, Ruth said, "Thank you for rescuing me." She unfastened the top four buttons on the dress Percy had bought for her and pulled it away from her skin, trying to get some air inside.

"Feel like walkin'?" Percy asked.

Ruth looked down at her heavy dress then looked at Percy and said, "How far are you planning on going?"

"Not far, but I reckon we can stop by the house and you can change into something else."

"Would you mind? I have that blue paisley summer dress we bought."

"Sounds perfect," Percy said.

Ruth looked at him and said, "You don't really care, do you?"

Percy smiled and said, "I prefer you naked. What you decide to put on is up to you."

She slugged him in the arm and said, "Percy Ridgeway, what am I going to do with you?" She took his hand and they walked over to what was now their house.

When they entered the bedroom, Percy sauntered over to the bed and sat down.

"Are you going to watch me change?"

"Might as well. I reckon I've seen everything there is to see."

Ruth unbuttoned her dress and pulled it over her head.

As Percy suspected, she had nothing on beneath it. He called her over and she walked across the room and into his arms. After a few tender kisses, Percy separated himself enough to reach into his back pocket and he pulled out a sheaf of papers and handed them to Ruth. "My wedding gift to you."

Ruth unfolded the papers and it took her a few moments to figure out what it was. When she did, she looked at Percy and said, "We're going to San Francisco?"

"We are."

She let the papers slip from her hand and took a step forward, pushing Percy back onto the bed before reaching for his belt buckle.

"We're not going on a walk, are we?" Percy asked.

"No, we are not."

For Emma it was all a bit surreal. After living so long with a void in her life, she now had someone to wake up to every morning, someone to share her fears and dreams with, and, most important, someone who loved her as she was. Over the last couple of months, they had learned to adapt to each other's quirks and the living had been mostly carefree and easy.

Reece leaned in and said, "It's hot in here. Let's go out to the front porch."

Holding hands, they worked their way through the throng and were disappointed to find the crowd had spilled over onto the front porch. Emma looked at Reece and said, "A walk?"

"Perfect," Reece said.

They stepped off the porch and turned toward the river. In celebration of their marriage, Emma and Reece had decided on a trip down to New Orleans later in the year. Emma had once visited the bayou during the summer months and quickly learned never to make that mistake again.

"Do you remember," Emma asked, "during the Land Run when I said we'd be telling our grandchildren about that day?"

"I do. I thought it was a touching moment."

"Well, in order to have grandchildren we first need to have what?"

"Children, of course." Reece looked around to see if anyone was close then lowered his voice and said, "Simon's occupied. We can go back to our place and do some more practicing."

"That's the thing, Reece. All that practicing we've been doing has paid off."

Reece pulled Emma to a stop and studied her face a moment. "You're pregnant?"

"I am."

"Hot damn!" Reece shouted. Then he remembered

where he was and looked around sheepishly to see if anyone had heard, but there was no one around. "Are you sure?"

"I'm sure."

He thought about it for a moment and his face fell.

Emma stepped forward and wrapped her arms around him. "I know what you're thinking."

His eyes were tearing up when he looked at Emma and said, "I can't lose you, too."

"You won't, Reece. I promise."

"How can you make a promise like that? No one thought Laurie would have any problems until she did."

Emma tilted her head up, kissed him gently on the lips, and said, "I'm not Laurie."

"Still, you can't—"

Emma silenced him by placing a finger on his lips. "I can. I gave birth to Simon when I was only fourteen years old."

He thought about that a moment and said, "You did, didn't you."

Emma, feeling his body relax, said, "I did and everything's going to be all right."

Reece took a deep calming breath and then it was like a steam engine had been switched on. "Well, then . . . we . . . we need to start thinking about names, and then we need to—"

This time, Emma stopped him by putting her lips on his and she was instantly consumed by that hunger which had been absent so very long. They broke for a breath and Reece said, "Our house?"

"Yes, please."

ACKNOWLEDGMENTS

The first round of thanks goes to you, the readers. Thank you for taking some time out of your busy lives to read.

Thanks to my terrific editor and good friend, Gary Goldstein.

A special shout-out to Doug Grad. Thanks for everything, Doug.

Thank you, Steven Zacharius. I'm eternally grateful to you and all the others who work at Kensington on my behalf, including: Lou Malcangi, Elizabeth (Liz) May, James Akinaka, Crystal McCoy, Larissa Ackerman, and Vida Engstrand.

A special thanks to two people who have made me a much better writer—my production editor, Ross Plotkin, and my copy editor, Randie Lipkin.

Thanks to those who hold a special place in my heart: Kelsey, Andrew, Camdyn, and Graham Snider, and Nickolas Washburn. Congratulations to my youngest daughter, Karley Washburn, who now sports a ring on her left hand. Welcome to the family, Philip Halpern! I love you all very, very much.

And lastly, to the woman who chose to share her life with me, Tonya. I love you forever and always.

Keep reading for a special excerpt . . .
The Ridgeway family faces their greatest challenge
when a devastating drought threatens to spark an
open range war, forcing them to fight for their ranch,
their dream—and their lives . . .

DEATH BY THE DEVIL'S ROPE

It's the summer of 1883.
A severe drought threatens to bankrupt
the Ridgeways' Rocking R Ranch and every rancher
in northwest Texas. The cattle are thirsty and hungry.
The ranchers are getting desperate. And a simple new
invention called barbed wire—the devil's rope—is their
only defense against illegal herders grazing on their
land. Percy Ridgeway and his brother, Eli, are working
overtime to stake a fence around their sixty thousand
acres. But someone keeps cutting the wires.
The Ridgeways keep fixing them. And soon Perry is
tangled in a high-stakes showdown with a thieving
cattleman named Northcutt and his cutthroat
henchmen. Let the battle begin . . .

History would call it the Fence Wars of 1883.
The Ridgeways would call it the summer they fought
back—come hell or dry water . . .

Look for **THE DEVIL'S ROPE,** *on sale now.*

CHAPTER
1

Under the light of a full moon, Percy Ridgeway repositioned his gun belt as he leaned against the trunk of a large oak tree, waiting. Using the deeper shadows created by the tree's enormous canopy to conceal his presence, it was now a little past midnight and he assumed they'd show up at some point after having done so the four previous nights. And Percy was determined to put a stop to the nefarious activity before things erupted into an all-out range war, something he didn't want but was preparing for anyway.

The spring and summer of 1883 had been as dry as the marriage chances for a seventy-year-old spinster, and water in sufficient quantities was scarce. That and a recent invention now spreading across the West had tempers flaring, turning longtime friends into bitter enemies. So, Percy was waiting, the time ticking down in his head and the sweat trickling down his back.

Along with the drought, the recent problems stemmed

from the convergence of two things—one an act of Congress and the other the aforementioned invention. Passed by Congress on May 20, 1862, the Homestead Act granted any adult citizen who had never taken up arms against the U.S. government the right to claim 160 acres of surveyed public land with the only stipulations that the owner file an application, make improvements, and occupy the land for five years. And now that the hostile Indians had been forced onto reservations, a great swath of land in the center of the country was up for grabs and homesteaders were crowding onto the open range, staking claims for their own pieces of paradise.

The second spark that threatened to ignite a range war was an unheralded invention that had been patented in December 1874 by a man named Joe Glidden on his farm a mile west of DeKalb, Illinois. And it wasn't just happening in Texas. Glidden's brainchild was now having major ramifications for ranchers all across the West. Using a short piece of wire and the guts from an old coffee grinder to create a small, sharp barb, Glidden had revolutionized the barbed-wire fence. During the first year of production, Glidden's company produced thirty-two miles of wire. By the time 1880 rolled around, the factory in DeKalb was cranking out 236,000 miles of wire a year, enough to encircle the earth ten times over. Seeing the end of the open range rapidly approaching, Percy and the rest of the crew at the Rocking R Ranch were early adopters. And they weren't the only ones. Barbed-wire fences were now going up all across Texas and some of the more unscrupulous ranchers had a bad tendency of throwing wire around land they didn't own. Roads had been fenced off and public buildings had been fenced in and it appeared that anywhere a man could string a strand of wire was fair game.

Hearing a twig snap, Percy stiffened as he was brought back to the present. He turned his head to see two shadowy figures approaching a section of fence that had already been repaired five times. When they were close enough to touch it, Percy lifted his Colt Single Action Army and cocked it, the four distinctive clicks loud in the stillness of the night. "Touch that wire and the next thing you'll feel is a bullet punching a hole in your forehead."

The two figures froze in place and Percy walked over for a close-up look at them. "You the same two that cut my fence the last four nights?"

"No sir," one of them said, a slight tremor in his voice. "We got stock that need water."

"Not my problem," Percy said, eyeing the two. They were a couple of pimple-faced boys who looked to be no older than thirteen or fourteen. He lifted his eyes and looked beyond them. "Boys, the moon is bright enough to read by and I ain't seeing any cattle or horses. They some special breed that makes them invisible?" Percy asked.

"We'll just be on our way, mister," the same boy said.

"Not just yet," Percy said. "What're your names?"

When neither of the boys offered their names, Percy said, "Either of you ever seen what a .45 caliber slug does to a man? I'll tell you it ain't real pretty. Now, answer my question."

The same boy said, "You ain't gonna shoot us, are ya?"

"Your name?" Percy said.

"I'm . . . Jimmy . . . Jimmy Martin and he's—"

"Shut up, Jimmy," the other boy said.

"Go ahead, Jimmy," Percy said.

"His name's Henry."

"Henry got a last name?" Percy asked.

When neither boy answered, Percy turned his pistol on Henry. "Well, Jimmy, I reckon you might get a chance to see what that big bullet'll do after all."

"Henry Parker," Jimmy blurted out.

"Henry Parker," Percy said. "Any kin to Ira Parker?"

"That's his pa," Jimmy said. "Please, mister, don't shoot 'im."

Percy slowly lowered his weapon. "Henry, did your father send you out here to cut my fence?"

"Look, mister—"

Percy held up a hand, cutting Jimmy off. "Henry's mouth was workin' just fine a minute ago." He turned to Henry. "You got lockjaw, Henry?"

"No," Henry said. "We's workin' for someone else."

"Who?" Percy asked.

Henry bristled at the question. "It don't matter. We ain't cuttin' your fences, are we?"

"No, but I reckon that has more to do with my pistol and not a sudden change of heart," Percy said. "Now, who are you working for?"

"Cal Northcutt," Henry said. "Can we go?"

Percy holstered his pistol and said, "If I ever see you within ten feet of one of my fences again, I'll shoot you on sight. Understand?"

The two young men nodded.

"One more thing," Percy said. "Tell Northcutt I'm comin'. Now git."

Jimmy and Henry turned and took off like a pack of wolves were nipping at their heels. Northcutt, like a half a dozen other men in the area, hadn't invested in fencing and hadn't toiled to string wire around their property because they had none. Him and others like him were open-range ranchers and now that fences were going up, they were being squeezed out. It used to be a man could put together a herd, brand it, and turn it out on the open range along with all the other cattle then cull them out at the next roundup. But that was all changing now, and water for the remaining open-range cattle was as scarce as a virgin in a whorehouse. As far as Percy was concerned, if they wanted access to water, they ought to fork over the money to buy some land just as he and his family had done. Walking down the fence line, he untied his horse, mounted, and rode for home.

It wasn't just the fence cutting and the drought that were weighing heavy on Percy's mind. Cattle rustling was a constant problem and, unfortunately, it was directly related to the Rocking R Ranch's location. Situated hard against the Red River in northwest Texas, a majority of the headaches were caused by the riffraff who hid out in the lawless lands of Indian Territory, just across the river. A den of sin and a refuge for killers, the Territory was home to outlaws of all stripes, most of whom had no legal claim to a single blade of grass in an area that stretched across seventy thousand square miles. Those lands were under the control of the United States government and occupied by another headache-inducing group of people—the Indians. And there were thousands of them, all hailing from dozens of tribes who had spent an eternity stalking and killing one another. The only common trait they all shared was their hatred of the white man, and the ranch was only a stone's throw from some of the meanest, cruelest, and deadliest Indians to ever walk the planet—the Comanches and the Kiowas. They were only a few years removed from raping and killing whites all across Texas, and Percy had his own run-in with them after they kidnapped his niece Emma Turner and held her for over a year. It was just plain old bad luck, Percy thought, that they would all spend the rest of their days in such close proximity.

When he reached the barn, Percy quieted the noise in his head and climbed down from his horse. After unsaddling the mare and slipping off the bridle, he turned her loose in the corral and exited the barn. Exhausted, he knew he would be in for another long day tomorrow. Every day was a long day when you ran ten thousand head of cattle on a ranch that sprawled across sixty thousand acres. And, on top of that, he would need to carve out some time to have a chat with that asshole Cal Northcutt. Climbing the steps to the back porch of his house, Percy pushed off his boots and slipped inside.